BETWEEN

C000089644

By

P. J. Roscoe

Cover by

Loraine van Tonder

Edited by

Denna Holm

Published by

Crimson Cloak Publishing

ISBN 13: 978-1-68160-182-3

ISBN 10: 1-68160-182-6

Publishers Publication in Data:

Roscoe, P. J.

Between Worlds

1. Fiction 2. Time Travel 3. Drama 4. Mystery 5. Murder 6. Paranormal 7. Medieval 8. Hypnosis 9. Mediaeval

For the women in my life who truly live.

ACKNOWLEDGEMENTS

I would like to sincerely thank Liz Monks for reading my novel and giving me honest feedback. Maria for helping me to understand hypnotherapy and patiently answering my questions, even when they were ridiculous! As always I thank my family and friends who continue to support me in my adventure, especially Fiona who listens to my constant jabbering about 'my books'! She was also kind enough to give me feedback on this book which helped me considerably. My heart and soul go to my darling husband Martin, always, and our daughter Megan who believes in me unconditionally and my Dad Ken and step Mum, Eiko san for always being enthusiastic about my work, however small an achievement.

PROLOGUE

I dream that I am flying like a great bird. I can't turn my head; I didn't need to. I trust my instincts and follow them without question. I can hear the sound of the wind as my wings spread out, caressing the warm and potent air that allows me to soar closer toward the sun. I'm free and happy and know that I am loved. I have no cares to worry about. I'm young and vibrant and full of life with my world stretching out before me. This feeling of freedom is new. I'm merely a fledgling, protected by my parents with their barrier of devotion that keeps all harm out of my reach. I am alive, truly alive, and the dark is long gone.

All at once I feel the blistering heat against my skin. I climbed too high and without warning the sun is burning me, causing me to shrink away from it as I envelope my face and body with my wings to protect myself. Thus I fall towards earth; no longer caressing the sky but plummeting to my doom. I know that there is no one to catch me and nothing to break my fall. I will die alone.

I wake with a shudder and the bed jolts as though I've landed upon it. I curl up in a ball and weep. I am abandoned. All hope is lost in my ability, and fear has taken hold. I have fallen.

I will never return ...

CHAPTER 1

"Emily? Emily, my lovely, come on, you lazy thing. Wake up and hear the birds sing!"

I heard the words drift into my dream, but I was warm and didn't want to open my eyes, safe and away from the nightmare that was my life if I kept my eyes tightly shut. However, the insistent rocking back and forth, accompanied by the unrelenting singing of my name over and over, forced me to crack open one eye and glare as best as I could at my roommate.

"There you are, sleepyhead. Come on, Emily, out of that bed. It's time to eat and breakfast is ready. So come on, Emily, ready and steady ..."

I should probably have pointed out at this stage that my roommate had a dependency to speak in rhyme. Much to mine and everyone else's annoyance, it was apparently her only coping mechanism, though I had no concept of how rhyming words helped her cope with her trauma.

"Come on, come on, it's a beautiful day, hip, hip, hurray!"

"Oh, fuck off!" I snarled and pulled the covers back over my head. Sadly for me, Mary, who'd always been nice to me, was passing the open doorway at the time.

"Emily, you not up yet? Feeling okay, child?"

I heard her soft footsteps approach my bed, and with a loud sigh, I peeped out from under the covers. "Sorry, no, just getting up, if Jane would leave me alone for a moment ..."

Hearing my hint, Jane clutched her arms around herself and drifted off into the corridor, "Oh my, oh my, time to fly ..."

I sighed again and caught Mary's eye. She was one of the kind nurses, and although I was twenty-six, she still called me child, as she did everyone else. I liked it. It made me feel loved, and I'd told her once not long after arriving.

"I'm glad," she'd said, "because to me, you're someone I'll strive to protect and care for as if you were my own ... but don't tell the other nurses, they don't like us getting too close. Know what I mean?"

She'd winked at me then and given me a friendly nudge. Now, Mary looked down at me with concern and just a hint of disgust at hearing my choice of language.

I immediately felt contrite. "Sorry for my language, Mary. Jane was annoying me."

"Oh, I see. Being woken isn't pleasant, but let's consider our language in future, if you please, Emily ... Good dream was it?"

I nodded, but found I couldn't form the words to describe my adventure. I could feel the dream drifting away and knew that soon I'd have forgotten it. I felt a strange sadness at the thought, as if I needed to keep hold of how it had made me feel—like it was important. However, it was already fading.

"Well, you know the rules, child. Time to get up and have something to eat. The canteen closes in half an hour. They have that yogurt you like. I saw it this morning."

I smiled and pushed myself into a seated position, and yawned. "Okay I'm up. I'll do anything for one of those yogurts, you know me so well, Mary."

Smiling, she left the room and the happiness left with her. I gazed out at the empty corridor, feeling the terror return with the dreary prospect of suffering another day in that hellhole. I swallowed hard and licked my lips as I forced down the urge to scream and shout at the injustice. After some deep breathing, I felt able to get out of bed and visit the bathroom. Washed, with my golden-brown hair brushed and tied back, I dressed in jeans and an Alice Cooper T-shirt. My slippers finished my ensemble, and I followed the nauseating aroma of fried food.

After my small breakfast of yogurt and red berries, a large mug of stewed tea and a piece of Galaxy chocolate, given to me by a fellow inmate, I wandered back down the corridor towards the common room. Today was my turn with the psychiatrist Doctor Marian Griffiths and I had half an hour to kill before my appointment. However, because they didn't like us going back to our own rooms, we had to congregate in various places to keep the staff happy.

Upon entering the large room, I was surprised to see it empty. It was rare to find anywhere in this place unoccupied, even for a moment. Always someone drooling, crying or wandering aimlessly around the room—all because of their meds—or merely sitting and staring off into space, lost in their own little worlds. That in itself wasn't so bad, considering the scenarios I'd witnessed since my arrival nearly three months ago. Still, another person invading my space annoyed me, when all I wanted to be was alone with my thoughts.

I wandered over to one of the large oval windows that lit the room with morning sunshine and closed my eyes against the warm glare. I didn't need to see outside to appreciate what lay before me. Central, was a perfectly mowed lawn that stretched out for about an acre. West of the lawn was a waist-high bush of blooming rhododendrons, while on the east, a perfectly cut hedge of lavender and rosemary. Planted close together there were no gaps between the herbs, the scent exquisite as you passed by. Along the bottom of the lawn stood the ten-foot-high brick wall made to look pretty with red and pink roses creeping up and over.

The old hall had been built in the early nineteenth century for some rich person who'd died without having children. Apparently his wife had suffered from depression and hallucinations and, as he couldn't bear to see her go into some insane asylum, he'd turned his own home into one. On her death years later, still screaming about the "visitors," he'd handed the hall over to the local authorities, before dying himself of cancer. All in all, the place was dripping with irony.

I'd read the brief history in some pamphlet left lying around the ward and asked if anyone knew who those visitors were? No one had given my question the time of day, fobbing me off with some incoherent answer. I'd not asked again. I had my own theories anyway. I was convinced that the place was truly haunted. I mean, it was the perfect setting, wasn't it? Old hall, lots of tragic history, and now a home for the sick and insane. So much negative energy must have conjured up the presence of some kind of spirit? It simply lurked in the eerie air and clung to you like a heavy, woollen winter coat.

Besides, I'd heard strange noises in the night. Footsteps were normal, as were groans, moans, screams and profanities, but those footsteps echoed and were loud, as if a giant were roaming the hallway.

"Whatcha doin'?"

I sighed loudly, opened my eyes and looked at the younger woman staring at me with intense interest. "Mia, what does it look like I'm doing? I'm leaving this place in my head."

Excited, she nodded and hugged her raggedy doll tighter to her small chest. "Oh, okay. Well, come back soon ..."

I smiled. "I will, but first I have to go see the doc. Are you all right?"

Mia chewed on her inner cheek for a moment and rocked herself before leaning forward as another inmate shuffled in. "Not really. My baby won't wake up, and they're blaming me ... again."

"Ah, I see." And I did, of course, as Mia told me the same thing whenever we met, which was most days. Her doll clutched to her bosom – and the sheer sadness and grief of what she had done etched into her face.

"Well, maybe she will soon. I'll see you later, Mia. Goodbye."

Picking up her doll's hand, she made it wave at me before shuffling off into her favourite corner of the room where she'd make a little den of the chairs to play house with her baby. The nurses would encourage Mia to put the chairs back, but after a few minutes, she'd make another den and it would begin all over again.

I'd been horrified the first time I heard the reason for her incarceration. Aged seventeen, she'd become pregnant after a gang rape of four boys, aged between fifteen and nineteen, who'd done it as a dare. Mia had been considered a little slow by the children and adults in her village, and nobody believed her until the evidence of that night became clear.

Her father owned a farm and, on seeing her swollen belly, had taken a shotgun and found the boys one by one, blowing off their weapons and leaving them to bleed to death. One boy survived, but he'll never rape another woman again. Afterwards, Mia's father turned the gun on himself, leaving Mia and her mother to cope with the aftermath of his actions, and the consequences of the attack.

Five months later, Mia gave birth to a healthy boy. Her mother left the room for a few minutes to visit the bathroom. On returning, she found Mia alone, calmly sitting up in bed holding a raggedy doll to her breast. The hospital staff searched high and low for the child, eventually finding his tiny broken body in the bushes beneath Mia's window, ten stories up. She'd flung him away like garbage.

I watched her for a moment as she began to turn the chairs to make her little den that would help her feel safe for a short while. The horror of what she'd done three years ago was not evident on her face, as it hadn't been the night she killed her baby. She'd never admitted it or shown remorse for her actions, but had merely slipped away into her own safe world and not returned.

The evil of men had brought her to this. Despite her action, Mia was an innocent, yet it felt like nobody had considered that. If the boys hadn't attacked her, she wouldn't have been pregnant. Though Mia's father had dealt out the justice, the boys' parents demanded her incarceration for life because the death penalty was not allowed in Britain anymore. Personally, I wish it had been, for rapists as well as murderers. Would those parents have still wanted it then if Mia's father hadn't provided his own? I doubted it.

Movement near the doorway caught my eye, and I turned to find one of the nurses watching me. One of the newer ones who still wasn't sure if this was the job she really wanted, and always became anxious if a patient espied her. This one nurse would quickly glance around to check where the other nurses were in case we mad bastards lunged at her.

11

"You have an appointment this morning with Doctor Griffiths in ten minutes ..."

I continued to stare at her. "I know." I couldn't keep the contempt at being reminded out of my voice, and I saw the flicker of fear on her face.

"Right, okay then ..."

I watched, and smiled, as she quickly left the room, and then I let out a long breath to try and help relax my shoulders. It felt like I had a permanent knot in them, and my neck was sometimes so rigid from tension it hurt my head. I gently rolled my shoulders and gazed out of the window. I could hear Mia mumbling to her doll in the far corner - a sound of surreal sweetness that comforted me. It was a few minutes' walk to Doctor Griffiths office. I wasn't in any rush.

I didn't move as more inmates tottered into the room in ones and twos, like Noah and his Ark. Bibles littered the bookshelves around the room, but nobody read them. We had a priest who came once a week to "save our souls," but I never gave him much thought and from what I saw, neither did anyone else. He came to make himself feel better. Or perhaps he got a perverse joy at seeing so many troubled souls in one place, making him feel superior? Who knew? I didn't, nor did I care.

Eventually, I sighed loudly and departed, the corridor no longer silent, as people filled it. Most were moving at some pace, either coming or going, usually escorted by orderlies, heavily built security guards or nurses. A few stood looking lost, staring up at the whitewashed walls, or down at their feet. Eventually someone would come to them, but they weren't in a rush. Those poor souls were harmless, doped up to the eyeballs, and I often wondered how they even managed to stand upright.

I hurried towards the double doors and was met by a security guard and an orderly who, after checking the appointment book, escorted me through the secure door. Together we climbed the two flights of stairs, as I preferred them to being cramped in a lift with two men, all the while cameras following our progress. We entered the corridor where the consultants and specialists were housed. Carpeted, it smelt clean and fresh, with windows—a few that someone had left open—running the length of the corridor, letting in beautiful sunlight and fresh air.

The security guard left us here with a nod to the orderly. Returning the way we'd come in, while the aloof orderly and I turned right. We moved to the side as two women orderlies escorted a patient from another office. The elderly woman looked fairly sedated, a newbie—you could tell them a mile off.

I knocked on Doctor Griffiths' door and opened it before she bade me enter. My one rebellion, my one tiny bit of control in this place— which Doctor Griffiths readily understood. I slammed the door in the orderly's face and grinned to myself.

As always, Doctor Marian Griffiths was dressed impeccably in a loose black skirt and a white shirt with a maroon scarf hanging around her slim neck. I couldn't see her feet, but guessed she would be wearing short heels to lift her five-foot-six stature just a couple of inches. Her dark ginger hair was piled high on her head and, somehow, it always looked perfect, even though loose strands fell all around her head. I wondered if she spent hours in front of a mirror to make it look that way. She never wore much makeup; she didn't need to. Quite attractive, I guessed her age to be late forties. No wedding ring, possible lesbian. I'd ask her one day.

"You checking me out as usual, Emily?" Marian smiled, and I grinned back, having been caught in the act. Admittedly, we both were more at ease in my referring to her by her first name—save the initial formality of "Doctor Griffiths" while the burly, surly orderly was still in earshot.

"Of course, Marian, you always impress me with your wardrobe."

Marian inclined her head in what I presumed to be a 'thank you' whilst indicating the armchair opposite her desk. I sank down into it listening to the squeak of the leather, and shuddered as the coldness penetrated my thin T-shirt.

Marian noticed. "If you prefer the couch...?"

I glanced at the beige two-seater that sat along the far wall and shrugged. "This'll do for now."

"Okay then, where would you like to start today, Emily?"

I shrugged again. "No idea. I wish I could remember stuff to tell you, but I can't."

Marian looked down at her notes. "Is that true? Do you really want to tell me? Can you recall our last conversation?" At my nod, she continued, "You became quite upset with me when I pushed you to remember. How do you feel at this moment?"

"At this moment, I feel pissed off with my roommate and sick of being here. I hate being dictated to, and I hate being kept inside. I want to be outside in the fresh air."

"I understand that, Emily, but last time you attempted to leave, do you remember that?"

"Of course I do. I punched that nurse pretty hard for grabbing me like he did, so you put me in confinement for my own good."

"You still sound angry about that."

"Wouldn't you be? I'm put into a place for crazy people and my rights taken away and treated like a third class citizen ... Of course I'm angry."

"You think you're third class?"

"I don't have any say in what happens to me, do I? So yeah, I'm a slave to you and this place."

Marian wrote a few notes and closed her file. "All right, Emily, I understand. You've been here nearly three months, and it's been slow progress, which can be frustrating for you, but we have to try and get to the bottom of why you did what you did and help you remember it. You chose not to speak for such a long time. Do you remember that?"

I shrugged, refusing to engage or agree, and looked towards the window. Thoughts flew through my head, and I tried to keep my face blank as the memories flew past like a videotape on fast-forward. I remembered everything. How could I ever forget, but how could I ever tell them? It was impossible, and the irony was that if I told them the truth, they'd lock me up! I think that was partially why I kept silent, but also, staying in my own bubble kept me close to them and to him. The grief was still so raw.

"Emily? Where did you go just now?" Marian's voice filtered into my awareness, and I quickly blinked away the burning tears.

"Nowhere. I just zoned out."

"I see. And during this 'zoning out' did you recall any details about why you are here?"

I began to bite my nail nervously under Marian's gaze. I knew what she wanted me to say—that I'd killed a man. Then we'd talk about blame and guilt and repercussions and forgiveness, and then they would do one of two things, keep me here in this secure wing indefinitely or send me to jail for murder for a very long time. I doubt they would release or forgive me if I told them the truth. Being here was the better of two evils, yet I didn't have to like it.

Without my bidding, his face swam into my consciousness and the breath caught in my throat and the emotion from the loss that came with it choked me for a moment. I fought to hold it at bay, but a couple of tears escaped before I angrily wiped them away. His beautiful face. I knew every detail of it, although all they ever questioned me about was that security guard. I never saw his face and I refused to look at pictures. I didn't want to remember his face. The man they say I murdered. The man who ruined everything.

I became aware of Marian watching me carefully, and I quickly pulled myself together and waited for her obvious questioning.

"Who were you thinking about just then, Emily?"

"No one of importance. I can't remember." I folded my arms, but realised she'd think I was doing it for defensive reasons and quickly unfolded them. I felt uncomfortable under her scrutiny. I'd let out my emotions in front of her. It'd taken me by surprise and I didn't know how to behave. For nearly eight weeks, I'd not spoken, preferring to lose myself in silence, locked away in my grief. Now I was finding it more and more difficult to hold it together. I couldn't give them anything that might provide them with enough evidence to hold me here indefinitely.

"No one of importance? I see. So it wasn't the security guard?"

"Security guard? You mean the one I'm supposed to have killed? Why would I think about him when I don't remember?"

I knew she was trying to read me, so I kept my body as still as possible. I fought the urge to scratch my nose or look away. Eventually, she gave a little nod and returned to her notes. "This will be the seventh session with me, how do you feel it is going?"

I shrugged. It didn't matter how I felt. It would continue until they decreed otherwise. I watched Marian carefully as she seemed to be weighing up something. I couldn't help my curiosity. "What is it?"

She looked surprised for a moment that someone else should be asking a question in a therapy session. "Well, it's just that I was wondering how you'd feel about hypnotherapy?"

So there we were at last. The authorities were sick of waiting to see if I'd confess to murder. They'd given the go-ahead to try other techniques. Marian's sessions weren't working quickly enough.

I looked away from her prying eyes. Marian saw too much and I hated being under her scrutiny. I couldn't let her hypnotise me. I had no idea what would come out, and I didn't know enough about hypnotism to know if I could fake it. If I spoke of what had happened to me, they'd lock me up and throw away the key for sure, yet how could I not tell them under hypnotherapy? It would all come out about the security guard and the tragic circumstances of his death. His wife and family were already baying for my blood, believing I was hiding behind the hospital. In that, they weren't wrong.

I could feel Marian watching me suspiciously and abruptly stood up, unable to bear it any longer. I walked to the bookshelf and glanced quickly through the variety of books, not really seeing any of them, but needing to go through the motions.

"Emily?" Marian's voice penetrated the long silence and brought my vision into view. My sharp intake of breath sounded loud to both of us and Marian quickly came to my side. "What is it?"

I swallowed hard to stop the rising bile and shook my head as I backed away from the books. "Nothing ... nothing, I just, I mean, I have to go ... can I go?" I felt sick, my head swam and I began to see black spots in front of my eyes. I reached out, blindly clutching for anything stable and vaguely heard Marian shout for help. I staggered, remembering the couch nearby and I aimed for it. However, strong hands caught me before I fell into oblivion and, for a moment, I felt his hands, and I wanted to weep.

Marian watched as the two nurses laid Emily on a stretcher and wheeled her out of her office. Once the door closed behind them, she went back to the bookshelf that ran along the length of the wall. She scanned the books looking for any clues to this latest development, but apart from her array of counselling and psychological books, her medical and self-help volumes, Marian couldn't see what had caused Emily to have an extreme episode.

She tried to gauge exactly where Emily had stood. As they were both the same height, Marian looked through the books at eye level, surprised to find an old book which she'd forgotten she had lent to a friend. She must have placed it on the shelf without thinking, hoping to return later to take it home. She pulled it out and flicked through the pages, finding no reason for Emily to behave in such a manner over any of her books, but this one least of all. She laid it flat on her desk to remind her to take it home, yet her gaze kept returning to it. Eventually, Marian reached out and gently caressed the glossy cover, running her fingers over the title. The calligraphy was beautiful, making the title all the more enticing: Medieval Britain, the Dark Ages.

Marian frowned, and absentmindedly chewed her lower lip. It was the first time Emily had shown any emotion. In fact, most of the time, her manners demonstrated a complete lack of interest and, since Emily had resumed speaking in normal patterns, she barely said a word, if necessary. Marian glanced at her clock on the far wall and sighed heavily because she didn't have time to contemplate this now. She quickly wrote down her notes and tried to focus on her next patient, due in ten minutes. However, something didn't feel right—she felt it in her gut. Somehow, this book was the clue.

CHAPTER 2

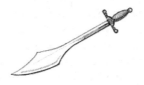

I listened as the nurse went about her work, with no notion of how long I'd been out. I also had no doubts that she wasn't alone. Cracking open one eye, I saw one of the broad-shouldered male orderlies leaning against the wall, watching the nurse's backside with a slight smirk on his face. This one was a fairly new black man who had a secretive air about him. I didn't like him. As if he could feel my eye on him, he abruptly turned his head and caught me.

"She's awake." He stood up straight and unfolded his arms, as if he expected a fight of some kind. He reminded me of a burly fighter I'd once known, with thick, muscular arms that were bigger than my thighs. Like the actor, Arnold Schwarzenegger, except so much more violent than anyone I'd ever conceived before. This orderly was similar, but there was no kindness in this man's eyes. The man I'd called 'boxer' was always ready for a fight, and if one wasn't forthcoming, he'd make one happen anyway, just for fun. But even with all that energy to fight, he was still the sweetest man I'd ever known, with eight children and another on the way, and he'd loved them all.

I fought back tears and slowly sat up. I didn't recognise the young female nurse who came to stand in front of me. She silently handed me a drink of cold water and I gulped it down thirstily and thanked her. She took the empty cup with a nervous smile. I sensed rather than saw the male nurse move closer as she held out the blood pressure tube. I slipped my arm in-between and silence ensued as the machine did its work. Finally, she announced I was all better and free to leave, stepping as far away from me as possible as the male nurse took over.

"Right, let's get you back to your room, shall we. You've already wasted enough of everyone's time, haven't you, Miss?"

I clamped my mouth shut as he took my arm and pulled me roughly off the bed. His fingers dug into my muscle, bringing memories flooding back to me to a time when another man had used the same force. I walked quickly, trying to keep up with his long strides, and was glad when we arrived at my door. Opening it, he pushed me inside and closed it without a word. I stood staring at the door handle for ages, my head trying to make sense of the morning. I heard the lunch bell and felt a wave of anxiety. I'd been out for hours; surely that wasn't normal.

Eventually, I sank down on my bed and curled up, facing the wall. I desperately needed peace and quiet and wondered if it was worth making a scene so they'd put me in solitary. I thought about the consequences and gave up on it. Yes, it would get me privacy. However, they'd probably drug me, which I hated; it stopped my thoughts from flowing, and I needed them to be clear at this critical juncture.

The book had been unexpected. Since my enclosure, I'd not had any contact with the outside world. I never watched television, preferring to listen to my MP3 player when allowed it and lose myself from the noise and the smells within music. Seeing those words, the writing, had been too close for comfort, and my body shut down. I wasn't ready to see pictures, or be reminded of the clothing and behaviour of the people of that time or, worse still, see a name I would recognise. Every face was too clear, so I fought them back into a little hole I'd constructed, allowing me not to hurt as badly.

*   *   *

Marian let out a long sigh, loosened her top button and removed her shoes. Putting her feet up onto the stool, she relaxed into the armchair and closed her eyes for a moment. She usually enjoyed this part of the day, when the patients had been seen and there was a lull, a quiet time before she had the energy to face the traffic home; however, today was Thursday and tonight was her weekly session with her supervisor, Carla.

It wasn't that she disliked the woman. In fact, she respected her attitude to life. Brought up in a mining village somewhere in south Wales, Carla had followed a rather rough path until her mid-twenties when she got herself into rehab and changed the course of her life. She now followed a more spiritual path, mediations, sound baths, you name it, Carla did it. The scent of lavender followed her around, and she hugged everyone, even Sidney Brown-West, the head honcho, who glared at everyone with a mixed look of distain and superiority.

She glanced at the clock, and right on cue, Carla waltzed through the door.

"Darling Marian, how's your day going, dearest?" Settling herself on the couch, Carla waited patiently, a slight smile on her face.

Marian considered for a moment how to begin. "Not too bad, I suppose. I'm still pushing for Rebecca to be released into day care and continued support on home visits, as I'm worried she has become too dependent on this place. Eight months is too long, but we've already spoken about that haven't we?"

Carla remained silent, waiting. Marian knew what she was waiting for, and finally gave in. "Okay, okay, it's been a pretty shitty day and I'm worrying about Rebecca's progress, and Mary is not progressing one little bit, so far as I can see. Then there's Jane who refuses to talk normally at any time which is damned annoying, I almost lost my temper. And Mia is, well, Mia just is, poor thing. I feel terrible whenever I think about Mia for too long. She shouldn't be in here. The crime against her was so despicable. She is the victim as well as that baby, but nobody seems to want to dwell on that."

"Is that all?" Carla's voice was encouraging.

"No, there was Emily today. The girl flabbergasts me. I know she's playing with me, hiding the facts. I'm pretty sure she remembers everything, but plays the game regardless and it infuriates me."

Carla leaned forward. "Today sounds as if it's been an emotional day for you, Marian. I wonder why you are allowing yourself to feel so much for your patients? Empathy, remember, instead of sympathy. You need to encourage a barrier between yourself and these women, otherwise you'll drive yourself mad."

Marian nodded. "I know, but sometimes, especially with Emily, I feel such frustration, I want to yank the information out of her and say, 'there you go. It was there all along!' and see them get better."

"Get better? Is that your job?"

Marian saw her mistake and huffed loudly. "Shit! No, of course not. I can only guide them. They have the ability to heal themselves."

She glanced down at the forms on her desk that needed to be filled in to start the process of release and support. The silence dragged on as she tried to process her thoughts. Carla sat back and watched and waited. Carla would never press her. Instead, she would wait and know that Marian would get there in her own time. Marian's thoughts returned to Emily. As her first patient, Emily set the tone for the day. Something hadn't felt right about Emily for weeks. She couldn't quite put her finger on the problem, though she was convinced Emily was playing the system. But why, she could not fathom, beyond the obvious; Emily did not wish to go to prison. Yet, she wasn't convinced of this being her motive either. Today, it seemed as if she'd been afforded a peek into what it was, but couldn't quite see the picture.

She finally looked up and found Carla quietly waiting as always. "I think I'm fed up with this job. I'm allowing myself to get wound up by the patients too easily. After Emily this morning, the rest just bored me ... no, bored is the wrong word. Infuriated me so much, I couldn't be bothered listening or attempting to listen to those barely willing to talk to me. I gave up on Mia almost completely and Jane didn't even last the hour. I don't feel proud of myself today, Carla."

"We all have days like that. Seems Emily started you off on this negative thought pattern. Can you tell me why?"

Marian considered the question. "Emily is something of an anomaly to me as a patient. I've seen evil, we both have. True evil has sat in this very office. Wickedness drips off people who have done terrible things like black tar, and it creeps into every orifice. Emily sits in that chair and there is nothing. Twice I've had to look at the file to remind myself of the crime she's been accused of and, according to the police running the investigation, there was little doubt that Emily wielded the weapon that killed the man, yet there's nothing 'evil' about her."

Carla nodded. "I agree. Emily does rather have a sense of innocence about her, and yet, she has a secret. It is obvious to anyone willing to truly see. The girl has been through some kind of trauma which may or may not have ended in this tragedy; but why is it affecting you so badly?"

Marian rubbed her tired eyes. "Have you seen the police photographs? Emily butchered the man. No head, missing fingers, blood everywhere, with Emily sitting among the remains, the murder weapon in her hands. The police report states that she attacked the officers first on the scene. They said she'd been wild-eyed and sobbing uncontrollably. Screaming words over and over that nobody could understand, Emily was tasered as a last resort and brought here to the maximum-security wing of Owl Haven Hospital. I'm just not convinced that this is the best place for her."

A memory flashed into her brain, and she abruptly stood and went to the large window. The murder weapon had been a sword and, when forensics finished testing it for evidence; they'd allowed the British Museum, located in central London's garden-laden Bloomsbury area, to take a sample for carbon dating, announcing recently that it was from the sixth century A.D. No one believed them, and had even mocked their tests, as the sword was in impeccable condition. The murdered man was evidence of its sharpness. However, the results were being checked again, but archaeologists were convinced of its authenticity. There was a growing line of people who wanted to speak with Emily but, as yet, she'd refused to speak with anyone of authority.

"So Emily is talking a little more now?" Carla's question broke into Marian's thoughts.

"Yes, more or less full sentences now, though she's still obviously angry and frustrated with being here. Makes a change from complete silence, I suppose. It has helped knowing her name. She has a brother, a man called Brian. Though from her lack of information on him, I get the feeling they are estranged. He's an obvious alcoholic and no use to Emily's recovery."

Marian reached for the book that had caused such a strong reaction from Emily and showed it to Carla. "I think it was this book that caused her to react today, though I can't be absolutely sure."

Carla took it and flicked through it. "Why this one?"

Marian shook her head. "No idea and, as I say, it's only a guess, but it would tie into the sword. The archaeologists are going wild about the murder weapon."

"Yes, I heard. From the sixth century apparently." Carla flicked through the pages and marvelled at the intricate Celtic artwork that covered the pages. It was mostly artwork found in churches and scrolls with a chapter on 'How they lived through the medieval period,' showing various dress codes and differences between the rich and poor. There was a chapter on foods they ate, diseases and medical knowledge, which was minimal and barbaric in many cases, and the general way of life. It had a chapter on the wars and the rulers, but nothing stood out as to exactly what could have affected Emily so profoundly.

"They say she'd been half-naked when found, wearing the remnants of a long dress. Bloodied, bruised and very thin, so I was told. The doctor who examined her found various scars on her back. Some resembled whiplashes and were fairly recent. Another scar on her thigh looked like a knife wound. I heard theories were circling the police and hospital staff, all trying to search for answers to the crime and who Emily was in the world. What's your theory?"

Marian took back the book and put it on her desk. "I think she was abducted by someone. The police discovered that nobody had seen Emily for months before her appearance and, on visiting her home, they'd found mail littering the floor, with thick dust and food rotting in the cupboards and fridge. It was evident her home had not been lived in for a long time. The police guessed at least eight months going on the letters."

Carla nodded. "I agree, I believe she has been through some terrible ordeal that hasn't ended yet."

Marian shrugged. "Losing the baby must have been a difficult experience, if the child was her abductor's. To be raped is bad enough, but to endure a pregnancy afterwards is abhorrent surely?"

"How far gone was she?"

"They think about ten weeks."

"And did Emily show any emotion after the miscarriage?"

"None."

Marian considered her own theories regarding Emily. An alcoholic brother moving away, she had lived in the family home alone after their parents had been murdered. Moving from job to job, Emily had met someone who'd kept her somewhere for at least six months, judging from the state of the house. Finally escaping, mad with pain and fear, she'd lashed out at the first man who'd found her. He might have attempted to touch her, keeping hold of her while he called the police— the latter an act akin to a death sentence, as men touching meant pain and suffering to Emily.

She'd pondered these possibilities weeks ago when Emily had first come in and her mind had not been changed yet, though many theories raged around Marian's head. Now she wondered about the book connection. Had the man been a medieval fanatic, perhaps that was why Emily had been found in an old-style dress? Moreover, though, it might explain her violent reaction to the book.

The authorities were trying to be tolerant and hadn't rushed her so far. If Emily was a victim of a heinous crime, then they didn't want to be seen to be harming her any further. Meanwhile, the security guard's family members were baying for her blood, demanding the girl be charged with his murder and sentenced. Marian had been approached to try new techniques to see if any novel ideas or concepts emerged; everyone needed answers quickly. She'd been given the go-ahead to shake the tree and see what fell, but her gut feeling was that whatever dropped would not be what people wanted to hear, and she was pretty sure Emily knew that too.

CHAPTER 3

I feel his breath on my neck and bend my head so he can nuzzle closer. His kiss against my hot skin sends tingles through my body and I lean into his strong arms, encouraging him to continue. He does not disappoint. His arms squeeze tighter around my waist and his kisses became more passionate, moving up and down my neck, onto my bare shoulder and back up to my ear. His breath is becoming hard, as is something further south, and I turn into his arms with a mischievous grin. "You want me? You'll have to earn me!"

I feel his smile against my cheek and knew I'd pleased him. His language is so harsh, but I'm learning fast. A hand roams down to my backside and moves to the front of my dress. "I can make it worth your while, my lady ..."

His eyes gaze down into mine, full of wanting and love, as I smiled seductively. "We'll see, shall we."

"Emily ... Emily ..."

I turned to the sound of my name, a smile lingering on my face, but it instantly vanished when I saw Jane hovering over me. "Go away, Jane!"

"No, no, can't be done, have to get up before the day is gone ..."

"Jane, you and your fucking rhymes are doing my head in. Why do you do it?" I sat up, so quickly it made me feel woozy. The room spun, and I blinked a couple of times. The light in the room was dull. "What time is it?"

"Time for tea for you and me, time for tea for you and me ..."

"Tea? You mean I've slept all afternoon?" My stomach growled to remind me I hadn't eaten since the morning. I stood a little unsteadily and used the bathroom, splashing water on my face and trying to stop myself from crying. The lustful dream was still fresh in my mind, and my body's reaction to it was complaining that it hadn't reached any conclusions.

Sex. I missed it. Not that I'd been a slut, but I'd had a boyfriend since fifteen, and lost my virginity the night before my seventeenth birthday to a complete arsehole who, having enjoyed two days of celebrations and my body, proceeded to dump me the day after my seventeenth birthday. The only thing he'd taught me was that sex could be good. My next two boyfriends showed me how it could be better, while he had shown me how making love could be fantastic, leaving me wanting more, and he'd obliged without question.

I heard Jane outside the bathroom door getting agitated as the dinner bell rang. She had a thing for being on time, as well as singing her sentences. "You go, Jane. I'll catch up," I shouted through the door, hearing her leave with a sing-song about the corridor. Relieved, I opened the bathroom door and enjoyed the solitude that I knew wouldn't last for long. Sure enough, I heard the nurse doing her usual routine as she checked to see who lingered in the rooms, opening the bedroom doors as she went without a care for privacy.

She reached mine, and I instinctively pushed myself away from the bathroom wall. "I'm going," I bellowed, more than loud enough to pierce her ears. Pushing past her, I walked fast, passing the other inmates who shuffled along the long corridor to the cafeteria, the smell of food acting like a magnet. For now, it was the sustenance I needed, and hoped it would help me forget, if only for a short while, the memory of my love and the time my life really began.

Mary looked up from helping an inmate to feed herself and watched as Emily joined the short queue for dinner. She looked agitated and kept running her hands through her hair while glancing around nervously. Mary spooned more soup into the open mouth and smiled warmly, as the woman known as Lily reached out and took the spoon from her to begin feeding herself. Dearest Lily was always the same at every meal. Cursed the staff for trying to poison her, but once she had a mouthful of food, she fed herself, until the next meal.

Leaving Lily to it, and walking slowly along the table, Mary smiled at inmates who caught her eye, but all the while remained aware of Emily, who was now helping herself to mashed potato and a vegetarian pie, along with her mixed vegetables. Next she chose a chocolate mousse and a large cold drink, then went to sit at an empty table. Emily always tried to sit alone – an easy task most of the time. Mary wondered if the other inmates instinctively knew to stay away from her. Emily did emit a negative energy and a deep sadness that emanated off her in waves. This sadness is what drew Mary to Emily every time she saw her.

A few other nurses had warned her not to get close or too involved. They called Emily all kinds of nasty names after what she'd done to that man. Mary wasn't stupid; she'd been doing this job for thirty-two years and seen every kind of evil—but Emily did not fit any template. Sure, she could believe the other nurses, who insisted Emily was a fantastic actress, yet her gut feeling told her this wasn't true either. She was sure something traumatic had happened to the girl.

"Good evening, child." Mary remained standing on the opposite side of the table, sending out an air of authority to avoid giving the other nurses something to shake their heads in disgust about.

Emily glanced up, her mouth full, and she quickly chewed and swallowed. "Hello, Mary."

"I'm not surprised to see you hungry. I'm told you've slept most of the day and had a fainting spell this morning. Feeling all right now though, I see?" Mary smiled kindly, hoping she didn't sound as if she was judging her. But Emily didn't seem bothered and shrugged non-committal, carrying on eating.

"Yeah, I'm fine, thanks." She spoke with her mouth full. Mary took the hint and with a nod, she walked away to help Jane, who was making a tower with her mashed potato whilst singing some rhyme about potatoes and magical faeries.

I watched Mary walk away and felt bad about the way I'd treated her, since she was a good woman. However, my mind was going ten to the dozen, and I needed time to calm down. Once I got my food, I found I had no appetite, but shovelled the potato into my mouth enthusiastically to keep the nurses from watching me. I'd realised they tended to home in on an inmate who wasn't eating. Food, rest and exercise, apparently the three things to magically make these people better. I learned that lesson on my arrival when I'd refused to eat, and they had put me on a drip for a while. I'd barely cared.

I glanced around the large white painted room. From the large window nearest to me, I could see the top half of an ash tree and dark red bushes, punctuated by the blue-grey sky dotted with white clouds—a hint of early evening approaching. I'd lost a day, which to me didn't seem too bad, but it meant night was coming. In another hour, the sun would set, and we'd be herded into the common rooms to "socialise" before being locked into our rooms for our own safety.

I hated being locked in like some child, with only Jane for company. It was enough to drive me insane, unless I was in solitary confinement-where I could be alone without any sounds of singing, and mumbling, or occasional screaming, to pull me out of my dreams. Except for the camera hidden in the wall, I felt free of people and could usually drift back into my mind and escape, recalling everything in perfect detail. A bittersweet thing to do, but a compulsion I found increasingly harder to stop. Being stuck in this hell-hole made it compulsory to leave at every chance I got, even if it was only in my head.

I stared down at the vegetable pie and gravy and weighed up my options, nurse or patient? I pondered waiting as I quite fancied my chocolate mousse, light and easy on my stomach. With quick decision, I spooned it into my mouth, and savoured every mouthful. Finished, I decided to let fate make my decision for me. I stood up and flung my tray away from me. I enjoyed the seconds of silence, before the screaming started, and the shout of the nurses and orderlies, as they rushed me as one. I fell to the floor under a barrage of hands and arms, half-choking me in their quest to subdue me. I considered their behaviour well over the top, but I didn't fight. As they dragged me to my feet and escorted me out of the dining room, the wailing of an inmate deafened my ears.

"You've done it now, Emily my girl," the hefty nurse whispered with heavy breath in my ear. I could feel the adrenaline coursing through every one of the five who now walked me quickly towards the confinement area and, very briefly, I considered trying my luck. I'd fought five before—perhaps not in this situation where two of them had me in a choke hold and another held my arms behind my back, while the other two took guard duty, front and back—but it might be worth it, just to see if I could.

I decided against it and let my body droop. I didn't bother answering her. Besides, I probably couldn't have anyway, fighting for breath, and walking so fast it was almost a jog. The black guy was fairly new, as was another orderly, but I recognised the other three nurses who opened and shut the doors, keeping an eye on me in case I dared to struggle.

On reaching the block, I was taken to a room and forcibly sat down. Finally released, I carefully rubbed my neck, flexed my arms and rotated my shoulders. My left one hurt a bit, and I massaged it to ease the ache. One of the female nurses on duty saw me and came over. The black orderly stood between us.

"I need to check her neck and shoulder." It was a statement said with such bland disinterest. As she bent over my neck to examine me for injuries, I fought the urge to hit her.

"She's fine," the black orderly replied. He glared down menacingly at me, his disdain evident. "She just needs some time out after a tantrum in the dining hall."

The female nurse shrugged and turned away to fill in her report. "Number two is free. She can go in there till the morning when the doctor can come and see her then. I know he's busy with another patient right now, and if she's just having a little tantrum, she can wait."

"I'm sitting right here, you arrogant bitch! You can address me!" The words were out of my mouth before I could think about the consequences.

Thankfully, she merely glanced at me with as much interest as she might an ant and turned back to her monitors. I was pulled roughly to my feet and pushed towards the locked doors. I knew where the number two room was and walked there myself, aware of people on both sides of me. One of the nurses opened the door and gave me a little push inside, slamming the door shut. I was finally alone.

CHAPTER 4

The light through the small window gave just enough illumination to find the narrow bed in the corner, but I avoided it and sat down heavily on the floor. The window, barely a foot across and down, was high up in the wall, and the evening sun was around the front of the building. I guessed to have around two hours before full darkness descended, and I closed my eyes.

The noise of the hospital couldn't reach me in here, and vice versa, which I guess was the point of the room. It smelt of damp and the residue of the previous occupant, who'd vomited and urinated judging from the faint odours invading my nostrils. Most likely Jane, who relived something horrendous. She had episodes where she would just make herself sick and wet herself with fear. If she made the mistake of attacking a nurse whilst having one, she'd be thrown into one of these cells to cool off, until the doctor could be found. I knew she'd had one yesterday, but still had no idea why Jane was in here.

I truly felt for her. She was older than me, but not by much. Like Mia, there was something childlike about her. Perhaps the singing, her voice so high-pitched reminded me of a child. I'd attempted to have a 'normal' conversation with her when I'd first decided to talk, but realised almost immediately two things. Firstly, conversations were impossible, Jane well and truly locked in her own safe world. And two, she annoyed me too easily for me to be around her for long.

That wasn't to say I didn't feel her pain. Sometimes I'd watch her and could see the anguish on her face. Just a fleeting moment when she thought no one was looking, before the blanket would drop down again and she'd be lost and safe within her own bubble.

I could relate to that sorrow. One born from man and his actions. I had seen it first-hand and recoiled from it. We witnessed injustices and cruelty on a daily basis, watered down on television, films and games, but not like this. This was day to day brutality that had been born and bred, and nothing could sway its nature; it was on a grand scale. Men killing men, women and children, just because they could, or worse, because they had been told to do so by one man, and they'd revelled in it. A cruelty nobody in this civilised society could comprehend unless they were living in war-worn countries. There were horrors of war, murders, terrorists, but it was diluted and chosen by the governments, deciding what we could witness and what we couldn't. I had seen it raw, without compromise, and I think Jane had also witnessed it in some way. I yearned to tell her, to open up, and find out if we shared a trauma, but I daren't in case it backfired on me.

I had been one such victim of what men considered 'sport'. They took great delight in making me suffer for their own pleasure. I thank the gods daily that I'd had champions who came to my rescue, and saved me from a terrible fate. Yet, I cannot help but wish sometimes that they had let me die that day, because then I would never have had to endure this torture.

"Emily ..."

The name was whispered in the air, so delicate that I held my breath, as if the very movement of my chest could destroy it.

"Emily ..."

My heart hammered, so loud to my own ears I could hardly bear it. I wanted silence so I would not miss the sound whispered so faintly on the air. I let out my breath slowly and it shook as I released it. The tension in my body increased and the silence dragged on. Eventually I could stand it no longer. "I'm here, my love ... will you not find me ...?"

Only silence answered me and my body sagged against the wall. The sob that escaped me sounded loud after such stillness, and I fought to choke it back, an impossible task now. The tears come swiftly now. I

31

hadn't realised how difficult it had become to hide them. It's why I'd made a scene in the dining room, to have some semblance of peace. For a few brief moments I forgot the camera, hidden high in the wall, and I let all of my grief out onto the vomit-stinking floor.

Marian watched the screen with a slight frown. She'd heard through the grapevine that Emily had attacked another inmate and come to see for herself. Of course it had all been fabricated, passed from one mouth to another, but she was glad she hadn't gone home immediately, hearing of this now instead of tomorrow. Though tired, Emily intrigued her, and as she watched her sobbing on the floor, her curiosity heightened even more.

This young woman had shown nothing beyond anger and frustration, but mostly indifference, aimed at the staff, following weeks of a coma-like state. Her behaviour was not unexpected, of course. Marian had always thought there was something else lurking within Emily. Something so well hidden it scared her how she kept it locked away. Not many people could do that without breaking at some point, either by action or words, but not Emily. She had chosen to release herself from her own induced state and reveal her pregnancy before returning to her silence.

Her attempted escape had come as no surprise to Marian, neither had her level of violence when she'd been caught. A black eye, a bloody nose and various other bruises in the groin area on four of the security staff were part of the job. No, it was the level of transition from completely calm and inward, barely speaking or acknowledging her surroundings, to a killing machine. She'd taken on the security guards at the hospital like a ninja, and done considerable damage before she'd finally been restrained. Her fury at being caught evident judging from her language as well as her fight. Now, Emily was displaying sorrow. She was hurting and felt safe enough to instigate a night in solitary to allow herself time to cry. This was something new, and Marian had seen a glimpse this morning. This heightened her interest, but it also frightened her, though she wasn't quite sure why.

"Can you rewind it?" She glanced across at the nurse on duty.

"I can, but what are you looking for?" The elderly nurse didn't wait for an answer but went about rewinding the recording.

"I thought I saw her lips move. I want to hear what she said."

The nurse shook her head. "Sorry, Doctor Griffiths, there's no audible on these cameras to provide the patient with some privacy—apparently it's their human rights." The nurse shrugged and continued the DVD recording.

Marian sighed loudly. "Of course it is, I forgot." She watched for a little longer, but Emily seemed to have stopped crying and was sitting facing the window, her back to the camera. She's remembered it's there, Marian thought and smiled to herself.

She left the room abruptly and headed for her office. Emily was breaking. She'd move all of her appointments tomorrow and make sure Emily was brought to her first thing. If she had to, she'd get a court order to hypnotise Emily and get to the bottom of her mind. Her instincts told her she'd be astounded by whatever Emily was hiding.

Brian downed another pint, and caught the eye of the old barman, who was watching him carefully. Having already apologised for his behaviour the night before and paid for the damage, Brian could tell that he was still angry with him, and it made him feel uneasy. "Hey, George, how about another, and get yourself one on me, eh?"

George took the offered empty glass but shook his head. "I don't drink during the day, Brian." He began filling the glass with frothy ale. "Wouldn't get much work done drunk now, would I?"

George looked him in the eye as he placed the pint down on the bar. Brian felt a pang of regret and shame at his behaviour. He enjoyed his time here, one of the oldest pubs in the village, dating back to the 17th Century when it had been a drover's inn. He liked the atmosphere. No noisy machines, no music blaring, and George knew how to look after his beer. If George sent him away, Brian knew he could walk down the road to the Four Daggers, or to the Cross Keys further out of the village, sure he could stagger two miles, but he liked it here best. He wanted George to like him, but the ruffians last night had spoilt the man's opinion of him.

Brian smiled and thanked him as he handed over his last five-pound note. Food would be cheap biscuits for a while. "Thanks, George. Again, sorry about last night. Four against one was not my best odds and I did try to take it outside. You understand why I had to fight him, don't you?"

George shrugged. "Not really. Was it worth it?"

Brian downed half his pint before answering. "Yeah, it was. My sister is innocent." What else could he say? It was that simple really.

George moved off to serve another customer. Brian knew he didn't trust him. He'd heard when George took over the pub nine years ago that he'd jokingly asked the regulars one night if he needed to watch out for anyone, and the answer had simply been 'Brian'.

Brian, only thirty years old, looked more like forty, the drink obviously having taken its toll on his body. Over the years there'd been many tales involving Brian, most outrageous, though not the one about his lost younger sister. Some of the stories said she'd run off in the dead of night to escape his vicious bouts of depression following the murder of both their parents and the family dogs. Brian didn't like to talk about it since nobody had ever been caught and the murders remained unsolved.

When it happened, Brian had been in college training to care for the environment, or some such course. His sister had been in bed asleep, home for the school holidays. Their parents, both teachers, enjoyed walking their three dogs early in the mornings before work, and during the holidays kept up the routine. One day, they never returned. His sister woke to an empty house, and waited all day for their return. Finally, in the early evening, the police had come to the house. A farmer checking his fencing had come across their bodies, and those of the three dogs. All had been shot.

Brian left college and stayed as his sister's care-giver until she disappeared herself. People talked of course. The murderer was never caught, and Brian was questioned, but students could vouch for his whereabouts. His sister, on the other hand, no one could give her an alibi and the tales flew around the village, even though she'd only just turned sixteen. When she disappeared, some said Brian had found out her guilt and killed her. This sad tale backfired on everyone when lo and behold she turned up a couple of years later having travelled the country, working her way around Britain and France. She found a job in some cafe and stayed in the old family home, but then disappeared again, until her picture appeared in the paper, accused of murdering a security guard. She was now locked up in Owl Haven, the hospital for the mentally ill, for evaluation.

34

The ruckus last night had been about that. Some stupid youth hadn't learned to keep his mouth shut in Brian's earshot. Brian had been there since leaving work and was on his third pint when five young men came in, ordering lager before they sat down. They'd been quite loud, though the bar was fairly empty on a Wednesday night. Brian didn't give them a glance as he focused on his pint and the newspaper he'd been reading. Within the hour, they'd drunk another two pints each, and were getting louder and more rowdy by the minute. The regulars left, but not Brian, who remained sitting with his back to the group, slowly drinking, face emotionless.

One of the lads came to the bar to order another round. He happened to look down at the newspaper and saw the article on Emily's incarceration and the murder. The lad paid a heavy price for mouthing off with two black eyes, a broken nose and a fat lip, before his mates could drag Brian off. Four broken glasses and a smashed picture frame was apparently a 'light night' for Brian.

Beryl, George's wife, come up behind him with a plate of chips and set it in front of Brian. "There you are, Brian. No use drinking on an empty stomach now, is there, love." She passed him a fork along with the salt and vinegar and, with a wink, went to serve someone on the other end of the bar.

Brian stared after her retreating figure, then down at the steaming chips. He swallowed hard before picking up the fork and began to slowly work his way through the meal. A single tear ran down his cheek and Brian quickly looked away, keeping his head down.

George frowned on seeing this show of emotion, then walked away to serve another customer. He was grateful to Beryl for suggesting he give Brian another chance.

CHAPTER 5

The bed jolts, and I turn towards the warmth that suddenly emanates from my side. I could smell his musky scent, and the cold water he'd used to freshen up after his exertion before returning to me. With my eyes still closed, I traced a finger along his hairless chest and upwards towards his neck, collecting the stray water droplets as I went. Reaching his chin, I retrace my journey only this time I open my hand to touch more of his skin.

A large hand abruptly clasps mine as I reach his erect nipple, and kisses my palm passionately, before moving to my eager lips. I open my eyes as he gently eases himself above me, his body warm, inviting, and strong, and I catch my breath, and ...

I caught my breath and felt my heart convulse with pain when I saw he wasn't there. I lay perfectly still as the dawn light reached me, aware the nurse watching through the camera would pick up on any sudden movement. My eyes brimmed with tears, and I hastily blinked them back before they were also noted. I'd already given too much away with my weakness yesterday, no need to give Marian any more ammunition.

I was strong. My survival here had proved that. Not that I needed any more proof, but I was dreading today. I knew without any doubt that Marian would have acted upon my show of weakness yesterday and I wouldn't be surprised if she had been told of my confinement. Had she witnessed my sorrow last night? If not, it didn't mean she didn't know about it by now. It would be more fuel for her to use. Marian would fight for hypnotherapy or some other psychoanalysis to reach inside my brain. The truth would render me mad, and this would be my prison for the rest of my life.

I hadn't truly considered the murder charge, in all the mayhem that had occurred since. I cared about the dead man. He had been an innocent man in the wrong place, in the wrong time. Why had he appeared in that very moment? What had I been wishing? Thinking? Could Marian make me confess to his murder? I still wasn't sure who had wielded the sword in that very second. I don't think it mattered anymore. If Marian got inside my head, the game was over.

Nurse Edwards was taking notes, which she did every hour after rounds. She rubbed her eyes, the early morning shift due in half an hour. She hated doing the "graveyard shift" as they called it, eleven till six. Not much happened as most patients were tranquilised.

Last night had been one of the quieter ones, only four in solitary, three of whom were drugged to the eyeballs. Emily was not, but she hadn't made a sound all night.

"Good morning, Nurse, how's the patients today?"

Edwards jumped on hearing Marian's voice and her head peeked around the office door. "Christ, Doctor, you scared me!"

Marian came fully into the small office and glanced down at the monitors. "Sorry. Couldn't sleep, so thought I'd get an early start. Is everyone doing okay?"

Edwards wasn't fooled. She'd spoken with Mary last night and heard about Emily's therapy sessions and Marian's involvement. The authorities wanted Emily to either confess or give up her accomplice apparently, and Marian was the woman for the job. "Yeah, everyone is fine. Sleeping all night. No problems."

"And Emily?" Marian kept her voice light, probably hoping not to arouse gossip.

Edwards shrugged. "She's as well as can be expected under the circumstances."

Marian turned towards her. "What do you mean, Nurse?"

Edwards blushed, but there was no backing down now. "It's just that, I feel sorry for her. She looks so lost and she's grieving, though she tries to hide it."

Marian smiled encouragingly. "I think you're right. She's grieving her baby, but is she grieving the father? Is she sad about the murder? There are people waiting ..."

Edwards looked away first. "I know that family need answers, but sometimes it feels like we're punishing an innocent woman to make them feel better. I know about grief and, well, it just seems cruel, that's all."

Marian nodded. "I'll be gentle, I promise. Hypnotherapy is a pleasant experience and relaxing. She'll come out of it feeling much better."

Edwards sighed. "Yes, I had hypnotherapy following the death of my fiancé a few years ago. The therapist did help me finally sleep, and I was able to release my anger at his dying."

"Then you know it's safe and you can reassure everyone who is gossiping about it, can't you?"

Edwards glanced up at Marian, who was looking down at her with a blank expression, but her tone had made it quite clear. Stay out of my business. Mary had warned her to keep her thoughts to herself. The doctors did not appreciate hearing that nurses were feeling sympathy, or empathy with the patients.

A movement in the corner of her eye made her glance up quickly and stare at the monitors. "Who was that?"

Marian looked at the monitor. "Who? Nobody has got up yet."

Edwards stared at the screen that showed Emily's room. "I could have sworn I saw.... Never mind, it must have been dust on the camera lens."

Marian said nothing, but turned and left. Edwards felt the goosebumps run down her spine, and the hairs on her arms stood to attention. She'd heard the story about the ghost of the wife who'd gone mad and now wandered the hall. She wasn't convinced about such things, but sometimes, especially during the night shift, she couldn't deny that she'd had a few experiences that were making her question her beliefs. She stared hard at the monitor and considered checking the room, but dismissed the idea as quickly as she thought it. Whatever she thought she'd seen was gone. The sooner she got home for a well-earned sleep, the better.

Brian woke to the sound of his alarm. The blare of 'You spin me right round' was abruptly cut short as his fist found the snooze button by instinct. He opened one eye and groaned, realising he was going to be late again. He'd lose his job at this rate. Joe would not be happy.

Pushing himself out of bed, his skull throbbing and his mouth tasting as if something died in it, he rummaged around for his cigarettes, finding them on the floor, soggy. Then he recalled peeing outside the pub and they had fallen out. He left them while he dressed quickly. Using the shared bathroom, he ignored the stranger who passed him on the landing. So many men came and went in this pigsty. Grabbing his boots, some loose change and his jacket, he was out of the door and walking fast. He hoped they had coffee going on site and a few biscuits in the tin.

At the building site, Brian saw a few of his workmates hanging around the main entrance. Some were smoking and he felt the lack of nicotine in his own system. Those guys wouldn't give him a cigarette. One of the younger men he didn't recognise was reading the local newspaper and Brian's heart jumped in his chest. Brian knew he was going to have a go. He could see it in his body language. As he approached the gang, the worker with the newspaper made a big show of fluffing it open to a middle page. "Says here, the family of that murdered security guard are demanding justice and want to know why the murderer hasn't been charged? Maybe we should ask someone who knows the killer personally, eh?"

Brian stopped dead and slowly turned back to face the worker. His friends gathered around the guy, five on one, not good odds, especially in his state. "You got something to say, Keith, you'd better speak up. I'm a trifle deaf this morning." Brian made a point of fiddling with his ears in a comical manner and turned away. He'd get him later.

"Maybe it's not just sisters who murder people, eh? Maybe brothers, or possibly sons, have something to do with certain deaths as well ...?"

He'd stepped over the line, the last part reference to his parents' murder. Brian felt his blood boil in his veins and his hands began to tremble. He turned to attack, but a strong hand held his shoulder, and he twisted around to find Joe holding him tightly. "You and me need to have a chat, Brian." He looked towards the small group. "And you lot, I take it you don't fancy a pay packet at the end of this week? Get going!"

He walked Brian to the makeshift office, which would one day be someone's garage, and indicated one of the four seats in there. Brian slumped down in the nearest one and rubbed his face. "Okay, I know what you're going to say and I'm sorry...."

"Half an hour late, Brian? Come on, I can't allow that, not with this group. They think I'm giving you special treatment, and they're right."

Brian rubbed the back of his neck, stood up and began pacing the small office. "I know, it's not good. Do you have any pain killers, Joe?"

"Pain killers? Fuckin' Christ, Brian. Are you still pissed or just hung-over this time? I have to let you go, mate, I'm sorry. I'll pay you what you're owed, but dammit, I hate losing you. You're one of the best bricklayers I've got, and fast too, when you arrive."

Brian grinned sheepishly. "I don't blame you, Joe. I know I've let you down—"

"You've let yourself down, Brian. You're good at this. You have natural talent, and I've seen your designs for the gardens." Seeing Brian's surprise, he hastily added, "I wasn't looking. I just happened to notice them on the table. You must have left them there by accident."

Brian's shoulders slumped. "No worries, Joe, I just did those on lunch break, you know, doodling. You can use them if you want. I owe you." He stepped close and held out his hand. "Thanks for having me here. I appreciate the chance you gave me...."

"If you'd only cut down on your drinking ... I understand why. Emily is a lovely girl you know ... but ..." Joe shrugged, what more could he say? Joe shook the offered hand. Brian held on a little longer than expected before releasing him.

"She's innocent, you know."

Joe nodded. "I believe you. When was the last time you saw her?"

Brian thought for a moment. The image of her, the last time they'd met was all he had, that and her photo plastered all over the bloody papers. Sadly, none of them were good images to remember. "Been a few years. I did something despicable and she said she never wanted to see me again. I didn't blame her then, and still don't."

Joe offered Brian a rolled cigarette, and lit it before asking, "What did you do?"

Brian inhaled deeply before answering, "I stole some money from her purse to buy booze. I feel shame whenever I remember that day. I also remember how she kicked my arse. I was bruised for days. Damned black belt ninja! But Emily would never kill."

Joe waited to see if Brian would tell him anything else. When he remained silent, Joe stepped closer. "You do know I've been given the contract to build the extra rooms for the Owl Haven Hospital, don't you, Brian?"

Brian stared at the older man. "What are you saying?"

Joe shrugged. "No idea, but I don't fancy losing my best worker just yet. I knew you both as kids. I never met Emily as an adult, but I never believed you were both killers back then, so how about you pull yourself together, Brian."

Brian grinned. "I'll take the job."

Joe laughed. "I didn't offer it, 'ya cheeky bugger!"

Brian stared at him, with a look of gratitude for a moment before smiling warmly. "Yes, you did. I'll meet you there tomorrow with the new crew. Appreciate the chance, Joe, I won't let you down."

CHAPTER 6

Marian was slowly twiddling the pencil between her finger and thumb as she spoke with the leading detective on the telephone. "So you have doubts, Inspector?" She could almost see him calculating how to phrase his sentences and smiled.

"We have a few questions we'd like answered by Emily as soon as possible, to clarify some details we've found."

"Details?" Marian began pushing the pencil along the desk, bored with this conversation. She wanted to prepare for Emily's arrival.

"We have some doubt about Emily's ability to wield such a heavy sword. Mr Dawson's head was cut off with one swing. We've also found a smudged thumb print beneath Emily's fingerprints, so ..."

Marian sat up. "So, are you saying Emily is innocent of this murder, or not? You know she has a black belt in karate, don't you?"

She heard the inspector sigh. "Yes, yes, we know about her skills, but this man wasn't killed by a karate blow, but a sword. Anyway, I've spoken with everyone regarding Emily and nobody speaks ill of her. How is she behaving?"

"Emily is 'behaving' like a woman trapped within a cage she isn't meant to be in." Marian struggled to keep her irritation from showing. From the tone in Inspector Richards' voice, she'd failed.

"I see. So you believe she is innocent too, do you? I'm afraid I have to go on facts, and the fact is, we found her sitting in the man's blood wielding the murder weapon, and she refused to speak a word to us on the subject. Now, I've heard that she is speaking, I'll be returning for an interview with Emily."

Marian leaned forward. Her hand clutched the phone tightly. "I'm not sure that's a good idea, Inspector. She's only just coming out of her shell, having endured a terrible ordeal, and then losing a child ... I'd prefer you to wait until I've had a few therapy sessions with her."

"I was under the impression that you were her therapist, Doctor Griffiths. What sessions are you talking about?"

"I've been given the go ahead to try hypnotherapy with Emily, to see if I can unlock her memories. If she sees you again, she might shut down and go internal again. She doesn't trust the police."

"She's told you that, has she?"

Marian felt herself getting warm. She was overstepping herself. "Well, no, not exactly. But following the murder of her parents nine years ago, I know she was under suspicion for a while. She associates authority with blame and I can't have that."

"Yes, I see. I read though their parents' murder file. Horrible business. No one ever brought to justice for that. A shame. All right, I'll leave Emily with you for a few days, but no longer. I need answers from her."

Twenty minutes had now passed since she'd said goodbye to the inspector and called Carla to steady her nerves. Carla had given her some breathing exercises to do and wished her luck. The go ahead had been given by them upstairs, but she still felt anxious. She'd already paced the floor, fumbled around with the blinds, rearranged her desk and flicked through the 'Medieval Britain' book once more, hoping to find something to use in her session today. She felt so close to the truth of what happened, it was difficult not to go and find Emily and shake it out of her.

She glanced at the wall clock. Emily would have her breakfast before being assessed by Dr Gilmore on whether or not she'd be allowed back into the main building. Everyone knew Emily had done it deliberately, except Gilmore—an old fossil who hated women and loved nothing more than to put a woman in her place. He would consider another day in solitary punishment, stupid idiot. Emily would see that as a holiday.

A smirk on his face, Gilmore left, pushing his little round glasses farther up his nose. Nurse Mary swiftly followed him, and the black orderly slammed the door shut behind them without looking at me. I heard the start of Mary's argument, that I'd deliberately placed myself in solitary and that it was silly to keep me here.

The door shut and silence returned. To make a point, I waved and smiled at the camera, hoping the old fool was watching, then turned my back to the door and sat down. I glanced around the small room, already knowing what I'd see. The remnants of my breakfast still sat on the tray which lay on the bed. I could still smell the hot porridge and my mouth watered. The bowl was empty, but I reached out and ran my finger around the edges and licked it. They did good porridge and fruit, though lacking in a decent cup of tea. It was always stewed. What I'd give for a decent cup of warm ale.

The emotion that almost choked me was instant. I had said that once before and the memory of it was like a kick in the guts. Suddenly the porridge didn't feel too good in my stomach and I rubbed the area, fighting off the building nausea. A minute or so later, I felt better and I sipped the water in my plastic cup, which sadly already tasted of it. I could remember tasting clean, crisp water, fresh and freezing cold, like clear crystals in my mouth. Too much, too quickly and I'd get brain freeze. We'd laughed about that.

I choked back the tears and, to keep myself occupied, I began to rock myself, which gave me a strange kind of comfort. I got into quite a rhythm when the door opened behind me and Nurse Mary stood within the doorway.

"Come on, Emily, my child, time to go."

"But Gilmore said ..."

"Yes, well, never mind what that idiot said, time to go. No more time off, my girl."

I caught the sly wink and grinned. I'd been found out! I did wonder how long I could get away with my antics just to get some peace and quiet. Next time I'd have to do something really bad!

Heaving myself up, I stood a moment while I got the feeling back in my feet. As the pins and needles cleared, I gingerly stepped out of the cell and into the bright corridor. "What gave me away?" I asked with a grin.

Mary sighed and shook her head. "We all knew, Emily. We just prefer to indulge you on occasion, only this time Doctor Griffiths has asked to see you and your little 'wave' at the camera forced Doctor Gilmore to concede you were happier in there than out here, so he changed his mind."

"Shit!" I huffed and rolled my shoulders to ease the tension in them.

Mary smiled. "Indeed, now come on, child, and no messing about or John will have to restrain you."

I noticed John loitering nearby and smiled sweetly at him, which only made him scowl deeper. The big black orderly hated me and I knew it was a bad idea to antagonise him, but I couldn't help myself; it was the 'wild-cat' in me. That thought made my smile disappear, too many references to old memories today. I needed to pull myself together.

I obediently followed Nurse Mary out of solitary and up the flights of stairs, aware of John who followed us closely. Mary knocked on Marian's door and opened it on hearing her shout, "Come in." I stood a moment in the doorway surveying the woman I'd had to talk with for weeks and felt a stab of apprehension; she'd been given the go ahead to hypnotise me. I could see it on her face.

"Well, come in, Emily, we don't have all day." Marian spoke in a light-hearted manner, but her eyes betrayed her impatience, and I stumbled in. The door was immediately closed behind me, and I felt much like a fly might feel when caught in a spider's web.

Mary headed back to the main building to start on the medications for the day. She smiled at everyone she passed, but her mind was troubling her. Emily looked absolutely terrified just now, although she tried very hard not to show it. She wasn't due another session with Doctor Griffiths for another week, so she'd been taken aback when told to escort Emily to her office. She'd heard various things through the hospital grapevine about Marian Griffiths, and how she portrayed herself as a professional, caring human being. But there was another side to her, a darker side, if anyone crossed her. She was determined to climb the success ladder, and what better way than to climb than to use patients as case studies in her career. Emily would surely be considered a few rungs if she could somehow get her to talk about what happened.

Reaching the Pharmacy, she wished the elderly man behind the desk a 'good morning' and went about her daily routine of checking the medications he was already preparing. She noticed Emily's medication wasn't on the chart.

"Has Doctor Griffiths already got Emily's medication in her office?"

Neil stopped his preparations and turned towards her. He glanced through the names and shrugged. "She must do. If Emily is not on my list, it's nothing to do with me ... or you." He added with a shrewd look. "Take my advice, Mary, don't get in Doctor Griffiths' way. If she deems it necessary not to medicate Emily with Prozac today, then leave it. Besides, Emily usually spits them out, I'm sure of it."

"You think? Yes, you're probably right, but surely, even if that is true, Emily should be given smaller doses over a period of time, not just ..."

"Leave it, Mary. Nurses do not question the doctors here. It won't be tolerated. Emily is a patient, so don't get attached. Now, get on with checking Mrs James' meds, I'm sure she has two, but they have her down as one today."

Mary bit her lip and turned back to the list of names and medications. Nurses never questioned doctors, and that was part of the problem. They felt like gods and saw these poor patients as guinea pigs to further their careers. Emily was nothing to these people other than a mystery and Doctor Marian Griffiths was determined to be the one who solved her: and Mary couldn't think of a damned thing she could do about it.

Marian was watching me carefully and no doubt using her findings to calculate how to approach this session. I kept my face as passive as possible by moving directly to the large window and looked out with interest. The morning sun was just reaching this side of the building and a patch of sunlight warmed the window sill. I put my hand in the yellow glow and closed my eyes. Unbidden, a memory rushed in of when I had done the same at a different window only this time hands had twined around my waist and lips had nuzzled my neck in an attempt to tempt me back to bed. I quickly withdrew my hand and thrust it into my trouser pocket, but kept my back to Marian.

"Not talkative today, Emily? Well, I have some good news. I'm going to help you with that, if you'll let me? I think you have memories that make you feel anxious and sad, am I right? Hypnosis can help you with that, if you let it. There's also the problem of family needing answers, perhaps the same answers you need to be happy ... I'm sorry to throw this at you without really talking about it first, but you've left us with no choice. For the family's sake, Emily, for yours, will you comply and allow me to do this therapy with you?"

My heart raced in my chest, how could I allow it? What if I talked of him? Of them? Of what happened to me? I would never leave this place, that was for sure. Yet, she was right, of course, the security guard's family needed some closure, but I didn't have those answers for them, did I? All I had would be considered the ramblings of a mad woman under a delusion. Maybe that would be enough? Maybe if it did all come out, they would leave me alone, believing there was nothing left to learn and they could get on with their lives? So many possibilities. I had no idea how it would go, in my favour or against me, but I had no more options left whilst stuck in this place, unless I could fake it?

"What if it doesn't work? I mean, many people can't be hypnotised, especially if they don't believe it would work. You can't force me, can you?"

I turned and looked at Marian. I saw my question hadn't taken her by surprise. She'd been expecting an excuse of sorts. "No, Emily, I can't force you, besides, hypnosis only works if you want it to. You have control. I can't make you do anything you don't want."

"Is that true? I'd have to want to remember ...?"

Marian nodded. "I can't make you act like a chicken or not feel pain, unless your mind wants it on some level. Besides, I wouldn't do that. Hypnosis is merely to help you relax and perhaps your mind will access those hidden memories ... or not ..."

"No pressure then ..." I smiled weakly at my own joke. I couldn't deny the temptation of visiting my memories, though I remembered so much, I had heard that hypnosis can make things seem so real. Could it take me back to them and feel real? What a sick and twisted thing to want if I could never have the real thing again. Perhaps this way I had control over where or when, and maybe, just maybe, it would return for me and let me go back. My thoughts of family had returned me, perhaps memories of them would allow me to go back and be happy again.

Marian was watching me carefully. She finally smiled and indicated the armchair opposite her desk. Reluctantly, I went to sit in it and curled my feet underneath my body, removing my pumps first.

"I understand your concern, Emily, but please let me reassure you that I am merely going to relax you. I won't be expecting you to act like an animal, or find yourself in another life!" She smiled again, but I merely raised an eyebrow and waited.

"All hypnosis will do is relax you into a state where your mind will be free to access memories that are hidden from you. I will not let anything happen to you, Emily, you must try and trust me. Can you do that?"

"No. I can't trust anyone in here, but you already know that. I don't feel as if I have a choice in this, do I? So, when do we start?" I didn't add that her comment on living another life had struck a chord in me, but let it go.

Marian sighed loudly at my statement. I knew I'd hurt her, but she quickly shook it off and put on her professional coat. "If you feel up to it, Emily, we could try a short session now and see what happens?"

My stomach dropped and panic overwhelmed me, but nothing showed on my face. I swallowed hard and drew a shaking breath. "Sure, okay, I just need to use the bathroom first. I won't be able to relax if I've got to pee ..."

I saw Marian's jaw tighten, but she quickly pressed a button and like magic, a nurse appeared in the doorway. "Please escort Emily to the ladies and return her immediately please." Leaving my pumps on the floor, I walked ahead of the young nurse to the bathroom. Behind me I heard Marian press her intercom and tell her secretary to cancel her morning appointments. Reaching the bathroom used by the doctors, I quickly slammed the door in the nurse's face.

My legs buckled and I leaned against the bathroom wall. It smelled of pine and bits of the floor were still wet from the cleaners. The bathroom on this floor was large to accommodate the disabled staff. We mere patients weren't supposed to use it. I felt honoured. Marian must be desperate to allow me to use her bathroom. I quickly sat on the toilet, used it and flushed. I knew the nurse would be timing me. I had perhaps another minute left before she'd bang on the door.

I splashed cold water on my burning face and rinsed out my mouth. My toiletries had not been given to me that morning and I yearned to clean my teeth. In fact, I longed for a long, hot bath with bubbles, but I was not getting one of those anytime soon. I splashed more water and jumped as the banging began. "I'm coming, you big hulk! Hang on!"

I would have to try and fake it. Say anything. Talk about another assailant without mentioning the rest. Surely forensics would have found his prints on the sword? He had hold of it as we wrestled that one last time and I lost him forever. The possibilities of going back were tauntingly close. If it were possible that Marian took me back, what the hell would they say about my sanity? Whatever I said, it was a risk. I couldn't win.

The door opened and the nurse stood there glaring at me. "It doesn't take that long to piss, Emily, get back into the room and stop messing Dr Griffiths around."

I glared back at her, but walked out of my sanctuary with a plan and a hope that it would work.

CHAPTER 7

I focused on the feel of the couch under my fingers and attempted to keep Marian's voice from interfering with my head. She tried so hard, I almost felt sorry for her, her soft tone quite calming, too calming, and my eyes were beginning to feel heavy. Panicking, I scrunched my hand into a fist and then splayed out my fingers, feeling the softness beneath my fingertips. I did it again and began to recite anything that sprang to mind.

'There was a young man from dale, who thought he'd swallowed a whale, but on opening his mouth ...' Shit! I couldn't think of anything ... 'Mary had a little lamb; her fleece was white as snow ...'

"Emily, relax your hands, your fingers, breathing in and out ... listen to my voice, Emily ... breathing in and breathing out ..."

No, I couldn't let her take over my mind, they would lock me up. I tried again to think of a song, any song, but nothing came to mind.

I feel the biting chill of the wintery air, and shiver, wrapping my arms around my freezing body. My fingers touch the warm fur of the cloak that I've been given and I caress it, searching for some remnants of warmth to help bring feeling to my icy fingers. I feel guilty at having the fur, as I've always fought against animal cruelty and try to be a good vegetarian, though I slip every now and then and eat salmon, or a bag of fish and chips was a temptation I rarely said no to, but I haven't eaten meat for many years. Now, here I am enjoying the pelt of some slaughtered animal and relishing its warmth. I pull the cloak tighter around my body, close my eyes, and feel his gaze on me.

Shit!

I jumped off the couch, stumbled and fell to the floor. I knelt on all fours for a brief moment, before easing myself into a seated position with my head in my hands. I fought down the nausea and breathed deeply, hoping the panic would subside quickly. I tried to slow my breathing, the room spinning if I moved too quickly.

"Emily? Can you hear me, Emily?" Marian's voice cut through the spinning void and I nodded, unable to focus on words, not trusting what would happen if I opened my mouth. "Emily." Nearer now. "I want you to drink this water for me. Can you do that?"

For ten minutes I couldn't move my hands as they supported my head. It felt so big and heavy, while the rest of me was weak, but eventually I felt strong enough to look up into Marian's face, and took the offered glass of cold water. My hand shook, and I quickly grasped the glass with both hands to steady it as I brought it to my lips. The cool liquid helped calm me, and by the time I'd finished drinking it, I felt much better. The dizziness had disappeared, but the panic hadn't.

Had I spoken out loud? How much time had passed?

I handed the glass back to Marian who took it with a smile. Her face gave nothing away and I began to breathe easier. "Sorry, Doctor Griffiths, I guess it didn't work ..."

Marian watched me for a moment before asking, "Why did you jump up, Emily?"

I sighed. "I don't know. I felt sick."

"I see." Marian sat down behind her desk and crossed her hands on her lap whilst watching me intently. "So, it wasn't that you felt cold and were glad of the cloak he'd lent you?"

I stared dumbfounded, searching for something to say. "I, erm ... no idea what you mean, Dr Griffiths ... What cloak?" I made a point of looking around the office, hoping to look sincere, but I wasn't fooling anyone, especially Marian.

She merely watched me for a moment longer, a slight smile on her face, before glancing down at some notes she'd been taking. "You're a vegetarian, I believe, is that right?" She didn't wait for my response. "So touching fur would be a problem for you?" I stared back, unsure what to say. My throat felt constricted. My heart beat was going ten to the dozen. "How long do you think you were hypnotised, Emily?"

"Hypnotised?" I eventually managed to croak out. "It didn't work on me."

Again, Marian watched me before returning her gaze to her notes. "I see, well, perhaps we could try again tomorrow. Now that you've had a small taster of what to expect, you might relax a bit better?"

I shrugged and pushed myself off the couch. My legs felt like jelly, but I managed to walk to the door as John was opening it and finally left Marian's scrutiny.

"I'll see you tomorrow at ten, Emily, thank you," Marian called after me, but I didn't acknowledge her, and I didn't wait for John as he closed the door behind me. I'd seen the clock on the wall as I'd stood to leave, five to twelve, which would mean I'd been on the couch for over an hour. She'd done it, she'd hypnotised me and I'd lost time. What the hell did I say? But I had been there. It had, for one brief moment, felt so real again and I hugged myself, trying to find the same warmth from that fur cloak—but I never would.

Marian took a long deep breath after Emily left, and waited for her hands to stop shaking. She'd hypnotised a few clients over the years and heard everything. Nothing astonished her anymore, until today. She was fairly sure Emily couldn't have faked it. Why the hell would she? Something like this would put someone in a loony house and Emily wanted out, not in, but if what she'd said was true ...?

Marian immediately dialled the number of a friend who had a strong interest in history. It went to voicemail and she hung up impatiently. The sad fact was that Dean was probably in the bloody library where he always was with his head in one book or another. She dialled his number again and this time left a message asking him to get back to her as soon as possible.

Replacing the telephone, she sat down heavily in her armchair and let out a long breath. She re-read the notes she'd made while listening to the tape recording of the session. Emily's voice was barely audible, she'd have to change the angle of the recorder next time and move it closer. Emily was whispering, her voice sounded frightened, in awe of what she was experiencing. Marian had reached out tentatively and gently touched Emily's fingers, they'd been icy cold, just as she described. It had been that touch which brought the session to an abrupt halt, and she kicked herself for doing it.

Emily's description of a place of stone, the archway and square yard that held the stables, and a bakery, and the vastness of the moors that surrounded the building, was very evocative. Marian knew she had to be careful not to influence Emily in anyway, in case this was merely a snatched memory from childhood perhaps. Maybe she'd visited a living history museum of this period and it'd come through as a real event in her life, although it didn't explain her icy fingers. It was warm in the room, yet Marian was convinced she'd touched the wet, cold fingers of outdoors.

She sat back in her chair once the recording finished. She had to be careful not to project her own thoughts onto Emily. Perhaps her body language had subtly inclined Emily to do something like this. Perhaps on a subconscious level, she'd hoped Emily would follow this past-life progression because of the medieval book? Emily did do strange things, and act as if she was elsewhere, always thinking and daydreaming, and now she'd caught her showing emotion, but for what, or possibly whom? It was also conceivable that Emily's mind had imagined this place so vividly, that her body reacted to it, believing she was in this cold place. There were many avenues to explore. The paranormal elements could wait.

Unable to remain seated she began pacing the floor. Emily had something to hide, they all knew this. Forensics said it was possible Emily hadn't been the one who wielded the sword that killed the guard. Another strange thing, the sword, it was ancient, but in excellent condition, and apparently that wasn't possible according to the scholars. She caught herself and sighed. Okay, possible, but very doubtful. Where had the sword come from? They were fairly certain the sword had come from England and the date narrowed it to around the 6th century. Experts were desperate to speak with Emily, but the authorities had denied it, for now anyway. Money and influence would soon break that barrier.

She stopped and looked out of her window. An hour before her next patient. She needed to get her thoughts clear for Jane, but Emily's session refused to go away. She didn't believe in ghosts or past lives, and yet, after many debates with her friends who did, she'd begun to believe something, just not sure what. Did we die, or become resurrected? Possible, she'd read a few research papers on the subject of past lives, but why did only a few people remember? No, for now she considered Emily's episode as a childhood memory, perhaps combined with a film she had watched. A nice, romantic fantasy with a man from the dark ages ... But wasn't that the same era as the murder weapon? She would break Emily and find out the mystery behind her behaviour. Marian smiled to herself, sure this would be the catapult to moving her career further up the ladder.

*   *   *

Mia bounded over to me as I entered the main block, her doll clutched to her chest. Mia rarely wanted any physical contact, which was understandable, but today she grabbed my hand and kissed one of my knuckles. "Love you, Emily!"

Flabbergasted, I stared at her, then my hand, which she had let go. "Mia, are you okay? You seem happy?"

Mia nodded. "I am happy. I'm going home today."

I frowned. "Really? Are you sure, Mia?" I felt my heart sink for her. Mia wouldn't get out for a very long time, not until a judge decided she wasn't a threat to any more children. It angered me that they hadn't taken into account the circumstances of her pregnancy, and the impact it'd had on Mia's life. Her mother rarely came to visit and, when she did, only stayed half an hour. She felt shame for her daughter and most likely guilt along with grief for a dead husband and grandson. What a mess!

Mia was grinning like a cat. "I'm going home. I'm leaving. I just wanted to thank you, Emily, for helping me."

Before I could answer, Mia turned and skipped away, waving to anyone, including a nurse who passed her in the corridor, though the nurse didn't acknowledged Mia as she carried an arm full of charts. I watched her skip away with a strange sense of sadness. Ten months of being cooped up in this hell-hole, I'd barely bothered with any of the other inmates, preferring to keep my distance, and my silence, in case they talked with staff. I trusted nobody, except Mia. Her innocence shone through regardless of her crime. I'd miss her.

I sat down in a high-backed armchair and turned it away slightly from the half a dozen other inmates in the lounge. The television was on, but barely audible and easy to shut out. I needed time to think about what had just happened in Marian's room. I'd been there. She'd somehow managed to do it or she'd made my mind think I was back there again. I clenched my fingers, they were warm again, but the freezing coldness and his touch were still fresh. I rubbed my fingers together hoping to feel him once again, but I knew he was gone.

Damn Marian! I was trying to save my life so that I wouldn't be locked up here for the rest of it, but she made it harder by giving me a possible avenue back to him. My memories were all that I had, but today, under hypnosis, my memories had, for just a brief moment, become real again and that temptation was too great. To be so close, yet be so far away, was so much worse than never. I had to find a way of stopping the sessions, but that very thought brought a mixture of emotions I couldn't organise properly in my head.

I stood up and began walking to my room when I heard the wailing begin, quickly followed by the emergency siren. Nurses came running from all over and I deftly moved to the side of the corridor out of their way. They were all running towards Mia's room and my stomach dropped. 'I'm going home' she'd said. I walked quickly, almost jogging as I followed a male orderly around the corner. The wailing was coming from Mia's room-mate Andrea, who suffered with terrible depression for long periods of time. She'd connected with Mia on her arrival and so the consultant had put them together in the hope of helping each other. Andrea was kneeling in the doorway of their shared bedroom and her clothes were covered in blood.

I started to run towards her, but a nurse was already pulling Andrea away from the scene. Another nurse I didn't recognise abruptly appeared and together they marched her away, their reassuring words going unheard over Andrea's screams. Seconds later a doctor ran after them, a syringe in his hand. The screams died away and a strange silence filled the corridor.

A small group of patients had gathered outside Mia's room and a couple of orderlies were shooing us away. "Come on now, ladies, nothing to see. It's all right, Mia has just had an accident. Come on, Emily, move away ... Now!"

I looked up into John, the orderly's, face and back to the closed door. I resisted his slight shove and remained leaning against the wall, the shock of it sinking in. Tears began to fall down my cheeks as I continued to stare at the door. "I should have stopped her ..."

"How could you?"

John's answer surprised me. I hadn't realised I'd spoken out loud. "I mean, just now, I should have questioned her more about going home ... I knew it couldn't be true. Who told her she was going home?" I felt a deep anger and resentment building inside me. Whoever it had been was responsible for Mia's death. She was dead, I was absolutely positive now.

John was watching me carefully, a frown on his face. "What do you mean she was going home? I think you need to tell Doctor Gilmore what you discussed with Mia last night."

"Last night? What are you talking about? I spoke with Mia only minutes ago and she said ..."

"She said fuck all, Emily, so stop this nonsense. We don't need this crap from you right now. I was outside Doctor Griffith's room most of this morning, so you and I both know you hadn't spoken with Mia before she did this." He shoved me a little harder and my legs gave way. He caught me and roughly walked me away from the scene a little before releasing me. "Keep walking, girl, or I'll put you in solitary, understand?"

I stared open-mouthed at him. "But ... Mia ...?"

A nurse passing by saw my pain and came over, dismissing John with a tilt of her head. "Yes, Emily, we're all sorry for Mia, poor girl. Are you okay? Do you need to lie down?"

"No, I ... I feel confused, Nurse, about Mia. Why would she, I mean, she was going home, right?"

The nurse smiled kindly and shook her head, "Oh dear, Emily, we are a little confused this morning. I don't think you've had your medication today? Weren't you with Dr Griffiths this morning?"

"Yes, but Mia ..." I was getting agitated.

"There was nothing anyone could do, Emily. If someone is going to take their own life, then they find a way. She must have done it after breakfast when she knew no one would check on her for a while. It'll affect Andrea terribly ..." As if realising she was speaking to an inmate, she coughed and smiled reassuringly before leaving me cold, statue-like and fighting the nausea that threatened to overtake me.

After breakfast, she'd said, but that had been four hours ago. I'd just seen Mia half an hour ago, hadn't I? I sat down suddenly on the nearest chair as my legs gave way completely. My body trembled as I tried to take in what had just happened. I had seen her. She'd kissed me, which had been strange as physical contact was not something Mia encouraged, and yet ... I gently touched the knuckle she'd kissed and let the tears fall for Mia.

CHAPTER 8

B rian carefully moved the brick and gave it a little wiggle so it fitted perfectly within the crevice. He dipped his trowel into the cement and efficiently covered the brick on all sides before moving onto the next one.

"It's like watching an artist at work."

He smiled to himself on hearing the comment. "And if you can name one artist, I'll buy you dinner!"

He grinned as those nearest heard the good-humoured banter, and laughed while they continued their own jobs. Brian glanced across at Johnny, the Geordie lad who'd shouted the comment, and wasn't surprised to see him frowning in concentration. The possibility of his dinner being paid for was a big challenge, as the man was renowned for eating his own weight in burgers, yet he still looked fairly trim compared to others in the group.

"Anything spring to mind yet, Johnny lad?" Brian didn't turn to look again as he concentrated on his wall.

"I'll think of someone and then you'll be sorry!"

"Aye!" shouted another builder nearby. "He'll have ya skint and you'll be beggin' to borrow cash from us till pay-day. Well, ya can fuck off from me."

Brian ignored the comment, knowing it was meant in jest, but there was also truth behind it. He had borrowed money off most of the crew at one time or another, but he'd always paid it back when he could, and he'd always buy a round if he could afford it. Most of the crew who knew him shook their heads at the comment, but said nothing, not their fight.

Johnny scratched his head on hearing the comment, shrugged and got on with his work. He wouldn't take Brian's money, he liked him, so he kept the artist 'Banksy' to himself.

Brian soon forgot the banter as he continued with his wall. He'd been there one whole day and had barely touched a drop of alcohol. Last night, after leaving the other job, it'd been hard to stop at four pints, but he'd left on a fake errand, and gone straight back to his bedsit to smoke himself to death while he contemplated his plans.

Emily was less than half a mile away. The hospital complex was fairly big and the new buildings he helped with were at the far end of the large grounds where the old stables had once stood. Considered too fragile to be left, they'd been knocked down to make way for this latest development for out-patients due to open next year. Emily was deep in the heart of the old hall, central to the surroundings, and safely kept prisoner behind bars, walls and medication. He had no idea how he was going to get her out, but he had to try. She couldn't be guilty of this murder, or that of their parents and dogs, which had been implied at one stage by the investigating officer.

Brian didn't have faith in the system. Not since their deaths and nobody had been brought to justice for it. Now the murder of the guard made the authorities question their parents' murder once again. It wasn't fair. Both were innocent, yet they had been treated as suspects, unable to truly mourn their loss. He'd eventually found solace in booze, Emily in fighting. When their parents had been alive Emily had dabbled in various keep fit groups, but after their murder she had drifted towards the more energetic fighting skills, using the force of kicking and punching to ease her pain. After trying kick boxing and Judo she'd settled on karate, and joined the school team. It surprised him, as 'karate' is more about peace of mind than violence. Maybe she'd needed both.

Emily was now a black belt, and he had no doubts she could, and would, handle herself in a situation. But murder? No. Nobody would convince him of that, not in a million years. He was all she had to fight in her corner in a world that was desperate to pin this murder on someone. He couldn't let her down now, not again. Booze, his crutch, would have to take a back seat. He would need all of his wits to free her one way or another before he lost her to the system—who merely medicated the brain and body so the soul was lost forever.

*   *   *

Mia's death was obviously the main topic for the rest of the day. Patients and nurses alike wandered around the hospital in a daze, in shock at such a violent death happening so close to them. The nurses tried hard to hide their horror, and for some it was easier said than done. I noticed many tears being wiped away when they thought patients were not looking, and most had red eyes, but their professionalism shone through. Most of the orderlies didn't give a shit about Mia. She was merely a job.

I let my tears fall freely until I couldn't cry any longer. For the rest of the day nobody was allowed to return to their bedrooms to find solace. Instead we were herded into one of the many lounges and common rooms and spied upon, watched for any signs that another might self-harm or worse. Eventually, the head doctor deemed it unethical to keep us cooped up and we were let out to wander the halls and rooms like passive ghosts. I made my way to my room, yearning for solace, but Jane had got there first and was singing her rhymes over and over in some attempt to console herself. I needed a quiet corner to think, but solitary wasn't an option now. They knew I wanted to be there, so they'd only put me there in restraints and dope me up. I needed a clear head.

The nurse had of course been right, I'd dodged my medication by going to Doctor Griffiths' room and now Mia's death had meant they'd been preoccupied and forgotten again. My head was probably clearer than it had been in a while. I was absolutely sure that I hadn't been hallucinating and Mia had kissed my hand and skipped past me. I went over it again and again and gently touched the knuckle she'd tenderly kissed. It didn't feel any different from the last time I'd touched and examined it, but it reassured me that, for whatever reason, Mia had shown herself to me, and I found just a smidgen of comfort in that.

The more I thought about it, the more I should have known something wasn't right. Mia touched no one if she could help it. The chairs were her only barrier to keep her from touching other people. As she'd skipped past nurses and other inmates, nobody had acknowledged her, in fact, I'd swear to the nurse not even seeing Mia as she'd not stopped in her stride and Mia skipping by would have made some impression as Mia never moved anywhere fast, preferring to creep about so as to be forgotten.

No, the more I considered it, the more I knew Mia had come back to me as a spirit to thank me. I'd like to believe it was because I'd been her friend and had never judged her, but I couldn't be sure. I didn't think I'd done anything out of the ordinary, but perhaps Mia did. I sat down in the corner of the lounge, close to where Mia would set up her fortress, and silently thanked Mia and wished her peace.

Movement opposite made me lift my head in time to see Mia's mother walk in, a tissue clasped to her face as she controlled her tears by frantically wiping at her eyes. I wondered if she was even crying at all, or merely making them red with all her wiping. I felt nothing but disdain for this pathetic excuse for a mother. This woman had let down her child by not protecting her, then not believing her, then abandoning her. Thoughts of my own mother flooded unbidden to mind, and I quickly pushed them away. No use thinking of her now.

I continued watching her as the circle of concerned nurses and doctors grew, and the group walked into the main office, the door firmly closed behind them. I could visualise the conversation. The doctor would go into pathetic overdrive of sincerity and how they had done all that they could for poor Mia, but somehow she'd managed to find something sharp. It was no one's fault, and there would be an enquiry, but the hospital would of course be exonerated and Mia would be forgotten. Mia would be just another statistic. I hoped Mia's ghost would find peace now.

Mia's ghost. I felt a ripple of goosebumps along my spine and I quickly shuddered, but felt no fear. When did my perception of all things supernatural become so mundane? Seeing a ghost, should have had me quaking in my slippers, pissing my pants and diving for the bed covers, but no. Instead I felt a great sadness and an inevitability that I would experience more paranormal occurrences in my life.

And I would accept them without question.

The strings of life seemed so fragile. One action affected everything else. Nothing shocked me anymore. Nothing scared me beyond never seeing him again. Consider that fateful day in the field. Someone else could have come across it. My life would have been so different if only I hadn't walked that route. Did I choose that walk, or did some higher being? Was it fate or predestined? I would never have ended up here accused of murder. Or was that always in my timeline? And my parents? What of their future? Had it already been decided so I would be found walking in the field on that particular day?

My head hurt from thinking, so many questions bubbling up at once. There was no way of knowing one way or the other. I didn't believe that a 'God' had any power over my destiny, and yet, something had created this earth, the animals on it, and me. There was energy enough for ghosts and weird phenomena, and a powerful force that could push through time. My time. Twice. According to opinion, this was so improbable that it wasn't worth considering any possibilities, and yet, I had returned. Was that an accident, or was I meant to be back here, alone and in this place? What was my destiny? Maybe the only way I'd ever access any answers was to be hypnotised by Marian?

Lunch was nearly over, but Brian meandered across the lawn regardless of the warnings he'd had from the staff. He ignored a patient who sat staring off into the surrounding trees and the nurse who walked swiftly towards the bench. He smiled to himself, knowing from her expression that she'd forgotten that the patient was there, daft bitch! Could it be so simple that they'd wheel Emily out and forget she was there? He could steal her away! But he doubted they'd ever allow her in the garden, and that pissed him off.

Emily was an outside child, always had been. She'd wander off for hours with the dogs to go exploring. She had friends, but it seemed to him and his parents that they were only necessary on a part-time basis and they'd said as much to her on numerous occasions.

"So what?" she'd replied one morning over breakfast. "I don't get in their face all the time, and they don't get in mine! We enjoy each other's company when we have a girlie get together, but I don't want to talk about boys and periods and makeup all the time, it's boring!"

Brian had laughed at her outburst and she punched him. It hurt, but he'd put on a brave face and tackled her, tickling her till she begged for mercy. His parents had merely shaken their heads and watched in despair. The five-year gap between them caused both problems and a strange connection. He hated and adored his little sister, and he knew she'd felt the same back then. He was supposed to have saved her, but it turned into a mess. Now she merely hated him.

"Excuse me, can I help you?"

A stern voice to his right made him jump, and he turned towards the huge black man striding towards him. He wore the white uniform of an orderly and Brian smiled. "Yeah, perhaps you can. I'm here to see my sister, but I can't remember the visiting times?"

"Who's your sister?"

"Emily Rogers."

"I see. Well, you have to make an appointment to see her as she's in the high security wing, Mr Rogers?"

"The name's Brian, and why is she in high security? Have you already found her guilty?"

The sarcastic tone wasn't lost on the orderly and he grinned unkindly. "Not yet, but she attempted to escape, so she's been transferred. She's mostly in solitary ... doesn't behave that one, gets herself into all kinds of trouble. Best place for her. Now you'd best be on your way."

Brian clenched his fist and quickly released it. The man wanted a fight, he could see it. It wouldn't help Emily to antagonise him. He obviously had some kind of beef towards his sis', so it wouldn't do to make it worse for her. "I'll be sure to make an appointment then, at the front desk in reception."

"Better to telephone or write."

"No need for that. Besides, I'm very close by. I can be here in a few minutes once I'm given the all clear." Brian turned and walked back towards the building site. He could feel the man watching him, gauging his whereabouts. He suddenly turned left, away from the hospital and headed towards the main entrance and onto the road. He waved to the security guard at the gate and made a point of being seen walking away. It had occurred to him that if they found out he was one of the builders, they might make trouble for him and Emily. The animosity on the black man's face had scared him. He hated that Emily was surrounded by people who might be feeling ill will towards her, and wondered what she had done to provoke such a reaction. He felt a small sense of pride in her.

Emily wouldn't give up without a fight.

Doubling back on himself, he entered the building site through a small doorway half hidden behind a large skip. It had once been an entrance into the sizeable gardens, as it still nestled within the huge brick wall that surrounded the grounds. It was now used as the door to the impromptu toilets if the portaloo was busy. As he scuttled in, he almost ran into Johnny relieving himself against the wall. He laughed as the lad jumped, almost peeing down his leg. Brian moved swiftly past him and with a quick glance around to make sure he couldn't be seen from the upper garden, he donned his safety helmet and got back to work. Emily was alive, causing trouble, and he would make an appointment to see her very soon.

CHAPTER 9

Marian moved the tape recorder closer, wanting to be sure nothing was missed. Emily had gone under quickly. It surprised her knowing Emily's anxiety on the matter, but something within Emily wanted this, or it wouldn't work. Marian held her breath and waited.

*　　*　　*

I felt it before I saw it. Like a shift somewhere within the atmosphere that my brain couldn't fathom. It was like knowing that change had taken place, and I turned towards it automatically, every sense alert. But as I squinted against the sun, I couldn't see anything I would consider threatening. The meadow was empty, though cows grazed on the other side of the waist-high hedge. My gaze took in the whole of the field searching. It took me a while to see it, so slight I must have missed it a few times. A shimmer, like a heat haze, yet stronger. I could see the grass beyond it, but it looked different, darker perhaps, no, changeable, as if clouds were moving across the sky in that one spot, yet it was a blue, cloudless day.

I moved cautiously towards the strange anomaly, and stopped a few feet away. The air around it was colder, not a heat haze after all. More like the autumn breeze that I expected in a couple of months' time. Yet, it wasn't blowing outwards, but inwards, and it was getting stronger. Intrigued by what I was seeing, I leaned closer to inspect it further. Jolted by a sudden gust of cold wind, I instinctively reached out to steady myself and recoiled in fear as my fingertips seemed to disappear for a fraction of a second. I held my hand, nursing it, as though it had suffered some trauma, yet on inspection, all my fingers were fine and normal, though chilled.

I stared hard at the shimmering sphere. It looked to be around six-foot high by three-foot wide, and the sides seemed to be taking on a coil-like shape, as if a small tornado was growing around the edges. I stepped back finding the shift of energy disagreeable, curiosity quickly replaced by a growing fear. I retreated faster, but the shimmering followed, or seemed to, as I couldn't get away from it. Was it growing or actually following me? I had no idea, but panic jumped in and I broke into a run.

I remember my legs moving, and my arms pummelling the air to get away, but I wasn't moving, at least not forwards. Pulled backwards, I screamed, nothing but air to cling onto. The force that pulled me backwards grew stronger with every second. It reminded me of the terrible gusts of wind experienced in England years before. I'd watched the news and marvelled at the devastation, footage of people attempting to walk forward, but literally picked up off their feet and swept backwards. Yet, around me it was only calm and sunny, the same as only moments ago when I'd first been enjoying it.

I lost my footing, yanked backwards, my legs flying freely in the air, my hands grasping for anything to save me, but there was nothing, and I went through the shimmering. The cold hit me immediately as I lay on my back gasping for breath, and mentally taking note of any injuries. Besides a bruised backside, and a slight throbbing of my head, I considered my body to be okay. My summer dress and denim jacket did nothing to keep me warm though, and I quickly sat up and hugged myself as I stared around at an unfamiliar place. The shimmering had gone. I quickly stood and waited for my legs to stop shaking. They felt as if they would give way at any moment. I suffered from terrible motion sickness and this was very similar. I felt as if I was on a moving ship, sick and faint, and I put my head between my knees.

I became aware of being watched almost immediately and slowly looked up. He stood a few feet away in mid-piss. His mouth was open and he looked absolutely terrified as he looked me up and down. I swallowed hard, aware of the growing knot of terror in my stomach. Everything about him told me he wasn't from North Yorkshire, or from anywhere I knew. Or anytime I knew. I had excelled in history as a child, gaining a decent 'O' level, but as I looked at this man, covered in furs and leather, with a sharp looking sword, and an axe hanging from his thick waist, (that looked like nothing from any books or pictures I could think of in that moment), I vomited.

I saw the granola cereal I hadn't long eaten leave my stomach and tried to comprehend what had just happened. I glanced back at the man, who hadn't moved an inch, his hand still holding his flaccid penis, his eyes fixated on me. I quickly looked at where I was, the meadow gone. Trees surrounded me, not empty fields with cows grazing. I looked back to where I knew the farm stood, finding nothing but trees. I think I knew in that instant what had happened, but my brain argued with itself. The only logical answer of time travel was impossible, and yet....

These trains of thoughts, and the emotions that followed, seemed to go on for ages, but it must have been no more than a minute or two. Another thought that brought a swift, but meaningless, possibility was that I'd completely tripped out on something without my knowledge and was still safely somewhere in my own time, perhaps my own bed, and later this would all be a very bad story.

Finding an old tissue in my pocket, I wiped my mouth, blew my nose and shoved the tissue back in my jacket pocket. All the while, my eyes were locked with the stranger. The man didn't move, not once, frozen in terror, his hand on his dick, his piss long dried up. As we stared at each other, my mouth trembled with fright, but someone had to say something. I swallowed hard and took an uneven breath and blew it out slowly.

I'd trained for years in karate and had gained my black belt three years ago. I tried to focus on my breathing techniques that helped me to relax and focus. I stepped around my pool of vomit feeling my legs go wobbly, but I managed to stay upright. "Hello ..."

The man finally replaced his penis back into his trousers in a hurry and turned towards me, pulling out a long dagger from his waist as he did so. Seeing it, I quickly stepped back and held out my hands in surrender. "No ... please ... wait. I just ... where am I?"

The man snarled as he ran at me. He was quick considering he was extremely overweight; his bare belly bulged out from beneath his grey, unkempt tunic and bounced as he ran. I barely jumped out of his way as he lunged at me, the dagger splitting the air close to my face. I stepped around him quickly, and felt my years of training kick in. I forgot everything except that I was faced with someone hostile and intent on killing me. I had no idea why that should be, but at that moment, it didn't matter. Fighting was normal, it focused my mind, and I desperately needed that right now.

He lunged again, almost whimpering, and I smelt the alcohol on his breath which gave some clue as to why his aim was way off. It'd been close though, and I thanked whatever gods were around that he was drunk. He lunged again and I moved around behind him, and kicked him in the small of the back, sending him staggering forward through my vomit which made me gag. He didn't notice as he quickly regained his footing, turned and threw the dagger. I felt the piercing sting on my arm as it scraped my skin and landed somewhere behind me. I didn't have time to react to the fact that it had gone through denim and cotton, as he quickly followed his throw with his own body. He was on me in seconds, pinning me beneath his weight, his breath hot and foul on my face. Spit drenched my cheek as he yelled words I didn't understand. All I knew was that I had to get out from under him, or I'd die from suffocation, or something else.

I got a hand free and quickly slapped his ear. When he reacted, I had a fairly good aim for his nose and I bloodied it, blinding him momentarily. I got a knee up and caught him somewhere around the liver and he rolled off long enough for me to get to my feet. I was breathless and bleeding from the cut on my upper arm, but it didn't feel too bad. He was already on his feet and coming at me again, so I kicked out and winded him. His breath was knocked out of him long enough for me to turn and run to the dagger that I'd glimpsed lying nearby. I knew he was right behind me and I had seconds. I reached it, picked it up and turned just as he reached me.

The impact of the dagger as it went into his throat was enough to make my hand go numb and I let go. He looked as startled as me as the blood gushed outwards, covering my dress and bare legs. My legs gave way completely, and I pushed my body backwards along the muddy ground as he fell in front of me. I watched his back rise and fall once, then remain still. Every cell in my body wanted to scream, to panic, to do anything to make sense of what had occurred in those last ten minutes, but a cry from nearby jolted me and I looked towards the sound. A man dressed like my attacker was pointing towards me and shouting. I hadn't taken much notice of the shabby building, but now half a dozen men were running out, some with tankards in hand, to stare dumbfounded at me and the man who lay dead at my feet.

A roar of fury from one of the men was enough to get me up and running, and enough to move the men into pursuing me. I had a hundred yards or so head start, but with no idea where I was, or where was safe, I just ran blindly. I saw a small wood in the distance and instinctively headed for it, but my stomach cringed as I heard the tell-tale sound of hooves. I could not outrun horses, I was going to die, but I ran anyway. I ran until my breath was nothing but rasping sounds and my lungs were on fire. I dodged around trees and pushed my way through bushes, tearing my dress and my arms as I ran full pelt, but I couldn't stop.

The force of the blow sent me flying forwards and my face hit the hard ground with a thud. Blood poured from a split lip and my cheek burned from a graze that felt like half my face had been lost. The man nearest to me jumped down from his horse, yanked me upwards and punched me in the stomach, hard enough to knock every last bit of breath from my lungs. I fell to the floor fighting for breath through the pain. Meanwhile another man had jumped from his horse and was starting towards me with an evil look on his face. I instinctively turned away and was glad I did as his boot met the backs of my thighs, the other way would have been my stomach as well. As it was, it hurt badly, and I tried to curl up into a ball as more kicks hit their mark.

I heard a shout and a few angry exchanges before I was pulled to my feet by two men, who held me while a third man looked me over carefully, a deep frown on his face before he slapped me hard. I felt as if my jaw had left my face and he slapped me again on the other side, and my head flew the other way before it was yanked back by my hair to face my abuser. It was becoming impossible to breathe or see as blood gushed from every orifice, but the two men held me firmly while the third one walked around me. I presumed he was inspecting me.

Eventually, he was in front of me again and I spat out blood, more to try and breathe, and not swallow my own blood, than to be haughty, but as I did so, I saw he thought the latter and grinned wickedly. Shouting something that sounded like an order, one of the men holding me pulled off my denim jacket and threw it at the man in charge. He caught it, smelt the fabric and touched it with a frown, before letting it fall to the ground. He reached out and lifted my dress, showing my knickers beneath. He said something to the other men, who laughed loudly. Reaching out he pulled down the thin straps of my dress and flicked at my pink bra with interest, before groping my breasts through the thin fabric. I felt utter revulsion but could do nothing with two large, muscular men holding me. With an evil smile, he walked behind me and I waited for the inevitable assault.

I didn't have time to react before the whip broke my skin. Of all the horrors I hadn't expected that. I screamed. An instinctive reaction, and I tried to turn my body from the pain. Another lash and I involuntarily cried out. The man walked to me and grabbed one breast and whispered something in my ear. The others laughed and I caught the eye of one of the men holding me. His lecherous grin and the way he rubbed himself told me exactly what they had in mind before they killed me, and my stomach clenched in terror.

Letting go of my breast, he sniffed his hand before he walked away, saying something that amused the men holding me and the others who stood watching. I closed my eyes, knowing what was coming, but instead, I was suddenly on the floor as my two captors abruptly let go and began shouting. I heard the clash of steel and the whinnying of horses, and one of my captors suddenly dropped down dead next to me, his eyes staring blindly from what was left of his face. A blade had almost severed the top of his head. Gagging, I stumbled to the nearest bush and crawled through. The sounds of fighting were all around me, but I focused on the ground ahead, refusing to look left or right, and never behind me.

I was abruptly brought up short by a pair of legs, horse's legs to be precise, and squealed in terror. But on looking up I saw it was a rider-less brown mare that was looking down at me with little interest, obviously one of the men's horses. In that instant, I saw a chance to escape. Mercifully, the horse kept still long enough for me to pull myself up onto its back, with some effort. Every part of my body was in pain and trembled badly. I wasn't a brilliant rider, but a horse was no stranger to me having ridden whenever I had found a job near a stables. Kicking it into a canter, I fled the battle behind me, clinging onto the bridle with every last ounce of strength. I could barely see, both eyes swollen and blood flowing from everywhere, but I had to get away, nothing else mattered at that moment.

I heard him coming. Somewhere it registered that it was just one horse coming up fast behind me. I knew I'd never out-run him, not in my condition, and I was barely able to hold onto the strange bridle. Without stirrups my legs were flying all over the place. I abruptly pulled the horse to a stop and dived off its back, then ducked to my left under low hanging branches and fought my way through the bushes. Panicked, my breath rasped, but fear and a need to survive giving me the strength to push on.

I abruptly stopped. I couldn't hear my pursuer's horse and I stared around me, but all I saw was thick bush where anyone could hide. I took a moment to fill my lungs, but I was shaking badly, adrenalin making it difficult to breathe. I had no idea which way to go, but thought heading right might take me farther from where I'd left the horse. I pressed on, aware that I made too much noise and anyone with ears would know my direction.

I was suddenly in a small clearing with bushes behind me and a grove of trees ahead. My stomach shrank away, too vulnerable out in the open, and the men would see me. I turned to head back into the undergrowth and screamed as he rose up before me. I hit out at his face, his neck. I aimed for his groin, anything that might slow him down, but he blocked each blow or didn't seem to notice them. Reaching out he wrapped his solid arms around me and lifted me as if I was nothing more than a child, but I fought on with every ounce of strength I had left.

I kicked my legs, though they met nothing but air. I yanked my head backwards and heard him exclaim as it hit its target. I felt the blood from his nose wet the back of my head and I tried again, but he was too quick this time and I hit nothing. I wriggled and twisted and swung my legs about, trying to free my arms that were stuck to my side. After a few minutes of struggling I realised he was speaking, just one word over and over. "No."

He wasn't shouting and he didn't sound angry, if anything he was calm. He and I both knew I couldn't escape, but there was no hint of malice or spite, only a quietness. My captor was attempting to instil a sort of peace, I guessed, so I would stop hurting myself, because I certainly wasn't doing too much damage to him.

Eventually I did stop. Every muscle ached badly and I went limp. My lungs fought for breath as sweat soaked my ripped dress. I was fighting to stay awake as my body went into shock and I wept for what I had endured and the horrors I imagined were to come. My mind went into overtime as I tried to calculate what I could do given a few minutes to rest. He wore a sword at his side and a dagger of sorts. Could I grab it and kill him like the other man? My hands shook terribly from the memory of the dagger in his throat and I gagged. That had been a lucky strike, the man had been in shock, and drunk, and not fast and ready for a fight, not like this man, who still held me tightly.

My breath began to slow down as the adrenalin rush subsided. I began to feel all the pains of the last hour and my mind whirled with questions I couldn't answer. My brain was still trying to catch up with the rest of my experiences, but if I wasn't going mad, a bunch of soldiers had just chased me for miles for killing one of their own. They spoke weirdly, but left me in no doubt as to what they intended to do with me after their chief, I presumed, had whipped me for a bit. This man silently holding me could be one of them.

The thought of being gang-raped and whipped to death sent a fresh surge of strength through my body and I yanked, twisted and threw him over my shoulder, as I'd been taught so many times before. He shouted in alarm, but I was off, running for my life again. I didn't get far. He rugby tackled me and the wind was knocked out of my lungs again as we grappled on the grass. In shape, he had more muscle than I did, pinning me to the ground with his own solid body. Our eyes met and I stared into the deepest brown eyes. They stared back at me with such concern, I was taken by surprise, before I turned away and resumed my struggle to be free, but we both knew it was pointless and I gave up and waited for the inevitable.

I remained still, fighting for breath, his full weight pinning me to the ground. It was obvious to anyone that I had no fight left in me, but he continued to stare down at me, a slight frown on his face, as he now had time to take a good look. He moved slightly and I froze, his excitement becoming evident. I caught him grinning at me. Not in a horrible way, but almost like an apologetic grin. He even shrugged slightly as he lifted himself off, easing the weight on my chest.

We both turned our heads at the sound of horses' hooves getting closer, and he muttered something under his breath while I felt sick to my stomach and lay still. I didn't recognise any of the men. None of them wore the same type of clothes the other group had worn. That said, they still looked a deadly lot, swords, daggers, bows and two axes swinging down the side of their saddles. Most of the weapons were covered in blood, as were some of the men, their hands and faces spattered with it. The blood of my attackers no doubt, and the words of an old quote entered my head. 'The enemy of my enemy is my friend,' and I looked at each man in turn.

One man was leading a grey horse and on seeing us, he laughed out loud and dropped the reins. My captor jumped to his feet and grabbed the trailing reins while I remained perfectly still, glaring at each man in turn, daring them to touch me, but none of them were staring at me in a lecherous manner. If anything, they had looks of concern, surprise and curiosity.

There were six in all, and they began talking amongst themselves in a language I didn't recognise. Every so often one of them would look towards me, but they didn't expect me to run, there was nowhere to go, and six horses could outrun me any day, especially in my state. I sensed no malice among these men and some of my terror subsided just a little. My captor watched me closely and after a brief word with the man I decided was the leader, he leaned forward and offered me his hand. I hesitated, but what else could I do, I had nowhere to run or hide. I took his offered hand and he pulled me up with no effort.

My legs thankfully held me up though they trembled badly. My back blazed as if it was on fire and I felt blood trickling down into my knickers. I crossed my arms to hide my breasts as the cotton had been torn in so many places it wasn't leaving anything to the imagination. My captor saw this and with a quick word with the other men, he walked to the back of his horse's saddle where he untied a bundle which I saw was a blanket. He shook it out and moved to wrap it around me. I involuntarily flinched away and that stopped him in his tracks. He considered for a moment, before holding the blanket at arm's length and waited patiently for me to take it. I did, gratefully, and attempted a smile.

The men spoke again. They were obviously discussing me as they freely pointed and gestured in my direction. I guessed these to be the attackers who had given me the chance to escape. Judging from the state of them, the battle had been bloody and brutal, but I felt nothing for my abusers, only gratitude towards these men who so far had shown me kindness, though I kept my guard up just in case. I still had no idea where, or more importantly, when I was, and the terror returned two-fold.

I hoped they wouldn't take too long and they'd let me go soon. My body was in agony, shock and fatigue. The blanket warmed me a little, but it didn't reach my bare legs, or my summer pumps that were soaked through and freezing. I had to find the field I'd arrived in or whatever had happened. What the hell had happened, a time-slip? A very bad acid trip? Judging from the pain from my back, I doubted that one, or surely pain would bring me back to my senses? It had to be time-travel of some kind, or I was having the most realistic dream ever. I needed to ask the way back to that inn, or whatever it had been, and look for the shimmering. I refused to consider the possibility that it wouldn't be there, but I thought that time would be of the essence. It was getting dark and I had lost my bearings.

I took a deep breath. "Excuse me ... Mr ... whatever ... I need to ..."

The men stopped talking and frowned down at me. A few looked at each other and shook their heads. The one I thought might be the leader urged his horse closer. He wore a red cloak fastened by a gold brooch at his shoulder. He was big, muscular and bloodied from the fight, but he had kind eyes and smiled down at me. He said something that made no sense to me and I shrugged. He nodded and seemed to understand my lack of their language.

He unexpectedly shouted something and the men turned their horses as one. My captor rushed forward and before I could fight him, he'd picked me up and thrown me onto the back of his horse, jumped up behind me and we were off on a canter. It was all I could do to hang on. He must have felt my fatigue as he wrapped his arm tighter around my waist so I didn't fall off. I heard a couple of shouts from the other men, who laughed at their own jokes. My captor merely grunted and urged his horse onward.

An hour or so of riding and I saw ahead of me a large castle. The sun was just setting behind it and to my eyes it looked enormous. I thought I could smell the sea and as we rode closer I saw a deep estuary that divided the land so I guessed the sea to be close by. We rode across a narrow bridge and entered a small hamlet of thatched roofs and muddy tracks with a stench that made me gag. Slowing to a trot, we crossed another, wider bridge that connected the outer stone wall and went through a large gatehouse. We rode up a slight incline, through another smaller gatehouse and stopped in a square courtyard.

From my vantage point, as we rode up, I had thought the castle completely built of stone. I was wrong. The huge outer wall was thick stone as were the gatehouses, but within its walls, most of the buildings were thatch and wood. A huge hall two storeys high stood in the far centre with other buildings surrounding it. Around the outside, lean-tos made do for various workshops, and here and there small rooms had been built into the wall. The blacksmith and bakery caught my eye and my stomach growled as the scent of fresh bread filled the air, mixed with dung, unwashed bodies, sweat and blood. My hunger vanished in an instant.

The circular courtyard was wide enough to accommodate our horses plus a multitude of people without hindering our movements. People moved about freely. Everyone seemed busy. Young boys came and took hold of the horses' reins while women bustled out to welcome the men, mostly with kisses and cries of delight. The men picked them up and hugged them back, leaving me in no doubt as to what they would be doing later. The women wore dresses of dull colours, most muddied and stained, though nobody seemed to care. I noticed a few women standing in a doorway watching me with open curiosity. Their eyes fixed on my bare legs and bloodied skin.

It was too much, and I began to feel the tingling, warm sensation of a faint. Black spots appeared before my eyes and I was falling. One of the men detached himself from his woman and ran over to help me as my captor shouted a warning. He had me by the waist, but the other man, a huge giant with a shaven head and piercing-blue eyes caught me and carefully pulled me off the horse. He held me like a child in his gigantic arms, before surrendering me to my captor, who had leapt off his horse and was holding out his arms to take me back. With a grin, the giant surrendered me immediately. The other men laughed, shouting things as he carried me towards the hall.

I was aware of people staring, whisperings and pointing, but between my captor and the man in the red cloak, I was transported to a room with a large bed. My captor laid me down and I thought, reluctantly stepped back. The two men turned away from me and had a whispered conversation, in which I wanted to intervene and tell them how frustrating it was. I understood nothing. They could have been talking Klingon for all I knew. I could only wait for more pain and humiliation to start and hope it would be quick. Perhaps they preferred to rape a woman in the comfort of a bed? The appearance of four women took me by surprise.

The man in the red cloak, who I was now convinced was their chief, spoke softly to the group of women, looking between him and me with a variety of pity, sympathy, curiosity and fear on their faces. After his speech, he turned back to me and gave me a single nod, a reassuring smile, which I found encouraging and then strode out. My captor was watching the women as they moved around the room pouring water and bringing in bottles of what I thought might be soaps. One woman was carrying a basket of herbs, and behind her an elderly woman stood in the doorway watching me carefully. She had a strange expression on her face. She didn't fear me.

The women approached the bed, and one carefully rolled me over onto my front, and gently stroked my hair off my face. I heard one of them shout something, and I turned to see two of them pushing my captor out of the room, but in a good naturedly way. He left with a laugh and a wink, though I thought I detected a hint of regret. Was that because he cared for my well-being, or was he just a letch hoping for an eye full?

The women talked excitedly together as they warmed water in a small cauldron that hung over a nearby fire. The one who'd stroked my hair sat on the bed and proceeded to gently pull off the remnants of my summer dress, exposing my bare back. I heard a gasp from everyone in the room and immediately turned my head. "What? Is it that bad?" Forgetting in that moment that they couldn't understand me.

I caught one woman pointing at my lower back and I suddenly remembered my tattoos. Were tattoos normal in this time? My captor had a tattoo on his right arm, but could a woman have them? I hastily looked around the room as I sensed a change in attitude, and my eyes locked with those of the elderly woman, who still stood perfectly still by the doorway. She nodded to herself as if making a decision, then abruptly began shooing the other women away.

I lay perfectly still as she closed the door behind them all and leaned against it for a moment watching me. She seemed to be weighing up something because she abruptly pushed herself away from the door after locking it and walked over to the cauldron. She began rinsing out cloths before walking slowly to the bed with them and a jar. I hadn't moved. My back still exposed to the warmth of the room. The whiplashes stung terribly, as did every cut and gash and bruise, and I knew I'd be suffering worse tomorrow if I survived that long.

The woman dipped a cloth into the sweet-smelling jar and gently began applying a lotion to my back. I winced as it stung badly, and she stopped for a moment, but almost immediately continued, gently cleaning away the blood and muck from my back and arms. It hurt like hell. Where was paracetamol or co-codamol when you needed it? As if reading my mind, she lifted my head and urged me to sip something lukewarm. It tasted bitter, but I drank a little more and let her continue.

Finally satisfied, she laid a warm cloth over my back, and the scent of lavenders filled my nostrils. I felt myself dozing off to sleep despite the pain and fear. I woke abruptly moments later and cried out as the movement jolted my wounds. The elderly woman sat watching me, her expression empty. Eventually, she seemed to make up her mind and pushed to her feet and came to sit beside me on the bed. Her gaze travelled down my back and she exhaled loudly.

"Where did you get your tattoo done?"

I stared open-mouthed. She had a soft Scottish accent and she spoke English. She laughed at my expression. "It's a good one. A green goddess, I think, yes?"

"Er ... yes. Who are you? Where am I?"

A look of sympathy crossed the old woman's face and I felt a stab of fear. This woman was about to tell me something bad and I didn't want to hear it. She moved closer and gently rested her warm hand on my shoulder. "Let me ask you a question first and then we'll see where we go from there, okay?" On my nod, she took a deep breath and leaned in closely. "What I'm about to tell you will be a shock to ye, aye, so perhaps you'd be wanting a large Gin and tonic about now, eh?"

CHAPTER 10

I woke with a jolt and groaned loudly, as every part of my body stung in retaliation for the movement. I froze and eased myself back down on the bed and took a few deep breaths to steady myself. I had been dreaming of my parents and the last time I'd heard their voices, calling up to me to get out of bed and go for an early morning walk to gather blackberries for a pie. I'd muttered something incoherent and rolled over, enjoying the comforting warmth of my duvet to a chilly September stroll through bramble covered tracks. I'd help make the pastry when they returned.

They never returned and I lived with the regret of not going with them every day. Of course, I'd have probably been slaughtered along with them and the dogs, but that didn't ease my guilt at being alive when they were not. Tears welled and fell onto the warm blanket beneath my head. Tears for them, but also for me as the memories of my ordeal came flooding in.

I became aware of someone as my sobbing subsided. Turning my head slightly, I saw Ayleth, my elderly helper, sitting near the fireplace watching me with sympathy and concern on her face. Her brief conversation and introduction last night filtered into my consciousness and I stared open mouthed at her. The story she'd told me last night, had been incredible, but I couldn't think about it now, as the pain took over my every thought.

She got up stiffly and went to a small table that held a jug, two goblets and a plate of what looked like bread. The smell of cooking wafted towards me and I saw Ayleth stirring something in a small cauldron that hung over the fireplace.

Ayleth poured us both a drink and she helped me to drink mine. I coughed and recoiled on finding it to be weak ale, but she encouraged me and I drank a little more. "It becomes easier, drinking in the morning. But you really don't want to drink the water unless it's boiled first, and even then it's a risk. I tend to go out onto the moors and find a fresh spring and fill up a jug or two to last the day. I'm collecting herbs as I go, so it's not a wasted journey. Here, nibble on this bread, it's fresh, while I get you some broth."

She helped me roll onto my back and eased me into a seated position. I yelped with the pain, but we persevered and finally got two pillows supporting me, with another warm, lavender-scented blanket on my bare back. The rest of me was covered in blankets and a couple of sheepskin rugs, which I felt awkward with as I'd always been against animal cruelty, but the room was chilly.

Ayleth was busy spooning out two bowls of broth while I tried to nibble on the bread. It was good, fresh, but my lip was split, and I had cuts on the inside of my cheek, and my jaw was terribly swollen, though Ayleth assured me it wasn't broken. My lip began to bleed so using the end of the blanket I dabbed it clean and tried again, wincing with each movement.

"This might help. It'll soften the bread so you won't have to open your mouth so wide." Offering me the small bowl, she sat opposite and began dipping her own chunk of bread into the hot broth.

I sniffed thoughtfully. "What is it?"

"Chicken broth, you need to get your strength so you'll heal. Though I've found that I don't tend to get sick, perhaps the germs in this time can't fight all of my twentieth century antibodies."

I attempted a smile and carefully licked my lips. It did smell good, but ... "I'm vegetarian."

Ayleth looked aghast for a moment, then reached forward and gently patted my hand. "I salute your morals, my girl, but if you want to live in this world, you'll have to leave your principles behind, or you'll die. In this world, we need the animals for their meat, their warmth, and their transportation. I'm sorry." She gave me a long look before returning her attention to her meal.

I hesitated, but my growling stomach suddenly didn't care about the well-being of animals, only me; and I dipped the bread into the broth. It was delicious and it did help my lip. I managed half a small loaf before I began to feel sick. I hadn't touched any of the floating chicken, but merely dipped, so I felt fairly certain it wasn't eating the meat which caused my stomach to gurgle noisily. Ayleth heard it and grinned. "You must need the toilet, my love."

Now, going to a toilet in a stranger's home is never a comfortable experience, more so if you're sure it's going to be a disgusting bodily function. Shock, horror and trauma, followed by revelations and eating chicken broth was too much for my insides, and Ayleth barely got me to the required hole in time.

I expect toilets to be disgusting places, but this hole in the floor was pretty foul. I could remember seeing them in ruined stone castles on visits with my parents and we'd wondered at the stench. The guide had said the ladies would leave their dresses nearby so moths would be deterred from nibbling at their fabrics, although the smell of the dresses would be astounding. I saw no dresses as I staggered inside the small, narrow room. The muddy walls were cold and the air was chilly from the gaping hole. Ayleth had handed me a wad of small square pieces of old looking fabric before closing the door shut behind me.

Grateful, I almost fell as I squatted over the hole and let nature do whatever it needed to do. The rush of air occasionally made for interesting sensations on my arse and I felt weak and sickly afterwards, as if every last ounce of myself had been discarded. I wobbled back into the warmer room where Ayleth offered me a small bowl of hot water to wash my hands and face before she helped me back into bed.

"They use large leaves mostly, but I tend to keep hold of any discarded fabric as I prefer it on my backside!" Ayleth smiled and busied herself with cleaning up the bowls and pouring out more ale. I took the offered goblet and sipped.

"I think it tastes like John Smiths, though it's been a long time now of course, how about you?"

I took another sip and shrugged. "Perhaps, but I'm more of a wine girl myself."

"You'll have that later, no doubt." Seeing my expression, she laughed. "Oh, aye, they drink anything and everything around here. Weak ale with breakfast, wine, mead and more ale throughout the day. Water is not really an option, though I've tried to show them ways of cleaning it up a bit. The well is in a much better state now, thanks to me, I think, and my Lord is working on a way of bringing the mountain spring closer to the castle so it's not such a trek."

I sipped the ale and began to relax into my pillows. Drinking ale always made me sleepy, and drinking it in the morning was a decadence my body wasn't quite ready for. I didn't drink too much at home, a glass of wine here and there, and never before the evening after I'd eaten a significant amount to soak up the alcohol.

"I know you told me bits last night, but can you tell me again? I can't seem to retain information right now. I feel all muddled and teary ..." As if on cue I began to cry again.

"I understand. You've been through a terrible ordeal. What those men did is unthinkable. At least, it was to me before I came here. When I arrived I wasn't physically attacked as you were. You know you're safe now, right? Lord Artorius' people killed those men."

"Artorius? You mean the man in the red cloak?"

"Yes, he found me wandering the moors when he was a young man and brought me here to his father, who kindly let me stay. He saw I had knowledge and I became known as a seer, a wise woman, which served me well."

"Jesus, how long have you been here?"

"I was forty-five when I came. I'm sixty-three, I think. I lose track of time here, but it's gotten easier as the years go by, though I miss so many things, and now seeing you here, I miss them even more!"

I sipped the ale, trying to digest this information. "Does time run alongside then, do you think?" Seeing Ayleth shrug, I continued, "So, you left in nineteen eighty-five?"

"Yes, when ra-ra skirts and big shoulder pads were hip. Are they still? No, of course not, but I'll ask you some questions of my own soon. For now, I'll answer yours."

"What was your name?"

"Elizabeth Montgomery, but everyone called me Betty. I lived near Glasgow, and worked as a home help for the elderly."

I watched as Betty's eyes welled up and she coughed, clearing the emotion that threatened to show. "I had a partner, a woman." Seeing I didn't react, she smiled gratefully and went on. "Her name was Melinda and we were trying to find a man who would donate sperm to give us a child. I often wonder what she thought had happened to me. We'd had a terrible row that night and I'd stormed off, taking our car and just driving, you know, not really going anywhere."

She was talking faster and faster, as if finally having someone she could tell was overpowering and she had to get it out. "I ended up down some country lane near the English border and started looking for a B&B for the night, and then the damned car ran out of petrol and I had visions of me sleeping in it all night. I had to pee so I got out of the car and walked through an open gate into a field. It was dark, cold and spooky, but when I'd finished, I noticed a light coming from somewhere in the distance and thought it might be a house.

I began walking towards it. It was a strange kind of light. It had warmth, like a heat lamp and I began to think it wasn't the light from a window, but something else. I couldn't stop walking towards it, the warmth was so inviting, and then I felt a pull, like a hard yank on my body and I know my legs left the solid ground because I had the sensation of flying, then hitting the ground hard that knocked me for six. I looked up and it was dawn, here on the moor and that was that. I'd left the English border in early February and arrived here, dawn of early summer in the late 5th century, it seems. It's now the sixth."

"Sixth century? Fuck!"

"Indeed. And so I pretended to have lost my memory of who I was, the bruise and nasty cut to my head helped my case, and eventually they called me 'Ayleth' after the last wise woman who had died a couple of years before me."

"Was that woman from our time, do you think?"

Ayleth shrugged. "I've no idea, but made me wonder why wise women are wise? Where did the knowledge come from?"

My head hurt, as did the rest of me, and I lay back carefully. My back stung so badly I had to ease myself over onto my side. Ayleth watched me with a sympathetic look on her face. "Do you want to tell me what happened?"

The tears came without conscious thought and I sobbed my heart out, my aching body racking with each mournful howl. I clutched at the pillow, now soaked with my tears, and tried to stifle the noise. Ayleth gently reached out to stop me.

"Let it out, you've been through a terrible ordeal, and it isn't over yet."

Her words stopped my crying. Lips trembling, I frantically wiped my hot face. "What do you mean? Are those men going to hurt me too?"

Thankfully Ayleth shook her head. "No. If this was a film, these would be the good guys. However, they'll want to know who you are and where you're from, and I can't think straight right now. It's like a miracle to me, it is, havin' ya here, though I guess it feels different for you, eh? Seein' ya there on the bed all bloodied and beaten, ya were a wonderful sight, lass ..."

I attempted to return her smile, but it came out awkward and my lip started to bleed again. Ayleth tutted to herself and handed over a clean cloth. I dabbed the sore, then sighed loudly. "I guess I'll start at the beginning and maybe we'll think of something?"

With a nod from Ayleth, I proceeded to tell her everything. I let the tears fall as I related the beating and the whipping, and Ayleth shook her head as I told her what I knew the men wanted to do to me. She grinned when I told her about my captor wrapping his arms around me and saying something that sounded like 'no', refusing to let go. She chuckled when I told her about throwing him over my shoulder.

"Aye, but you're a canny lass and no mistake, those fighting skills will come in handy around here, though I'll need to prepare you for their ways and customs. Ladies here are, shall I say, more submissive than twentieth century girls, and they allow the men to look after them. Men are men and women are women, each has their own place, ye' ken?"

Ayleth stood up and fetched more ale, but on seeing it empty, she shrugged and went about collecting the bowls and cups. Suddenly she looked up. "I guess we'd better start with your name, lass?"

"Emily, I'm Emily Rogers, aged twenty-five. I have a brother and no parents. I don't think anyone will miss me ... and that worries me."

Ayleth came to sit on the bed. "Emily, it doesn't matter whether someone misses you or not, they'll never find you, and you can't get back. I'm sorry, lass."

CHAPTER 11

Ayleth let the shock of her words sink in. I stared hard at the bed, the stone walls, the faded tapestry that depicted some fight or other. I glanced at the open narrow window and stared down at the goosebumps rising on my arms. Finally, I looked back at Ayleth who hadn't moved. "Never?" The word almost stuck in my throat and it came out no more than a croak.

"Aye, Emily. I'm sorry, but there it is. I've been here all this time and revisited the place I came through, but I've never seen or heard of another doorway. That's what I called it, and I've never met another from my time, or any other. I've never presumed it is just a phenomenon of our world, and have often hoped to meet a traveller, but I've not."

Ayleth shifted her position and leaned forward, as if sharing a secret. "When I was younger, I can recall reading about time-slips, where a person would be walking in full view of their family or friends and they would suddenly disappear in front of them. I remember reading about a man who was running in a race, and at one point, in full view of spectators and friends, he seemed to slip, fall forward, but he never reached the ground. He disappeared before hitting it."

"Is that true?" I stared dumbfounded at such a story.

"Aye, it is. I read it in a book about ghosts and strange phenomena, so it can't be a lie, can it?"

"And none of these people came back?"

"No, I don't think so."

I slowly eased myself into a seated position and leaned forward. "Ayleth, Betty, I can't stay here. I'll be killed, or raped, or raped and killed. Ayleth, those men were ... Oh, God!" I threw my head in my hands and cried.

Ayleth reached out and gently patted my hands. "I know, it's a shock, and a scary one at that, but I survived and I was alone, and a lesbian. How do you think that went down with the lads?"

Wiping my eyes, I attempted a smile. "Was it that bad?"

"Terrible. None of them could understand why I never fell for their so-called charms. At my age, I'd hoped to have been done with all that, but some of the older men were worse than the younger ones! After a while though, they let me be, especially once they learned I had healing skills, and I could tell them the future."

"You did that? But, wouldn't that change things?" I was becoming interested in Ayleth's tale, an idea forming in my head.

"I only told bits that they already knew, kind of anyway. Like the battles that came with the Saxons and who would rule. My partner was more of the history buff than me, but I knew enough to save my skin anyway." I saw the flicker of emotion as she mentioned her lost love and it was my turn to reach out and touch her hand.

Ayleth patted it and with a big breath, she heaved herself up and stood looking down at me. "Okay, we need a story. I'm not sure Emily is a known name in this time?"

I suddenly remembered something my father had once told me. "Actually, it might be, though spelt and said slightly different. 'Aemilia' is the Latin name and apparently 'Emily' is Teutonic and means 'hard-working'. You said the man in charge is called 'Artorius'? That sounds Roman to me. He might accept 'Aemilia' as it comes from the Roman 'Aemilius' meaning industrious."

I smiled triumphantly that I'd remembered my dad's words and I felt a sting of emotion. He'd have been proud that I'd listened, and taken it in. Ayleth looked pretty much the same as I'd expect him to look.

"Well, that is impressive, my girl. It might actually do. But, where have you come from?"

"Maybe we can say I ran away, from somewhere, I'm not sure yet of the details. Perhaps we can say, news reached me that my Great Aunt still lived and I escaped my captives to see for myself. We could say I have the same gift or something. Maybe it runs in the family?"

"Maybe, but you'll have to have enough knowledge of a place and people to make them believe you. Can you do that?"

"I don't know. I was pretty good at history, but nobody knew much about this era."

"What did you do as a job?"

I blushed and hated myself for it. "Well, I did bar work when I left school. I could mix a mean cocktail. Then I travelled around the country doing odd jobs, picking fruit, waiting on tables, worked in a record shop for a while, then went to college and did a couple of 'A' levels in English and Biology. After that I did more bar work, worked in a cafe for a while ..."

"I see, so at twenty-five you haven't settled down yet?"

"No." I looked down, ashamed. How could I tell her that after my parents were murdered I just couldn't be bothered grasping life? What was the point? Brian fell to pieces with drink, and I got a job at the main pub he frequented to help keep an eye on him. Before he threw a bottle at the boss and we both got chucked out. "I applied for an Open University place, but I guess that's off the table now."

"What was the course?"

"Midwifery."

Ayleth smiled. "That might just do, Emily. You're quick, you have knowledge, and it might just save your life."

"Save my life? But you said these men were the good guys?"

Ayleth sighed loudly. "They are, Emily, but they don't just accept any woman to offer protection to. You have to earn their trust and earn their respect. These men are what is left after the Romans deserted this land. They're a mix from all over, but they fight together, and try to keep some law and order, at least in this part of the country. Hadrian's wall is not far from here, and it's an amazing sight. Obviously, I'd seen it in my own time, but by then, of course, it's nothing but ruins. Here, there is constant fighting between Saxons, Picts or Woads, as they're also known. Farmers fight among themselves for the scraps the Romans left, and then there's the Roman British, who stayed to make a life here. That's Artorius."

"Artorius? Is that Latin for Arthur?" On seeing Ayleth's excited nod, I felt my own stomach turn to butterflies at the possibility. "As in, Arthur of the round table, Arthur ... and his Knights? You mean the King Arthur and Guinevere and Lancelot and the Holy Grail Arthur?"

Ayleth smiled. "Stories made up by some medieval bloke, Emily, but based on this man, Artorius, I think. I haven't met any Guinevere or Lancelot, but I have met his Knights, as did you yesterday. They fight to protect. Isn't that wonderful? Like our own police force, only with swords and axes instead of batons and riot shields!"

"Shit."

"Indeed, my lass, and you'll have to be careful of your language. I'm not sure how they'll take your flowery expletives in this time."

"And just when is this time exactly?"

"511 AD. The new century celebrations are still talked about. What a night and day that was!"

A knock on the door brought us both up sharp and I winced at my sudden movement.

Ayleth glanced quickly at me and called out, "Come in. Oh bother, I mean ..."

The door opened anyway and Ayleth smiled gratefully. "I'd forgotten my languages. I haven't spoken modern English for such a long time."

She looked up at the young boy who stood within the doorway, glancing curiously at me. "Wit?"

The boy edged forward and spoke quickly into Ayleth's ear. She nodded and he scampered away with a backward glance at me. "It seems Artorius is curious about his guest and wishes to come and visit you. He asked if you were ready for his presence."

My stomach did flip-flops and the ale I'd drunk threatened to rise up. "What the hell am I meant to say?"

"Well, thank him for his kindness at saving you from those drunken soldiers. They sounded like Roman soldiers who'd perhaps deserted and become mercenaries; Artorius and his men hate them. There's quite a lot of them who hated going back to Rome, as they'd made a life here and they saw this country as the perfect hunting ground for riches and land. Then lay into your story of escaping a life as a slave in a bar or tavern, as you'd heard that I lived. You sound foreign, so make it somewhere like Wales, or even Ireland, if you know the country."

I shook my head and she shrugged. "Okay, Wales then, yes?"

I sucked my lower lip, tasting blood, very nervous. "I loved Wales. I went there as a child on holidays."

"Great, that'll do for now, aye. Artorius has only been that far south as a young man, and as a slave you won't be expected to know lots of details. Although, as a slave, he won't behave the same as he would a lady, know what I mean?"

I think I did and nervously licked my lips. "I'm not a woman of low birth and neither are you. We came from a good Welsh family, and somehow you ended up in England, where he found you, while I was sold into slavery or something and ..."

A loud knock on the door interrupted me. Ayleth looked nervous as Artorius entered the room, but she quickly hid it and stood to greet him. He was alone, and with a quick glance at Ayleth and myself, he shut the door firmly behind him and walked slowly to the seat nearest the bed. With a slight bow, he sat down and waited.

CHAPTER 12

B rian looked up and down the corridor again before daring to venture out of his hiding place. He'd timed his visit with those of the lesser guarded area and had brought a large bunch of flowers that he'd pinched from the graveyard nearby. He wasn't proud of that, but when he saw them, he knew they'd help with his story.

He pretended to be visiting a patient and got talking with another family as he walked in. From any casual observer, they were all together and nobody stopped him. After detaching himself from his newfound friends on the pretext of visiting his own patient, (a man he'd made up as being his uncle) he began making his way farther into the complex. He knew he'd never get into the high security area, but if he could see the man in charge, he might be able to push his reasons for seeing Emily. He had a whole speech ready on human rights and violating their human rights by keeping family apart without proper authorisation, but he wasn't convinced it would work.

A couple of nurses walked past without seeing him and he moved farther along the empty corridor. It felt eerie and he kept looking behind to double-check he was alone. It felt like eyes were watching his every move. He rounded a corner and came to an abrupt halt as three burly orderlies stood leaning against the wall chatting idly. On seeing him they all abruptly stopped and barred his way.

"Can I help you, sir?"

Nervous, Brian looked around and casually ran a hand through his hair. "Yeah, mate, I'm looking for the man in charge of the secure wing, a Mr Hastings, I think his name is, or the doctor in charge of Emily's treatment? I can't find his office. I seem to have got a bit lost, you know, it's like a maze."

The three men smiled shrewdly. "Do you have an appointment?"

"Well, no, but I was hoping to make one, or see if he was available to speak with now ..." Brian knew it was game over and shrugged. "I thought I'd give it a go, you know, I've been trying to visit my sister for weeks, but nobody gets back to me."

One of the men nodded sympathetically. "I understand, but this area is out of bounds unless you have an appointment. Who's your sister?"

"Emily Rogers. I just want to know if she's okay?"

The three men were slowly moved him backwards as they descended on him. "You mean the killer?" said one man, and the other gave him a shove.

"Hey, nothing's been proven yet, come on."

Turning to Brian, he shrugged. "Sorry, mate."

Brian stared hard at the men and stood his ground. "Is this the attitude my sister is facing in here? Are you telling me she's being treated as if she's guilty before she's even had a trial?"

The behaviour of the men changed slightly. Two looked appalled, while the one who'd made the comment continued to look smug. The guard in charge stepped in front of the other two. "No, no, of course not, sir, I'm sure she's getting the best care."

Brian held his ground. "I don't believe you! I want to see someone ... please. Let me check she's okay and I won't make a complaint about his attitude ..."

Both men glanced across at the other guard and glared at him. The guard grinned back. "And who'd believe him?"

They nodded upwards. "The bloody cameras might, you prick!"

Brian looked up, surprised. Of course, no wonder he'd felt eyes on him, they were. He hadn't expected cameras until farther into the buildings, stupid mistake.

He felt the two men wavering as they glanced at each other. "Look, I just want a chance to speak with Mr Hastings, or the doctor in charge, or at least get an appointment. Can you help me, guys, come on ...?"

"All right, we'll take you to the office. I'm not sure if Hastings is in today, but his secretary is and you can work something out with her, okay? The doctor in charge is Doctor Gilmore."

Brian nodded eagerly and quickly followed the men back up the corridor, through a locked door and farther into the lion's den where Emily was incarcerated, alone and innocent.

*   *   *

Artorius listened to my story without interrupting me. At times he raised an eyebrow, and at one point reached for a goblet of wine that a servant had brought in not long after his arrival, along with fruit, two other goblets and a large jug. I hadn't touched anything, but Ayleth was drinking every so often and helping herself to an apple.

Artorius held my gaze and I saw only concern and kindness there. When I finished, I let the real tears fall. I'd begun to believe my own story, and it was heart-breaking how I had been sold into slavery as a young child while my aunt had been taken away, and I thought her dead. Both my parents had been killed while fighting to protect me. I had been taken to a family in deepest Wales, the 'Jones' where I'd been kept as a prisoner on pain of death if I attempted to escape.

I'd managed to finally escape when a small group of Saxons had come to pillage and taken over the village. They'd killed the man holding me prisoner and I'd run for my life. As I'd got closer to England, I'd felt the strange connection of my aunt. We shared the gift, and I'd followed the trail. I'd been set upon by those soldiers, intent on rape and murder: and I finished off by thanking him for his kindness.

Ayleth was interpreting everything I said and at this final sentence, she bowed humbly, and I quickly copied her with tears running down my cheeks. I surely looked the part of a terrified, broken woman.

We waited impatiently as Artorius took a deep breath and finally got up from his chair. He looked down at the ragged pile of my clothes, picked up the cream dress, or what was left of it anyway, and turned to Ayleth. He said something brief, then frowned hard, while chewing the inside of his cheek as if considering my tale. He glanced back at me. He said something while staring at me, but turned back to Ayleth and waited for her answer.

Ayleth merely shrugged before interpreting what he'd said to me. "No family resemblance!"

I gave a nervous laugh and shrugged as well, as Ayleth talked non-stop about God knows what. I felt absolutely exhausted after relaying my impromptu story and my body hurt badly. I must have made a noise as Ayleth suddenly stopped talking and came to my side. She turned to Artorius and said something sharp before helping me to lie down carefully on my side.

Artorius watched us sympathetically before finally nodding to himself and strode to the door. Opening it, he shouted out what sounded like orders and, sure enough, three women appeared laden with clean cloths, a jug and plates of food. They were so quick I thought they had been waiting just outside for Artorius to either believe me or have me thrown in the dungeon. I hoped the former. A reassuring smile from Ayleth helped me feel a little better and I thankfully sipped the weak ale offered by one of the women and sank back onto the bed. Artorius watched me from the doorway, a frown on his face, but he was watching the proceedings with interest, not anger, and I felt myself drifting off, sure that I could trust this man.

*   *   *

Artorius headed for the great hall where he knew his men were breaking their fast. He heard them long before he saw them, their laughter and chatter filling the corridor with noise. He stood in the doorway a moment taking in the scene before him. Most were busy eating, while passing crude comments to each other in-between mouthfuls. Tristan and Merek were standing near the fireplace in deep conversation. Rulf was kissing a wench in earnest, while his cousin Dain was shaking his head next to him in despair. Rulf was always in some embrace with a woman if he could help it. He said it kept him alive knowing he'd be kissing a woman at some point during the day.

Tristan, he knew, was watching out for his reappearance and sure enough he caught his eye. On seeing he'd lost his companions' attention, Merek turned to see who he was watching, and smiled. "I see you're more interested in how that lady is faring than my own story, Tristan, not that I blame you, a fine woman, indeed."

Tristan threw him a playful punch in the arm as he went to hear from Artorius. A man of few words, he preferred the company of animals to men, and had indeed trained all the horses in Artorius' stables. On finding an orphaned wolf, he'd brought it home and trained it. Now it followed him everywhere. He glanced across at Domitius, named by Artorius as it meant 'to be trained', who stared back at his master, and with a loud fart and a sigh, he closed his eyes again.

Artorius was smiling knowingly as he approached, and Tristan felt his cheeks burn. He'd had his fair share of wenches over the years, but no woman had ever captured his heart, and not through lack of trying either. This woman in strange dress intrigued him. The feel of her body beneath his own had caused not only a growing lust, but something else. He felt a strong urge to protect her.

He bowed slightly as Artorius reached him. "My Lord, get it over with. I've heard the jests from the others already."

As if on cue, shouts of bawdy content were called from around the room, followed by mimicking of various sexual positions. "Tristan's in love!" "No, he just wants to see something new!" "I'll wager he has her by the end of the day!" "Me thinks Tristan is too much a gentleman for that diabolical behaviour, am I right, Tristan?"

Tristan ignored them all and waited as Artorius shook his head and smiled. "The lady is healing. And might I remind my fellow men that while under my roof she will be treated with the respect due a lady ..." He spoke lightly, but his words carried true meaning, and every man nodded his acceptance.

"So, she is indeed a lady?" Borin set down his bread to hear the story of the woman they'd saved.

Artorius walked further into the room, patting Tristan reassuringly on his shoulder as he passed. "She is. Her name is Aemilia and she has been through a terrible ordeal. It is in God's grace that she found her long lost Aunt Ayleth whom she thought dead."

"It is indeed the gods' gift that they have found each other." Borin shoved a large piece of bread into his mouth and chewed thoughtfully. But which god? Artorius was a Christian Pagan, but most, including himself, followed the old pagan gods. He kept his thoughts to himself. He'd talk quietly with his friend Brom later.

Tristan looked thoughtful as he stared towards the doorway Artorius had just entered. Aemilia. A beautiful name for such a strong and beautiful lady. The need to look into her blue eyes again was overwhelming, but he kept it to himself. As if sensing his restlessness, the wolf abruptly stood and walked over to his master. Tristan obliged by absentmindedly stroking his neck.

Artorius looked back at his friend and guessed his thoughts. "She is resting now, Tristan, perhaps a visit later to introduce yourself might be wiser? Come, we have work to do. I want a patrol to check our borders. Those mercenaries came from somewhere, though I did not recognise their dress, and none carried a mark for whom they fought. I also think it is time to begin our sword practice, if you have all finished filling your bellies."

Artorius led the way and men and women reluctantly finished their meals and got on with the day's work. With one last look of regret at the doorway that led to the guest chamber Tristan followed the others out towards the fighting field. Her window looked out on that area, perhaps he might glimpse her?

"Did Aemilia tell you Ayleth's true name?"

Artorius shook his head. "I did not ask, my friend, I did not ask."

*   *   *

I woke with a start and stiffened as the pain on my back ripped through my body. I was immediately surrounded by concerned faces, who encouraged me to lie back gently. Pillows were propped against my back so I was cocooned between pillows that smelt of lavender. A goblet of wine was held to my lips and I sipped it carefully as my lip felt very swollen and sore, as did my jaw and gums, though I'd already checked for any loose teeth, thankful none were missing, (or likely to be). I felt the heady rush of alcohol hitting my system and stopped. It couldn't be more than midday. Drinking so early was definitely not good for my body. I handed the half-full goblet back with an apologetic smile and grimaced at the bruise on my jaw.

I understood nothing of what the three women said, but from the tone of their voice, they sounded kind and concerned and not telling me what a trollop I was and how much they wanted to slit my throat. I glanced behind them and scoured the room for Ayleth. One lady guessed my query and shook her head kindly before mimicking 'sleep'. I nodded to let her know I understood and gave her a smile. She smiled back shyly before walking briskly away to the fire where she proceeded to ladle out something into a small bowl.

The other two had moved to a far corner where they were busying themselves searching through a large chest that contained various fabrics of greens and browns. They lifted a mustard-coloured dress out and held it to the open window, before shaking their heads and diving in again. Their chatter excitable, I considered how I must have looked to them yesterday, my short summer dress torn to shreds. I had no idea what happened to my denim jacket, but it felt important to try and get it back somehow. I doubted denim had been invented yet. The women here wore long dresses with tunics over them, or aprons, depending on their job. I'd have to ask Ayleth what they thought of a woman who turned up with bare arms and legs, not to mention tattoos on her back. I guessed it wouldn't be accepted without numerous questions as to my status.

My attention was brought back to the third lady, who now held out a small bowl of stew of some kind and a large chunk of bread. Nervous, I took both and sniffed the contents. It smelt of animal and as I dipped in my spoon, I saw I'd guessed right as a large piece of what I presumed to be beef came into view. My stomach heaved slightly and I gagged. I couldn't eat this. Thankfully, the woman turned away and was busy pouring herself some. The broth Ayleth had given me yesterday had been watery enough for me to just drink the juice. This was quite thick.

The woman had sat down next to the fire and watched me carefully. I lifted the bowl and shook my head in what I hoped was an apologetic way. I didn't want to hurt her feelings if she'd made it. She came over immediately and took the bowl, but indicated the bread in my hand. I nibbled at it and nodded my head in a positive manner. She smiled and returned to her own bowl, and the other two eventually joined her.

The bread was fresh again and I soon finished it. I was strangely hungry considering my ordeal and considerably thirsty. I heaved myself up determined not to be waited on. I attempted to get out of bed trying to reach the jug of weak ale, when the room went dizzy and my body began to shake. I blindly reached out to try and catch myself, as the floor seemed to move beneath my feet, but there was nothing, and I hit the hard wooden floor with a bang. I vaguely heard someone scream and hands were on me, trying to turn and lift me, but I was a dead weight and blackness became my friend away from the pain.

I woke briefly and felt as if I was floating in the air, but I didn't care and closed my eyes. I abruptly felt the soft bed, propped up on my side with blankets draped carefully over me. The thin chemise I had been given felt sticky against my back and I knew my wounds had leaked. Sure enough, careful hands plied the fabric away from my skin and I felt a small trickle and a throbbing pain emanate from my back. I grimaced and wished for the blackness to return, my oblivion, but I stubbornly remained awake, though groggy, I kept my eyes tightly shut to stop the spinning and nausea.

Enduring the cleaning of my bare back, I dared to crack open my eyes and I saw faces, but I only focused on one. Dark brown eyes came into view. My captor stood next to the bed, sweating. He looked as if he'd been running. I quickly glanced behind him and saw Artorius, and others I couldn't focus on, and then there was Ayleth shooing the people out. She touched my captor's arm and said something kindly, and with one last glance at me, he reluctantly turned away and followed the rest of them out of the room. Ayleth twisted the key in the lock and leaned against it.

"You gave everyone a fright, young lady! Poor Brunhilde thought you were dead and Artorius would blame her for it. Apparently you didn't eat her stew?"

"No, it had beef in it. Sorry if I frightened her, maybe I should apologise...?"

Ayleth sat next to the bed. "Maybe so, when you see her next, aye. As it is, best to let everyone settle down." She laughed suddenly. "Gave the men a scare too, hearing Brunhilde screamin' away like she did. I heard her from my own bed and came runnin'. Silly woman."

"I don't remember much. I think I just fainted." My head was mushy and my throat dry. As if sensing it, Ayleth reached behind her and offered me one of the tankards that sat on the table. My arm and hands felt very weak, but I managed to sip half of the ale before handing it back.

"Aye, ya did that, and then went and knocked yourself out on the hard floor, along with opening the wounds on ya back! Brunhilde is not a woman who likes blood, aye!"

I smiled politely and drew a long, deep breath. "Who was here?"

Ayleth grinned, "I think near everybody. Though it was Tristan who reached ya first on hearing Brunhilde scream. Every man on the field ran like the devil for this room!"

"Tristan?"

"Aye, a gentle soul that one, except in battle, so I'm told. He's fierce and a good fighter. Beautiful brown eyes, reminds me of a horse, or perhaps a Labrador's eyes. It's been so long since I've seen one. Think he likes you, my dear."

I shook my head and grimaced as the pain shot through my skull. Ayleth immediately went to the fire and brought back a smaller goblet filled with a dark liquid I'd drunk before. "Willow bark tea," she told me. Disgusting, but effective and I forced down a few mouthfuls.

"Thank you, but I think you're wrong about Tristan. I'm just a prize to him. He caught me and brought me back here."

"And if he hadn't, you'd be dead by now, my girl. Out there is no place for a woman alone. I was terrified the whole six days I wandered the land, hiding from anything that moved. I thank the gods every day that Artorius found me and not ... well, anyone else without morals. Tristan did you a favour, Emily, never forget that."

After finishing the rest of the offered ale, I felt my eyes beginning to close. This almost constant exhaustion was most likely shock, my oblivion from this nightmare, so I welcomed it and didn't fight. Although, it could have something to do with time travel, but I was too tired to contemplate it at the moment.

My mind wandered and Tristan's eyes popped into my head. Ayleth was right, of course, despite everything. Tristan had saved me. I hoped I could trust him and any of the men here. I suppose time would tell. Their running to my room on hearing the maid scream was a tell-tale sign of concern, or had they'd considered that it was me hurting Brunhilde? Trust would have to be earned both ways and if Ayleth was right, then I had all the time in the world to achieve it. I abruptly pushed that notion firmly away and focused on those deep brown eyes.

CHAPTER 13

I woke with a terrible thirst and automatically reached for the usual glass of water I always kept by my bed. The sudden movement made me flinch, and I moved slower to reach for a glass that wasn't there. It took but seconds for my addled brain to acknowledge it and I lay back as a fresh wave of panic and terror enveloped me.

The thought of never returning home was one I'd barely dared to stop and contemplate, refusing to deal with it. The wounds kept my mind focused as the pain ebbed and flowed with each movement, reminding both my body and mind that I'd been abused and violated. All I wanted to do was curl up and pretend none of it was real. I was living through a traumatic event, yanked from my own time and hurled to what I considered the "dark ages" and what historians of my time knew very little about.

I squeezed my eyes tightly closed, stemming the onslaught of more tears and drew a shaky breath. I turned my head slightly and stared up at the wooden ceiling through swollen eyelids. I needed a mirror or something to see the damage done to me. I could hear someone walking around and they had a nasty chest cough. I listened to their wheezing and immediately thought, a cough mixture might help, or honey, whisky and lemon, but did they even have those things here in this time? As the reality of my situation slowly sank in I felt a deep terror and anguish that I hadn't felt since my parents' death.

Was this my life now? Could I actually survive it? Ayleth had been lucky and, to some extent, so had I. Artorius was a kind man, but not a fool, and I doubted he believed our pathetic story. For now, he indulged us, I think more for Ayleth's sake, as it was obvious he was very fond of her, and her knowledge of the future invaluable. My history was very rusty, so what could I use as proof that I could be useful enough to keep alive?

I gently eased myself into a seated position. I could see Ayleth sleeping on a trundle bed near the fire, brought on her insistence. Poor woman. What must she be thinking on seeing me, a woman from her own century? After all this time it must have been a shock to see my tattoos and my summer dress. She'd had to lie to these people, learn their language, and blend in as best as she could. She reminded me of my grandmother. Granny Rose had been sixty-four when she died, nine months before my parents' deaths. I can remember thinking when Granny died that I couldn't bare anything else to happen, and then the worst had.

I manoeuvred my legs over the side of the bed and rested them on the cold floor for a moment to get my balance. I felt weak as a kitten, flu-like, as every part of my body ached from the exertions of fighting, and running, and the shock of being flogged, and travelling through time. At this point, I wasn't sure which one freaked me out the most, so I pushed both thoughts firmly away. I tentatively reached over my shoulder and winced as I touched the bandage that covered my wounds. It felt very tender and bruised and I hoped it wouldn't scar. Then again, who would ever care if it did?

I sniffed as fresh tears fell, and pushed myself onto my feet. I hadn't cried this much since my parents were murdered and I'd hated it then. Tears were weak. I needed to focus on something, anything, to try and bring some semblance of normality into my life, and at this moment, peeing was it. So far so good. I felt light-headed, but not as dizzy as before. Holding onto tables, chairs and walls, I managed to use the toilet again and balked as it hadn't gotten any better in the interim of my last visit. The night air chilled my body as it raced up the chute, making my arse feel like a plucked chicken.

On my way back to bed, I had an overwhelming need to look outside the closed door. I'd been carried upstairs by Tristan, of that I was fairly certain, but I'd been in no fit state to recall my surroundings. Now, I was sick of lying down and annoyed at my weak body. I wanted to explore my new home, for want of a better word, if indeed what Ayleth said was true, so with a quick glance at Ayleth's sleeping body, I crept to the door and turned the large iron handle. It clicked loudly and Ayleth muttered something in her sleep as I pulled the door towards me.

I didn't see him immediately. The short corridor was lit by a single sconce in the wall that barely gave off any light as it was waning. I peered into the semi-darkness and could just make out the top of the stairs, leading downwards. It was the growl that alerted me and I froze. I heard a sharp command and my eyes turned towards the voice. My eyes were getting used to the surroundings and I could make out a vague shape of a man sitting on one of the steps. Below him on the next step lay a wolf or a large dog, its eyes glowing as it stared back at me.

"Who's there?" I whispered, not wanting to alarm the animal again. My voice shook and my heart hammered against my chest. My legs suddenly felt very wobbly and I clung to the door handle.

The man in the shadows stood, stretched and came into the light. I instinctively stepped back and he stopped. He lowered his gaze slightly and gave me a slight bow in a way that let me know he meant no harm. I was suddenly very aware of the thin, white gown Ayleth and the women had found and they'd torn the back so my skin was exposed. From his slight smirk, I guessed that he was aware of it too. I didn't think he would be able to see through it in this dim light, but nonetheless I moved so the door hid most of my lower body, and I peeped around it.

"What are you doing out here? Don't you have a bed? And what the hell is that?"

Frowning, Tristan stared at me and shook his head, not understanding me. I pointed at him, the stairs and the big dog thing, then at the door, and shrugged.

He seemed to comprehend that, but just smiled and pointed to the chamber.

"You're not coming in here, mate."

"No, he's telling you to get back into bed, ya daft woman! Whatcha' doing out of it? You'll catch a chill in that chemise."

I jumped as Ayleth came to stand beside me. She spoke sharply to Tristan who merely grinned, bowed to us both, and with a whistle to his animal disappeared down the steps.

I didn't have time to get a better look at it before Ayleth closed the door chastising me all the way back to the bed. With a sigh, I eased myself under the warm blankets and furs. My legs and feet were freezing and I was thankful for an extra blanket from Ayleth who wrapped it around my chest as she checked my bandages.

"What was he doing out there with that thing?"

"Keeping an eye on you, my dearie, and that 'thing' is his wolf. Follows him everywhere, and God forbid anyone even looks at Tristan funny. Now, you get some sleep, it'll be dawn in a couple of hours and then we'll see if you're able to walk around a bit, and get acquainted with your new home, eh?"

Her words chilled me to the bone and I shivered. On seeing it, Ayleth shook her head, gently patted my arm and went back to her own warm bed. My new home. Having had that very thought not so long ago, hearing her say it out loud made this ordeal all too real and I curled into myself for comfort. It felt like ages before I finally fell into an exhausted doze, but that's when her other words sank in. 'Keeping an eye on you, my dearie.' But why?

Ayleth watched Emily for an hour from her own warm bed nearer the fire. Her bones ached more frequently these days and her asthma was a constant threat as the chill seeped deeper into her aged body. She found herself searching for the fire in each room she entered, and barely left the sanctuary of the castle if she could help it. The men laughed at her as she bustled past them to reach the soothing flames and she grinned good-naturedly back at them. Let them laugh at her, they'd feel it themselves soon enough, if a sword didn't get them first.

Her head ached from lack of sleep. Though she'd fallen into a deep sleep earlier, from absolute exhaustion, she now found herself staring at the face of a woman she yearned to question. Yet fear prevented her from doing so. She'd made peace long ago with the fact of her being stuck in this time, but now, seeing another traveller, for want of a better word, she felt the old stirrings of homesickness, and grief for the people she'd lost. But more so was a renewed possibility of getting back to her time. To have Emily here proved that 'doors' were still opening around this area, for whatever reason.

Emily was a huge surprise, and yet, somewhere in the back of her head, Ayleth must have known there would be others who'd suffered the same misfortune. Shocked at seeing such a person, to speak her old language after such a long time had felt foreign to her lips, but the words still flowed quickly and easily.

Emily was in a strange way, alien to herself, a time-traveller, coming from her own future. Ayleth remembered the eighties with all its pathetic fashions and politics, yet Emily had barely been born in that decade. Emily had knowledge of what came after, having travelled from the twenty-first century, and she was desperate to know what happened to people from her own era. Such as Margaret Thatcher, did someone kill the bitch? Those poor miners and their families, what happened to them? Even mundane things like the price of food, petrol, and what had happened to music? Was Duran Duran still going? And if so, why?

Of course, Ayleth knew Emily wouldn't know anything about people closer to home. What of Melinda? How long had she hoped for her return? Did Melinda believe that she'd run off and left? Had the police helped? Did anyone hold a memorial for her? Would her death bring Melinda and her family back together? She hoped for that scenario all the time, so Melinda wouldn't be alone.

She wondered about her own parents, and her brother Robbie. Her father had disowned her for being a 'disgusting specimen' as he'd put it, demanding that she leave his home for good when she'd plucked up the courage to tell them she was gay the day after her twenty-first birthday. Her weak mother had not argued, but hung her head in shame as she'd packed her bags. Robbie, only two years older, couldn't understand it, and refused to see her. Friends fell away, and she'd moved away from Edinburgh to start a new life in Stirling, then Perth, then eventually finding Melinda and they'd moved to the outskirts of Glasgow. What happened after she disappeared?

Sleep finally found her as the birds woke and began singing their morning songs near the window. Somewhere in her dreams she heard the songs and smiled. At least the birds hadn't changed over time, their songs were just as sweet, thank God.

CHAPTER 14

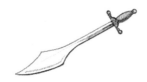

I woke to the sound of bustling and cracked my eyes open to be greeted by a woman's smiling face. On seeing me awake, she called out, and immediately I was surrounded by three other women, all chattering to each other and gently coaxing me to sit up. I did as I was told, too tired and confused by the goings on to fight them. On sitting up, I blinked my eyes a few times as my head swam a little, but I had no time to think about it as my bedclothes were ripped off me and one woman grabbed my ankles and swerved me round so my legs were dangling over the side of the bed.

I guessed their intentions as my attention was on Ayleth who was just pouring a large bucket of water into a wooden bath. It had the same shape as a bucket, but four times its size, big enough for a person sitting with their knees drawn up I presumed. She caught my eye, shrugged and replaced the empty bucket on the floor. She clapped her hands and shouted something which I guessed to be 'get out' as every woman scurried past her with various facial expressions before slamming the door behind them.

"Come on, Emily, this will do you good. There's Lavender and Rose oil to help your scars."

It did smell nice, now that I was coming round. I eased myself off the bed and walked slowly towards the tub. After a moment's hesitation, I let my stained chemise fall to the floor to mingle with various towels on which the tub sat. I grabbed Ayleth's outstretched hand and stepped into the warm water. There was just enough room with my knees bent, and the water reached above my breasts. I winced as the warm water touched the wounds on my back and the various cuts all over my body, but I couldn't deny the pleasure of feeling warm water after such a long time without showering. I felt clean. Closing my eyes, I wrapped my arms around my knees, let out a long, slow breath and let the water do its job.

"Good, isn't it?" Ayleth's voice broke into my dozing.

I nodded and smiled up at her dreamily. "Heavenly!"

Pleased, she went back to the bed, stripped it and laid the old sheets by the door. "The other maids will put clean sheets on your bed once you've finished. I've told them ya felt a little shy about your wounds."

"Thanks, it's the truth. I'm not used to having a bath in front of people." Realising what I'd said, I quickly added, "But you're okay."

Ayleth laughed. "Glad to hear it. I'm not about to jump on a wee lass after all these years either, so you can relax! Now, I've got a dress made for ya, though I've had to guess your size. A twelve?"

She held it up for me to admire. It was of dark green wool with a round neck, long sleeves and a free flowing skirt that I guessed would reach the floor. Ayleth also laid out a clean chemise that wasn't torn down the back and green stockings, and then she held up a pair of brown leather shoes. She set the dress over the bed and then held up a lighter green tunic and a cream-coloured woollen scarf that seemed out of place. I pointed at it and she grinned. "Well, I had to introduce something of our age. I missed my knitting, so why not the woollen scarf—they love it!"

After the water cooled I reluctantly accepted Ayleth's hand. Who knew when I'd feel it again? I'd washed my hair with some kind of soap that smelt of animal fat and herbs and longed for the apple and mint shampoo at home. She held out a towel of sorts and I carefully rubbed myself dry before I let Ayleth dress me.

I found the stockings very weird as they tied just above the knee. They felt strange, and cold on my thighs.

"Where's the knickers ... and bra or corset thing?" I asked, gazing down at the clothes on the bed.

"None, I'm afraid. I've fashioned my own and I'll do some for you, but it'll take a few days ... if I can get hold of some spare linen. Are you due your period, dear?"

Shocked by the question, it took me a few seconds to think. "Er ... no, I mean, I finished last week. What do women do here?"

Ayleth sighed loudly. "That's a discussion for another time, my lass. Artorius is waiting for you downstairs. Drink some of this, it'll help with the pain." She handed me the Willow bark tea brewing on the fireplace and I took it gratefully.

"He is?" My butterflies returned and so did my weak knees. "What does he want?" I sipped the tea, grimacing at the taste, but feeling the pain on my back urged me to swallow.

Ayleth applied some lavender oil to my back and gently wrapped another bandage. "This is healing nicely, but we'll keep it covered as the chemise will irritate it." Taking the cup from me, she helped me with the chemise and the dress, both of which went over my head. It took a bit of jiggling as holding my arms up pulled on my wounds, but eventually we managed it. "He wants to introduce his guest to his household, of course. And no doubt let people know you are under his protection, as if they wouldn't know already, but he'll make it official."

The light tunic also went over my head and tied at the sides, then she helped me into the shoes. They felt odd because they didn't have a left or right and were quite slippery. Ayleth finished tying them on and stood back. "Aye, you'll do for now, girl. Here ..." Handing me the scarf, she added. "You'll need this in the corridors, they're full of drafts. Its autumn here and winter isn't far off."

I wound the warm scarf around my neck and pulled one side over my head to hide my wet hair. Ayleth smiled. "You look the part of a lady now, Emily. Shall we go?"

I wanted nothing more than to hide away in my warm cocoon. My back hurt and my body felt weak and vulnerable. I had not felt this way for years. Having trained in karate for many years, it had given me a feeling of power, giving me the ability to fight back if necessary. I had been in control of my life for so long. Since losing my parents I'd fought to keep that feeling in every aspect of my life. Outside this room meant danger from men, and anything else that lived in this time, and it terrified me more than I had ever felt before. But Ayleth's insistent pulling on my arm forced my feet to move forward through the door and slowly we descended the stairs, following the noise of voices.

I'd walked into a country pub once hoping to quench my thirst with a lager after a long walk last summer. As I'd entered, the few people, who I guessed to be locals, stopped and stared at me and all conversation died away. For a few seconds, silence invaded the space and I remembered feeling awkward and wanting to back out and run away. But I'd held my head high, nodded at a few faces who'd politely nodded back, and resumed their conversations.

Whether it was from a need to prove a point to myself, or hoping to annoy the locals, I became a regular, walking the four miles just to show that I wasn't going to be frightened away. I was in charge of my own life; besides, they did a nice wine. After a few initial raised eyebrows, they slowly warmed to me, and they'd call out to me as I walked in and we'd pass banter of one sort or another. They were mostly older farmers or shift workers. Rarely any women, so I suppose I was a novelty. I liked that, and wondered what they'd thought when I never showed up again.

I swallowed the lump in my throat and took a deep breath for my nerves. As Ayleth led the way into a large hall it felt like entering that pub all over again, as all conversation died away and people turned to stare at me. There were so many faces and piercing, curious eyes, I didn't know where to look. I chose a fairly young servant, who quickly blushed, dipped her head and moved away. I chose another, a young man who was carrying a large tray of fresh, small loaves. I gave him a shy smile and I was rewarded with a kind smile back before he abruptly moved to the side. I glanced up sharply to see why.

Artorius was walking briskly through the crowd and finally stood before me. He spoke kindly and Ayleth interpreted for me. "Our dear guest. Welcome, Aemilia, niece of Ayleth. May my fire be your fire, my food be your food, and my shelter be your shelter, for as long as you need it ..."

He waited patiently for Ayleth to repeat it in English, and I smiled up at him once I'd heard his words. He took my hand and gently escorted me through the crowd to a long wooden table where he indicated a chair. Ayleth had followed and sat next to me. I was nervously rubbing my hands together, unsure what to do, when Ayleth gently covered them with one of her own and smiled. "It'll be all right, Aemilia ... now eat something and regain your strength."

I glanced at Artorius who had seen Ayleth's action and he smiled reassuringly, offering me a plate of some kind of fish. I took it with trembling hands and passed it onto Ayleth. "You can't live on bread, Emily, you need to eat something."

"I can't. Maybe they have some apples, or cheese?"

Ayleth caught Artorius watching us and he pointed at the fish. Ayleth quickly explained my vegetarianism, and although Artorius looked flabbergasted at such a thing, he called one of the servants, who ran off immediately. Artorius gently patted my hand and offered me fresh bread and a bowl of honey. I devoured it. As I was helping myself to a second slice, a plate arrived with two apples, a pear and chunks of cheese. Followed by a large jug of weak ale. I smiled up at Artorius who was watching me closely. On seeing my gratitude, he roared with laughter and nodded happily. We may not be able to verbally communicate, but I'd made him happy for accepting his gift of a meat-free meal, and that made me feel happy too.

The breakfast was a fairly brisk affair as men, women and children bustled about, chatting with each other, but eating quickly before darting off to be replaced by someone else. There didn't seem to be any particular rules of status, find a place, eat, chat, leave, very simple. I mentioned this to Ayleth who grinned. "Aye, 'tis a time to break your fast before getting on with the day. This evening will be more leisurely."

After watching the comings and goings for a while, I noticed a tell-tale significant drop in people, which signalled the end of breakfast. Within minutes, the hall was almost empty, besides myself, Ayleth, Artorius and a few of his men who lingered nearby, chatting casually. I recognised a couple of faces and nervously smiled as they caught my eye. They nodded back and then abruptly turned towards the open doorway and shouted at someone I couldn't see. Whoever it was, he was the butt of some joke that I was beginning to think involved me.

I felt I'd hit the nail on the head when seconds later Artorius silenced the jesting with a curt word and the men came to sit around our table. I looked towards the door and my breath stuck in my throat. Tristan stood there, his wolf beside him. He was eating an apple with a long dagger, slicing off pieces with such ease. His gaze was fixed on me as he sauntered down to the table and I found myself looking away first and staring at the crumbs on my plate, hoping I didn't have any honey around my mouth. My heart and stomach were competing as to which one could go faster and my mouth felt dry.

Ayleth suddenly covered my hand with her own. I jumped and looked up at her questioningly, but she indicated Artorius and grinned knowingly. I turned towards him and saw that he was addressing his men. Ayleth moved her chair closer and whispered in my ear. "Pay attention now, Emily, Tristan can wait. Now, Artorius is saying that the men who attacked you came from across the border. They were a scout party of sorts to see what resistance, if any, would befall a raid. The problem was, they found a good inn before returning their verdict to whoever had sent them. However, it wouldn't be long before they would be missed and another group of mercenaries would come looking for sport and bloodshed."

I suddenly felt sick and quickly grabbed the half tankard of ale and finished it, feeling a little tipsy at drinking so early. Artorius was still talking and unexpectedly pointed to me, and I blushed as every pair of eyes turned to me. Tristan lingered longer than the others, before a sharp nudge from the large giant next to him brought his attention back to Artorius.

Ayleth whispered again, "He is saying the attack on you was abhorrent. One woman against six men for no reason is bad enough, and he hopes they rot in hell for the crime. He's thanking his men for risking their lives to save you, and thanks the gods for their honour and friendship ..."

I leaned in closer to Ayleth and whispered. "Should I tell them I killed one of them?"

The bread and cheese suddenly felt like a brick in my churning stomach and I grabbed the tankard of ale again, hoping the ale would keep it there, but there was nothing more than a dribble left. The memory of killing the man had thankfully been kept at bay for the most part, as

I'd battled to suppress everything else. However, now listening to Artorius, the image of his protruding eyes as he fell, and his tongue lolling out of his bloodstained mouth as he hit the floor, burst forth into my brain, along with the smell of warm blood on my hands and my dress.

No. The bread was not going to stay. I sprang up, covered my mouth and urged Ayleth to move, which she quickly obliged and pointed to a wall behind us, where I gratefully found a stinking hole in which to throw up just in time. Finished, I leaned against the cold stone and cried my eyes out. My limbs ached, my back burned, my face felt broken and torn, and now my stomach hurt, my throat raw, and I yearned to clean my teeth and scrub my mind of the images of my victim. I'd killed a man. I was a killer.

Ayleth appeared a short while later with a clean, wet cloth. Grateful, I took it and wiped my face while she disappeared again, returning with a small goblet of spring water. "Sip this and we'll go outside in the sunshine for a bit before I take you back to your room."

I took it gratefully and sipped as instructed. I swilled my mouth with some and spat it out. "I'm sorry. Artorius gave me veggie food and he must think I'm a pathetic woman and ..."

Ayleth hushed me. "Artorius thinks you are a brave woman who has been through a terrible ordeal and survived. Being whipped is not taken lightly, Emily, and neither is rape. Those men got what they deserved. You say you killed one of them?"

"I ... he ..."

Ayleth stopped me, "Not here, let's go outside away from this stinking pit, and you can tell me everything."

I followed her out and was thankful to see the hall empty save for a couple of servants who were cleaning the tables and floor. Ayleth led me slowly to a quiet part of the castle, a sun trap that overlooked the walled garden beneath. It was small with only a handful of herbs and vegetables on one side and a couple of apple and pear trees on the other. A servant was busy collecting any fallen apples and putting them in a basket.

"They will be made into apple sauce for the pork and cider. The ones still on the trees will be put into apple pies."

"Do they have those in this time then?"

"Of course. I introduced them to cider." Ayleth laughed. "I missed it so much, you know. I considered what harm it would do, and besides, who is to say it wasn't already known? And apple pies were my favourite desert ... now, tell me everything."

We sat in silence afterwards, staring out beyond the garden, past the moat and hills. We watched the clouds float along the sky and the birds that swooped down on the current. There were bustling people everywhere, but just here, right then, it was peaceful.

"I'd better go and tell Artorius about the man by the inn. He'll go and question the locals who are supposed to tell him of any strangers. He'll want to know why he hasn't heard of this man's death."

"I don't want to get anyone in trouble."

"You won't, they're already in trouble for not telling their Lord and master. Besides, he needs to find out who these men were and who sent them. No one recognised them and they had no crest, which bothers Artorius. If these men were working alone, so be it, but if they are part of something bigger, then he needs to know."

"Ayleth?" I remembered something else and touched her arm to stop her. She turned to me questioningly. "Before I was rescued, one of the men tore off my denim jacket. I don't know where it is ... I don't think they have denim here."

Ayleth shook her head. "No, lass, they don't, not for many centuries yet. I believe it was in the fifteen hundreds, so it can't be found in this time. I'll see what I can do. You stay here and keep warm for a wee while. I'll be back shortly."

I watched Ayleth make her way down the steps and disappear out of sight. I gazed around. From my vantage point I could see most of the fortress. I had been right. It was surrounded by a high thick stone wall, but all the buildings inside were wooden, though built into the stone at various points. It was three storeys in some places and covered a fairly large area. I could remember visiting various castles in Wales as a child and this one looked to be about half the size of Conwy in North Wales. I peeped over the side of the wall and saw a deep ditch ran around the outside and on the opposite side of the ditch long, sharpened spears protruded outwards to deter people from crossing. In the other direction, a small hamlet occupied the lower meadow near a narrow river.

I shielded my eyes against the glare of the sun and saw him. Tristan stood in the courtyard watching me. He was holding the reins of a grey horse, his own if memory served me, and another man was talking to him and laughing. Then he too looked up at me, slapped Tristan on the shoulder and walked away shaking his head. Tristan didn't move.

I felt my insides quiver and my breath quickened. In all of this madness how could I feel anything, never mind lust for a man I barely knew? Maybe this was hero worship? He did save me from being whipped and gang-raped. I looked away, back at the garden, and tried to gather my thoughts. He was gorgeous, there was no doubting that. I remembered the feel of his solid body on top of me, perfectly muscled, no fat or beer belly. He must be around five-foot-ten. He looked to be about the same height as Brian, though he stood proud where Brian slouched, usually behind a bar.

His long brown hair was kept off his face by two plaits, one either side of his head, and out of his perfect brown eyes. He had a short beard and high prominent cheekbones. Today he wore only a brown tunic over his woollen trousers and I could see some kind of silver pendant on his bare chest. He still wore his sword at his side and I noticed a dagger, probably the one he had eaten with, sheathed on the other side of his hip.

A low growl stopped my breath. I felt the hairs on the back of my neck stand up and my heart burst as it pounded in my chest. Suddenly a big wet tongue licked my neck. I flinched and turned towards it when another lick caught my cheek. I opened my eyes and stared into the face of a wolf.

A soft command brought us both up sharp and as one, both animal and I turned towards the man standing above us, watching our greeting. Immediately the wolf lay down at my feet and Tristan came to sit beside me. He said nothing as he stared ahead, his arms casually wrapped around his bent knees. For a few minutes I could barely breathe, but eventually I began to feel calm and allowed myself to enjoy the moment as he obviously was. So we sat in silence and watched the birds and I waited to see what my captor would do next.

CHAPTER 15

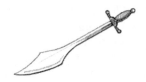

Brian stared straight ahead, his head busy doing calculations, working out times and plans. He didn't hear a shout until the man was running up to him and called again.

"Hey, mate, didn't you hear me?"

Brian turned to the large black man he'd met previously and cursed his luck. Anyone but him would have been better. He was catching his breath and glancing around nervously, which took Brian by surprise. "Not here, let's keep walking ..."

Brian was about to argue, but saw a nurse pushing a patient nearby and quickly changed his mind, following the man cautiously. He rounded a bend and Brian found himself near the walled garden. The orderly, walking towards it, disappeared behind a hedge. Brian glanced both ways and weighed up his options. He wasn't sure what this man was playing at; last time they'd met he'd been menacing, but now, he was acting completely different. He rubbed his chin and licked his dry lips before quickly following. If the man wanted a fight away from prying eyes, he guessed he might have a chance to throw one, maybe two, punches before he'd be knocked to the floor: the orderly was pretty big.

Brian wasn't some thin weakling. The building work had toned him, especially his arms, but he was out of shape from years of drinking and smoking. He knew how to hold his own in a fair fight with a man his own stature, but this man was out of his class .

He found the orderly sitting on a stone bench just inside the garden, lighting a rolled cigarette. He offered Brian one from his tin, but Brian declined and remained standing and vigilant. "Well?"

The man shrugged, lit his cigarette, coughed and grinned up at him. "Yeah, okay. Look, I know what you think of me, I can see it in your eyes ..." When Brian said nothing he continued, "You've come to see your sister, Emily?"

Brian nodded slowly and waited.

"Look, what I'm going to say to you can't go any further yet, okay?"

Brian was getting impatient, needing to get back to work before he was sacked. "Look, what is it? Something about Emily? Are they hurting her?"

The man shook his head. "No, worse than that. I think they're playing with her head."

Brian stepped closer. "You mean experimenting?"

"Maybe?" The man inhaled deeply and blew, watching the smoke disappear into the air. "She's under the care of Dr Marian Griffiths, and man does that woman want to get promoted! She'll do anything, and Emily is her ticket."

Brian finally sat down beside him on the bench. "What do you mean? And how do you know all this, you're only one of the orderlies?"

The man nodded while inhaling, "I am. I got this job so I could watch and learn and report back anything amiss. I see a lot of things here, wrong things, and your sister, Emily, is one of those wrong things."

"Report back to who? Tell me." Brian could feel his blood boiling. The fury he felt was intense, but he knew he had to hold it together or he'd never get her out.

"I'm a journalist, mate, okay. They say she's a murderer, but hey, no real proof. In fact, I heard just the other day that the police suspect someone else was involved, but they're keeping it quiet for now because Emily hasn't said anything and the family needs someone to blame, right? So, Dr Griffiths is using hypnotherapy sessions to play with Emily's mind to try and piece together the puzzle. If she succeeds, she'll be promoted and Emily will be left here to rot."

"I should go to the police ... or better yet, you should."

"No way. How would you know these details? I found them out, but they haven't been made public. You can't say a word, not until I have more evidence, and then I can blow it open. My editor is bristling for this story. I just need more time."

Brian stood and walked away a few strides before turning back, his hands in his pockets. "Why are you telling me all this now?"

The man laughed. "'Cause I know what you're going to try and do, mate. You can't get her out, you know, and your pathetic attempt might stop my investigation. I need more time and proof about what's going on inside this hospital. Can you give me that?"

Brian quickly ran a hand through his hair and shrugged. "What about my sister?"

"I'll keep an eye on her, I promise. If I think her life is in danger, I'll call it quits and blow everything whether I have enough or not. Just give me a couple more days?"

Brian walked away, but not far. He looked up at the roof of the hospital, which was all he could see from his position. Somewhere in there Emily was being played with. He looked towards the building site and he sighed loudly. Yards away and he could do nothing. He had no idea when he'd get to see her. He'd been allowed to speak with one of the consultants regarding Emily's incarceration, but he hadn't got the authority to offer him a visitor's pass. He'd been told that someone would contact him, but he wasn't hopeful. Maybe this man was her only chance?

"Okay. I'm not convinced I believe everything, and believe me, if this is bullshit, I swear I'll kill you, understand? What's your name anyway?"

The man finished his cigarette and threw away the stub. He stood up and grinned. "Okay, no problem, and best you don't know my name for my own protection."

"And what about Emily's protection?"

The man shrugged and walked away, back towards the hospital. "I guess you'll just have to trust me."

Brian watched the orderly walk across the perfectly-mowed lawn towards a side door before he turned and ran around to the building site. He waved at a few of the men who rolled their eyes at his tardiness, and he gave two fingers to a passing comment. Let them moan, he'd work an extra half hour after they all went to the pub, just so he wouldn't be tempted, and it'd make him look good. Besides, it also meant he'd have time to think while he worked, without constant interruptions, and that's what he desperately needed right now.

*   *   *

The silence stretched on uncomfortably. I became aware that I was getting sidelong glances and it occurred to me he was trying to work out how to communicate with me given our language barrier. Eventually, Tristan turned and stared openly at me. I shyly glanced up at him, but turned away embarrassed. He obviously wasn't, and reached out to touch my cheek.

His touch was soft, barely a caress, but my skin reacted like a heat wave, and my stomach trembled. My breath caught in my throat and I turned to look at him. He offered a reassuring smile and I managed to smile back, though I couldn't keep eye contact. His stare was too intense, raw and untamed. His feelings for me were clear and I found that openness hard to deal with. In my time, men were not so open, unless he was some lecherous sod who left you in no doubt as to what he wanted from you; a quick fuck and he'd be gone. Tristan may well want those from me, but he wanted something else too, he wanted to know me, to understand me and that was both a turn on and very frightening.

He said something, but knew immediately it was pointless. Without Ayleth to help, I understood nothing. He thought for a moment, and then put his hand on his chest. "Tristan." Then pointed at me. So, we were starting with the basics, fine.

I put my own hand on my chest. "Emily. Or how do you pronounce it? Aemilia."

He heard the difference and I said my own name again. After listening, he repeated my name several times until we were both happy with it. He seemed very pleased with my name and said it to himself over and over while absentmindedly stroking the wolf.

What followed was an hour or so of miming and short spoken words to establish my marital status, my age, my family, any animals, where did I learn to ride? Where did I learn to fight like that? Could I show him how I flipped him over my shoulder?

Without waiting for my consent, he quickly stood and reaching down, pulled me to my feet. I flinched at the sudden movement and he immediately became concerned. I tried to pretend I was okay, but he grabbed my hand and held onto it longer than was necessary, and his large thumb gently stroked the inside of my wrist where my pulse was beating fast. With a grin, he turned and gestured the steps downwards and we took the steps slowly as the skirt and shoes hindered me, as did a wave of pain and exhaustion that made me see spots before my eyes. I was thankful for the stone wall and Tristan's presence, otherwise I might have tumbled over.

Making me sit on the third step, he abruptly left me, but came back almost immediately with some ale. He held it with me and carefully poured the warm liquid into my mouth until I dribbled some down the sides of my chin. Having a drink himself, I watched the muscles on his throat move as he drank thirstily. Finished, he left the jug on the steps and produced two apples from his pocket, offering me one of them; I took it gratefully, and offering me his hand, he gently pulled me back onto my feet, hooked his arm through mine and leisurely walked me out of the courtyard, aware of everyone watching.

Just before reaching the small hamlet, he turned me right towards the meadow next to the river. I guessed that was where we were heading and within a few minutes he had sat me down on a rock and was throwing stones into the water. His wolf was knee deep trying to catch them. After a while, his wolf got bored of that game and came to lie next to me, which made me feel very apprehensive, but he merely licked his lips, gave a loud sigh and promptly fell asleep.

Tristan laughed and I grinned sheepishly, knowing he had guessed my fear. I was beginning to feel uncomfortable, not just with Tristan's silent stares, but my dress was getting warm and my back was stinging as sweat trickled down to my bum. I must have been fidgeting as Tristan's manner changed completely from watching me with such an open look, to one of absolute concern. He swiftly pulled me to my feet and was about to pick me up when I let out a yell to stop him, the thought of his arm rubbing against my whip-lashes as he carried me abhorrent. He seemed to quickly understand and bowed apologetically before offering me his arm instead. I took it gratefully and he slowly walked me back towards the castle.

A shout brought us both up short and we turned to the caller. Ayleth stood with her hands on her hips. "And just what the hell do you think you're doing, my girl? Have you forgotten how badly bruised your body is?" Turning to Tristan, she glared at him. "And you? Just what the hell do you think you're doing? I leave her for ten minutes to sit quietly in the sun and you gather her up and walk her for miles." She must have noticed my discomfort as she swiftly moved in between us, taking my arm with one hand and slapping Tristan across the head with her other. "I'm sure there are easier and less harmful ways of flirting than half killing the poor lass. Now off with you, Artorius wants you!"

He laughed and I stood shocked, staring from one to the other, before he bowed politely to us both and strode away. My face must have shown my thoughts and Ayleth grinned. "No, dear, he doesn't know our language, but I've taught him some of our words and phrases over the years and besides, he knows an angry woman when he hears one regardless of language, eh, Tristan?"

Hearing his name, he abruptly turned, bowed again and disappeared through the doorway that led into the kitchens, clicking the wolf to heel. I was left feeling breathless, in a lot of pain, and yet very hungry. Guessing all three, Ayleth laughed and putting her arm through mine, we idled back to my room, where I knocked back a cup of ale, and fresh biscuits dribbling with honey before I sank into oblivion.

I slept through the rest of the day and most of the night. My adventure outside had drained me completely, and I'd opened up some of the wounds on my back, which made Ayleth cluck like a mother hen and reapply lavender- and honey-soaked linen on my naked back after I'd eaten. I fell asleep that way and woke in the same position with such an intense hunger I felt sick. Thankfully my dearest friend, Ayleth was on hand and quickly pushed herself out of her trundle bed by the fire and handed me freshly baked bread and a small bowl of vegetable broth, followed by oatmeal biscuits and two cups of weak ale. I wolfed them down while she nibbled on a biscuit and we ate in companionable silence.

Finally, as we began to hear the dawn song of the birds, we crept back to our beds in silence and I drifted off into a fitful sleep, trying to ignore the throbbing pain in my back. I hadn't managed to look at the wounds. I'd only gingerly felt some of it with my fingers, straining to reach, but even that had caused me to bleed and I'd given up. I longed for, and at the same time dreaded, a long mirror to see what damage had been done and how much scarring I'd be left with. I had many scrapes and grazes all over my body and my eyes were still swollen, but didn't feel as tender. I had a large cut on my temple hairline and a bruised jaw. I must look a sight, but I needed to see it. I hadn't voiced my concerns with Ayleth, but I didn't doubt that she already knew.

I woke feeling groggy and irritable and wished people wouldn't keep sneaking into my room while I slept, as two servants were carrying a large cauldron between them, placing it over the roaring fire. Someone had already been in to bring fresh jugs of ale and Ayleth was quietly watching everything. Noticing me awake, she grinned and swept her arm around the room, "A wash, some liquid to quench your thirst before going down to breakfast … Oh dear, you don't look happy ..."

I moved carefully and recoiled as I caught one of the linens that had slipped off in the night, but still clung to some dried blood. It pulled at the wound and I cried out angrily. "Fuckin' shit, bollocks!"

Ayleth merely raised an eyebrow, while the two servants on their way to the door looked startled by my outburst. Ayleth said something softly and they nodded in sympathy before leaving us alone.

"Hurts?"

I glared at Ayleth for asking such a stupid question and continued to carefully climb off the bed. I reached the jug of ale and poured us both a cup before gulping mine down, leaving me gasping for breath. "I don't think I'll ever get used to drinking first thing in the morning!"

"Aye, well, there's also spring water in the other jug if you'd prefer."

I heard the teasing and looked up at her. "You could have told me?"

"Aye, I could have, but after your outburst, I felt too afraid."

I sighed heavily and peeped into the other jug and poured out a cup of freshly boiled spring water and drank it thirstily.

"I've organised another wash for you, so when you're ready, come here by the fire and I'll help you. It's only a strip wash today, but I'll leave the warm linen on your back to help it heal."

"Is it … I mean, will I be scarred?"

Ayleth shrugged, "No idea, though it is pretty deep in two places, but if you'd only behave and not over do things, it would heal better and quicker. You pulled your wound open yesterday, and I've chastised Tristan for it."

I let my loose chemise fall to the floor and knelt down on a towel before the fire and began rinsing a hot flannel. Ayleth took it from me and gently placed it on my back. I flinched at first but it felt so good I eventually relaxed, and washed the rest of me while every so often, Ayleth would re-apply a fresh hot flannel to my back. She helped me wash my hair with a rosemary scented concoction and then she finally helped me into my gown and tunic. She'd been brewing willow bark tea and she gave me some to help with the pain. Eventually I was as ready as ever when Ayleth smiled broadly and produced a roughly cut pair of knickers with a flourish.

I gasped, delighted, and quickly put them on. It felt so cosy covering up my bits, I hadn't realised just how much I'd miss wearing them. "They're brilliant Ayleth, thanks."

"Glad they fit you. I did them while you slept yesterday. I'll make some more once I get spare linen. You'll just have to wear them one day and clean them the next. I have several pairs now that I clean halfway through the week so they dry while the others are being worn. It's about getting into a routine and hiding these." She pointed to my groin before sitting down in a chair next to the fire. She closed her eyes in bliss and sighed.

"Why do I need to hide them?" I sat opposite her on the smaller chair.

"Because knickers haven't been invented yet, so far as I'm aware, so we cannot alter history now, can we?"

I thought about that. We could so easily change something so small and insignificant here that might have repercussions further along in time. I wondered what I'd have done if I'd come to the beginning of the World Wars and had a chance to kill Hitler, or change the outcome and stop World War I? I voiced these thoughts to Ayleth.

"Yes, I've thought of that too. Producing a pair of knickers in this time seems so insignificant, but I have no idea who actually designed them, or when. If they are already in existence, then how would that affect the designer? Killing Hitler would undoubtedly change history, but would it merely happen through another, much worse, means?"

I shrugged and we fell silent. "Knickerbockers!"

Ayleth laughed out loud. "You're right, I'd forgotten those. Weren't they an eighteenth century invention? Didn't they make that into an ice cream sundae?"

I grinned, "Yes, I could never finish one. Sorry, I just got into the origins of knickers and that word came into my head. But surely women wore something to keep themselves warm?"

Ayleth shook her head. "Not that I've noticed. The chemise and stockings are all they wear, so please try and keep the knickers a secret. The servants here are very nice ladies and helpful, sometimes too helpful, and they gossip, so be careful." Easing herself out of the chair, Ayleth stretched. "Now, after breakfast, if it remains dry, I'll take you to my shed. Well, I call it my shed, it's actually more like a cave in the rock with a wooden overhang the men built for me. It's where I keep all my herbs and where I usually sleep. It's quite cosy."

I couldn't wait, and after an uneventful and lonely breakfast of warm scones and cheese, washed down by more weak ale, I followed her without question. I was ready to get out of my room and explore a little. I was beginning to allow myself to feel safe within the castle walls. So far people had been curious, but kind. Whether that was an order from Artorius or not, I smiled warmly at everyone we met, and hoped I could be accepted.

We descended the stairs carefully. My shoes were still an issue for me and I slipped a couple of times on the wooden steps and gangways. We went through a single door and I found that we'd entered the courtyard. The smell of horses, straw and muck reached my nostrils and I breathed it in. I coughed as smoke from the fire and the scent of unwashed bodies reached me. I smiled at a man who stood nearby, holding a horse's head while the blacksmith worked on its hoof the other end. I couldn't see if he was putting on a shoe, and wondered if they even did that in this time. He nodded to me, and Ayleth said something to him which made him smile broadly, displaying a lack of front teeth. I voiced my query to Ayleth who repeated it to the blacksmith. He moved to the side and showed me a leather boot type thing that he fastened to the horse's hoof to protect it from wear and tear apparently. I made a comment about nails, but Ayleth shook her head and moved on, thanking the men as we passed. I looked around at the busy courtyard and suddenly felt overwhelmed by it all. There were familiar things, and yet nothing was the same.

A few people nodded a greeting as we passed, but most were too busy and we reached her little home without interruptions. It was indeed cosy, no bigger than ten feet by twelve. The back wall was stone, as was half of one side, which created a slight alcove. The rest was wattle and mud like all the other buildings. The stone wall was lined with boxes and herbs hung from the roof. I touched one bundle and sniffed, rosemary. I rubbed another, sage. I rubbed my fingers on the leaves and inhaled the familiar scent, immediately thinking of 'sage and onion stuffing'!

A narrow bed took up most of the side wall and a small fireplace and chimney had been cut into the rock. It was roughly done, but adequate, as Ayleth had told me, and she began to make up a fire. Within minutes, a fine blaze was going and the room's chill quickly disappeared. In fact, after half an hour, I was sweating and moved back to the doorway to cool off.

Ayleth was resting on her bed and laughed, seeing me fanning myself. She invited me to open her door, which I did gratefully. I stood with my back to the courtyard and waited until the sweat subsided a little before re-entering to continue my examination of her room. I opened and closed pouches of dried herbs and bottles of various smelling concoctions that Ayleth said eased pain, or it could take it away permanently. Her words stopped my examination of one bottle and I gingerly put it down.

"Why do you have poison?"

"Why not? It may be that I need it for myself, or it may be that it would be the kindest act to do for someone with a serious injury. Death is accepted here, it's part of their world. Death is merely another journey."

Her words frightened me, reminding me of this precarious time which was too easy to forget cocooned in this cosy room with a woman from my own era. Yet, she was right, of course. In our time people rarely thought of death. Death was never spoken of until it was too late. Here, death was always around, a constant companion, and I felt vulnerable again.

"I know you're scared, Emily, and you should be, but you have to sort yourself out. You obviously have some skills in fighting if you could take on a mercenary. Why not use those skills? Teach the men. I'm sure Tristan would be interested. You obviously have skills I never had?"

I told her then about karate and why I trained. She listened quietly as she gently stirred something sweet smelling and fruity over the fire. Eventually she handed me a goblet and I sniffed its contents and grinned. "Ribena!"

"It's an experiment. I had left over berries last week, so I've kept them cool and mixed them with spring water and honey. What do you think?"

It was extremely sweet, but tasty and non-alcoholic. She laughed when I mentioned that and abruptly stood up. "Come on then, I'll take you to my spring. With you to help I can carry more jugs back. Come on before it starts raining." She rummaged under her bed and produced an empty bottle and gathered three more large jugs, handing me two. "Come on, it's a good walk up on the moors, we'd better get going."

I hesitated. "Will we be safe? I mean, alone up on the moors? It's a bit open, isn't it, anyone could see us?"

Ayleth shrugged. "Aye, they could, but if you want to live here, you cannot give in to fear, otherwise you'll never leave this castle and you'll go mad. Now come along. We'll go slow."

"But, Ayleth ... Betty, I don't want to live here." I sank down on the bed and cried.

Ayleth reached out and patted my shoulder. "I know, Emily, it'll be hard, I'll not lie to ye', but it's something you'll have to get used to. Besides, I've seen a young man who is more than willing to help make your time here bearable, eh?"

"Very funny." I sniffed, wiped my nose and pushed myself up. The thought of Tristan did make a little difference, I couldn't deny that, and catching Ayleth's eye, I saw she knew it too. "All right, lead on then." My body hurt and I was terrified of leaving the confines of the castle with only an old woman to protect me, but truth be told, I did need a good walk to stretch my legs, I missed walking, and the fresh air was tempting.

I followed Ayleth out of her cosy shed and shivered at the autumn chill. Clutching my scarf closer, I walked beside Ayleth who shouted to one of the guards and he opened a narrow door in the wall that allowed us to reach the other side of the castle quicker. We carefully picked our way down the steep incline and huffed and puffed our way up the other side of the ditch. As we stood catching our breath, I stared out at the open moors that surrounded the castle. I carefully rolled my shoulders, feeling the pull of the wounds but no tell-tale signs of them opening, and once we'd rested a moment, we left the safety of its walls behind.

CHAPTER 16

Artorius watched the two women walking towards the outer wall and beyond from his hidden place within the smithy. He'd been having a conversation about the expected foals when he'd seen them walk into the courtyard. He'd been about to show himself, but stopped as he watched the lady Aemilia. She looked as frightened as a rabbit caught in a snare and although he could see Ayleth was trying to help her, she had a look in her eyes that reminded him of when his father had first brought Ayleth to their home.

He could not imagine life at the castle without Ayleth. Her knowledge of medicines had saved many over the years, and her sight of the future had also helped him in his quest for peace, knowing he would be victorious when he had no choice but to fight. So he never questioned her regarding her true reason for being on the moors that day his father had found her. But he was no fool and Ayleth knew it. There was something mysterious about Ayleth and now he felt the same towards Lady Aemilia, if that was indeed her true name; he wasn't convinced of it.

The women reminded him of the first time he had witnessed the birth of a litter of kittens. He'd stared open-mouthed at the sight, watching as the newly-born kittens stared back at the world (once their eyes opened) and they saw for the first time their new home. They had a look of both awe and wonder at everything around them as though they had never seen such things before, and it terrified them. Ayleth rarely had that expression anymore, though on occasions he'd catch her by surprise and she'd have a strange look on her face, before quickly hiding it away. He decided to check on their mission and walked quickly towards the guard. Having ascertained their whereabouts, he returned to the courtyard. He knew Ayleth ventured outside of the walls every few days, and she had shared her visions with him in regard to fresh running water, but for now they had a well and he couldn't see any logic in directing running water to the castle from her hidden spring.

He glanced around and saw Merek flirting with the servant girls whilst sharpening his knives. Brom was eating a chicken leg and passing comments with Merek about the size of the girl's arse. There was no sign of the others, though he knew exactly where they'd be. He thought for a moment. His scouts reported nobody in the vicinity yesterday, but a lot could happen overnight. The women would be on the moors by now and he felt a stirring of unease. "Merek, Brom, when you've quite finished assaulting the poor girl and stuffing your face, I want you to follow Ayleth and my guest, the Lady Aemilia."

Both men immediately stopped what they were doing. Merek sheathed his knives and came to stand before Artorius, while Brom gathered his sheepskin coat.

"They have gone over the moor." He indicated their direction with a nod of his head. "I worry about them, especially as we know mercenaries are in these parts recently. I'll see my ladies unharmed ..."

Merek bowed and turned on his heels, catching Brom as he was walking towards him. "Come, we have care duty."

Brom glanced between both men, shrugged, and turned to follow Merek. He never bowed to any man and Artorius knew it. They had a silent agreement, Brom would never bow to him, but he'd be loyal and that suited them both. Merek on the other hand liked to know where he stood in the order of things. Having known Artorius for a number of years, he knew he didn't have to bow, Artorius never demanded it, but it was just his way. A habit he'd never grown out of, and neither had his family. Growing up as a servant, he'd shown promise as a young boy with knife skills that Artorius' father saw and encouraged. By the time the boys were young men, they'd become strong friends and battles won together had sealed that trust. Merek knew it embarrassed Artorius, but it was ingrained into his very being and so it went unchallenged, for now.

As they reached the outer door they met Rulf and Borin talking about their new swords, and Tristan was nearby helping settle in some of the new horses acquired from their fight to save Aemilia. They raised their hands in greeting, but carried on walking fast, out through the back of the castle; they ran down the steep incline and up the other side. A shout stopped them. Turning, they saw all three men catching them up. It was inevitable, they all fought together, why not go on a protection duty together?

"No need to follow, my brothers. It is only Ayleth on one of her hunting trips for the last of her herbs to see us through the winter, and fetching her water." Merek grinned. "Although, she does have a certain lady with her ..."

Tristan shrugged and said nothing, accepting the teasing remarks and punches with a smirk.

"May the gods bless him. He's so in love he cannot speak." Brom laughed loudly.

"It is not speech he wants to use his mouth for." Rulf howled with laughter as he tried to simulate kissing on his sleeve.

"Will she be your first, Tristan? I'll ask her to break you in gently." Borin guffawed and leaned on Merek for support.

Merek shook his head, "No, my lords, she will not be his first, but certainly the prettiest, I'll wager? A fine woman, Tristan, how far have you got? I saw you with her, did she reject you?"

Tristan smiled sweetly and shook his head. "I shall not answer any of this. She is a lady and ..."

A scream broke the mood and all five men turned as one towards the sound. They moved swiftly, branching out, searching for any signs as to where their women were in danger. Another shout and they ran at full pelt towards it. Over a slight rise and they saw below them four men circling Ayleth, who was lying on the ground, and the lady Aemilia was standing over the older woman, swinging a jug and shouting.

As they ran towards them, the men were too preoccupied to see they were outnumbered, as they jeered and taunted the lady. One man moved in to attack and was knocked sideways by the swing of the jug that broke into pieces, which was swiftly followed by a punch that had him out cold.

All of the other attackers stood stunned for a second, before it was too late. The five men of the castle were upon them and they were dead in moments, their throats cut and their bodies sliced. Tristan moved to the Lady Aemilia in one swift movement, as he neatly slit a mercenary's throat from behind in one motion. He stood between her and the assailant to block her view of his death, as she stared open-mouthed and shocked from what had occurred.

A groan from the ground caught her attention and she immediately bent down to Ayleth who was clutching her cheek where a nasty gash was visible, blood oozing between her fingers. Aemilia delved into Ayleth's pockets and found a piece of linen which she held against the older woman's cheek. Brom came and knelt behind her, holding her up with his knees, so the blood flow slowed down. Aemilia smiled up at him gratefully.

"We need to get her back to the castle." Tristan's orders were immediately done, and Brom gently bent down and picked up Ayleth, as if she weighed nothing. Tristan reached out and lightly held onto Aemilia's arm and walked her back to the castle, while Merek and Rulf roughly dragged the unconscious mercenary behind the women. All men glanced between each other and back at Aemilia, who hadn't said a word. Tristan could feel her shaking and longed to hold her. He cursed himself for not moving quickly enough. They should not have mocked him and taken their duty lightly, and now Ayleth was wounded and the Lady Aemilia in shock. Artorius had forbidden anyone to leave the castle without an escort. Ayleth knew better than this, but had disobeyed anyway. This attack would not go unpunished.

They laid Ayleth in Aemilia's chamber as the fire was burning brightly to keep the chill from the room. Aemilia stood over her, unsure what to do, but Ayleth said a few words to the two hovering servants and they ran off, he guessed to her cave of herbs. The wound would need stitching and he quietly stepped forward. Ayleth saw him and nodded her approval. Tristan was the best at doing stitches. His hand was always steady and he was able to make them small.

The women returned within moments carrying a small basket with an array of herbs and bottles. A cauldron was placed over the fire and a cloth placed inside, which they used to clean away the blood and filth. A small goblet of wine was brought to cleanse the wound, and a jar of honey, as Ayleth had shown them. She flinched as they washed her wound, and they poured her another large goblet of wine to drink before she turned to Tristan and indicated she was ready for him to sew. He leaned in gently, whispered something to her and she closed her eyes, remaining perfectly still as he sewed quickly and neatly. Eleven stitches later, he sighed loudly, rinsed her cheek with more wine, dabbed it dry and smothered honey onto the wound. He swallowed the last few mouthfuls left in the cup and stroked her hair. He stood, stretched, bowed to Aemilia and left the room followed by the rest of the men, leaving the women to care for each other as only women could.

I'd watched the proceedings as if I was watching a film. From the moment those men had jumped out on us, I'd felt detached somehow. Seeing the knife and then the blood, I'd felt something else. I wanted to kill and I knew how to do it. The skirts hindered me and I'd lifted them so I had enough leg movement. The men had thought this was some kind of invitation and made the mistake of stepping towards me. A hard punch in the throat followed by a kick in the abdomen was enough to make him back away, gasping for breath. I doubt I'd hit him hard enough to crush his windpipe but it had been enough to stop him in his tracks. Another had moved in and I'd swung the jug at his head and punched his nose with an upward movement that would give him brain damage and possibly death. I'd wanted to kill him.

I was so consumed with fighting, I hadn't noticed Tristan and his friends until they were behind our attackers and killing them. The spray of arterial blood is something I will never forget, and thanked God I wasn't close enough to get too much of it on me. As it was, my sleeve was stained with Ayleth's blood and I glanced down, sorry for it, as I liked this dress.

The tears came thick and fast then. How pathetic that I should be crying over a stain. Ayleth beckoned me to sit on the bed and I did. She held my hand and waited for the sobbing to subside.

"Better?"

I wiped my eyes on my stained sleeve. "I don't know. This is all happening so fast, I can't take it in. Being attacked again only three days after travelling through time, is a bit much, don't you think? And now you've been hurt and somehow I feel responsible ..."

"Responsible? How on earth are you? It was me who suggested the walk. I thought we'd be safe within sight of the castle. My spring is only a few hundred yards from where we were. If anyone's at fault, Emily, it's me, lass. I've never been in danger before, but I didn't take into account your attack."

"Why should that have any bearing on today?" I went to fetch us both a goblet of wine from the jug a servant had left us. It tasted sweet and warmed my chest with each swallow. Ayleth saw me close my eyes and sigh.

"Aye, it's a lovely taste. Not a bad vintage if I may say so. Comes from abroad, Spain I think. Artorius trades with his old comrades from Rome who trade with everyone. There's also mead, though it's saved for special occasions. It is the closest thing to a decent whisky at this time for me. There are monks who live on an island a few days' ride from here who make it with their own honey bees. It is delicious. I've asked if someone could bring me a small jug, as it will help numb the pain and help me sleep." She drank down the wine before handing me the empty cup. "A wee bit more would suffice please."

I smiled, but held the empty goblet. "If you're having mead as well do you think another glass of this is good for you? I mean, I'm pretty sure they say alcohol is bad for you in cases of shock and ..."

"Aye, shock, but I'm not in shock, I'm in pain."

"Perhaps I can brew some willow bark tea ...?"

Ayleth scowled. "Give me the fucking wine ..."

"All right, I'm not your mother." I immediately filled her cup to the brim and handed it back. I sipped mine, savouring the taste, but wishing for a cup of 'Typhoo' instead. Besides it wasn't even midday yet, I couldn't imagine getting tipsy so early.

Ayleth drank it down again and I took the cup and put it on the table. "Are you hungry?" I noticed some fresh bread and honey had also been left, with some cheese and a couple of apples. My diet, it seemed, from now on.

Ayleth shook her head. "No, but I am tired now. I'll doze a little, if you don't mind. Perhaps you'll wake me when they bring me the mead?"

I walked away and sat by the fire, a chunk of bread and honey in one hand, the goblet in the other. I sat quietly, nibbling while I tried to gather my thoughts and wits. I was right when I'd said everything was going too fast. It felt like I was jumping between scenarios at one hundred miles an hour and I couldn't stop it. Sitting here quietly was so nice and uncomplicated, and I wanted it to last.

My back throbbed and I knew throwing a punch had pulled the wounds open again. My shoulder felt bruised, as I hadn't warmed up and it felt stiff. The cuts on my legs, arms and shoulder were healing fine and had become itchy, especially so close to the fire. I was mending physically at least and I couldn't deny that defending Ayleth in a familiar way had made me feel better than I had for a long time.

"I saw what you did."

I started and turned back to the bed. "I thought you were asleep?"

Ayleth smiled drowsily. "I am, kind of. I wanted to say thank you for saving me. That was one hell of a punch."

I shrugged. "Karate. Black belt. And I didn't save you, you got hurt. I froze in that moment, but seeing your blood made me feel such anger, I lost it. I might have killed him."

"Let's hope so, because if I know these men, they'll have his balls for what he did, but not before they have some answers."

I was about to ask what did she mean when I saw her eyelids droop, and she was asleep within seconds. I considered her words and shivered at whatever barbarous torture the men of the castle would inflict on our attacker. Whatever he had done, surely he deserved a trial? I remembered my earlier thoughts on killing him and took a long, deep breath. I was wrong. Killing was wrong, first rule of karate, it is purely self-defence, creating peace of mind, and yet I'd fought to kill, knowing exactly where to hit to have the desired outcome. I didn't like that at all.

CHAPTER 17

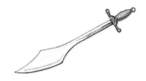

"Explain yourselves." Artorius had his back to the window, the light almost blinding from the midday sun as it warmed the area the sunbeams touched, leaving Artorius silhouetted by the rays.

Merek knelt before him. His sword lay on the floor at his foot. "I cannot, my Lord. We failed in our duty as we did not take the threat to our ladies seriously. Now Ayleth is hurt, and your guest, the lady Aemilia is in shock. I am disgraced and ashamed, my Lord."

Artorius frowned and hid the smile that threatened to rush forth. Merek took his vows very seriously, and a quick glance at the others showed they thought the same. Brom rolled his eyes and kicked Merek from behind. "Get up! We didn't get to the ladies in time, but we got there before any worse harm was done."

Merek glanced behind him at the others, huffed loudly, and stood, replacing his sword in its sheath. "I suppose that's true, though I do feel shame, my Lord, that our dearest Ayleth was hurt."

Artorius nodded. "I feel that too, Merek, but we are not to know everything that is to pass. You saved the ladies from further harm and that is all that I can ask of you. The blame lies on me." He raised his hands to stifle the protests. "No, my friends, I should have insisted Ayleth and the lady Aemilia be escorted. I know of Ayleth's expeditions onto the moors for fresh water and herbs and wild flowers, yet I've never sent out a guard with her. I have merely asked them to keep a watch from the walls as I'd never considered her in danger. That was my mistake and one I will never make again. I knew of her leaving the safety of these walls and did not act upon it. I will talk with her about this matter, but later."

The men mumbled between themselves. He could see how angry they were that this had happened, and felt a little pity for the prisoner. If he woke up, he'd wish he'd been slain like his friends once his men had finished with him. Ayleth was well loved among his people, having shown a great kindness to everyone and saving many lives with her skills. Her knowledge of the future had helped him greatly and he wondered if the gift had passed onto her niece, if she was truly that, which he doubted. However, Ayleth was considered one of the family now and whatever her reasons for lying about lady Aemilia, he wouldn't question it until he had to.

There was something strange about his guest. The men had told him about how she'd damaged their prisoner. He'd heard of fighting such as this, using hand and feet techniques to kill an enemy, and the women gossiped about the strange markings on her body. Maybe she was an assassin, but if so, she'd had plenty of opportunity to kill him. But if a killer, how had the men managed to whip and beat her? Perhaps six against one was too much even for an assassin, if that is what she truly was?

He knew of Tristan's interest in her, and on hearing about her markings, he'd become even more intrigued, as he bore his own from an early age on his face. The men had jested that it was an excuse to see her naked and although Tristan had not denied this, he guessed that the woman as a whole attracted him. He couldn't deny that lady Aemilia was a fair beauty and something of a mystery, and this was enough to light his inner fire. If Tristan hadn't voiced his interest, he would have considered pursuing the lady himself. As it was, anyone with eyes could see that the attraction was mutual, and he considered Tristan a lucky man.

He worried about Tristan most out of all his friends. They had all been brought together as boys to learn to fight. Every one of them had shown an interest in the girls, yet Tristan would not bed them immediately. He wanted to know them, court them, and only then would he bed them, if he liked what he found. Many maidens had fallen for his quiet, intense personality and had enjoyed the moment, but later had become tired of his brooding and broken the relationship. Tristan barely noticed, so long as he had his animals, he was happy.

Now something had changed. It was subtle, but all the men noticed it. Tristan had a fire within him for this lady, who was not falling into his arms, but her body language screamed out to him. She burned when he was near and he answered like a moth to a flame. He knew that Tristan wanted more. He'd never met any woman such as the lady Aemilia, none of them had, and she'd proved to be a topic on many occasions since her arrival. Tristan would listen and enjoy the jesting, but he refused to be drawn into any conversations regarding the lady. His fighting skills were not diminished in any way, yet he was distracted. Every man could see his attention was elsewhere, searching for any sign of the lady, like a young, sweet love as Rulf noted, which only got him a smack across the head.

"So, dear friends, let us see if our friend downstairs has woken or shall indeed wake at all considering what you have told me, Tristan. It looks like the lady Aemilia has hidden gifts that may well save her life?"

Tristan grunted and followed Artorius out into the corridor. The others brought up the rear and the group headed down to the dungeons where they had thrown the prisoner. Torches in sconces in the walls lit their way. Merek shivered as all heat left his body, as the dampness of the caves seeped into his bones. Rulf saw it and poked him from behind. "Nay worry, dear friend, we'll protect you from the ghouls that lurk down here in the dark."

The remark earned him a hard thump on the arm. "I'll break your legs and leave you down here with said ghouls if you don't shut up." Merek grinned evilly before quickly catching up to Artorius, who had reached the cell. All the men fell silent as they stared into the semi darkness of the chamber. The prisoner was still lying where they'd thrown him, on his back, and even in the dimly lit cavern it was obvious he was dead.

"Get him out of here and bury him quickly. I don't want the lady Aemilia to know of his death until we are sure it will not shock her too much. I believe she has been through enough lately, though I must admit to wanting to see this fighting skill she possesses if it kills a man. Are we agreed?"

Brom and Merek dragged the body back up the steps and together managed to get him out of the castle walls without too many people seeing it. There would be talk, but hopefully not in front of their guest. They took him down towards the woods to a clearing where they began the horrible job of disposing of his body. To burn him would be seen, so with a nod from Merek, Brom took out his large sword and handed his axe to Merek. Together they chopped him into smaller pieces they buried in a shallow grave. The man deserved no honour, the wolves could have him, and they quickly walked back to the castle to find a wench to help them forget.

*   *   *

I watched the two men walking back over the narrow bridge and into the courtyard. I kept well back in the shadows as the sun had moved and my room was now in shade, and I shivered from the chill. Away from the fire it was hard to keep warm and I suddenly missed central heating worse than ever, wondering how my parents had coped in the forties and fifties with frost on the windows and nothing but coal fires to heat the rooms.

A quick glance at Ayleth showed me she was fast asleep and her breathing was nice and regular. I didn't want to remain hiding in the room, because if I stayed here, I might never venture out again. It felt like a 'get back on the horse' thing and besides, I wanted to speak with Artorius and find out why those men had attacked us.

They hadn't ridden up to us. We'd almost stepped on one of them as he'd been hiding in a patch of long grass. He jumped up and grabbed Ayleth while another came out from behind a nearby tree. The other two slunk out from behind a couple of boulders, and it looked like they had been there a while, judging from the coldness of their hands and faces. Which could only mean one thing; they'd been watching the castle.

I made my way down the steps and found myself at a junction. I couldn't remember which way to go to the hall. I'd been so nervous yesterday I'd barely acknowledged any of my surroundings. Thankfully a servant girl hurried past, her arms laden with sticks, and after a little sign language and pointing, she indicated one way and I followed quickly, finally finding myself standing in the doorway of the great hall. Artorius was just walking down some narrow steps opposite me, followed by one of his men who closed a door behind him. I stepped further inside the hall and he saw me. I was rewarded with a warm smile and he immediately came to me, reaching for my hand and gesturing towards the chairs by the fire that was burning brightly, and I gratefully accepted.

He spoke slowly and used lots of hand gestures, which meant I had a pretty good idea that he was asking about mine and Ayleth's well-being. I reassured him as best as I could and gratefully accepted a goblet of wine and freshly baked biscuits he'd ordered from a serving girl. Once she left, I tried my best to convey to him my suspicions regarding the men who attacked us. I think I managed fairly well as he leaned closer and gently patted my hand in a reassuring manner.

At which point, he spoke for several minutes and gestured so eloquently that I began to understand him much better as I picked up familiar words. He spoke of how I was safe here and he would allow nothing to harm me, and he apologised for today. A guard would be with me from now on. I heard the name 'Tristan' and fought to control my facial expressions. I don't think I did a very good job because he smirked at me.

As if on cue, he looked behind me and welcomed Tristan and the other men into the hall. Each man nodded towards me and I smiled back. I hoped my 'thank you for saving my life again' was received well. I think it was judging from the returned smiles and a few winks. One man, Merek I think, who I'd just watched return to the castle, gave me a formal bow and I bowed my head back to him. I was rewarded with a glowing grin from him and he received a few slaps on his back from the men. Obviously an inside joke, but perhaps I'd made them feel valued and it felt good knowing I had them on my side.

I turned back to find Artorius watching me, a smile on his face. He said something to the men and Merek, then mimed what I'd done to my attacker. When he'd finished, all the men watched, waiting for an explanation. I guessed a woman fighting was a rarity in this time. What the hell was I supposed to say? Our lie had been I'd been sold into slavery in Wales. Did they have karate in Wales during this time? I doubted it, but I had no choice, I had to make something up.

So, through a lot of miming and gestures, I made up an oriental character from a faraway country who'd secretly taught me a few moves that might save my life. Half an hour later, Artorius had me showing his men a couple of easy punches, which had them all messing about and laughing at each other. They got so overly enthusiastic that it became a bit of a playful brawl that had me moving backwards and keeping out of their way. Fists flew and a bit of wrestling took over. It mainly centred on the large giant they called Brom who, having thrown everyone else off his back, got into a playful fight with Artorius. Sometime later though, I wasn't so sure it was a playful one anymore. Artorius ended up with a bloody nose and Brom had a swollen eye and a gash down his collar bone. It did have the men exchanging a few coins and excitedly urging them on. It finally ended when both men ran out of breath, bloodied, sweating and smiling at each other. They toasted with two full tankards of ale and finally sat down with a heavy sigh and an obvious release of tension.

I realised then why they had continued to fight, they'd needed it. I suppose pretending in this time didn't work well, not when you needed to kill or fight for your life for real. Being easy was not an option, so a few bruises and a bloodied nose was good compensation for a release of pent up anger and frustration. I'd guessed the man was dead. They had no answers. I'd killed the only person able to tell them anything. I'd killed a man, another one.

And I didn't feel anything about that.

I felt eyes on me and looked towards Tristan who was sipping a tankard while watching me. He didn't look away when caught, which always unsettled me. Men in my time rarely kept eye contact. They'd look away with a smile and play the game. Tristan didn't play games. He let me know as directly as he could that he was attracted to me. I licked my lips nervously and looked away as the man they called Rulf brought a jug of wine and refilled my goblet. I smiled and bowed my head in what I hoped was a 'thank you' gesture and he smiled back.

I felt his warmth before I'd even turned. Tristan had come up behind me and I felt my breath catch in my throat as adrenalin pumped through my body. He was so close we were almost touching, but he didn't reach out, but merely stood over me. I caught the eye of Rulf and grinned nervously. His own amused gaze moved between mine, and I presumed Tristan's, as he said something to which all the men laughed before falling into silence as they considered something. They were now all looking at me and I began to feel nervous. I slowly put down my goblet and stared at Artorius, who was frowning.

Suddenly he gave a sharp order and I flew backwards as an arm wrapped itself around my throat. I was pulled off my feet and I choked, grabbing at the arm. Knowing it was Tristan confused me and for a second I didn't try too hard, thinking that maybe he was playing around as the others had done. Then I caught sight of Artorius' face, his expression one of concern, but intrigue, and I knew then he'd ordered Tristan to fight me.

Damn the bastard! I guessed my free lunch was over. It was time to show what I could bring to the party. I abruptly turned, found a pressure point on his arm, twisted and he cried out involuntarily, his hold relaxed and I threw him down on the hard floor whilst pinning his arm upwards so he was in pain. Releasing him, I hitched up my dress, which amused the men greatly but with an order from Artorius they fell silent and watchful as Merek came for me. A punch to his stomach, a kick to his groin and his knee, and he was down. Tristan meanwhile regained himself and came at me again. A side kick sent him flying, followed by a punch to Rulf, who thought he'd join in.

A loud clap from Artorius brought the fight to an end. He bowed apologetically at me, but I merely gazed at him. I wanted to punch his face so badly I clenched my fists. He read the signs and backed off, hands in the air in surrender. I was breathing hard and was all too aware of the throbbing pain from my back and shoulder. It took a moment to regain some semblance of order and to stop shaking. I guessed I probably looked like a wild woman, with a hitched skirt showing my calves, (not the most lady-like look). I quickly pulled down my dress and used that time to gather myself, slow my breathing and gently rotate my shoulder. I hoped I hadn't opened the wounds again.

Artorius held out a full tankard of ale as a peace offering. I stared at it, wanting to push it in his face for doing that to me, but I eventually took it. I may never know or understand their ways in this time, but I'd proved to him that I could handle myself in a fair fight, though three men against one was pushing it. I drank down the ale and savoured the malty taste. At this rate, I'd be a raving alcoholic, I needed water or something non-alcoholic to quench my thirsts.

Both Rulf and Merek were holding their stomachs as they sipped their ale. They raised their tankards in my direction and grinned. They were proud of me. Tristan was standing by the fire, arms folded, watching me with a slight smirk on his face. Brom saw it and said something which made all the men laugh.

"He said that your fight has aroused him so badly, he's using all of his brooding skills to not burst!"

Everyone turned at the sound of her voice and Brom ran to the doorway as Ayleth stepped through. She was holding onto the doorway for support and she looked pale and drawn. He gently picked her up and carried her to the fireplace, though she protested loudly. I was so shocked by what she'd said I forgot to ask her why she was downstairs.

"Really? Bloody hell!"

Ayleth smiled and accepted a small goblet of wine. "Indeed. I gave up waiting for the mead." She quickly explained to Artorius who bowed apologetically, and sent a servant girl to fetch some. Turning back to me, she sighed loudly. "I see you've been fighting? You'll have torn your wounds again judging from the blood stains on your back." Seeing me try to twist round, she touched my arm to stop me. "No, don't make it worse. I'll get one of the girls to check it later. Rest now, and tell me all about it, and I'll see if I can help."

CHAPTER 18

M arian sat back in her chair and stared out of the window,
though she was seeing none of the foliage, but only the scene
that Emily had unfolded in her mind. She spoke so clearly and
with such detail, it was easy to summon images of those people in her
head. How real they seemed. Her favourite was Artorius. She'd heard
the name, and after digging around on Google, she'd found where she'd
heard it before. A contender for the origins of 'King Arthur legends', he
was a commander of a Roman army before they returned to Rome. He
remained behind with some loyal followers and helped to fight the
invading Saxons.

He had been based somewhere near Hadrian's wall, or so historians
believed, but it was all guess work due to very little being written down,
but in theory, he could have lived near the hospital. The wall was only a
few miles away. She'd walked half of the wall a few years back; lovely
scenery. Ruins dotted the landscape, so it was fairly conceivable that
he'd lived in a castle? Or perhaps one of the old forts that dotted the wall?
She'd have to do some research on him and the others.

Ayleth was an interesting character. She understood why Emily
would need another traveller in this time. One with more knowledge, and

someone who could help her find her way with all the various problems she'd encountered. A mother figure, of course, and understandable considering her own mother had been violently murdered. What had she called her? Flicking back through her notes, she found the name 'Elizabeth Riley. Preferred the name Betty. Lesbian from the eighties with a partner called Melinda. Said she disappeared in nineteen eighty-five.' Might be worth a quick look through missing persons? If nothing else, it would prove to Emily that she'd made her up.

Marian stretched and started shutting down her computer and tidying her stuff away. She felt a bit jittery, from either the unhealthy amount of coffee she'd consumed lately, or possibly excitement at the idea of finding a Betty who had disappeared in the nineties? What could that mean? Time travel was possible, or Emily had heard of the disappearance and lodged it away in her head?

Regardless, Emily's case was fascinating. Marian was so engrossed by what Emily said, she rarely kept to the hour. Today, Emily had been in the chair for almost two hours, it was like listening to a film being played out or one of those audio books. It left her riveted and not very professional. She could put Emily at risk by allowing her to go so deeply for so long, but she couldn't stop now. Besides, if Emily murdered that security guard, she deserved punishment, didn't she?

Marian had also become aware that one of the orderlies who brought and collected Emily was asking a few too many questions. The way he looked at her could be quite intimidating. Today, he'd grabbed Emily before she fell over, and picked her up in his arms. Emily remained passive and dazed, though coherent, having come out of the hypnosis in the usual way. Perhaps two hours was far too long. The orderly had looked back, stopping Marian from closing the door with his foot, a look of contempt and suspicion on his face. She'd have to be more careful, aware how tongues could wag in here.

"This girl looks overly medicated. What's going on here?"

Marian, shocked by his blatant question, took a second to gather her thoughts. "None of your goddamn business. Emily is my patient and I'll do whatever I see fit to help her! Now, take her back to her room and let her lie down for a while." To Emily she spoke softly. "Now off you go, Emily, have a little rest, and you'll feel so refreshed before a late lunch."

Emily merely nodded before Marian pushed the door shut. She glanced at her watch. Damn, it would be a late lunch. It was gone one already and she had another four patients to see today. Pulling a lunchbox from her large shoulder bag, she dived into a tuna and cucumber sandwich while sipping a fresh orange juice from a carton. She'd have to be cautious, people would begin to talk if she cancelled too many patients, and she didn't want any interference with Emily. She needed to get her to the point of the murder and see what actually happened, although Marian had to admit that the story getting there was really enjoyable.

Detective Inspector Richards sighed loudly as he listened to the archaeologist. The more the man spoke, the more confusing this case became. "Okay, so after all your initial testing, you're still saying that this sword is unique. I get that, but it's also the murder weapon, and I cannot allow you to keep testing it, not until after the trial in case your experiments ruin forensic evidence. You know that, Simon."

Simon turned away, he was getting agitated and he needed to take a deep breath. "Just let me have another look, take more pictures? I'll wear anything you want, but I need to look at the sword again. It's ... beautiful."

Richards smiled. He understood the man's frustration. The sword was beautiful. The handle was solid silver with two wolf heads carved into it that met in the middle and on the hilt, an ivory horses head, absolutely perfect. The sword looked brand new, so how these archaeologists could even suggest it was over a thousand years was too incredible to fathom, but apparently the analysis showed the metal fibres in the victim's body were from an ancient sword.

"Look, I can't let you have it, but if you want to see it down in evidence, I can get a PC to take you. But no taking it out of the bag, and you wear gloves. It's the best I can do right now."

Simon bowed his head in thanks and followed Richards out of his office, who summoned his sergeant Ian Mathews, who found someone who was free. Simon thanked everyone enthusiastically and hurried after the constable, who showed him down to the evidence room, almost walking into him in his haste to reach it. The pictures didn't do it justice. He pulled on the gloves and held out his arms for the sword. It felt fairly light considering. The carvings were immaculate, with no evidence of corrosion anywhere, yet the tests showed time and again the sword had been made around the late fifth century. Yet, what he held in his hands looked like it had been lovingly carved last week. It didn't make sense.

He desperately wanted to get the sword to the lab, and had appealed for that to happen, but so far he'd heard nothing. He wanted to do tests of course, but more than that, he wanted his friend Lucy to hold the sword. Lucy had a gift, one he'd never believed in as he was a scientist. Yet time and again, Lucy had been able to tell him in detail, about everything she was given to hold. Who it belonged to, where it had come from. It'd been uncanny.

He'd tested her, tried to give her fake objects, blindfolded her, put her in booths, isolated her, yet every time, she'd known exactly what it was and would give him a detailed description of its history. She said she felt the objects power and felt its vibrations. It showed her pictures in her head and he desperately wanted to know what Lucy could find out, and maybe it might help the murder case.

He'd even tried to organise a visit to see Emily Rogers. But he had been refused until her evaluation had been completed. Ever since they'd found another thumbprint on the hilt, Emily looked more and more innocent, yet she remained under secure lock and key. Something didn't feel right in this case and the sword had something to do with it, he was sure of that.

CHAPTER 19

My head swam and my legs felt very far away as I manoeuvred myself up the steps. My balance went completely and I clung onto the cold stone wall and thankfully righted myself before I fell backwards. The pain in my back had become a slight ache, as the alcohol dulled the pain. The wounds had been cleaned and fresh cloth applied hours ago by Brunhilde, but after the night's merriment, I doubted they still remained intact.

Ayleth had fallen asleep in the hall, having drunk an enormous amount of mead and wine. I remained sober at first, keeping an eye on her while trying to understand the many conversations that were going on around me. As the afternoon ticked by, more people started flooding into the hall, and food miraculously appeared on the trestle tables that littered the room.

Ayleth and I nibbled on various biscuits, bread, cheese, fruit from the orchard, and a fish broth, which I admit to knocking back, as it tasted as good as it smelt. Artorius was happy to see that I'd eat fish, and a few hours later, after a quick discussion with a servant, I found herring and a fresh salmon presented to me, which was delicious. I felt full and thirsty, but only sipped the ale and refused the wine, wanting to keep a clear head. All of that went out of the window when the singing and dancing began somewhere just after dusk.

The party, because that's what it had become, got into full swing with various people singing along to a homemade flute of some kind, what looked like a penny whistle made from animal bone, and some kind of square drum that Ayleth said was called an 'Adufe', made from pine and goats skin. I asked her why it sounded like rain every time they gently hit it and she told me they put seeds inside. I found it remarkable.

As the party got rowdier, the drum beat became faster and harder, until men and women were dancing and laughing. The men were twirling the serving girls around and around, and I noticed a few stolen kisses too. I caught Tristan's eye and blushed. Whether this was his cue, I don't know, but the next second I was being pulled roughly to my feet and propelled towards the middle of the room with the other dancers. Not knowing any steps, though I guessed it was a kind of free for all, he twirled me round and pulled me this way and that to the shouts of the men and Ayleth who was slurring her words badly by this time.

His arms were around me. I could feel his heartbeat and his hot breath on my neck as he picked me up and held me under the arms, lifted and spun me to the music. I squealed like a girl, loving the exhilaration and laughed along with everyone. He eventually brought me back down, but no sooner had my feet touched the floor, I was being spun again, only this time, Brom had come up behind me. Holding onto my waist, he lifted me four foot in the air, spinning from one man to another in time to the beat. Discos would never be the same!

When the song finished, I was given a tankard of ale, which I downed in six gulps, much to the men's amusement. So a goblet of mead was handed to me and I was so thirsty and hot, I drank that back too. With a quick glance at Ayleth and a reassuring smile from Artorius, I left her in his capable hands as Merek and Rulf had me doing a type of dance that thankfully kept my feet on the ground. But it was still fast and I kept getting it wrong, though no one cared.

By full dark, most people in the hall were pretty much plastered, me included. The issue with my bladder increased and I excused myself but on finding the toilet area blocked by couples, some of which had already begun fumbling with trousers and skirts, I turned away quietly and headed for a small door that I'd seen other women go through. I found myself outside behind the kitchen area. A servant girl had just finished relieving herself and jumped up as I appeared. After a few exchanges, she relaxed enough to keep watch as I gratefully squatted in the grass, and afterwards led me back into the hall. Without thinking in my inebriated state, I hugged her quickly, and after a moment's hesitation, she hugged me back, and hands wondered south, (a little too far for my liking), and I quickly detached myself with a cheeky smirk.

I swiftly headed back to my table and found my goblet full again, and Artorius grinning at me like a cat. Ayleth hadn't moved and snored quietly next to him. I leaned over and checked her bandage, but in my eyes the wound looked clean and the bleeding had stopped. The stitches looked good and the bruising minimal. In my inebriated state, I'd quite forgotten my own injuries which weren't hurting at that time anyway.

Artorius shouted a command and the music took up again. He jumped out of his seat and held out his hand for mine. I was so drunk, I thought it would be a great idea to dance again, so did the majority of people in the hall, though half had either become comatose with booze or had slipped out to follow other urges. Tristan stood watching me, and knowing that made my blood pump through my body, and my stomach jump with excitement.

This dance was fairly slow compared to the others, which was good for me as the shoes weren't getting any easier. I longed to kick them off, but wasn't sure of the etiquette of doing such a thing. Artorius' arm was around my waist, and he pulled me in closer as he moved me around the space allocated for dancing. He was drunk, but not so bad that he wasn't capable, and somehow he managed to convey to me that he was more than capable of doing anything that was needed. His gaze never wavered, and I felt my stomach doing flip flops for other reasons. I was glad when the dance was finally over and he let me go. He bowed and I had a go at curtseying which wasn't as steady as I'd have liked, but it was a perfect way to end the evening and I gestured I would be heading for bed.

Artorius immediately called to a serving girl to escort me, and with another gallant bow, he left me with her and returned to his men, who were either watching, or flirting with one woman or another. Tristan was nowhere in sight. I felt strange about that. Had he witnessed whatever had passed between me and Artorius? Was he jealous? Would it drive him away if his commander showed interest? I had no time to dwell on it as the girl walked briskly out of the hall and turning right, moved along the corridor, the light from her torch lighting the way. I recognised the steps that led to my chamber and tapped the girl on the shoulder, indicating that I was fine.

Reaching up, she pulled a lit torch from the wall and handed it to me. With a slight curtsey, she headed back towards the hall. A torch farther up the steps was lit, though the flame was low and cast moving dark shadows on the walls. I was suddenly sorry that I'd said I was fine, I wasn't, but I hadn't wanted the poor girl to take me all the way up when it was obvious she had better things to do. I also didn't dare try to carry fire in my hand and manoeuvre the steps in the shoes so I replaced the torch into its sconce and lifting my skirt, made my way upwards.

As predicted, I staggered slightly and my foot slipped on the stone steps. These damned shoes were going to be the death of me, and halfway up I took them off. The stone was freezing and damp and I shivered involuntarily, but I felt safer, steadier, and with a quick backward glance, I headed for my room. I felt very drunk, and in a weird way it comforted me. Being drunk in this time felt no different than my own. The similarity was reassuring, yet a wave of melancholy overwhelmed me and I leaned against the wall and cried.

I hadn't cared that I was slowly slipping down the wall, until a warm hand shot out of the darkness and caught me under my arm. I looked up into Tristan's eyes and sniffed. He pulled me up into some semblance of standing, though I was unsteady on my feet. A couple of times he had to catch me before I fell over, which he did, obviously amused.

Then he saw I wasn't wearing my shoes and spoke quite sharply to me before grabbing me around the waist and lifting me up. I protested loudly to put me down, but he'd already reached my bedroom door. Without releasing me, he opened it and stepped inside, using his foot to close the door behind us. My heart was in my mouth and my stomach did flip flops, wondering what he would do, but he merely lowered me to the floor and I reluctantly let him go.

My equilibrium temporarily off course, I found myself staggering backwards, until yet again, he saved me. His strong arm around my waist, he pulled me upright, which meant closer to him. We touched, chest to chest. I could feel his own heart thumping, or was it mine, vibrating through us both? His other arm came up behind me and both hands roamed my back slowly and gently, his eyes held mine as my breath quickened, and my nether regions let it be known they were willing and ready. I couldn't fight it anymore, this man was turning me on badly.

He spoke low and slowly, his gaze intense, never leaving me. His mouth only inches from mine I could smell mead, and his own musky scent mingled with my own of lavenders and rosemary from Ayleth's homemade shampoo. I didn't understand the words, but I thought I could guess his meaning. He wanted to make slow, passionate love to me, here, now.

His kiss was soft and light on my lips. A taste of what he was holding back. I could feel the rigidness of his body, the muscle and strength he used daily to kill now held in check, here in this room with me. Here, with me, he would be gentle, and use his strength to make our pleasure last. Our lust would not be sated easily and I was excited at what lay ahead with him.

His slight beard tickled my face, but it didn't cut my skin to ribbons as other men's beards had done in my time. Around his mouth he was smooth, no moustache, and I was able to feel his full lips as they parted slightly, tempting my own to divide and breathe him in. His tongue licked the top of my upper lip before his mouth closed round my own and drew me into a passionate kiss. His arms held me closely until he released me slightly, enough to allow his hands to roam, though careful of my injuries. He moved downwards and I willed him to continue, but he was teasing me, refusing to rush, which was driving me crazy.

He finished the kiss and looked deeply into my eyes, spoke a few words which made no sense, and let me go. His voice was hoarse and he licked his lips quickly, trying to regain himself, which I noticed was very difficult, and I stood a little unsteady, unsure how to behave. I was about to step closer when he abruptly bowed, turned on his heels and left, closing my door softly behind him.

I stared at the door, my drunken mind unable to make sense of what my body had expected to happen. What had actually happened? 'Cock-tease' sprang to mind and I knew that if a woman had done this to a man, that is what she'd be accused of in my time and probably here too.

I collapsed backwards onto my bed and winced as my body remembered the bruising on my back. The others were healing fine, but the bruising around the whiplashes was deeper and hurt when touched.

Was that why he'd left me? His hands had been gentle on my back and the odd pain had been easy to ignore, but had I involuntarily flinched and he'd read it as a sign, sex was off the table till I'd healed?

The fire in my room was nothing more than burning embers, but there was enough heat to keep the chill at bay; or did I merely have a booze coat on? I pulled myself up and relieved myself in the stinking pit, before staggering to the closed window. Opening one wooden shutter I shivered as the cold air penetrated the room. It was a moonless night, dark and eerie out there where anything or anyone could be hiding, watching me from the dark; I closed the shutter with a bang.

Throwing a couple of logs onto the fire, I carefully pulled my dress off and flounced into bed, settling onto my stomach to allow my back to breathe, aware of the warmth and smells of the animal skins and rugs and hating myself for loving the heat of them. I was too tense to sleep. I had a sexual urge to work off and my pride was hurting. No man had ever said no to me. Not that I was a slut, but I'd had a few, and for a man to leave a willing woman was just unheard of in my time. At least I'd never encountered it, and as far as my old friends told me, neither had they. A man followed a woman to her bedroom, a fairly done deal as to what would occur. Unless, there was something wrong with me?

Tristan fancied me, of that I was absolutely sure. His kiss and roaming hands had assured me of it, I couldn't have been mistaken. Perhaps it was my wounds that had put him off? Or maybe Artorius had warned him off? I thought about that possibility. Artorius had certainly flirted with me during the dance. His arm around my waist had felt closer than was really necessary and his eyes had betrayed his thoughts.

That had to be it.

I thought about the consequences of that possibility. Artorius was a good looking man. He was big, handsome, strong, kind and honourable, though he'd shown that he also had a wicked side when he'd ordered his men to attack me just to see what I'd do. He'd fought battles and commanded armies, a roman legion no less, and now he commanded these men and they obeyed, not because they had to, but because they wanted to. They loved him and he them, honour between them, and I thanked the gods yet again for their rescue.

I liked him, quite a lot actually, but he didn't make my stomach tingle and my insides go like jelly when he held me. Artorius made me feel safe and honoured as a lady, but Tristan moved something within me that touched my basic need as a woman. I couldn't deny there was probably a bit of awe there as he'd rescued me from those bastards, twice no less, and when he'd held onto me that very first time, something had passed between us. A trust that he would keep me safe, and I'd acknowledged it in that frenzy of fear on some subconscious level.

Perhaps if it had been Artorius who had held me in that moment, it might have been different, but there was no going back now. Artorius was the leader, the man who had commanded my safe keeping, Tristan was the man who would see it done regardless of his own well-being, and that both frightened me ... and turned me on badly.

CHAPTER 20

John gently closed the door to Emily's room and walked briskly away. His shift had finished, but he'd felt an overriding need to check on her before leaving. He'd planned to meet her brother again at a local pub, and he wanted to be able to tell him she was okay. He'd just heard that Brian's appointment to visit Emily had been cancelled due to some pathetic excuse, and wondered if he'd been told yet. But he barely spoke to anyone in the hospital and didn't dare change his act now or they might become suspicious. Being the grumpy orderly did have its downfalls, no one shared anything with him. He couldn't start looking too eager now, he'd just have to bide his time.

He was meeting his informant later tonight, who'd hopefully have more details on the murder enquiry. They kept Emily against her will, he was fairly sure of that, though being inside was possibly safer for her in theory. But whatever Doctor Griffiths was doing, he'd have to stop sooner rather than later or Emily's mind might never recover.

He pulled on his coat and nodded to another orderly who looked up as he passed. Keeping his head down, he made his way quickly to the back entrance for the staff, and pushed past two nurses who were having a quick smoke during their break. He heard one mutter something about his attitude and he grinned to himself. How easy it was to make people believe anything so long as he kept up the facade.

Nobody recognised him. And why should they? Nine years ago he'd been nothing to them, a mere patient who dribbled his way through the day, and slept the night away drugged up to the eyes. His stay at the hospital had been a nightmare before he'd convinced the doctor he wouldn't attempt to kill himself again. Instead, he'd turned that anger at the world, and returned to his love of writing. Focusing his attentions on perceived injustices, he'd slowly gained a name for himself in the magazine world. He was always careful only to use a photo of the back of his head, which intrigued his readers and he'd changed his name so nobody here would have a clue who he was.

Over the years, John had exposed sleazy goings on in back-alley bars with politicians and actors. He'd opened up a can of worms in banks and corporate businesses, and proved that all men in suits couldn't be trusted. However, he'd never forgotten this place and, after proving abuse in five residential homes, he moved his attention to the Owl Haven Hospital, the place that had given him nightmares for many years afterwards. He figured doing this would be good therapy, and he'd been right.

His editor had been interested almost immediately, and almost bitten his hand off for an exclusive, once he'd shown him evidence of malpractices (that had strangely disappeared a few years before). Along with secret photographs taken by a nurse who'd been dismissed, showing patients sitting in their own shit and screaming for help, it was enough to hook anyone in. Five months ago, he'd disappeared, re-invented his name, his references, and got the job.

The death of Mia had put him in a panic. He'd spoken to a couple of nurses and the doctor about his concerns only days before, but he'd been ignored. Thankfully, he'd recorded the conversations with the consultant, Doctor Griffiths and two nurses with their nonchalant replies made for alarming listening. Now Mia was dead and her roommate Andrea in bits, needing round the clock medications and supervision. It affected all the patients in one way or another, but nobody noticed their pain. He understood how they felt. They were unnoticed, but he'd not let Emily become invisible for a crime she hadn't done. And John was convinced of her innocence. He'd save at least one.

*   *   *

I woke with a dry mouth, a mushy head, a yearning to piss and the sounds of shouting down below. I forced myself up and was glad to see someone had already been in and relit the fire. It blazed hungrily, and its warmth reached my body. Taking deep breaths, I used the pit, and then went to my window to see what all the fuss was about at such an hour. The sun wasn't too high, so I figured it was still early.

Early or not, the activity in the courtyard suggested I was a lazy bitch having stayed in bed. Men on horseback were fighting to stop their horses from bolting, while men and women darted here and there fetching pails of water from the well, and offering bread and meat to the men on horseback, who'd grab at the offered food while holding the reigns of what looked like wild stallions. I saw the men I knew among the group, and there was Tristan standing beside his grey mare, stroking her neck while conversing with a soldier. As if he felt my stare, he unexpectedly looked up before returning his attention to the man. They laughed together before the soldier walked away, and Tristan heaved himself into the saddle.

Artorius came into view and spoke sharply to the assembled men, who cheered at the end of the speech, before the large gates were opened and Artorius led the group out, his brown mare itching to get going. Once through the archway, the horses broke into a gallop, and I watched them fly over the moor until they disappeared from sight. I closed the shutter quietly and returned to bed to wait for someone to tell me what was going on. Ayleth had taught me a few words and sentences, and I'd recognised a few of what Artorius had said. Death seemed to play a large part of whatever they were going to do, and I waited impatiently for my friend.

What was left of the morning dragged on. Hours later, Ayleth finally arrived, escorted by a servant who deposited her in the chair by my fire, curtseyed and departed quickly, slamming the door behind her. Ayleth offered me a weak smile and huddled beneath the blankets I brought her. I built up the dying fire and then stood, unsure what to do as the door opened again and another servant brought a jug, two tankards, bread, cheese and honey to break our fast. Ayleth took one look at my face, and said something to the young girl, who nodded and disappeared.

I stared at the jug of ale and felt my insides squirm, feeling nauseous. The bread was fresh and I pulled off a small chunk and began chewing it slowly, aware of Ayleth watching me, a smile on her face. Not trusting myself to speak, I merely shrugged and continued forcing it down. The door abruptly opened again and the girl returned with a larger jug, placed it on the table, and left.

"Here's what we both need, I think ..." Ayleth said.

I glanced between Ayleth and the jug, before venturing over to sniff the contents. Water, pure, non-alcoholic water! I gratefully poured us both full tankards and handed one to her. She accepted it with a large grin and downed the lot. I sipped mine, cautiously at first, but on seeing me doing it Ayleth reassured me it was from a spring farther up the moors, and it had been boiled twice, and strained through a muslin cloth just in case. I drank thirstily.

Pouring us both another tankard, I sat opposite Ayleth at the fire, as we both nibbled on bread and water. "Serves us right, I suppose. Don't drink so much usually, lass, but it helped dull the pain on my face. Doesn't seem to stop the men though. Up at dawn and eagerly mounting their horses, each one able to ignore any throbbing heads!"

I leaned closer and gently pulled open the padding I'd covered her wound with yesterday. "I think we should leave this off now, let the air get at it. Tristan's done a fine job."

Ayleth tentatively touched her cheek. "Aye, he's a fine tailor, is Tristan. He'll make a fine husband one day."

I caught the under meaning and shrugged. "I like him, but I don't think he's interested."

Ayleth laughed, but abruptly stopped as it pulled the stitches. "Oh, aye! Not interested, is it? My God, girl, he's not stopped looking at you since you first arrived. Did I not hear this morning, that he was seen escorting you to this room last night?"

I blushed under Ayleth's stare. "Well, yes, he helped me up the stairs. Those damned shoes will kill me!"

Ayleth leaned forward. "And?"

I took a long drink of water. "And nothing. He kissed me, but left, and now he's buggered off with the rest of them ... Why have they gone riding?" With my hangover slightly diminished, I could focus on other things, like the group of men in the courtyard. Besides, Ayleth's stares were making me feel uncomfortable.

Ayleth sat back in her chair and pulled the blanket higher. "Aye, Tristan's gone out with Artorius and the others to scout for more enemies who might be lurking. They figured when the four men watching the castle don't return, it might force whoever is watching to send out more men. They mean to try and capture at least one alive to find out information."

"Information on what? I mean, I know I've come to the fifth century, but my history is pretty bad. Is there a battle coming? Do we win? Should I be more scared than I already am?"

Ayleth reached out and gently touched my hand. "My dear, there's always a battle coming during this time. The Saxons are determined to rule somewhere in this country, if they cannot get all of it. We have the Picts and Gauls and Jutes to contend with too. Everyone wants to claim a small area as their own. So far, Artorius has made this area below Hadrian's wall his own, but he is constantly fighting to keep it."

Ayleth sat back in her chair and sighed. "However, Artorius is not convinced that it's the Saxons who attacked you. Those men were mercenaries. Men who'll kill for money. Men without honour, and it was the same men who attacked us. Now, most mercenaries ride in groups, usually small ones, but these men seem to be part of something larger, so Artorius is out there trying to find out who that is."

"Are we in danger?" The bread seemed to have stuck in my gullet and I felt sick.

"We're always in some danger, girl. Even in our own times, we were never truly safe, just under the illusion that we were. Life here is raw. There's no half measures, it's all go all the time. Everyone has a job to do and it gets done or everything stops. They have rules and if they are broken, there is a penalty, same as in our times, only they carry it out. As I remember it, criminals got away with too much in my time. Tell me, did they ever bring back the death penalty in your time?"

I shook my head sadly. "No, I really wish they had. All they do is whinge about crime, and how much it costs to keep criminals locked up in prison, which is more like holiday homes with all their human rights.

It's pathetic. We treat criminals better that our elderly in my time." I shrugged apologetically. "I'm all for the death penalty for murderers and rapists and paedophiles. It would soon free up the prisons for more minor offences ..."

"Minor offences, eh? I wonder who'd decide that. A robbery to one person is the worst ordeal ever to another. A home burglary is a fear I can remember having as a younger woman. My biggest fear here is being captured by an enemy." She sipped her water and stared at the fire, thinking. "You know, here they kill all of those types of criminals without mercy, without trial. I saw a rapist being killed once. He'd raped two young virgins, sisters, I think they were, down by the river. He made one watch while he raped one and then raped the other.

"Artorius was a commander of a Roman legion then, a group who had chosen to stay in Britain and make a life. Artorius had left Rome as a boy with his father, so had no ties to it. They made a life here, near where his grandfather had been stationed as a commander. With other likeminded men, they re-built this castle using stone from the wall and creating some semblance of law and order here. Artorius' father, Horus, was a fairly old man by the time I knew him. Had Artorius late in life. His mother died weeks after his birth. Horus wanted to return to the place his father had spoken of during the Roman occupation, and so he did. Horus was a good man, honest and kind, but ruthless in his dealings with filth. He taught Artorius well.

"The rapist begged for mercy. Said he'd been drunk and couldn't remember a thing. No one argued with him, he had no defence, only judgment on his actions. The two girls were brought into the room, bloodied and broken, and Artorius asked them what they'd like him to do to their rapist. Apparently they went into great detail and everything they said was done. He lasted four days in great agony before he finally bled to death, his cock and balls shoved into his mouth in front of everyone as a warning. As far as I'm aware, there has not been another rape in these parts since, until your attack."

The bread sticking in my throat decided which way it was going and I ran to the stinking pit and threw up. Ayleth slowly followed me and offered me a cup of water on my exit. "Sorry, just thought you should have a better idea of how it is here, and also just how angry Artorius and his men are about what happened to you. Any attack on a woman is considered the worst crime, and honourable men will not sit back idly and allow it to continue, not if they can stop it."

"So this is my fault that Artorius and his men are riding out to meet a possible enemy ... and might get killed ...?" I slumped back in my chair.

Ayleth frowned. "Your being attacked is now your fault, is it?"

I shrugged. "Well, no, but ..."

"All I'm saying is Artorius is letting people know attacking women is not accepted. He thinks, perhaps, the last time he dealt with the rapist has become too far in the memory and needs to be remembered? Also, he's letting whoever it is know that the castle's inhabitants are protected and will not go down without a fight."

"Last night he had his men attack me, why?"

"The men were amazed by your skills, Artorius wanted to see for himself, but guessed it wouldn't be impressive if staged, so he made the 'attack' as real as possible to see how you reacted, and he was very impressed. I believe he is hoping to talk you into teaching his men some more skills."

"Is he? I suppose I could. It's the least I could do for them after saving me twice, though I wish he'd waited as it broke open my wound a bit ... Ayleth, did they have karate in this time?"

Ayleth shook her head and leaned forward to inspect my shoulder. "I don't believe so, dear." Then quickly changed the subject. "It's not too bad, healing nicely."

I let her words sink in about my wounds and karate and let out a long breath. "And there lies the problem, doesn't it? If I teach these men an art that isn't here yet, will it change something?"

We both sat back in our chairs and sipped our water, pondering the question. If I refused to show them some skills, I'd have to explain why, and to refuse was very rude considering all they'd done for me. However, the problem remained about changing history, a problem I guessed would never be an easy one to solve.

CHAPTER 21

M arian frowned at the orderly, something about his nature that made her feel uncomfortable. He always looked at her with condemnation and he would glance quickly around the room every time he brought Emily for her treatment. Perhaps he suspected something was amiss, but frankly, he was nothing more than a servant in the hospital, fetching and carrying for the nurses. Her word would be taken over his if he spoke out about anything, but this knowledge didn't make her feel any better.

Not that there was anything untoward happening anyway. Hypnosis was a common form of therapy and she could prove that Emily was engaging in it, and leaving feeling positive. The nurses could verify that. The only feedback she'd been given was that Emily was sleeping more and eating less. Something she could rectify in her therapy session while Emily was under the influence.

Although, she didn't want it to detract from what was actually going on. Marian was convinced that Emily was displaying signs of a past life which she found fascinating. She'd had a few debates over the years regarding such a notion and usually concluded that people had taken on bits from books, films or stories heard in passing and amalgamated these pictures into something that represented a life, which they interpreted as having had in another life. Hearing it from Emily was making her question these theories as Emily constantly displayed reactions to each scenario and the details were phenomenal. Though what a past life had to do with the murder, she had no idea. All the same, she was reluctant to stop the story, and move her forward to that night. If Emily needed to tell this tale to reach that night, and feel comfortable about the telling, then so be it.

"Thank you ... John is it? Emily will be fine with me till lunch time."

John glanced between the doctor and Emily before reluctantly releasing Emily's arm and stepping backwards to the open doorway. "I'll make sure I'm back at midday."

His impertinence was beginning to annoy her and she walked forward and gently led Emily farther into the room. "There's no need, orderly. I'll call down when Emily has finished her treatment. You can go now, thank you."

She tried to keep her voice even, but the last words came out sharp, and the orderly glared at her for a moment before he turned on his heels and left, closing the door hard behind him.

Marian forgot him in an instant. "Emily, you're looking so well. Have you eaten breakfast? Shall we make a start?"

*   *   *

The sound of the horses woke us both from our slumbering in front of the fire. My left cheek felt hot to the touch and I carefully rubbed it. I looked over at Ayleth who snuggled further into her blanket, and closed her eyes again, unwilling to wake. I envied her, but my curiosity got the better of me and I reluctantly stood, stretched, and went over to the shuttered window. The cold air hit my face immediately and I shivered, closing it over slightly, so it was no more than a crack, but enough for me to see down into the courtyard. It looked like all the men who'd ridden out earlier were back. Horses, men, women and dogs occupied the square yard and every one of them seemed very animated in their movements and voice. I wondered how they'd got on. A minute or so later, I saw exactly how, as bloodied men, hands bound and of various states of injury were marched into the yard.

There were seven men, each one bruised and battered in varying degrees. One was limping badly, while another had so much blood running down his face I wondered how he was able to see. I guessed many punches had already been passed between the men of the castle and the enemy. I saw Brom and Merek dismount from their horses and take a rope from Rulf. Together, they led the men away, I presumed to the dungeons. I couldn't see Artorius or Tristan and my heart sank.

A loud knock on the door made me jump and I turned towards it as it opened without waiting for an invitation. Artorius stood in the doorway. His left eye was puffed and he had a cut on his cheek, but what caught my attention was the amount of blood on his tunic and cloak. I found myself moving towards him involuntarily, as one might to any injured person, and my concern must have been plain on my face as he saw it and quickly reassured me and Ayleth who pushed herself out of her chair. He spoke to her, and to me he merely smiled and pointed to his tunic, shaking his head. Ayleth collapsed back in her chair, relieved, and he immediately went to her and spoke shortly. She nodded, and with a quick bow, he left us.

"What the hell?" I hadn't moved, paralysed from what I had witnessed.

"They found a camp not too far away, and it seems they had a little skirmish with said mercenaries, killed most of them, caught a few, but they know some men got away. Tristan and a few others have gone after them. Tristan can track anything. He wants us to help the injured. Two of our soldiers were killed."

"Anyone I know?"

Ayleth gave me a strange look before she began gathering her things together. "No, dear, no one you know, but it's men we know."

Humbled by her words, I followed her out into the corridor and down to her cave where I helped gather herbs, clean clothes and prepare a large cauldron for boiling water. Ayleth carried her bottle of strong wine she kept hidden for such emergencies, as well as a basket of garlic cloves and willow bark to make tea.

She was right to have looked at me in such a way. I felt shame as I followed her into the great hall. Why would it matter if I knew these men or not? They were human beings and deserved my compassion and respect for fighting to keep us safe. In the past, death had happened to the people I loved, and it hurt badly, so I'd pushed any emotions about death away, refusing to allow myself to feel anything—until I'd come here and I'd been forced to face my own mortality. I'd explain it to Ayleth later; for now, we had work to do.

Blood had never bothered me, but I'd never seen it in such quantities before. It seemed to be everywhere, covering everything, clothes, skin, the floor, the benches—even the dogs that sniffed around the injured men before being kicked aside. Women bustled here and there, offering water, wine and ale, and helping stem the blood flow of their men folk. Some cried quietly, but most were focused on what had to be done, and did it with a smile, a kind word, or touch.

I counted eleven injured, most were fairly minimal. Ayleth cared for one man with a bad gash on the back of his head. I held the wad of cloth while she rummaged around in her basket, before indicating I take it off to check it. The cloth was drenched red. I abruptly replaced it, smiling reassuringly at the man. He looked familiar. He'd danced the night before with one of the servant girls. He didn't smile back, but gazed unfocused, as if he couldn't really see me.

"Concussion," Ayleth spoke in my ear. "We will have to keep an eye on him over the next few hours."

"What could happen?" I whispered back, though it was plain to see that the man had no idea what was happening.

"He could die if he gets pressure on his brain. For now, I'll need to stitch up his wound before he loses all his blood through his head, but I daren't give him any sedative as I need to watch his eyes."

"You mean stitch him up without painkillers? Jesus."

I spoke louder than intended and a few people nearby glanced over.

"Indeed, and let's hope he's with this man tonight, eh? Keep him steady and talk to him."

I moved around to the front of the man so Ayleth was behind him with her wine-soaked thread and home-made needle, which she quickly

162

held over a nearby candle. "For extra hygiene." She caught me watching her. "This alcohol and the fire is all I've got to sterilise this stuff, now talk to him."

"About what? He can't speak English, can he?"

"So bloody what, woman. His name is Dalibar and he's a fine stone mason, now talk!"

Fifteen minutes later I stood back against the cold wall, needing to feel something solid behind me. I felt quite light headed and fought the urge to vomit. My hands and part of my right sleeve was caked in blood, and I viciously tried to wipe off the excess as I watched Ayleth moving through the men, checking each one for further injuries. It looked like Dalibar had been the worst one; except of course for the two soldiers who had been killed. I busied myself with the tasks Ayleth set me, throwing the willow bark into one small cauldron and the garlic cloves into another.

Death was so close here in this time, as if it walked beside me. I wondered if I'd ever get used to the feeling as these people did. Death was something that happened on the television, in films, on the news and in my case, to my parents, but I hadn't been there. I hadn't witnessed it up close, only the aftermath—the police, the press, the funeral and the loneliness. Here I'd experienced so much in such a short space of time. It seemed too much to bear that this was my life running pell-mell every day with death standing by.

A sob caught my attention and I watched an older woman bend over the shroud of one of the soldiers killed, his mother I suspected. Ayleth was close and went to her immediately to comfort her. I stood feeling helpless and very much alone, more so than at any other time since coming here. Everyone had a place, a job to do, and they got on with it; whereas I stood against a cold stone wall like a fifth wheel with the smell of garlic in my nostrils. I must admit to being intrigued by what Ayleth had told me about garlic and its antibacterial properties. Since her arrival, she'd saved many from infections and death. I knew first-hand how reliable willow bark tea was in reducing pain. "Apparently, it has properties like aspirin. Native Americans used it," Ayleth had told me when I'd enquired.

"My lady, are you hurt?"

I didn't react at hearing those words as I stared down at the now bubbling cauldrons, though I wasn't seeing them; miles away, back home opening a packet of paracetamol after a heavy drinking session. Life had been so easy.

"My lady?"

I finally turned at the slightest touch on my sleeve. Tristan stood within arm's distance. He dropped his hand slowly, and had the decency to look ashamed as I glared at him, the realisation hitting me like a hammer.

"You can speak my language? You ... you ... son of a bitch."

I abruptly blushed, remembering some of my comments spoken out loud within his hearing and he'd pretended not to understand. "Damn it, man, why?"

Tristan shook his head and gently pulled me away from the wall. He guided me to the little sheltered nook in the castle wall where Ayleth had first taken me to look out on the moors. A cold breeze whipped up, but once I sat down on his cloak, the wall gave me shelter and I curled into it, now needing the solidness more than ever.

"Well?"

Tristan shrugged. "I not good at Ayleth tongue, but learn. Ayleth call it old English, yes?"

I said nothing. His voice was like silky chocolate, deep and rich. His lips smiled and he leaned closer and pulled me into his arm, kissing me gently on my forehead. I attempted to pull away, feeling betrayed and hurt. With a grin, he tried again, pressing his lips harder against my skin, then used his finger to raise my chin and pressed gently against my lips. Unwillingly, I gave in and kissed him back. Feeling the change, Tristan shifted closer, so our bodies touched and he wrapped me in his warm embrace. My hands travelled behind his back and pressed him close. When we finally pulled apart, I was breathless.

"Okay, I forgive you, but it would have been nice to hear you speak when I arrived."

He seemed to get the gist of what I said and, with a slight bow, he placed one hand on his heart. "I sorry, my lady Aemilia. We be careful of you. Ayleth has spoken true of you."

"Has she? I'm glad."

His piercing grey eyes gazed down at me with such raw emotion, I felt overwhelmed with an urge to open my legs there and then, but the cold wind kept my lust at bay. I wasn't sure if it would do the same for Tristan.

After a moment's hesitation, he smiled as if he could read my mind and backed away, but not too far. His hand reached out for my hand and he held it tightly. It was hot, not cold like mine, and calloused and big. My own hand was almost lost within it. I looked down at the contrasts of my lily white, unblemished skin, tinged with blood and his own hands, brown from being outdoors, bloodied and rough and I longed to have them on my body.

A shout from below caught our attention and Tristan waved at the young boy who was now gesturing him to come. Tristan abruptly stood, and I quickly followed, offering him his cloak. He held it to his nose and sniffed. "Smells of you, my Lady, I treasure it." And with a quick bow, he left me there to make my own way down.

I stood for a long time, taking all of the latest information in. Tristan could speak my language and I'd have to thank Ayleth when I saw her. I sank back down on the now cold rock and pondered what to do. The cries of the wounded had long died down, and people were milling about without the urgency of an hour or so ago, so I didn't feel guilty about not returning. I watched a young boy and I presumed his older sister collecting abandoned shields and bits of leather, bloodied swords and axes, and piling them in a corner for the owners to find when ready. I watched an old man wiping his bloodstained hands on an old rag as he also watched the children. I finally saw Ayleth walking slowly out of the home that had become the makeshift hospital. She stretched and flinching as the movement hurt her own wound.

I was about to get up and meet her when Artorius strode out with a few of his men and stopped before her. He spoke for a moment and then barked an order to Brom who escorted Ayleth inside the castle. The manner of his tone caught my attention, as he sounded angry, and it made me feel uncomfortable. Once he'd gone, I slowly made my way down to the courtyard and headed for my chamber where Ayleth sat looking into the fire. At my entry, she turned and the look on her face made me run to her concerned.

"What is it Ayleth? What's happened?"

"The Saxons are coming, Emily, and it'll be a slaughter."

CHAPTER 22

B rian rubbed his chin. "What kind of experiments?"

John leaned back in the car seat and shrugged, "Not sure, some kind of hypnosis ..."

"Hypnosis? But that's harmless, isn't it, unless she's making Emily act like a fuckin' chicken or something?"

John smiled thinly. "Maybe, but her sessions are going on for hours now. When Emily first arrived, it was for an hour a couple of times a week, but now she's seeing her every day, and the sessions are lasting for hours. Emily is leaving the room in a daze, barely eating, but sleeping for most of the day and night before another session. Some of the nurses have voiced their concerns, but Marian, Doctor Griffiths, has ignored them. So far the other doctors have also ignored the concerns and it's worrying me."

"So, can we put our fears to anyone else?"

"The board perhaps? But they are merely money grabbers. They have no real interest in what happens in the hospital, so long as they get their money every month. I need proof of backhanders going on. There is a Doctor Dowling who is retiring soon. He's a fairly decent doctor, but ill health has made him work part time these days, and everyone knows Marian Griffiths wants his job. He has a beef with Marian, hates her, I've been told. Maybe I could talk to him?"

"Do it. You can't keep your cover anymore, not if my sister and other patients are suffering, surely?"

John shrugged. "I've seen things you wouldn't believe, but I'm not ready to blow my cover yet. I know I can get more. When is your visitor's appointment?"

Brian licked his lips, shaking with fury at the thought of Emily being hurt. "Tomorrow afternoon. They moved it again. I've been left four messages on my mobile, but I'm refusing to answer. Do you think it's this Marian who's trying to cancel me again?"

"Most likely. She'll say something along the lines of, 'she's in a bad way at the moment and can't deal with visitors.' How close were you two?"

"Not very. In fact, before all this, we'd barely spoken. My fault, I'm an alcoholic who is trying to go sober."

"How's that going for you?"

"Not bad. Four days without a drink. Two weeks without passing out drunk. I see that as a plus."

"You'll need all your wits about you once you go in there, so no booze today, eh?"

"I had no intention anyway, mate." It was a lie, of course. The half bottle of brandy under the car seat would attest to that, and he hoped it wouldn't roll out. He was very scared about the visit tomorrow, with no idea what he'd see or how Emily would react. The last time they'd spoken, it was more of a screaming match and she'd told him to 'fuck off and drown in your own piss!' Sometimes it felt like he had.

"Okay, so we don't know each other if you see me in the hospital and good luck." With a quick look about, John hopped out of the car, rounded a bush and was gone. Brian felt reluctant to leave. The hospital and Emily were so close, but he needed to at least attempt to sleep and he started the car and sped away.

"Sleepy head, sleepy head, time for you to get up ... There's soup for you to sup ..."

I listened to Jane's song as she repeated it over and over until I couldn't stand it any longer and I abruptly sat up. She stopped mid-sentence, smiled and skipped out of the door. "Emily's awake now,

Emily's a lazy cow. Emily's awake now ..." her voice finally grew fainter as she moved further away.

"Sadly, she's right, my dear child, you are lazy lately and you're not eating." Nurse Mary stood within the doorway, but came to sit on my bed. She looked genuinely concerned. "Have you seen how much weight you've lost, child? You're looking more like a scarecrow every day."

I gingerly touched my face. My cheekbones did feel more pronounced, as did my collarbone. "I just feel so tired lately. All I want to do is sleep."

Mary nodded. "I see that. Do you feel hungry at all?"

"Not really. Thirsty, but not hungry."

"Okay, well I've spoken to Dr Gilmore and he wants to see you tomorrow morning for a little check-up, just to see if everything's all right. And you have a visitor tomorrow afternoon."

"A visitor? Me? Who?"

"Your brother... Brian, isn't it? Now, come on, even if you try a little soup for me, it'll be better than nothing. I'm not leaving you until you've eaten something."

I let her help me with my dressing gown and slippers, and support me as I walked the corridor. Every step was an effort, as if I had run for miles. My arms ached, as did my back (which burned in a strange way). I wanted to cry, to beg her to stop, take me back to bed, back to oblivion where I could hide in my dreams and be with him again. But I said nothing and did as she asked, supped on a small bowl of mushroom soup and even managed half a bread roll. We shared a scone with jam and butter and I drank a cup of stewed tea before I was released from her gaze.

I began walking back to my room, but the orderly John barred my way. "No sleeping yet, Emily. Go and watch television or something, mix with the other patients."

"And what if I didn't want to watch T.V?"

He didn't answer, but glared at me and folded his arms in a manner that let me know he wasn't moving. Yet again I had no choice in this hell and turned on my heels and walked back down the long corridor to the lounge. I felt his eyes on me the whole time, and was glad to reach the busy lounge of people, where I headed for the far corner and sat down heavily. Since when did a fucking orderly care what I did? I felt riled and annoyed and glared at anyone who dared to look my way.

A couple of nurses did make the mistake of glancing at me, but the other patients helped keep their attention. A nature programme was on the large television that stood in the corner, the sound turned down low, nobody watching it. I wanted my own television in my head. My memories were far better than anything conjured up by the BBC. I'd tried so hard to reject it, to keep it from her, but somehow she'd triggered something within me and it poured out. I was terrified about what would happen, but I also had an overwhelming happiness that didn't feel natural, so I guessed she'd programmed that into me? Or was I so happy to be back there, even if it was through suggestion?

My fear of what would happen had dissolved with those first images in my mind. I could hear my words clearly as though I were being told a bed-time story. Dr Griffiths barely spoke beyond the first few minutes. She never interrupted me and I found myself talking much more than I'd intended, and I enjoyed it. In those moments of being back with him and Ayleth I realised that I didn't care if I was locked up for being crazy. Being locked up would mean I could remain in my head, with him, and not return to this awful world that I now found so abhorrent. There was nothing here for me anyway.

Brian. His name popped into my head like a headache and I shook my head to rid it of him. If he was coming here, he was either in trouble, needed money, or to gloat, and I wanted none of it. He was my reality and reality meant I was further from Tristan and I couldn't face that. I wanted nothing to do with my alcoholic brother and I'd be damned if anyone could force me to see him. I'd told him to 'fuck off' and I'd meant it.

"She's looking much worse today. I think we should talk to Doctor Griffiths."

Mary walked back into the nurses' room, but hovered by the large window that looked out onto the patients' lounge.

Belinda came to see who she was looking at, and frowned. "I wouldn't bother. Doctor Griffiths is taking full control these days. I tried talking to her the other day regarding Jane and her treatment, which seems to have gone south lately. She wasn't interested and made some comment about priorities."

"What priorities? Aren't all the patients a priority to her?"

Belinda shrugged. "Apparently not any more. Your favourite, Emily Rogers, seems to be the be all and end all right now."

"That's not right, surely. What has Dr Matheson said, or Gilmore, or Dowling? Surely one of these damned doctors cares?"

"Not much. Dowling's ready to retire and his attitude towards the patients changed since his illness. I think he'd happily lock them all up in solitary just to get some peace. Tracey thinks he's worse than Gilmore!" Belinda retrieved her cardigan and put it on. "As usual, it's down to us nurses to hold the fort while the doctors decide who wins the pissing contest. I have to administer afternoon meds, see you later."

Mary watched her go before returning her attention to the lounge. Emily looked far away, deep in thought, with a strange, wistful look on her pale face. She'd never looked healthy. On admission she'd been diagnosed as malnourished but had slowly built up her strength over the weeks. Now though, she looked ill. Dark circles on her grey skin, though she slept almost constantly if they let her. These treatment sessions with Doctor Griffiths were not normal, everyone knew that, yet no one ever said anything. Well, she would, as soon as the opportunity presented itself.

CHAPTER 23

Brian woke with a hangover from hell and despised himself. Dragging his sorry carcass to the bathroom, he vomited, emptied his bowels and showered before retching again. His head split and he felt groggy but it was nearly midday and he had to visit Emily at one o' clock. He forced two cups of black coffee into his system and nibbled on a crust of stale bread with the last of his margarine that barely lubricated the surface. He choked it down and drank a pint of water before getting into the car. He had no doubts that if stopped, he would fail a breath-test. He could smell it on himself.

Turning the key, the car refused to start. After four more attempts, he saw the fuel gauge and slammed the wheel in frustration, empty. It was four miles to the hospital, he had no option but to run and hope his body didn't collapse, or projectile vomiting wouldn't occur. Slamming the car door shut, he walked fast, wishing he had some pain killers, but needing the pain to keep going. This was his penance for weakness and he deserved it all.

This was not how he'd wanted the first meeting to go, but weakness had over-ridden his promise to himself to just have a couple of pints to help him sleep. He couldn't remember leaving the pub, or how he'd bruised his cheek, but he touched it gingerly and noticed scrapes on his knuckles. A fight then? He wondered who and why as he broke into a jog, anything to keep his befuddled brain occupied at what reception he knew he'd get.

*   *   *

The evening meal was sedate, well, more sedate than the others anyway. Artorius gave a speech, Ayleth translated it for me. He spoke of the two men who'd given their lives to keep peace and of the injured who would recover in time, and he thanked everyone for helping. The men had been Pagans, so their families had taken the bodies to a site farther up the hill, a place of ancestors, where they would be laid to rest. There were a few moments of silence and then a young woman sang a beautiful song. Ayleth gave up trying to translate. Besides, I didn't need her to. The voice was so pleasing to listen to, it didn't matter about the words. Everyone banged on the tables in appreciation when she finished and then the feasting began.

It was fairly quiet at first, but as the wine flowed it became rowdy, yet I couldn't feel pleasure in anything I saw, barely touching my food as I gazed at the goings on. I noticed a few tears, but no wailing melancholy, only a sadness of loss of a loved one, an acceptance of life, and the routines needed to keep it going. The threat of battle and death was merely an inconvenience that wouldn't get in the way of a good party. Artorius noticed my lack of appetite and asked after my health. Ayleth explained something and he nodded knowingly before resuming his conversation with Merek on the other side of him.

"What is it, Emily?" Ayleth leaned closer. She smelt faintly of blood, urine and pickled herring.

My stomach contracted, but I swallowed hard and breathed through my mouth. "Nothing, it's just as you said, the Saxons are coming and if memory serves me well, didn't they do a lot of damage?"

"Aye, they did. Saxons have been 'coming' for a while now. Raiding a village here and there, but they've been driven off. Now the Romans have gone, this country is ripe for picking. I told Artorius this last year and now it has arrived."

172

"So those mercenaries I met were working with Saxons?"

"Aye, a large party of mercenaries who'd been promised money, gold and women if they helped to steal this part of the country. The small party you met were going to join the bigger one that Artorius fought yesterday. Of course, they didn't make it. One of them was the brother of the leader, a vicious bastard called Sagarus. He'd heard rumours of a skirmish with Artorius and sent scouts to find his brother's body, or what was left of him anyway."

"What was left of him?"

Ayleth had the decency to look uncomfortable. "Well, yes, dear, you know, bits for the crows to eat. Mercenaries tend not to leave anyone of no value alive, so they expect the enemy to do the same. Honour is not a word they know or understand, so they expected Artorius to behave in the same dishonourable manner."

I felt sick and pushed my chair backwards in readiness of bolting for the hole. The manner of deaths here were so violent, and always present. My body felt like it couldn't recover from one shock before another took hold. "And did he? I mean, the bodies ...?" Ayleth reached out and took my cold hand.

"It's all right, lass, take a breath. We're safe for now. The castle is well guarded. Besides, the Saxons are miles from here, on the coast. Artorius would have searched the bodies for anything of value to give to the innkeeper, who no doubt suffered in one way or another, and then they would have buried the bodies or burnt them. Leaving decomposing bodies lying around is not a good idea. The other leaders around the county will have sent soldiers to talk with the Saxons and see what they want. Artorius' problem was the mercenaries."

"Was? Does that mean they're gone?" I sounded like a small child.

I saw Ayleth fight with herself, but eventually she decided on the truth. "No, they are not gone, Emily. Artorius killed many today, but they want you."

"Me!" My voice carried, and those closest to us looked over. "Why? What have I done?"

"Well, you killed one of them ..."

173

I saw my attacker's face as easily as looking into Ayleth's. I saw the blade as it disappeared into his neck, and the look of shock in his eyes. A woman had murdered him. Expressions of disbelief, horror and fear mingled with his foul breath, until he fell away from me, and death took over. I swallowed hard and fought the black spots that pulsated before my eyes. I felt hot and found it hard to breath. "I ... I ... did ... He was ... oh, God."

Tristan was there. I sensed his urgency as he pushed people out of his way to reach me. I saw Ayleth look up, and then his strong arm was behind my back and holding me closely against his chest. Somewhere in that fogginess, I heard Artorius and registered his concern. I heard Ayleth reply, but all I could truly focus on was his arms, holding me against his warmth.

Tristan lifted me easily and I felt like I was floating in a safe haven. The scent of horse, his musky smell, and the aroma of beer reached me and I loved every one as it was a part of him. I never wanted to be released and clung onto him as he relinquished me onto the cold bed, causing him to stumble slightly, and he sank down beside me. Ayleth's clucking shoved him aside and I heard some witty banter between them. I wanted to speak, to say, 'stay' and for Ayleth to leave, but it was her cool hand on my brow, not his, and I forced myself to come around.

"Sorry."

Ayleth smiled down at me and gently covered me with a blanket. The fire was lit, but its heat barely touched the rest of the room yet. "What do you have to be sorry for? Unless, of course, you're doing it on purpose just to feel Tristan's arms around you? Then you could be sorry for wasting my time and I'll call him back ..."

I saw her smile and I pretended to contemplate her idea. "Well ... no, not just now. I need to gather my thoughts."

Ayleth thanked a servant girl, who'd brought up a tray of food, and poured us both a goblet of wine. "Now, sip this and relax. Artorius isn't going to hand you over. You are his guest. He swore it, and he will protect you."

I felt some panic leave me, but it was quickly replaced by another. "That's nice, but what about these people? I can't let them suffer because of me."

Ayleth took a long drink before answering, "Aye, well, there is that, of course. The band of mercenaries are quite a large force of a few hundred led by this 'Sagarus' who demands you are brought to him for killing his younger brother, Aldus. No one here will do that, Emily. I doubt he even cared about this brother. He's using it as an excuse to provoke a fight, and Artorius knows that."

"But why?"

"I think they've known each other before, but Artorius is keeping his reasons to himself. Besides, having a woman kill his brother is unheard of, and Sagarus needs to tip the scales back into his favour. I've no doubt that his men will be thinking less of him because of this weakness."

"Weakness? I was fighting for my life!"

Ayleth leaned forward and gently patted my thigh. "I know, I know, but they won't see it like that. A woman here is to be protected, bedded and used as a pawn in alliances. Woman is mother, sister, wife, never warrior, and you, my dear, are causing tongues to wag among the ladies of this county, especially of this castle."

I was surprised at this and said as much. "Surely women are taught to fight as well?"

Ayleth laughed. "Haven't you seen the awestruck looks you get from the servants? For a woman to fight, especially without a weapon, has never been heard of, unless you are an assassin. That's another reason Artorius wanted to see it. He needed to convince himself that it was possible, and now he knows it is. I've heard of some women of noble birth in court being taught knife wielding and some sword fighting, but it isn't taken as seriously as it is with the men. I spoke to Artorius a couple of years ago about showing the women of this castle fighting skills. Eventually he agreed to archery. The women of this castle are pretty good now and welcome the chance to prove it."

I drank back my wine and refilled our goblets. I felt breathless and warm as the wine filled my stomach. "Is he mad at me?"

"Mad? Of course not, though I think he's a bit upset you aren't an assassin. He could do with one on his side. He's impressed if anything and he still awaits your lessons. Remember, my girl, I started the women's movement here long before you arrived. Getting a bow and arrow into a woman's hand was hard on both sides, but eventually after a lot of persuasion, they realised it made sense to have back up. I meant what I said, the women here are pretty good."

I pushed myself upwards and walked around the room, unable to keep still. My head still felt fuzzy, but the need to move was harder to ignore. "But, Ayleth, I can't show him anything, can I? It'll change history and God knows what will happen ..."

"I've considered that and it's worth the risk. If you only show his men some moves then it may help them in battle, but the reality is that not many, if any, will see old age. Battles, usually small skirmishes, are fought so often, the chances of survival are small. The chances are that these women would have been shown archery eventually, so who is to say it wasn't me who put it in their minds to learn? Just because I'm not named in any history book doesn't mean I wasn't meant to get them started, begin a women's revolution or something? I take it I'm not in any history books ...?"

The look on my face stopped her and she sighed loudly. "I'm sorry, Emily, I got a bit carried away, but you need to get to grips with your life here now. Tristan is a damned good fighter, but I've stitched him up a good few times over the years, and he's had some lucky escapes. His luck and fighting ability won't last forever. There is always someone who is better and one day he will meet that person."

"You've got to old age." I sounded like a sulking child and hated it.

Ayleth pulled a face. "Well, of course I have, and as I've already told you, meeting Artorius was my lucky day, otherwise.... Besides, I'm not out there fighting my arse off most days to keep women and children safe now, am I?"

"Sorry, I'm being pathetic, I know. It's just so much has happened in only eight days, and I never dreamt I'd feel so overwhelmed by someone and the thought of losing him now that...." I stopped suddenly, realising what I was saying. I felt the heat rise up my neck and burn my cheeks a deep scarlet. Saying how I felt out loud made it all too real and I clamped my mouth shut.

Ayleth gave me a knowing grin and pushed herself up from her chair. "It's all right, Emily, you don't need to say anything. The pair of you have it written all over your faces, much to the amusement of the men in the castle. I'll send up one of the girls with a pitcher of hot water and you can wash off the blood and sweat of the day properly, I'll be doing the same before an early bed, I think."

I watched her walk to the door with Tristan in my head and suddenly remembered our conversation. "Ayleth, why didn't you tell me he could understand us?"

She stopped and thought a moment before looking at me directly. "It wasn't for me to tell. Besides, he only knows the basics. I needed to hear my own language. Good night."

I watched the door close softly behind her and slumped down in front of the fire. I needed my head to stop. I'd been here just over a week, and during those few moments of time when I was alone, my thoughts still ran at full pelt, my stomach always in knots from anxiety. I carefully stretched my hand over my back and touched my wounds. They were scabbing nicely. Another hot bath would be lovely.

Sure enough, a light knock at my door heralded a multitude of girls and two young boys carrying the bath tub while others carried steaming buckets of water. One young girl poured something into the bath and the room filled with the aroma of lavenders. Finally alone, which I had to enforce as two of the servants tried to insist on scrubbing me, I quickly disrobed and eased myself into the tub. It only reached my waist; if I moved my backside over, it reached my shoulders but it meant my legs were dangling over the side. I moved between both positions as each part became chilled.

I hadn't heard him come in and have no idea how long he stood watching me, but he was suddenly there, holding another bucket of hot water. After my initial shock, I gave him permission to pour it carefully over my shoulders. I closed my eyes in ecstasy, enjoying the sensation of warmth and the closeness of Tristan. On opening them, I found him sitting beside the tub, his face close to mine. I saw his want, his need matched my own, but I didn't want it to end quickly and neither did he.

With a smile that made my stomach quiver, he gently placed his hand into the water and stroked whatever he found there. As it happened, it was the top of my thigh and my breathing quickened. Our eyes remained locked. Slowly, teasing, he moved his fingers up my arm, my neck, and caressed my cheek before leaning forward and kissing me, his tongue gently parting my lips before his kiss became demanding, as passion held in check was released.

I answered it with my own, wrapping both arms around his neck, drawing him closer. One hand moved slowly downwards and touched my breast, his thumb stroked my nipple and it sprang to life, sending ripples of pleasure down my body. Involuntarily, I opened my legs and, as if he sensed it, he moved downwards, his fingers like electric eels surging through every pore. God, I wanted this to last while every ounce of me wanted him to plunge himself deep within me right there and then.

He finally arrived at the top of my pubic bone, and laying his hand flat, he explored that territory with a knowing hand. I felt a slight change but I didn't care at that moment what the problem was, as he was driving me insane with his fingers. Our breathing became heavy, Tristan was soaked from my bath, and he finally pushed himself away. With one quick motion, he pulled me out of the bath and into his arms, where he transferred me to the bed with a smile.

He knelt over me taking in everything. His gaze rested on my lower regions, and I realised his earlier shock. I doubted women of this time waxed their bikini lines and mine was just beginning to grow back. I felt myself blushing from his scrutiny and leaned over to grab a cover. He stopped me and pinned me to the bed. His face close to my own, our breath mingled before his mouth was on mine, and I responded with my own lust when he let go of my wrists and I began undoing his clothes. After some minutes of fumbling, he broke from our kiss and pulled them off over his head, leaving him bare-chested.

His muscles were an absolute six pack, if ever I saw one. He was lean and muscular with a small triangle of dark hair on his chest. A multitude of scars littered his skin and I bent upwards to kiss them. I pushed him over and lay on top of him, slowly licking his neck, his earlobe and down to his nipples, his scars. I heard his intake of breath and felt his need beneath his trousers. I used my hand to tease him before rubbing my body against his groin at which point, he flipped me over onto my back and pushed his trousers off.

Naked at last, his hands roamed every inch of me, followed by his lips and tongue. I was so close to orgasm it was driving me mad. He slipped inside me with a grunt and he exhaled loudly as I sighed with pleasure. Our mouths found each other again and he moved slowly, but we both knew it wasn't going to last as long as we'd hoped, and he rode me with great thrusts that made me gasp for air. I came first and two thrusts later, Tristan followed me, holding me tightly as the intensity died away, leaving us both breathless and limp.

He quickly pulled the covers up over us and I nestled into his chest. His arms held me tightly, as one hand gently stroked my hair. He was saying something softly, but I didn't understand it, nor did I care. I was at that moment, happy, safe and that was all that mattered to me.

CHAPTER 24

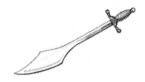

I woke sometime in the early hours to the feel of lips against my back. I smiled lazily and pushed my backside against the man who was making it very clear what he was after. Tristan whispered my name and continued kissing my wounds, which had bled a little after our night of passion. I hadn't noticed. Now, he caressed my back gently with the tips of his fingers before slowly moving downwards. Unhurried, he parted my legs and entered me from behind. I felt as drowsy as a kitten until he began to move rhythmically against me, pushing my legs farther apart as urgency took hold of us both. We came together and sank back into the bed with a loud sigh of content. I'd never experienced anything like Tristan before. He was both animal and gentleman. I fell asleep again with his arm holding me tight and one hand cupping my breast.

I woke hours later to Ayleth clucking away as servants brought in breakfast. One woman placed a cauldron over the already burning fire and left with a slight curtsey, and a smirk on her face that told me everyone knew who had shared my bed. I found myself blushing as I caught Ayleth's raised eyebrow as she indicated the now empty tub and warming water.

"I presumed you'd want to wash after your night of debauchery?" She said it with mirth in her voice, and a smile played around her lips. "I have some nice soap made with lavenders and roses if you'd care to try it?"

I waited until the servants left before getting out of bed, the sheet wrapped around my shivering body. Of Tristan, there was no sign. His clothes were gone, as were his weapons. Only his scent on the sheets was evidence of his being there. As if reading my mind, Ayleth nodded towards the closed door.

"Tristan left about half an hour ago to get his own breakfast. It was his suggestion that you might like a hot wash."

"Oh, did he? Am I sullied now then?" I felt a bit hurt at his words and needed a few minutes to compose myself. The stinking toilet was my only sanctuary and I remained quiet as I got my head around last night and my part in it.

Ayleth waited until I reappeared. "No, dear, not sullied, but Tristan is a thoughtful man, is he not ...?"

From the look on her face, I guessed her and Tristan's meaning and blushed again. No, not sullied, but the smell of our love making was very evident on me. I climbed into the bowl and squatted down to rinse my face and neck as Ayleth carefully poured the hot water over my back. Some of it splashed near the fireplace and it hissed like a snake.

I groaned in pleasure at the hot water and accepted the soap. Ignoring the underlying smell of animal fat, I lathered it up and scrubbed my body. With one final pouring of more hot water, I stepped out, wrapped my body in a towel and knelt over the bowl to wash my hair while Ayleth poured us both some weak ale, a glass of her spring water, and began her own breakfast of bread and cheese. I joined her, and towel dried my hair by the fire.

"So, you and Tristan, eh?"

I grinned. "I guess it was inevitable ..."

Ayleth shrugged. "I suppose it was."

I finished my water and reached for bread and cheese. "You don't sound too happy about it. Why?"

Ayleth shook her head. "Oh, I am, dear, truly I am. It's just getting involved with someone here might alter the future of someone else."

"You mean, another woman was supposed to fall for Tristan, and him her, but because I've come along, I may have changed that?"

Ayleth shrugged again. "It's a possibility, but maybe you were supposed to come here. Maybe, you were always supposed to be his? We'll never know."

We were both quiet for a while, nibbling at our breakfasts, each having more or less the same thoughts. "So, you've never got close to anyone, just in case?"

"It's a bit different with lesbians, I guess. If we fall in love and have sex, we don't create a life that perhaps would never have existed, but you ..."

I gawped at her a moment and it made her laugh. "You should see your face."

I quickly closed my mouth and became silent. I hadn't even considered children, and the thought terrified me. To bring a child into this world was too hard to contemplate. My thoughts must have been evident as Ayleth leaned forward and gently touched my knee.

"I'm sorry. It's something you have to consider. It was something I had to consider once. A drunk guest got a little too familiar and only the arrival of Brom stopped it from being rape. It also became obvious that Brom's father had a 'thing' for me. I doubt 'lesbians' are taken seriously in this time. I've not met many women who have come out. I think it's considered more of a pastime if women are intimate, have a laugh and go home to be fucked by their husbands."

"Have you never wanted children?"

Ayleth slowly shook her head. "I did, once, but not here. My partner and I had hoped to adopt a child or use a sperm donor, but it never happened, and now, seeing the horror of everyday life, and watching children die, when in our time they would be saved, is too hard for me to contemplate."

She stood, stretched and straightened her gown. "Time for me to visit the wounded. I'll see you later."

I stopped her as she was about to leave. "Ayleth?

"Yes?"

"How can I bring a child into this time when I hope every day that I will find another time hole, or whatever it's called, and return to my own time?"

She stared hard at me for a moment and shrugged. "I don't know how to answer that, Emily, but know this, the chances of you ever finding another is almost impossible. Decide what it is you will do while you are here, and get used to the idea that you will be here for the rest of your life. It'll drive you mad if you don't, if you want my advice."

*   *   *

There were families arriving in the car park and entering the huge front doors of the hospital. It felt like prison. Their eyes held a sad, desperate look that betrayed their need to leave as soon as possible. Brian could agree with the sentiments, a very depressing place, and he yearned to take Emily out of it.

He gave his name and identification, then was ushered into a large room with tables and chairs of various degrees of comfort scattered around the bland white room. Three large oval windows on one wall brought welcome warmth from the afternoon sunshine, but did nothing to banish the depression. If anything, it illuminated the blankness, and he felt a stirring of panic of his own, that he could ever be put in such a cold place.

A bell rang somewhere in the distance and slowly the inmates came wandering in. Most were accompanied by a nurse or orderly, but a few came unsupported and their faces lit up on seeing those waiting for them. The supported ones barely glanced up at the visitors, who gently tapped them on the shoulder, or didn't touch them at all.

Ten minutes went by and he was still alone. He kept glancing towards the double doors from where the other patients had come. Finally, he couldn't bear it any longer and went up to a nurse who was helping a patient out of her cardigan.

"Excuse me, I'm waiting for Emily Rogers ..."

The nurse looked embarrassed. "Sorry, I don't know where she is." Her attention was taken back to her patient, a woman in her late sixties who was attempting to yank off her cardigan. "No, Elsa, you can't do that. Let's do it gently, eh?"

"But I have an appointment to see my sister," Brian insisted. "Can you find out where she is? Visiting is only an hour and it's been ten minutes already...."

The nurse looked between him and Elsa with exasperation. "Well, I have to look after Elsa until her family come ... Oh, here they are."

Brian watched her hand over her charge, and with a thin smile she walked through the double doors and beyond. He was tempted to follow, but the stout guard on duty put a stop to any idea of sneaking past.

When the nurse finally reappeared, she shrugged. "Sorry, Emily is still in therapy with Doctor Griffiths. They've run over. Perhaps you could reschedule ...?"

"No, I bloody well can't reschedule. You go and tell this Doctor Griffiths that I have an appointment to see my sister, and visiting hours or not, I want to see her NOW!" His heart was beating fast and he could feel the blood pumping through his body, which only made his headache ten times worse. The fear and the fury he felt towards this place erupted like a volcano, and he glared down at the nurse, who'd taken a few steps back. The guard moved to her side.

"What's happening here? Are you all right, Nurse? Sir, I'm going to have to ask you to leave ..."

Brian moved his attention to the guard, who rose above him by four inches. "I'm going nowhere till I've seen my sister, and if you threaten me the newspapers will find out about this place and how you've locked up my sister and are doing experiments on her ..."

The nurse edged forward. "Sir, there are no experiments here, I can assure you, only good care and—"

"Then get my sister, Emily Rogers, right now!" Brian said.

"Okay, okay, calm down, I'll see what I can do. Mike, stay here and relax, okay…?"

Brian didn't like the sound of that and kept his gaze fixed on the nurse till she left in a hurry. He was aware of the other visitors watching the drama, and didn't care. Mike folded his giant arms and stood his ground, but said nothing else. Brian was tempted to goad him into a fight, just so he could prove to the papers that the hospital was at fault in some way, but said nothing ... for now.

Instead, he strode towards one of the windows and looked outside, trying to quell the rising fear in his belly. He felt awful, and no doubt the nurse and guard could smell the alcohol of last night, and he despised his weakness. He'd had to stop at a shop on his way to buy pain killers, but so far they hadn't worked. His head was throbbing badly and he felt very dehydrated. He walked over to a water butt and poured himself a large plastic cup of cold water.

"Mr Rogers?"

Brian spun around to find a young orderly standing by the table nearest to him. He was gripping Emily tightly on the upper arm, as if he was holding her up. Brian ran to her and the orderly let her go, as if she was contagious. She fell into Brian's arms and clung onto him for a long time. No sound, only a soft breath, and after a while he began to think she'd fallen asleep.

He glanced across at the orderly, the guard, and the nurse who'd also returned. All three stood at the back of the room surveying the visitors and patients. He had twenty minutes left, but damned if he was going to be pushed out on time because of their lateness.

"Emily? Emily ... can you hear me?" He held her tightly and looked across at the nurse, who watched him with some sympathy in her eyes. She eventually made up her mind and came to him.

"She may still be a little dopy from her treatment ... Emily? Can you hear me...?"

Emily made a sound and Brian tightened his grip. The nurse checked Emily's eyes and her pulse. "Yes, she's coming around now...."

She was right, he could feel Emily stiffen as she became aware of her surroundings.

"What treatment? I want to speak with one of the doctors," he demanded, but the nurse was already backing off to attend another patient, who was becoming distressed.

"Brian?"

His attention was brought sharply back to his sister who was pushing away from him. She looked confused, looking at him and past him as if she couldn't focus on anything. "Yes, Emily, it's me. What have they done to you?" Emily pushed hard enough to break free of his grasp, staggered slightly and half fell into the nearest chair. Brian moved as if to help her, but the look she gave him stopped him. "It's me ... Are you okay?"

"What do you want? Money? Fuck off. I've got nothing!"

The venom in her voice hurt him deeply, but he slowly sat down in the chair opposite. "I don't want anything, Emily. I've come to see you and try and get you out of here."

Her laugh was so sudden it unnerved him and he looked around nervously. "You. Save me. What a joke!" She leaned closer and sniffed. "You stink of the bottle you crawled out of. Go back into it and leave me alone."

She stood to leave and he reached out to stop her. "I know I've let you down, Emily, but this...." He moved his hand to take in her appearance. "This is not normal, Emily. What are they doing to you? Tell me. I can help you. I know you're innocent, so do they."

Emily turned to look him fully in the face. "Innocent? I killed him and more. I'm not innocent. I have blood on my hands and I don't care, they deserved it. Now go away and never come back."

He watched her walk unsteadily towards the nurse and orderlies, who were beginning to herd the patients back through the double doors. He stood while the other visitors hurried out of the room, thankful to be free of its stench. He turned unseeing towards the exit and made his way back to the car park, before remembering his was still sitting outside his bedsit. Emily was innocent of murder, he'd swear on it, but who were 'they'? She was obviously confused, and yet, something in her face had made him believe her words, and that scared him more than he could ever imagine.

CHAPTER 25

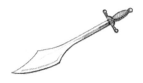

Weeks passed in a blur of tending the wounded, watching the men train hard and fierce, and catching stolen kisses from Tristan, as he was either out scouting the land, training with the men, or in meetings with Artorius. Every night I'd wait impatiently to see if he'd come to my chamber, but he never appeared, and I'd finally fall asleep in a mixture of frustration and anger, until I'd find out he'd been out all night tracking and killing scouts sent to spy on the castle.

His world was impossible to grasp sometimes. On occasion I saw a mere man, with a job, who was able to love and have children, but then the reality was that Tristan, like every man in the castle, was a killer. A warrior to serve his Lord, protect his women and his land, and he'd do it without question. I wondered if the killing played on his conscience. I had long moments when I'd remember the men's faces at the inn and out on the moor and I'd curl into myself, knowing I'd taken their lives. A large part of me rationalised that it had been self-defence, and they were bad men who did horrible things, but was Tristan any better than that?

I'd catch glimpses of him washing in the stream or a handy bowl in the courtyard. The water was always dark with blood and muck, and I'd fight the rising bile at seeing the sight. He knew I was there, of course.

I'd notice the sharpening of his shoulders, the ever so slight turn of his head and a touch of a smile on his lips before he'd continue his ablutions.

Not that I was idle during all of those times. My day was busy with the wounded, who all made full recoveries, thankfully, though Dalibar took a while longer than others and still complained of headaches on occasion. I was learning about the herbs from Ayleth, whose own wound was healing nicely. I got to talk with the other women from the nearby village. Well, they'd talk and I'd listen, hoping to catch something I could understand. Most of the time, a gesture made it obvious, but Ayleth was usually on hand to help translate. I did begin to notice though, that as time went on, I began to recognise more and more words.

"It's fairly easy, Old English to our English. Some sound a little the same, like 'Come in' is 'Cume in' and 'what?' is 'Wit?'"

I sounded some of the words much to the amusement of the women in the makeshift hospital. A sudden shout from above, made everyone freeze and look to each other in fear. Ayleth shouted something to the young girl nearest the door and she looked out. Almost immediately, she turned to the congregation and said a word even I could understand. "Saxon."

Instant terror rippled through the room. My stomach lurched at the thought of what might be coming. I glanced across at Ayleth, busy trying to calm a young woman who, from what I could understand, was begging her to kill her if they got in. Being gang raped was not something she contemplated surviving. I had to agree with her on that score.

We all jumped as the door was flung open and Tristan stood in the doorway. He quickly scanned the room, saw me, and pulled me to my feet. Turning to Ayleth, he helped detach the clinging girl and pulled her to her feet as well before leaving, expecting us to follow which we did willingly. He marched across the courtyard, up the stairs and into the great hall, where so many men were getting kitted out in various leather and helmets. Tristan walked us past everyone and up the back stairs to Artorius' own chamber. At our entrance, he turned to us smiling, though it didn't fool either of us.

He kissed my hand and hugged Ayleth briefly before indicating the two free chairs in his room. From here, I could hear a distant drum and my heart fluttered and my limbs went weak with fear. Ayleth was having a conversation, but it was so fast I couldn't understand until all three turned to look at me.

"What? He's not going to give me to the Saxons, is he?" Even as I said the words I didn't truly believe them, but I was terrified nevertheless.

Ayleth reached across and patted my hand, translating for Artorius' sake. He in turn rushed over and knelt at my feet.

"No." Turning to Ayleth, he asked her to translate. "I am going out there to fight this small army. My scouts tell me they are part of something much bigger, but these have a personal hatred of you. This is the brother of the man you killed in self-defence." He gripped my hand as I started to shake. "We will not allow him to use you as an excuse to kill, and that is what he is doing. He may be grieving, but it is not grief that drives this man to kill relentlessly. It is power and greed. You have my word, we will protect you, my lady Aemilia." He kissed my white knuckles again and stood, turned, and left with a quick nod to Tristan, who hesitated and looked at me with such longing before he followed his lord into battle.

*   *   *

Nurse Mary walked past Emily's room again and looked through the window. Emily lay on her back staring up at the ceiling, though she doubted she was seeing it. She'd heard that her brother had visited this afternoon which they'd hoped would help bring Emily out of her day-dreaming shell. It hadn't worked obviously.

She looked completely detached these days, but the complaints and concerns given to the other doctors went unheard. They used the doctor's privilege garbage, and Doctor Griffiths knew what she was doing. Emily might be hiding the truth of the murder somewhere in her head, and perhaps this was the only way to give the family closure, but at what cost? Mary and a few other nurses, even a few orderlies, had voiced their concerns for Emily's well-being to both Doctor Gilmore and Dowling. Both had given them the brush off.

The orderly, John, was coming the opposite way. When he saw Mary he suddenly straightened himself, gave her a nod and walked on by. She didn't trust that man. Something didn't fit. He was always looking around as if he was noting everything in his head. She'd even voiced her thoughts to another nurse as they shared the night shift last week. Liz had laughed at her idea of him being an undercover journalist.

"Who in their right minds would want to be put here for a job?"

Mary had smiled at the obvious and waited patiently for Liz to realise her mistake.

"Well, except us, of course. I mean, this isn't my dream job. I'm only here while I wait for an NHS job to come up that fits in with the kids, then I'm out of here. This place gives me the creeps, especially at night."

Mary was quiet for a while, before continuing the original conversation. "So, John doesn't strike you as being odd?"

Liz was filing her nails and looked up again. "No, he doesn't. He's quiet, of course, but I like that. I don't want to get into conversations with the orderlies, do you? Besides, I heard him speaking with another orderly yesterday, regarding Emily Rogers, and even he's uneasy, so he can't be that bad."

"I suppose not, though I like to pass the time of day with everybody, he never engages and politeness costs nothing...." She could see Liz wasn't listening anymore and returned her attention to the monitors.

Now she glanced behind her, to watch him disappear through the double doors and beyond. He turned right into the cafeteria area and she stood for a while, contemplating him. John had been with them for nearly five months. He'd never been late or taken a sick day so far as she knew. He was efficient and good to have around when a patient kicked off. However, his constant watching bothered her, and his manner towards some of the patients was a bit too close. He'd never shown any concern for Emily before. In fact, he behaved as if he despised her. That was fairly normal. She was accused of murdering a man in cold blood, but still, it wasn't his or her job to judge these people.

She looked back into Emily's bedroom and sighed loudly. She'd have to get her moving around. If only they could take her outside to the gardens. The tiny concrete enclosed garden, for the more dangerous inmates, was cold and flowerless. It had no features other than a bench, two birch trees and cameras at every angle. It could be walked around in fifteen seconds and, because it was enclosed on all sides, the sun barely reached any part of it, so it wasn't used much.

A cry from farther up the corridor had her running. Mrs Bridges, four bedrooms up, was throwing her knickers around again, and if not stopped, would escalate into more destruction, usually of herself and her bedroom. Last time she'd managed to tear her curtains into strips and shoved two of those pieces into her mouth before they'd realised what she was doing. To this day, she had no idea why Eileen Bridges felt she had to do that and, sadly, most of the time she didn't have the chance to find out. With one last look at Emily, she strode purposefully away to save another patient.

*   *   *

The thundering sound as the men rode out to meet the small army was a sound I may never forget. I'd never heard so many horses moving at the same time. Ayleth and I watched from Artorius' chamber and saw about a hundred men heading straight out, while Tristan and his gang turned left and disappeared among the trees.

"They have a plan, obviously," Ayleth said.

I said nothing as I stared hard towards the trees, hoping for another glimpse of Tristan and his brothers in arms. Artorius was leading the main troop and then even he veered off and was lost from our sight. It was cold at the window, but I couldn't move away. My fate lay with the men and their skills at fighting. If they lost, I lost. I turned then to look at Ayleth who was putting logs on the fire. We lost, I corrected myself, and felt the knot in my stomach tighten.

"Come away, Emily, there's nothing to see. The battle will be too far away, and we'll know soon enough if we lost. It's different for men in this era. To die in battle is an honourable death, especially if they are defending those they love."

"How can you be so calm? I'm shitting myself here in case I'm raped repeatedly, tortured, and then killed, and all because I walked through some fucking hole...."

"I'm not calm, Emily, it's just after so many years of sitting and waiting to see if the men came back, or a Saxon, Pict or some other mercenary hoping to make his mark on this torn land take over, I learned to keep busy. I sort out bandages and get cauldrons filled with water to boil. I steep herbs and willow bark tea for our men and I have a last resort if anyone else should break down our doors."

She produced a small clear bottle with liquid inside. "Foxglove. Deadly poison if necessary."

I slowly walked forward, and reached out to take it. It felt strange holding something so deadly in my hands. "And you'd take it?"

She looked me squarely in the eyes and took it back. "Wouldn't you?"

I knew I would. Compared to being passed around from one stinking rapist to another, before dying from my injuries, a quick death was certainly preferable.

"But let's hope it never comes to that. Now, help me get the room ready for our injured. We'll know soon enough if they failed. The archers on the walls will call down with news."

I followed Ayleth out of the warm room and shuddered as the damp corridor invaded my skin. We headed quickly to our makeshift hospital and I waited as Ayleth made mental calculations as to who should go where, and what we'd need.

"We need more cloth. I have some stored in my cave ..."

"I'll go. I need something to do."

Ayleth gave my arm a quick squeeze and I walked quickly to the back of the castle. I had just arrived at her cave when an arm wrapped itself tightly around my neck and yanked me off my feet. All breath left my body, but I tried to kick and twist. I heard harsh whispering behind me as I was pulled backwards. I tried to kick, to find a hold so I could free myself, but the grip was iron tight, as was the hand clamped over my mouth, making it even harder to breath.

I was yanked through a tiny door and saw it being closed by a young woman, who kept her eyes lowered. I recognised her from the kitchens, though couldn't recall her name. I tried to make some sound, to warn the men on the wall, but my captors kept to the darkness and stealthily moved in the shadows.

I gagged when I saw two dead men with their throats cut staring up at me, and knew them to be Artorius' scouts who kept watch on this side of the castle. The men, I counted four, dragged me, half-conscious, to a clump of trees where horses stood tethered. I was whacked on the head, and the last I saw was the horse's brown hair as my face made contact with it. My backside was slapped once in triumph as we cantered away. They'd caught their prize and I lost consciousness.

CHAPTER 26

"Emily is all tied up tra la la la la. She's taken very far tra la la la la. Emily is all tied up tra la la la la la ..."

I didn't know where I was for a moment and stared up at the ceiling. Jane's singing finally reached me and I turned my head. She was perched on top of her bed, squatting and wringing her hands, staring at me. The words of her song struck me and I slowly sat up.

"Did I talk in my sleep, Jane? Sorry if I woke you ... That's a weird song today ..."

Jane barely acknowledged me, but repeatedly sang the same two lines over and over. It was beginning to grate on my nerves and I took a deep breath, reaching out to her. She flinched backwards as if I'd slapped her, and she finally focused on me.

"That was a strange song to sing, Jane," I repeated. "Did I talk in my sleep?"

"Always talking in your sleep, you say such things it makes Jane weep ..."

I could see, now that I was more awake, that Jane was indeed crying. Her eyes were red and her cheeks were wet from tears. "Jane, I'm so sorry. What have I said that's upset you?"

Jane didn't answer straight away, but seemed to be mulling something over. Finally, she eased herself off her bed and came to sit on mine. "You are so sad, you are not bad, but something bad has happened, to make you feel sad. You were taken, and you were scared, but you survived and that has made you strong, and they were wrong to keep you."

I stared at her open-mouthed. Not from her words, but the way she'd said them. No sing-song voice, but normal. Yes, words rhymed, but for Jane, in all the months I'd known her, and from other patients who had known her longer, this type of talking had never been witnessed.

"Jane." I spoke softly and reached out to take her hand. "You didn't sing your words. Have I upset you so badly?"

She nodded enthusiastically and I gripped her hand tight. "What did I say, can you tell me?"

She thought for a moment, then nodded again. "I think I can remember. You were terrified. The men were from a mercenary and they kidnapped you from the castle. They killed men and they were going to hurt you, use you like a whore."

My stomach clenched as I remembered that terror. I relived it every day, but hearing Jane voice it made it so real again. I instinctively looked around the room to be sure we were alone. Jane saw me do it and yanked my hand to get my attention. "Silly Billy—no one here but us now."

I smiled, feeling stupid, but stopped as her words sunk in. "What do you mean by 'now'?"

Jane leaned in close. Her breath tickled my neck. "Doctor Griffiths lingers nearby. She watches you with a glint in her eye. Beware the woman, she has ambition." With a sudden jerk of her hand Jane stood up, did a little dance and skipped out of the room towards the canteen and breakfast. I could hear her rhyming as she went. Jane's high-pitched, school-girl voice a familiar sound: but which one was real? I think I'd glimpsed the real Jane before her need to withdraw pushed through again. I felt honoured and wondered if I should tell someone, but immediately changed my mind. Jane had trusted me enough to show me herself when I needed clarity. I wouldn't betray her.

So, if what Jane said was true, and somehow I didn't doubt it, Marian Griffiths was interested in my dreams now, and I knew how she would be getting her information. I looked directly at the tiny camera in the corner of the room and waved. Bastards! No privacy, not even in my sleep. I guess it was hardly surprising, as the therapy sessions were getting interesting and her need for answers to the murder of the guard would be causing her anxiety.

I turned my back, wrapped my arms around my knees for comfort and fought back the tears. I knew I'd not have the strength to fight her. Somewhere in my psyche, I obviously wanted to go back and be with Tristan again, but I hated reliving those horrible moments, and I knew what was coming next. I'd fought to forget the trauma and abuse, if only I could just be with him, but it seemed my mind was determined to relive every moment, and nothing was truly forgotten, just conveniently put away somewhere. Marian was drawing it all out of me. To feel his arms and his lips once more was both heart-breaking and glorious. Her sessions filled me with dread and excitement, and I found myself eagerly ready to go when the orderly came for me, something I would never have considered happening.

The sessions were going as I knew they would. Marian was getting excited by what she heard and the therapy sessions were becoming longer, more frequent. It was like a book she couldn't put down and that made me smile. I knew how she felt, except for me the book was real, skin and bone, blood and guts. These people were real. They had lived and loved and died so long ago, but were not forgotten, not by me. I would allow this to continue, it was like a drug to me now.

I quickly washed and sauntered down to the canteen. I was never hungry these days, as my body was convinced that I was eating elsewhere. However, to keep up appearances and having looked at my skeleton in the mirror, I decided I'd better eat in this century too and opted for a cereal, a small bowl of fruit and a large mug of tea. I just couldn't face bread and cheese but was surprised to find that I craved a flagon of ale. I giggled to myself as I forced the food in, unsure how the hospital would view ale for breakfast. I'd have to ask Marian if we could incorporate it into our sessions. Get pissed like in the old days.

Marian sat back in her chair and shrugged. The meeting with the hospital directors was not going as she'd hoped. Too many nurses had made complaints about Emily Rogers' condition, and her brother was making threats and accusations. The board could not turn a blind eye anymore. "I don't know what else to say, gentlemen. Emily is doing really well in our sessions together and making real progress in her treatment. If you stop now, I can't be held responsible...."

They looked unsure and that might be in her favour. She leaned forward, "Look, the police have every faith that I can help Emily remember that night, but the fact remains, there is another print on the murder weapon and Emily could very well be innocent. How will it look if it's found out that we've kept an innocent woman locked up? I have to finish this so we can all sleep with a clear conscience...."

That got them. It was a risk. The police had never said any such thing, but she was working closely with them and the directors knew it. She hoped it was enough to stop any further questions. Besides, keeping an innocent woman locked up for months was never going to look good, but at least if Emily was found innocent, they could say they tried everything to help find the truth. It covered their arse and they knew it.

Half an hour later, she strolled back to her office to see her other patients. Boring. She'd agreed to keep on top of her other work and in return, Emily would continue her sessions. But she must keep them to an hour, no longer. Her supervisor was very worried about her own state of mind, and had already questioned her motives for increasing the sessions to two hours or more every day.

She passed the nurse called Mary and gave her a smile. Mary was one of the nurses who'd made a complaint, she was sure of it. An old busybody who was always calling everyone 'my child', as if she was some kind of guru. Glad to reach her office, Marian closed the door on the rest of the hospital. Five patients today and then she'd see how Emily felt about another session tonight. It wasn't protocol, but if she was prepared to work late, the board shouldn't have a problem.

*   *   *

I began to wander the corridors as the day wore on and on and on. Bored out of my mind by mid-afternoon. A couple of orderlies and nurses grew flustered trying to keep an eye on me. Not that I could get out. The doors were monitored constantly with I.D badges, and a code to open them in and out. I smiled at the security guard who stood watching my approach with a resigned look on his face.

"Go back, Miss, you know you can't come down here."

I ignored him for a moment, looking beyond him through the thick glass and to the long corridor beyond. "I can go as far as the door actually. It's the other side I'm not allowed to go."

Frowning, he stared at me, knowing his mistake, but pointing back the way I'd come anyway. "Go on, before I have to call for help to restrain you."

"Restrain me? For what? For walking? Are you as bored as me?" I took a couple of steps closer, wanting to see how far I could push him, and he knew it.

"I mean it, Emily. Leave now."

I huffed loudly. "But I'm so bored. Have you any idea how it is to be innocent and locked up?" Too late I realised my mistake, and immediately turn on my heels to walk away. His gaze burned into my back and as I rounded the corner. I heard him talk into his radio. I'd never said a word about my innocence or guilt, and now I'd blabbed it out to a security guard. What was it about security guards? I either got them killed or I blurted out information!

I hurried to my room knowing I'd be visited at any moment. Sure enough, Marian came in, looking tired and flustered, but on seeing me waiting for her, she stopped abruptly, brushed back her hair and sighed heavily.

"I see you're expecting me, Emily."

"Well, of course. That security man must have almost wet himself when I spoke to him."

Marian slowly entered the room, closing the door behind her. "I see. And what you said to him, did you mean it when you said you were innocent, or were you just ... bored?"

I ignored her question and looked her up and down. "What were you doing when you got the call that I'd confessed my innocence?"

She actually looked uncomfortable for a brief moment, and I felt a sense of triumph. "I was with another client, but we'd just finished, so...."

I heard the unspoken sentence. So I hadn't dropped another patient to come running here, but I knew she had. I'd bet money the other patient had been kicked out of the door for her to get to me so fast. I hadn't realised until that moment just how important my story was to her. Marian's career obviously needed this to work in her favour, and I hated her for it.

"So, were you merely bored as you said, or are you innocent of the murder? Do you remember that night now, Emily?"

Her bluntness took me by surprise as I think it did Marian. What a risk. I appreciated that, but didn't let on. "You know I'm innocent."

Marian stared at me hard. "Do I?"

"You probably know more than me, but you aren't going to tell me. You want me to tell you, but I can't. Will you tell the police that I've confessed my innocence?" I saw the sudden change of direction had caught her by surprise.

"I'm not sure, Emily, because I can't work out if you're telling us the truth or merely playing, and why can't you tell me about that night?"

Now her change of direction took me by surprise. I smiled sweetly. "I have no memory of that night ... as you well know. I remember nothing. Perhaps you could fill me in on what I'm saying during our sessions ..." Game set and match to me, I thought.

Marian shifted uncomfortably. "Maybe. Although I'd like you to be able to remember them on your own. Do you recall anything?" When I didn't answer, she shrugged. "However, I'd like to continue our sessions."

"Really? I was under the impression they'd been cancelled...."

My knowledge made her feel even more uneasy and she quickly sat down on Jane's bed. I wasn't going to tell her that I'd overheard Nurse Mary telling another nurse about Marian's meeting that morning with regards to my sessions. I'd taken a guess at the outcome.

"No, not cancelled, but they do have to change slightly, in the times we proceed and how many sessions we do. Are you okay with that, Emily?"

I shrugged. "I didn't realise I had any say in my treatment."

Marian stared at me for a moment and I could see she was choosing her words carefully. "You always have a say, Emily. The sooner we find out the truth, the sooner your life can get better." She abruptly stood and opened my bedroom door. "I have one more patient to see, then if you're feeling up to it, perhaps you'd like another session before your evening meal, say four-thirty?"

She didn't wait for my answer, but gave me a knowing smile and left. She knew I wouldn't refuse. She knew I longed for the sessions just to feel again, and who could blame me? Why would I refuse when it took me back to him? To them. And I'd give anything to go back. Even if hypnosis and my dreams weren't real, it was better than this hell-hole. I hated Marian with every ounce of my being, as she had full control. She was like my drug dealer, who could withdraw the sweetness at any moment, make me bark like a dog to get my fix. The days of my fear of hypnosis seemed like another world. I was deep into it and never wished to return.

CHAPTER 27

The cold water splashed my face, soaking the front of my gown. The icy droplets made goosebumps stand out as it trickled down between my breasts and onto my stomach. I came to abruptly and yanked hard, realising almost immediately that my hands were tied with rope, and had been levered upwards, so my arms were above my head, which throbbed badly from whatever they had hit me with. My feet barely touched the floor and I kept sliding on the slippery stone, made worse by the bucket of water they had thrown at me.

I heard many men laughing and one threw the empty bucket into the small crowd before turning back to me. He was huge. A mountain of a man with arms twice the size of my thighs. Around six-foot tall with a thick red beard and long hair, matted and dirty. He grinned at me, but there was nothing nice about his smile. It left me feeling cold and sick with fear. I tried to wrench my hands free, but it was no use, the knot solid.

I was in a dark stone room, and stinking. A large fire lit up one area of the room, while sconces in the walls gave enough light to see my captors. There were perhaps twenty or thirty men, sitting around wooden tables, everyone had tankards and were drinking heavily. I pulled again at the rope, but on looking up at the low stone ceiling, I could see it was too tight.

He spoke, his voice like grit, deep and evil, as I'd expect the devil to sound. He repeated his words, but I didn't understand him, and I merely blinked at him, terrified. He turned to his men, yelled something and they roared with laughter. His attention returned to me, and he walked purposefully towards me. When he was about a foot away, he leaned in and spoke. As he spoke, he slowly pulled out a large knife that was in his belt and raised it to my face. I had no need for translation. I knew he meant to kill me slowly, and that I'd suffer first. I tried to shrink away but there was nowhere to go.

He nodded to someone behind me and I abruptly felt another large man pressing his groin into my backside. I squirmed away, but his hands roughly grabbed my breasts and twisted, which made me cry out in pain. The man nuzzled my neck, and then licked me from collar bone to ear in one lick, then said something to the watching crowd. They laughed and some whistled, so I guessed it was something offensive about my taste.

The devil watched me intently. He'd been given a flagon of something and held it, but didn't drink. His dagger was in his other hand and he absentmindedly tapped his chin, as if deep in thought. His gaze made me more nervous than what was being done to me. Behind those eyes, true evil lived and I dreaded what he would think up.

My abuser was now dry humping me, and getting himself very excited in the process, much to the amusement of the onlookers, most of whom looked the worse for drink. This was it. The repeated rapes from which I'd finally die and I'd be with my mum and dad again. Although technically, they hadn't died yet, or even been born and the possibility that they wouldn't be waiting for me only made me feel worse.

The devil suddenly shouted and the room fell silent. He shouted an order, and my arms were immediately released and they slapped against my body with a thud. Blood rushed to my hands with pins and needles causing me significant discomfort, but I showed nothing as I stared back at him. My hands were still bound and he grabbed the rope, yanking me towards him. The knife almost went into my neck, but I managed to pull backwards just in time and it glanced off, leaving a scratch. It still hurt and I cried out, but his lips found mine and it stifled the sound. He thrust his tongue inside my mouth and I gagged. He tasted of decay, sour ale and body odour. His hand grabbed my arse and he pulled me towards him. I could feel his erection and I tried to pull away, but his hand on my backside kept pushing me closer. He rubbed himself against me in a lewd manner, much to the men's amusement, and with cheers of encouragement, he tore at my dress, exposing my right breast.

The men roared and he dipped his head and began kissing and sucking and licking it in a vile manner. I struggled to move away from his intrusive mouth, but he held me fast until he'd had his fill. He lifted his head and gave the audience a slight bow. I tried to turn away from the stares, to hide my nakedness, and was thankful when he abruptly pulled me out of the large room and into a dark corridor. He pulled me along the cold corridors until we came to a wooden door. He kicked it open and threw me inside, shutting the door behind us. I lost my footing and fell hard on my elbow, yelping in pain. I stayed on my knees.

He spoke, but I had no idea of what. As he talked he slowly walked around me. He wasn't in any rush. He had all the time in the world to rape and torture me. Our men were being kept busy fighting, so there'd be no one coming for me. He walked over to a large table on which stood a jug and a few tankards. He poured himself something and drank it down. He saw me watching him and he smiled a cold, calculating smile that made my insides shrink away in fear. But I kept on watching him. It was as if I couldn't look away. I was daring him to kill me. I wanted it over and I think he knew it.

He moved so quickly I barely had time to react. He pushed me backwards onto the cold, stone floor, undid his trousers and masturbated on me. It was over in seconds and thankfully his aim was terrible and most of him hit my stomach and the floor. I turned my head and vomited. The smell and the humiliation, just too much for me.

He laughed and went back to the table and poured himself another tankard, but this time, he stood and watched me as I struggled to get to my knees, wiping my mouth on my sleeve, careful not to touch any of his semen. He was talking again and indicated my dress or boobs, I wasn't sure which, but I ignored him and slowly rose to my feet. I was angry now. Angry, pissed off and sick of his humiliations. I guessed this to be Sagarus, and unless I did something to either quicken my death or escape, he'd make my life a living hell for killing his brother.

I couldn't help but think about the battle. I had no idea how long I had been unconscious. Had it ended badly for us, because Sagarus was here and not fighting for his life? Maybe I could give him a fight? The rope binding my hands together was loose, though it would still take some work to get free. I stared up at him. Okay, he was definitely bigger than his brother and not drunk, but I was a black belt for God's sake, despite the hindering of the skirts and tied hands. I'd fought bigger men than this guy and won. I just needed to be rid of the dress and untied.

As if reading my thoughts, the devil, as I'd begun to think of him, launched himself at me, slapping my face with a swift backhander before tearing at my dress. With one loud tear it fell off me, leaving me standing in my torn chemise with a bleeding lip. It was all I needed. I took one step backwards to steady myself and abruptly swiped him with a kick to the chest, swiftly followed by another to his neck, and a punch to his face. He staggered backwards more in surprise than pain, but I hit him again. Groin, stomach, and a swift kick to the jaw. I heard it break and he fell sideways. Not daring to stop, I punched him hard with both hands still tied, across his ears, and he went down hard. I kicked his face and knew I'd broken his nose. He remained unmoving.

I stopped and listened. I was breathing hard and focused on my breath, slowing it down until I felt a little calmer. Nobody came, so I guessed he must have told them he was not to be disturbed, regardless of what they heard. I suppose they didn't expect a mere woman would, or could, fight back, especially with hands bound, and I thanked the gods for my training.

I picked up his dagger, cut the rope and massaged my sore wrists while I contemplated what to do next. I might be able to fight one on one, but there were at least thirty lecherous men out there, not counting the guards I saw standing at various points along the corridors, and I had no idea where 'here' was. I ran to the only window in the room, high up and hard to peer out of, but enough to show I was a few floors up. I stood back defeated. A ground floor room I would have had a chance to climb out of and sneak away, but this high up, I'd need a ladder ... or sheets?

I glanced across at the unmade bed and grimaced, doubting they'd ever been cleaned. But on further inspection they did look to be fairly good material, possibly strong enough to hold my weight. I quickly began tying the sheets and blankets together as best as I could. It'd worked in films, maybe it would work for me. I didn't think I was too high up.

The devil hadn't moved and a quick check showed me he was still out cold. It was only just getting dark and I didn't dare attempt the climb in the light. Much to my shame, I kicked him in the head before tying his hands behind him and gagging him with my soiled dress. I couldn't chance him waking before I'd even tried to escape. Then, I waited and sipped his ale. It wasn't too bad, but what I really wanted was fresh water. After so much excitement and fear, I felt dehydrated and exhausted.

As I sat there hunched up in the corner, terrified in case someone did come to check, I could hear men singing and laughing in the distance with the occasional clashing of metal. Sometimes I heard screams, and my heart wrenched for those poor women. I sent out a prayer for their quick deaths. I kept watching my attacker, but besides a small trickle of blood from his nose, there was no sign of life, and I felt nothing.

Finally, the sounds died away and all I heard were the sounds of a night owl and men talking softly from somewhere outside. I cursed my chemise for being white, but besides going naked, there was nothing I could do. I tied one end of my makeshift ladder to the bed and stood on a chair. I peeped out of the narrow window and checked it was clear before throwing out the bed sheets.

I waited for a shout, an alarm, but there was only silence. After another quick check on the devil, I climbed out of the window before I thought twice about it. The climb down was heart wrenchingly scary, as I expected any number of things to go wrong. The sheets to unravel and break, and I'd fall and die, or worse be injured and at their mercy. Sagarus would wake and raise the alarm. A guard would see and stop me, or all three. However, the only thing to happen, and only a slight inconvenience, was the sheets didn't quite reach the bottom and I had to jump the last five feet or so. It jarred my ankle, but I immediately rolled and crept to a bale of straw.

I was in a field. I had climbed down the outer wall of the building. My feet were frozen and wet as my toes squelched in something I'd rather not know. The field was soggy and I wondered where the river could be. I listened intently, but I couldn't hear a river, but I recognised a smell that gave me some idea where I was. I could smell the sea. That meant I had to turn inland and try to find Artorius' castle, and Tristan. The dark was intense, I had no idea which way, but knew I couldn't stay behind the straw. I chose a direction and tiptoed away, and keeping my back to the stone keep, I kept low and stopped every now and then to listen, but I heard no one. As I crept away I felt the darkness of the night envelope me and hoped it would keep me safe until I could find Tristan and the men of Artorius.

CHAPTER 28

The farther I moved away from the shelter of the castle walls the more the wind picked up and whipped my chemise around my legs. Barefoot and half-dressed, I was shivering badly, but not just from the cold. My adrenalin and fear pumped so fast I found it difficult to move, as any sound caused me to freeze. I'd duck down, and quake in my terror that the bastard hadn't died, and he and his lecherous band of rapists would hunt me down.

I had no illusions about just how easy that would be. For all I knew I was heading in the wrong direction, in a circle, or into worse danger, but I couldn't stop. I had to keep going, even if it was only to help keep me warmer from freezing, which wasn't much but it might keep me alive till I could find either shelter or help.

I had no notion of how long I walked, jogged and sprinted, moving from one action to another as bursts of energy hit my body. At one point I was running so fast all I could hear was my breath coming, thick and heavy, gasping for every last ounce of energy. I fell numerous times and hurt my knees, my hands, and my elbow throbbed from where I'd banged it on his stone floor. Stones loomed up in the darkness, or stumps of old trees and I'd mostly manage to dodge them, but on occasions I'd fly into one and find myself face-down sobbing into the drenched grass. The going was fairly flat, and at times, boggy, but other than that, I had no idea where I was.

I finally came to a stone wall and heard the sounds of cattle nearby. I smelt them too and slowed down to a tentative walk. I was petrified of cows and bulls, but even more terrified of what waited for me in that room. I walked slowly through the throng of large bodies, stepping in their crap, but ignoring it as I hoped my presence wouldn't alarm them or alert someone close by.

A few made noises, but most remained still, doing what cattle did and I was soon through them. Then I saw it, a light. Nothing more than a flicker, a candle most likely, but I ducked down behind a boulder. Not that it would hide me in daylight, but in this darkness, I might get away with it if nobody looked too carefully. The light disappeared a moment, before reappearing and I realised what I was looking at, people walking past a small window. I couldn't risk these people being friendly with the men, so I remained still.

I heard snippets of low conversations when the wind moved the sound my way, but on the whole, whoever they were, they said very little. My body ached to leave. I didn't know how far I'd managed to get, but not far enough, and not to the safe-haven of Artorius and his men. Finally, I heard what sounded like a door slamming shut and I strained my eyes to see, but all became still and quiet.

Edging out from behind my boulder, I moved farther up the field, keeping a good distance between me and the people. Once I was sure they were behind me, I found my feet again and ran. I ran until I had no breath left. I ran, ignoring the pain in my feet as I stepped on stones, and branches, and who knew what. I ran until I collapsed between two large rocks, where I gathered my wits and tried to think about what I should do.

I had no idea how long I'd been unconscious when they'd abducted me, so had no notion as to how far I was from Tristan, or in which direction. I could see nothing in the utter darkness, only vague glimpses whenever the moon peaked out from behind the racing clouds. The wind out in the open was freezing, but here I was slightly sheltered on three sides and it created a hint of warmth that I clung to. Without warning, my eyes began to droop and I dozed off from sheer exhaustion.

*   *   *

Brian paced his bedroom. His telephone calls to the manager of the hospital had resulted in nothing more than polite responses to his claim that Emily was being mistreated, and that they would be investigated fully. He knew what that meant—fuck all!

He put the glass of brandy to his lips, but stopped himself from glugging it all back, and instead carefully replaced it untouched back on the mantelpiece. He had to find that journalist orderly trying to expose the corruption; maybe he could do something. But he had nothing except the man's contact details through the newspaper. It would take too long and he needed to do something now. Every minute Emily was stuck in that place was a minute too long.

The loud knock on his door surprised him and he glanced at his clock. Nobody would visit now unless there was trouble and he psyched himself up ready for a fight. The two men waiting out in the corridor quickly informed him that they were police and he opened the door wider to let them in.

"Sorry to call at such a late hour, sir, but we needed to catch you. We have left several messages...." The taller of the two men indicated Brian's mobile phone.

Brian glanced over and shrugged. "Battery died and no credit. Okay, so what was the message?"

"Your sister, Emily Rogers...."

"Yes, she's being kept locked up for something she didn't do. And?"

"And, we're beginning to believe that there was someone else involved and we need to eliminate you from our enquiries. Would you be willing to come down to the station tomorrow morning to give us your DNA and fingerprints? We'd also like to invite you to be a witness when we interview your sister later in the day. Would you oblige us?"

Brian could barely contain his excitement. Only minutes before he saw no way out, a dismal future. Now, here the police were finally admitting they made a mistake. "Of course, Officers, of course. What time? I can come now if you'd prefer...? Shall I meet you there? I'm working on the site, so I'll be there from seven...."

"Working on site?" The officers exchanged a strange glance.

"Yes. I'm working on the extension the hospital is having. I'm part of Owen's group of builders."

"I see. And the hospital knew you had a patient inside?"

Brian chewed his cheek and shook his head. "Of course not. That would be unethical, to have a family member so close, wouldn't it?"

The two police officers exchanged looks again and shrugged. "I guess it would, Mr Rogers, but for now that shouldn't concern us ... in any way, right?"

Brian held his gaze for a moment before lowering his own. "I understand, but you've nothing to fear from me. I merely go where the work goes and this was pure luck to be so near my sister."

"I don't believe in luck, Mr Rogers. We'll see you first thing for your DNA test around eight and then we'll all go on to the hospital for nine o' clock if that is suitable for you?"

"Eight it is. I'll let my boss know."

Brian followed them out and watched them walk to their car. His heart was beating so fast and his breath unsteady, but it felt good. There was cause to doubt, and perhaps that would be enough to get Emily released. He checked his change, put on his coat and headed for the nearest public phone box to call Jim, to let him know about the disruption at work, but also to ask if he knew of any good lawyers. Then he dialled the number John had given him and left a message on the answering machine. It felt good to be active and for the first time, he realised he didn't yearn for a drink.

*   *   *

I squealed as the salivating monster licked my chin again, and I clamped my hand over my mouth. I could hear men on horseback, just below where I'd crouched behind the rocks. The licking creature moved to my ear before rearing his head and howling. I was almost immediately surrounded by men with torches, and my terror at being found by Sagarus and his men diminished in an instant as Tristan pulled me from the rocks, picked me up, and held me tightly, his wolf licking my bare toes. I didn't care, I was safe and the tongue warm on my frozen feet.

A cloak was wrapped around me, and I huddled into it, as Tristan passed me to Brom as he climbed up onto his horse. I was handed back to him, and I snuggled in, his strong arms holding me tightly as we rode away. I heard a few comments spoken kindly and Tristan answered, but all of his attention was on me and I cried silently in relief. We rode at full gallop and I had to trust that Tristan kept a good hold of me as I had no energy left, and my frozen fingers refused to grip the horse's mane properly. Dawn was fast approaching, and I had no idea how close we were to Sagarus. Exhausted, I felt like I might melt through his fingers and dribble onto the dirt, but nothing would tempt me to tell Tristan of my discomfort. Nothing could hinder our escape. The very thought of being caught and taken back made me fight down bile, and so I concentrated on holding on.

Hours later on reaching the safety of our castle, Artorius stepped forward and helped me down, before he kissed my hand, smiling. He barked an order, and people around him moved quickly. I didn't give them much of my attention, cold and trembling from shock and fatigue. Someone brought him a warm blanket, which he wrapped around my shivering body. The cloak had helped a little, but my feet and hands were like ice.

Then things moved very quickly. Tristan insisted on picking me up and carried me to my chamber. It was very reminiscent of my first encounter with him as he laid me on the bed gently, Ayleth close behind him. "Oh, my dearest, my dearest, are you hurt?" Ayleth pushed him aside to inspect me, while people hurried behind her with hot water, clean clothes and food. I saw Artorius standing in the doorway and my attention was caught by the blood spatters on his face, his arms and clothes. I looked up at Tristan, who refused to move, and saw the same. Brom was pouring himself a large goblet of ale and I noticed he had a fresh cut to his forearm and a black eye forcing his eye closed. Rulf helped a maid carry in a large cauldron, and he was also covered in bruises and blood. No one had cleaned up from their own battle.

"What happened?" I was looking up at Tristan. "The battle? Beadu?"

Tristan bent down and patted my arm, kissed me on the forehead and with a sharp glance at Artorius, he left me in Ayleth's care. The other men swiftly followed, and we were left alone.

I turned to Ayleth who was pouring more water into the tub. "Well? What happened?"

She sighed loudly. "The same could be said for you? What happened? Where did you disappear to? Some are saying you are a traitor and went back to inform Sagarus...."

I scowled. "Are you asking me or telling me?"

She stared at me for a moment before breaking into a grin. "Telling, of course. They found the two men with their throats cut, and someone saw you thrown over the horse. You hadn't gone willingly, so that thought was quickly abandoned. Now get in and clean yourself off, you'll want to get rid of his stink, and then you can begin healing ..."

I peeled off what was left of my chemise and gratefully stepped into the warm water. My scrapes and cuts stung but I lathered up and scrubbed myself clean of that foul man. I guessed what Ayleth was suggesting but didn't feel able to voice what had happened until I'd stepped out, and was wrapped in a clean gown and sipping ale before the fire.

"I wasn't raped, Ayleth, though ... he did other things ..."

I heard the tell-tale release of breath as she had her back to me, and when she came to sit opposite with her own ale in hand, I saw her eyes were wet with tears. "I am glad of it, Emily. We did fear what we would find this morning."

"Does Tristan think I am defiled?"

Ayleth nodded. "He does, as do all the men, which is hardly surprising as they found you in a ripped chemise and not much else. Artorius blames himself, and Tristan blames him also. They knew where Sagarus had made his home. Scouts informed Artorius a few days ago,

211

and they talked of fighting their way in to clear it of mercenaries, but it is not Artorius' land, so he had no right to it, besides the threat of Sagarus himself. It's a good three hours' ride, but still too close to have that kind of man as a neighbour, ya ken?"

I nodded, but said nothing.

"There were words spoken in the hall last night when they returned to find you missing. Some voiced their own theories about you being a spy, but when they found the two men killed and followed the tracks, poor Tristan went mad with despair to find you before ... well, before you were defiled and murdered. He was willing to go to the castle and fight his way in to rescue you. It has been a long night for all of us."

"I suppose I should put them right. How did they find me?"

Ayleth shrugged. "Tristan can track anyone. Besides, you were more or less on the right road, which was lucky, as that terrain is difficult with boggy areas on the moors. His wolf helped, I think...."

Ayleth fell quiet for a moment. "I'd leave your questions and confessions for now. They'll be back soon. They have their own wounds to attend to and men to mourn." On seeing my incomprehension, she shrugged. "We lost Cedric, and Merek is in a bad way. I may not be able to help him."

"Oh no. How can I help?"

"You can help by resting, getting your strength back and telling Artorius everything you know."

We sat in silence for a while, sipping the warm ale and nibbling on bread and honey. We heard them long before they arrived at my door. Ayleth set about pouring cups of ale for Artorius and Tristan who I noticed kept his distance. No doubt respecting my pain of being raped repeatedly by men, and I loved them both more for that. I quickly put them at ease, and saw both heave a sigh of relief when I told them everything that had happened.

"Did you see any Picts?" Ayleth was translating for Artorius and she explained what 'Picts' were.

"No men with blue paint, just lots of men in various forms of armour."

"How many?"

"In the room I was tied up in, perhaps thirty, maybe more, but the castle was guarded, so in my opinion, at least a hundred men."

"Did you recognise any accents or languages that might tell us where they came from?"

"No, but I think I killed Sagarus." I went on to tell them about his attack and my escape, and how he hadn't been moving.

Artorius was impressed and wanted me to show him my moves and perhaps teach his men these killing moves. Tristan said nothing. I could see he was wound up tight and needed to hit something, or he'd crack. Artorius knew it too and spoke softly to his friend. Tristan remained sullen and detached.

"Did you see if there were any outer defences and guards?"

I shook my head. "No, it was too dark and I was unconscious when they brought me to Sagarus. Is it a castle?"

Artorius smiled. "Of course. It's on the coast but it was sacked many years ago and left in ruins. Seems Sagarus has made it hospitable again to anyone wishing to earn money to kill."

He abruptly stood, bowed and thanked me. Tristan went to follow him out, but abruptly stopped and turned to look at me. "You brave, Aemilia. I am ashamed."

I watched him leave and stared at the slammed door. After everything that I'd endured, this moment pissed me off more than the abduction. To have a man I love act with such self-pity because he hadn't protected me was laughable. I said as much to Ayleth.

"See it from his side. He goes out to a battle to keep you safe, to keep us all safe, and on his return, fighting for our lives, you've been abducted, your name questioned as to your loyalty. He then finds you have managed to escape a full castle of mercenaries and possibly killed the leader. The very man the men want to kill themselves. It's a big one for his pride to handle."

"I don't care about his damned pride! I can fight, so he either likes it or forgets it. I can't deal with his nonsense right now." I pushed myself out of the chair and flounced to the window. I was angry and upset, and fought back the hot tears.

I half listened as Ayleth put more wood on the fire and poured us both another drink. My stomach felt as if I might throw up, but I accepted the offered tankard regardless and sipped the brown contents.

"These are fighting men. Their whole aim in life is to fight better than anyone else to keep their women-folk and lands safe from marauding Vikings, Saxons and Picts. They have been bred to fight from a young age, and Tristan is good at it. It scared the hell out of me when I first saw them fight in battle. It's not like films. It's blood and gore and stench and screams and shit and piss, and it's right in the face. He isn't angry at you, but himself, and shame will play a big part in his feelings right now too, so go easy on him, eh?"

I sat down heavily, my body numb. I could have sat before the fire forever and just drifted away to a happy place. "Do you believe we were meant to come here, Ayleth?" My voice sounded drowsy and slurred.

"Yes, I think I do. Everything happens for a reason, reasons we don't understand, but maybe one day it'll make sense. Sometimes I can close my eyes and pretend this is all a dream, an illusion, and I am safely home with Melinda, growing old gracefully. I have contemplated that notion on many occasions. That all of this is not real. I am at home in a hospital bed and this is my brain's way of dealing with some head trauma and soon I will wake and find that I've been in a coma for years and Melinda will be so thrilled I am back and everything will be okay. I believe you and I were meant to meet and maybe we've met somewhere before and you're part of my psyche on some level."

"But I wasn't born in nineteen eighty-five, so how could I be?" My eyes were drooping and Ayleth's voice was becoming distant. She'd drugged me and I didn't care. Sleep was my new best friend.

"I know, Emily. So if this isn't real and it's all an illusion, where would I come into yours? So it must be real, and we just have to accept it...."

I didn't feel Ayleth take my half empty cup from my hand or cover me with the thick blanket and tuck my feet underneath. I was away with the faeries in wonderful, dreamless sleep.

CHAPTER 29

"She's doing wonderfully. Her progress is amazing. Emily is engaging with staff and her fellow patients and her therapy is producing some interesting finds."

"Yes, of course, but has she mentioned the night of the murder?"

Marian looked at the two detectives with disdain, but quickly hid her look by turning back to the bookshelf, where she'd been searching for a particular book when the police arrived. "I cannot discuss her therapy sessions with you."

"Yes, you can, Doctor Griffiths, and I'd like to know."

She heard the irritation in his voice and turned back to him, a smile plastered on her face. "Well, you'll need a court order for that, and I see you don't have one so...."

The detective stepped forward. "We've had complaints with regards to Emily Rogers' treatment here and we intend to investigate the allegations fully. Starting with you, Doctor Griffiths. We can talk here, or if you prefer at the station...?"

Marian stared at him coldly. "Emily is fine, and as far as I'm aware she is being treated with care and—"

"That's not what we hear, Doctor Griffiths," Detective Inspector Andrew Richards interrupted. "We hear your so-called 'therapy sessions' are messing with her head, emotionally and mentally. So much so that any conviction might be deemed inaccurate, and we can't have that now, can we? If Emily is guilty, we need a clear conviction."

"My treatment is perfectly safe. Hypnosis is not dangerous in any way."

"Yet, you seem to be having a lot of sessions with Emily, and long ones too according to witness statements. Why is that?"

"Emily takes a while to go under. It helps to have her relaxed, that's all." Marian walked back to her desk, the inspector's gaze making her feel uncomfortable. The inspector followed her and sat opposite, while his sergeant lingered nearby with his notebook.

"I see. And I would like to hear these sessions."

Marian blushed, and picked up a pen. "I'm afraid that's impossible."

"Without a warrant?"

"Well, you'd need one, but I haven't been recording her sessions. At least, I was, but the tape recorder went funny and nothing recorded...."

Though feeble, it was all Marian could think of at the time. Inspector Richards took a deep breath, glanced across at his colleague, who was writing everything down. "I see. This happens all the time with these tape recording gadgets. I'll take it with me and all the tapes you thought were recording. We'll see if one of our clever people can fix them for you."

"I threw them away." She was sweating, and he knew it.

"I see. Shame that, and may I say, not very professional. I'll be in touch with the warrant to read through Emily's notes, but first I'll have a word with Emily Rogers herself."

"What? You can't." Marian jumped up from the desk. "She's resting.... She needs to rest and police make her feel uneasy and scared."

Inspector Richards smiled calmly. "Not a problem, Doctor Griffiths, we'll be very nice and calm with Emily. We also have one of her family to sit in with her. You're welcome too, of course."

"I have another patient. You should have informed me of this sooner."

"Things come up that need investigating without hesitation. We'll be in touch. Thank you."

Unable to think of anything to say that would stop them, she watched the two policemen leave with a sunken feeling of dread in her stomach. She'd barely slept, and had woken feeling awful and dazed. She hadn't handled that well and now they'd speak with Emily about her treatment, and it would most likely be investigated and stopped. She sat down heavily and raked a hand through her hair. She felt dishevelled and very tired, and definitely in no fit state to deal with her first patient in half an hour.

She went back to the bookshelf and searched for the book she'd thought of last night, and what had kept her head too busy to sleep. She'd finally managed to get hold of her historian friend, who'd reminded her of a book she'd borrowed from him regarding 'Artorius' and other possibilities of King Arthur.

"I'm not convinced he was King Arthur," Jason had said, "but there are a few historians who are. They even made a film about it based loosely on some new evidence. It was pretty good. Of course, it's a difficult one to prove with so little facts. I'll have the book back when you've finished. Fascinating to have a client who believes she's met him. Don't suppose I could meet her?"

Marian immediately put him straight and promised to return the book this time. The small book was hidden between bigger books on the shelf. She even promised to look for the film 'King Arthur'. It was a possibility that Emily had also seen this film and created her own illusion from those characters.

Sometime during the night, it occurred to her that perhaps there was mention of a wise woman, or a strange woman, in his time. Perhaps somewhere in those pages there might be some mention of Emily, or this Ayleth woman, in letters or descriptions. If she could find proof of sorts that all of this was made up in her head from different aspects of her life, then it might help Emily's mental state and clarify her innocence or guilt. However, she couldn't deny that finding a snippet of information that linked Emily to this time, would be amazing. A worm-hole or time slip would be incredible, and might just help her career even more, to find evidence of such a possibility. She flicked through the pages but nothing jumped out. Deflated, she returned it to the bookshelf.

*   *   *

I looked around the small library and squinted as the late morning sun blinded me for a second. The two burly men sat behind one of the tables that littered the room. An orderly stood behind the door and remained unmoving as one of the men indicated the chair opposite them. I sat down and rubbed my eyes against the glare, until the bigger of the two men abruptly stood and pulled the blind part way down to block out the sun. With it went the warmth and I shuddered at the sudden temperature drop.

"Miss Rogers, do you remember me?" He had a slight Welsh accent and I could very easily picture him playing rugby.

I stared at him as I rummaged around my memory trying to recall his name. I recognised his face, but from where eluded me. I knew I was becoming more and more confused as I slipped between worlds. Time and faces seemed to have the same look about them, as if I was seeing them in both times. Perhaps this was proof of past lives?

"Er ... yes, possible...?"

"I'm Inspector Richards from CID, and this is my sergeant Mathews. We're investigating the murder of Mr Paul Dawson, the security guard."

"I see, and how's that going for you?" I stared back at him challenging, waiting for him to continue.

He held my gaze before looking at his sergeant, who was rummaging through photographs. "I'd like your help with these photographs, if you can?" Without waiting for any response, he quickly dealt them out onto the table. I didn't look down at them straight away, but watched him. "Would you tell me if you recognise anything?"

I looked then and sighed loudly. I'd seen these before when I was first charged with the murder. Although on closer inspection some had been blown up. The ones taken of the sword handle and blade were at least twice the size of the others and clearly showed various prints left behind by the dust they'd used.

"We know they are your prints on the handle and on the blade, but you've never disputed that, have you?" He already knew I'd said nothing. I had not denied, or confirmed, that they were my prints, there'd been no need, the evidence irrefutable; and he slowly shook his head. I remembered swinging that sword, the weight of it. The sharpness of the blade had terrified me, and yet, I'd held such power in my hands. Now, sitting here humbly made me sick, but what else could I do? I wanted out, away from this place; and anywhere would do, be it in my mind, body or soul.

"Look, I'm trying to help you get out of here, Emily, but I can't do that without you talking to me. I know you talk with Doctor Griffiths, and we've heard of your treatment with her."

I slowly raised my gaze to meet his own. I could see in his eyes how much this murder was affecting him, and it was no doubt due to the pressure from higher up. They wanted this case sorted and forgotten. His family wanted justice and I could understand and empathise with that, but what could I say? If I spoke the truth, I'd be locked up forever. If I lied, I'd be locked up forever in another jail. It was a no-win situation whatever I did. I said nothing.

"Your brother is making demands for your release. He says you are being mistreated here. Is that true?"

"Is it? Who cares what happens to me so long as you convict someone"

"I care, you stupid bitch, now answer the man!"

I spun round and noticed Brian hovering in the shadows on the far side of the library. We stared at each other, but it was me who finally broke the look, and I turned my back on him. Seeing him and hearing the intensity in his voice, confused me, but I managed to calm my face, and look unemotional. I merely shrugged and sat back in the chair.

Inspector Richards leaned closer and tapped one of the blown up images of the handle. "It's not just your prints on this old sword, is it,

Emily? Whose is the other? And where did you get the sword from? Apparently it's very old and in such perfect condition, it is winding up historians across the country. Can I tell them anything?"

A smile escaped and I quickly pulled it back, but he saw. "It amuses you, does it? It doesn't amuse Paul Dawson's family. They are suffering. They need this to end, Emily, as do you, I think. Do you want to know what I think? I'll tell you. I think you are covering for someone who murdered Mr Dawson in cold blood. Slicing his head clean off and then leaving you alone to pay for his crime. This person left you to rot in this place ... alone. It's been nearly three months, Emily, surely it's time to tell us who this other person is?"

I stared hard at the large thumb print, seen clear as day next to mine on the sword handle. I saw again those dreadful moments when I panicked on seeing the man loom up out of the darkness, and the confusion, as had he. The security guard died within seconds. Too late to make amends, to turn back time and put it right. The deed was done and I would pay for it. I said nothing.

At last the orderly physically pulled me up by my arm, much to the displeasure of Brian, who made a move to stop him, but was held back by the sergeant. He escorted me out of the room and back into the patient lounge where he released me with a smirk. I saw the two policemen walk past with Brian firmly between them. We made eye contact again and I felt a stab of pain at seeing his discomfort at my incarceration. He did care, but I didn't know how to feel about that right now. I watched them till they disappeared through the security doors and I sat down with a loud sigh of relief. Nothing had been mentioned with regard to my hypnosis sessions so there was still a chance of them continuing, and for now my life would be made bearable again, given a way to escape this nightmare.

John watched the police leave with Brian. From their demeanour he guessed that Emily hadn't given them anything to work with. He felt a small stab of guilt for them. They were trying to finish this enquiry for the sake of the family, and he really wanted to help them, but his own agenda was too close in the finish to ruin it now with sympathy.

He helped an elderly inmate get out of his chair, and abruptly jumped back when he began to piss in a wild manner. Some got on his shoes and he hissed with disgust, letting go of Wilfred to step farther back from the spray. Wilfred laughed and moved his body as if he was marking his territory. When he finished pissing, he squatted down and began shitting himself. Horrified, John watched, moving farther away as the stench hit him. A couple of other inmates nearby began retching and he quickly moved them outside towards the bathrooms, in case they vomited. He was thankful that two nurses came rushing over to see what was happening.

"You can clean this up, John, we'll deal with Wilfred." The older woman held a hankie over her nose, while the other one held her nose tightly. Between the two of them, they slowly walked Wilfred towards the bathrooms and the showers.

John watched them go, looked down at the mess and walked away to find a bucket and mop. Surely the investigation wasn't worth this? He almost had everything he needed. Some of the other orderlies and a few nurses had spoken freely about what they'd witnessed over the years. A lot of their comments centred on Doctor Griffiths and her methods. If he could only get into her office and her computer; but there was never a chance.

He felt eyes watching him, turned and caught Emily. She was watching him with a strange look on her face, but when she realised he'd caught her, she abruptly turned away and he wondered if he'd actually seen it. She'd looked interested, suspicious, and he wondered if her brother had said something to her.

*   *   *

Like many of the other inmates, I quickly left the lounge area in search of fresher air. I was prohibited from going to the outside yard but there was a small garden that was open to the elements, though windows on every side meant it had no privacy, but convicts couldn't expect that, could we?

On arriving, I found one other person sitting on one of two benches, playing with himself, but on seeing me, he abruptly removed his hand and ran away. I noticed movement behind one of the net curtains that covered each window and figured they had been keeping an eye on Jim, who always had his hand down his pants.

I waved brazenly to each window and gave the finger to another. I got no response. I walked among the few small trees in the square shaped garden and let my fingers gently touch the bushes as I passed. They were nothing special, all of varying greens, and the few trees were silver birch. Two bird houses had been placed high up on the trees, but I'd not heard any bird song since being incarcerated here.

I saw movement behind the curtains and sighed heavily. I was allowed to be outside, but never alone. I always had company one way or another and it vexed me greatly. At home, I'd enjoyed my solitude. Not that I had no friends to speak of, though none had ventured to this place to see me. I guessed being away for so long, and my reappearance beginning this murder enquiry, was not something any of them wished to be involved in.

It stung a little that not one of the girls I'd worked with over the years in all of my jobs, considered me worthy of a visit. Not even a letter or card. I couldn't blame them, yet it hurt anyway. The jobs had been brief, yet I'd thought I'd made some impression on many of my fellow workers. Obviously not enough.

I heard Jane's high-pitched laugh, followed by her sing-song words and I smiled to myself. Strange how those inflicted with some mental disease could be so much more gracious and friendly towards their fellow man than those who considered themselves sane. Even Jim, who could always be found masturbating in some quiet corner somewhere, was not offensive in his manner. It wasn't particularly pleasant to find him cupping his balls or working on his shaft, yet he wasn't vulgar. Although a lewd act, he was merely trying to find his comfort, as innocent babies did every day and, as far as I knew, he never ejaculated.

I held my breath, waiting to see if Jane would join me, but she skipped past on some other mission and I released the breath. The sun was on the other side of the building now and most of the garden in shade and I hugged myself for warmth. Out here it was fairly easy, if left alone, to shut out the almost constant noise of the hospital, pretend I was free in some National Trust garden. I clung to that hope that I would be free again. But free to do what?

I abruptly stood and wandered again, feeling unable to remain still. What would I do if, no, when they found me innocent? How could I return to a life so dull and monotonous when I had truly lived in his world? I had endured every emotion, felt them at such a pace, that life in comparison felt incomplete and robotic. Television dulled the brain, yet film and drama tantalized enough to aid the watcher into feeling something close to emotion, though it couldn't be real. I had lived and breathed 'real'. I had smelt and tasted and heard real and this lifeless existence was all I had to look forward to now.

I glanced up and caught one of the nurses watching me. I stared hard back at her to see what reaction I'd get. Nothing. She merely stared back, raised an eyebrow in a limited interest type of way, and was gone. I was forgotten, dismissed, for more important matters, and I hated her for it. I considered making a scene just to feel something. Anything. But remembered the mind-numbing contents of the needle and sat down heavily on the bench.

Whilst sitting there I even considered the concept of telling the police that I murdered the man, see how exciting jail could be. Fighting with a jail full of naughty women, and fighting off big ton Bertha who wanted to make me her bitch might be more exciting than sitting around here. Perhaps reinvent myself into a hard woman who could get you whatever you need. I laughed out loud at that and caught the attention of Doctor Hill.

"Are you okay, Emily?" Without waiting for my response, he came in and stood before me. "It's nice out here, but don't catch a chill. I believe Doctor Griffiths is looking for you...." He watched me take in the information, then in a quieter tone, he continued, "Of course, you don't have to see her if you don't want to. How is your therapy going?"

She wanted me to continue the hypnosis sessions and I knew why, and my heart ached with the notion. I had another chance to see him, to return and feel again. I shocked Doctor Hill as I abruptly stood up and he took a few steps back, bringing his files up to his chest, as if to protect himself.

"Thanks, Doc. I'm fine, it's going well. I'll go and find her now."

I left before he could ask me any more stupid questions. I'd thought with the police becoming involved my therapy it might have been suspended, but Marian obviously had more clout than I'd expected. Considering I'd feared these sessions in the beginning, I was hooked. It brought back a variety of emotions, but more importantly, it brought Tristan back, and for that, I was eternally grateful.

CHAPTER 30

I dreamt of sinister figures that watched me from the shadows and, although I ran, they were always just behind me or next to me. I couldn't escape. My chamber remained dark when I abruptly pushed my body forward in a half-asleep state and fell onto one knee, crying out in pain and shock. The fire had burned down to embers, leaving the room chilly. I quickly huddled back underneath the woollen blanket. Although my backside was numb from falling asleep on the chair, I was reluctant to move into the cold bed. My head felt heavy and I cursed Ayleth for doping me. I tentatively reached for a nearby cup and gratefully found a full tankard of spring water. I drank it all down and felt more refreshed and awake.

My need to use the stinking pit became obvious and I reluctantly relinquished the blanket. Afterwards, I hurried back to the dying fire, and tucked the blanket tightly around me, all the way up to my chin. I was contemplating building up the fire when I realised I wasn't alone. How long he'd been sitting in the dark corner, I didn't know, or care at that moment. But I knew someone was in the room and peered anxiously into the farthest, darkest corner, noticing the boots. My stomach flipped over in fear until I heard the soft tell-tale growl of a wolf, and Tristan slowly stood and walked towards me.

I wasn't sure how to behave with him after his earlier behaviour, so I remained impassive.

"My Lady Emily ..." He gave a slight bow, and although my body was melting quickly, I tried to keep my reserve and not show my feelings.

"Tristan." I didn't move.

Neither did he. He stopped a few feet away and leaned against the large table, and the silence crept on. I broke first. "What are you doing here. Beo. Bedroom." I groped for the right word and wondered if I'd said it right, as he merely looked at me. His gaze gave nothing away of what he was thinking and I began to feel uncomfortable under his silent scrutiny. "Well, fuck off then! Faeca! Afierren!" I had no idea if I was saying the right way of telling him to 'go away'. Probably not, judging from the quick raised eyebrow, and smirk he abruptly hid by lowering his face before resuming his stare. I was getting really angry at his behaviour now. "Well? Go away! I don't want to see you. Go on! Fuck off, damn it!"

His wolf gave another low growl, but I ignored it and threw the blanket on the floor. My anger gave me heat and I flounced towards the door and yanked it open intending to leave him to his brooding, but he reached the door in four strides and, with one push slammed it shut. I stepped back, shocked by the sudden movement.

He stared down at me with a look I couldn't comprehend, and didn't have time to act upon when he forcibly pulled me to him and kissed me passionately and completely. I pulled away for air and raised my hand and slapped him hard across the face. It merely lit the match and, with one hand behind my head, he again forced his lips onto mine and held my head, pushing my face into his, bruising my lips and crushing my breasts against him. I could feel his excitement and I answered him with my own. My hands moved from his chest to grasp his backside and I pulled him towards me. It was all the encouragement he needed.

In one movement, he had me in his arms and threw me onto the bed. He lay on top of me and kissed me again. His tongue moving delicately to meet mine, yet his passion was aroused completely and I knew it took every effort not to ravish me too quickly. I was having my own issues with self-control. I wanted to tear him from neck to hip, but I couldn't explain why I wanted to hurt him so badly, only that I did.

I felt his change of position as one hand moved downwards to the hem of my dress and he yanked it upwards. The fresh air hitting my nether region startled me, as one pair of knickers had been ruined by Sagarus. Within seconds I was naked beneath him and he grunted with satisfaction as his gaze moved downwards. His tongue followed his interest and my breath caught in my throat as he buried his head between my legs.

It didn't take long for me to cry out in pleasure, and he came up for air with a look of satisfaction. I could have punched him, but he immediately dipped his head again and kissed my belly, my breasts, my neck, my ears until finally he kissed my mouth and I began yanking off his clothes. He wasn't wearing much, a tunic and his trousers. His boots hindered us for a few impatient seconds, but finally we were naked together. He pushed me backwards and he entered me without any forewarning. I felt him go all the way and gasped with the sensation. He looked down at me with no apology and I encouraged him to keep going. This was not love, this was passion and possession. I was his and someone had hurt me. He felt responsible and was reclaiming his own.

Minutes later we were both gasping for breath, lying on our backs. Our eyes met and he smiled lazily as he rolled towards me and started stroking my thigh. I grinned back. I felt completely spent, what with the recent events and now this, but Tristan wasn't done. He pulled me to him, and kissed me gently this time while pulling the covers over us to cocoon us. I felt snug and languid in his arms and was surprised when his kisses became ardent again and his hands began wandering my body once more. He was reclaiming his woman and I wanted him too.

A part of me felt too sensitive and tired, but a small voice was crying out for more. I had little choice anyway as Tristan was not taking 'no' for an answer. He bent his head to my breasts as his fingers moved downwards, pushing my legs open. I was slippery with his seed and my own excitement and without any preamble he abruptly flicked me over and mounted me from behind. I gasped and tried to pull away but he held me tightly against him, moving slowly, pushing himself all the way inside. I cried out but he kept going, and I couldn't fight him. I didn't want to anymore.

Tristan lay for quite a while afterwards, keeping me warm with his own hot body. I felt as languid as water. I didn't have any energy left in me and felt totally spent. Eventually though, he gently removed himself from me and covered me with a blanket while he dressed slowly, all the while watching me. He winced as the scratches on his back pulled with the movement and I grinned maliciously, and received a knowing look in return. He stood and stretched and went to the table to see what he could find. Pouring the last of the ale in a tankard, he brought back the plate of half a loaf and cheese and placed them on the bed beside me. "Eat."

He offered me a drink of the ale first which I took gratefully and drank half of it before handing it back. He finished it and took it back to the table. He then built up the fire, and once satisfied with it, he came back to the bed and sat cross-legged opposite me. We shared the meagre meal in silence, and though I watched him through lowered gaze, he watched me openly. I had covered my body with the blanket, but his gaze made me feel completely naked again and I found myself blushing.

I had so much I wanted to talk to him about. To share my feelings about the abduction, and to let him know he wasn't to blame, although in truth, I had no idea how he really felt about that. Ayleth had mentioned heated words between him and Artorius, but about what exactly, she hadn't said. He stood up and wandered to the window, looked out and grabbed his trousers and sword belt, putting them on. In that moment, I felt like a whore, used and discarded, and I wanted to scream at him, but the words would have been pointless. He suddenly smiled. "Sleep, Emily. I go. Find Artorius. Keep women safe. My woman." He bent and kissed my lips very gently before giving a low whistle and his wolf emerged from the shadows, where it had kept watch on its master. I snuggled back under the covers, and with a smile on my face, drifted off to sleep.

*   *   *

John remained absolutely still. He barely dared to breathe in case Doctor Griffiths saw the movement. He desperately needed to piss and his legs felt wobbly, but he remained standing and tried to ignore everything except what he was hearing. Emily's voice was clear, though she spoke in a low voice, she was obviously reading some saucy book, or something, but the way she spoke it was like she was reading her diary.

She kept saying, 'I' and 'we' as though she was dictating her own life, and if so, then that girl wasn't shy.

He listened carefully. Who the hell was Tristan and Artorius? That last name rang bells, but he couldn't put a finger on it. She was talking now about a fight and an army of Saxons and mercenaries, and the castle preparing for the siege. Had the girl gone mad? What the hell did any of that have to do with the murder of the security guard?

Now he heard Marian's voice calmly ask questions about the time and dress of the people. Where was the castle? Emily's voice replied and he heard what sounded like a book's pages being turned. Doctor Griffiths exclaimed and then seemed to change her voice, though he detected an excitement in her tone as she counted back from ten, quickly coughed and apologised to Emily.

"Emily, sorry about that, a frog in my throat. We were talking about your treatment and how you think it is going?" He heard Doctor Griffiths return to her chair as it creaked under her weight.

"I ... I think it's going okay ..." Emily sounded unsure, dopy, as if she'd just woken up. "You tell me, Marian. Is it?"

"I think we're getting somewhere, yes, however, we need to get further along than we are, otherwise we might have to stop the sessions if the hospital deems them pointless...."

"Oh, I don't think they're pointless, do you?"

He heard the tone in her voice, and wondered how she could talk like that to a Doctor and get away with it. It had an underlying threat to it, but Marian merely laughed. "I agree, Emily, totally agree. So let's continue our sessions and let's get to where we need to be as soon as possible."

He heard Emily rise as the leather couch squeaked. "We? Don't you mean where 'I' need to be? I presume you still want me to remember that night with the guard?"

"Of course. Of course. It is very important to everyone concerned, you know that, Emily. Unless there's something you remember now?"

He heard silence that seemed to stretch far longer than would be deemed comfortable and wished he could see through the curtain. Eventually he heard Marian shout, "Damien?"

He heard the door open and presumed Damien, the night shift orderly, was there, as Marian bid Emily farewell and getting no reply the door was firmly shut. He listened as Marian sighed loudly and poured herself something, drinking it and slamming the glass on the desk. "Damn the bitch! She's playing with me. We need to get to the fucking point but this is such good stuff."

He heard Marian clicking her digital recorder and then Emily's voice filled the office again, but Marian didn't listen to it all before he heard her tidying away. She put on her coat and left the office. He waited for a few minutes before cautiously moving out of his hiding place. The window was deep and the curtains were full length. Thankfully, as it was dark, they had already been drawn otherwise he'd have had nowhere to hide. As it was, it was pure luck she hadn't come to the window.

He quickly glanced around the office and went to her desk. He'd been snooping around, having been told of the skeleton key kept in Matron's office by one of the other orderlies. He'd found a lame excuse, got the keys, and prayed they would fit all the locks. They had, and Doctor Griffiths' office was finally available, but within minutes of his entrance, he'd heard voices, locked the door from the inside and hid.

Now he searched her desk. One drawer was locked and there was no sign of the recorder, so he presumed it was either in the drawer or she'd taken it with her. He saw a few scribblings on a notepad and he rubbed over them to reveal odd words and dates. He realised they'd been dates that Emily had said, so he took that paper with him. Next to this lay two books titled 'Castles of Historical Britain' and 'The True King Arthur'. A quick flick through told him nothing, no pages turned over or book markers but he was convinced that something in one of these books had got Marian excited. He made a note of the title and publisher to find another copy in a library.

He moved to the large book shelf and scanned through the books that lined the shelves. It revealed a few books on history among the psychology. He'd not expected that and suddenly remembered where he'd heard the name 'Artorius'. A film had been produced a few years ago using that theory. A pretty good one, if he remembered. He'd have to watch it again. But why did Emily talk about him as if she knew him? Nothing he'd heard in the last hour or so made any sense, and nothing had anything to do with the murdered security guard, so what the hell was Doctor Griffiths doing? With Emily talking about her sexual encounters with some guy, he couldn't see how anything tied into the murder case. It all felt very odd.

Walking swiftly to the door, he listened before using the key to open it a fraction of an inch. The coast was clear and he let himself out. Locking the door behind him, he walked quickly towards his car in the car park. He needed to get back to his office and look at all of the evidence so far, because as it stood now, he had no idea what the hell was going on.

CHAPTER 31

Brian stepped back from his work and nodded to himself. The wall looked fine and, as always, he felt a small sense of achievement when he finished building something. He felt a familiar slap on his shoulder and turned to see Jim smiling at him.

"Yeah, it looks good. Now I need you to help with the opposite wall. Larry is off sick, so they're one man down and I want that section finished by today."

Brian turned to look at what Jim meant, and saw the men were flagging behind, but mostly because they were busy talking and laughing—most likely about one pair of tits or another. He hated that. "I'm just going for a quick piss and I'll get onto it."

Jim frowned. "Okay, but don't take the hour-long piss you took the other day, eh? These men aren't part of our team. Fucking contractors brought them in to speed up the building work, but they just take longer so they get paid longer. Me and my men have to finish the job before we get paid our full wage. It's a hard business these days and I need my best man on it, okay?"

Brian grinned, feeling a sense of pride and humility as he walked towards the portaloo. The hour had, in fact, been closer to two hours as he'd perused the hospital site, made some calls, and met with John the orderly who'd informed him that he was going to attempt to get into Doctor Griffiths' office. Now he telephoned John's mobile but got the answer message. He didn't leave one and went for the genuine piss he needed.

Refreshed, he lit a cigarette and observed the other workmen, who were now showing each other their mobiles and laughing, but one of them caught him looking and warned the other two. He merely stared back and the younger man looked away and got back to work. He couldn't stand these young builders, who fit the typical stereotype of a builder. They whistled at passing girls, found pictures of vaginas and tits amusing, and shagged anything that opened their legs to them ... or so they said.

He cringed, remembering himself being like that. He'd let Emily down badly since their parents' murder, and he doubted anything he did would save their relationship. Not that he blamed her in any way, but maybe getting her out of this hell would compensate part of the way.

Throwing his cigarette butt on the floor, he swigged water and walked back to the site. The work so far was okay, though the pointing was below his standard and he said as much, which annoyed the lads. He didn't care. He picked up his own trowel and began working on the half-finished wall, knowing that he was being watched. After a while, he sensed the attitude change as they saw how he was doing it, and the three lads openly asked him questions on his skills.

By the end of the day, all the walls had been finished and everyone was heading for the pub. Brian remained behind. He couldn't see the back part of the hospital from where he stood, but he stared up at the top floor anyway. He needed this quiet time when everyone had gone to try and organise his brain, as thoughts and memories scattered so fast he could barely make sense of them while he worked. Emily had been on his mind more so today than usual, something about her that kept coming back that troubled him. Seeing her like a zombie had scared him, but there had been something else in her eyes, and the more he considered it, the more he was sure that he must be wrong. Brian would swear that she'd looked 'happy' and that couldn't possibly be right, not in a place like that.

*   *   *

The men rushed around, while the women fretted and made themselves useful preparing oil, hot water, bandages, salves and collected barrels of alcohol from the cellars, and Ayleth's herbs were brought from her cave to her makeshift hospital next to the bakery, where it was warmer than most other rooms in the castle. The smell of fresh bread wafted around the room while we hitched our skirts and moved pallets in lines for any wounded that would come in. It all felt very surreal as my stomach lurched, alternating between hunger from the smells, and terror from the sounds of a large army marching towards us.

I had been stirred from my slumber by one of the servants, who shook me awake, a look of panic on her face, shouting something at me which I translated as 'get up, get up' and then I heard the word I recognised, "Saxon."

I shot out of bed, washed quickly and dressed. I could still smell and feel Tristan on me, but there was no time to enjoy the memories as I headed down to the courtyard. It was bedlam as people ran in all directions preparing for the attack. I saw Ayleth and ran to her, and together we prepared the hospital. Now it was ready, I found myself twiddling my thumbs and allowing the fear to wrap itself around me. Ayleth caught sight of me and came over. "Here, take this. I pray you'll not need it, but the alternative is too vulgar to contemplate."

I looked down and saw the bottle of foxglove. "I ... I can't. What about you?"

Ayleth smiled. "I have my own method, and besides, I'm an old woman, I doubt I'd be on their list of rapes, most likely a sword in my gut."

She pushed the small bottle into my hand and I thrust it into my skirt pocket. Feeling the small, hard bottle bouncing beside my thigh made me feel strange. I had death on me. A means to leave this life in a fairly pain-free method rather than the awful alternative, and it felt empowering whilst at the same time terrified me. My time as Sagarus' victim in his castle had shown me a mere taste of what hell awaited any of us women, and what kind of man he was, or had been, if I'd actually killed him. He'd sent men to their deaths just to keep our men busy, so that I might be snatched from the castle. He cared little for human life, and men like that were marching again on our castle.

My old life seemed so very far away, and this bottle proved that. How many people in the twenty-first century considered carrying around poison just in case of gang rape? Then again, who lived this terror-driven life as death stalked the land? Our ancestors had, and now I was living their nightmare too. My old sedate life was nothing compared to this feeling. Death was everywhere, so these people truly lived and loved every moment—and I finally got it, and craved life so that I might enjoy it with Tristan.

"Where's Artorius and his men?"

"They rode out a few minutes ago to see if they could even the odds a little. I believe Tristan went out with his wolf and a large quiver of arrows. He, Brom and Merek are the best archers I've ever seen." Mentioning Merek's name made us both feel sad, as he'd slipped into a coma, or at least, that was Ayleth's diagnosis. "You did all that you could, Ayleth, it's up to him now."

She smiled gratefully and touched my hand, knowing of whom I spoke. "I know, but it's annoying to be so useless in his care. Besides the lump on his head, he had barely a scratch on him. His skills with the bow would be useful right now."

I agreed, but there was nothing more to say or do for Merek. If the Saxons got into the castle, he'd be killed outright in his sleep. If left alone, he might recover, but without extensive medical experience, we had no idea what the problem was. We guessed and that was the best we could do.

"Maybe I should sit with him in case they get in … I feel I owe him something."

Ayleth nodded and tried to smile as reassuringly as possible, but it didn't fool me and instead she hugged. "That will be very nice of you, Emily. I will call you if we need you in the hospital."

For a moment, we clung to each other before reluctantly parting. Ayleth watched me go towards Merek's chamber before suddenly running after me. She handed me something long and cold. "Just in case. Don't let him die by an enemy's hand."

I stared after her, knowing what she had given me and unsure if I wanted it, before I looked down at the dagger she'd placed in my hand. I felt like my head was going to explode. I felt so many emotions at that moment that I couldn't decide which one was the most dominant. Could I use this murder weapon on myself? Or on Merek? I'd killed a man before using his own, but that had been self-defence. And the man on the moors had not been intentional either, but necessary. Maybe one mad, axe-wielding man was much like another, be it Saxon, Pict or English. I shoved the dagger inside my pocket with the poison and walked quickly to Merek's chamber near the stables. I'd just have to deal with it, if and when the time came.

I reached his door and saw it was ajar. Pushing it gently, I peered into the gloom. Three candles were lit near the narrow bed and they illuminated Merek's face. He had a bruise that ran down the side of his left temple and his cheek. I could see a small cut just behind his left ear, but otherwise he looked fine. Ayleth had removed the bandages at some point last night, as she believed air helped wounds heal better than being bound up. She was probably right, but this wasn't the hygienic twentieth century, and I had no idea what lurked in the air. I could see no seeping, so presumed the bleeding had subsided.

A small bowl and cloth lay beside the bed, as did a small wooden cross, a bunch of various herbs, a goblet of spring water, and an unusual wooden carving. I picked it up and moved towards the candles to get a better look, and saw it appeared to be a large woman with huge breasts. I thought, perhaps a weird porn doll? Well, each man to his own and set it down where I'd found it.

I sniffed the goblet and thought it smelled fresh so had a small drink. I picked up the cross and moved my fingers over the smooth edges as I gazed out of the small window. It was peaceful in here. Chaos reigned outside, but in here, I could easily believe nothing was going to happen. That thought didn't last long and I began to feel restless. I paced the small, square room. I noted the rushes on the stone floor, the chest in the corner, the narrow table opposite, and the bow leaning against the stone wall. I'd tried archery once and I hadn't sucked. Maybe I might get lucky and hit something, but could I hit someone? After a moment's hesitation, I decided I could. If I could kill with a dagger and my bare hands and feet, then killing with a bow and arrow should be a doddle.

I caught myself then. Surely killing someone could never be a doddle? Was my attitude to human life really changing so quickly, and so ruthlessly? Yes, I decided. Here in this time, it was kill or be killed, or in a woman's case, kill or be raped repeatedly and killed. That had been my possible future if I hadn't killed Sagarus and I felt no remorse for it either. Though, I had to admit to myself, I hadn't checked him before leaving. The very thought of him being alive and of his crude act on me made me nauseous, and I drank a little more water.

I heard a shout, followed by another and knew it was starting. I had no idea how big this Saxon army was, but figured we were outnumbered by a large amount. I reached into my pocket and pulled out the dagger and the bottle and placed both on the bed next to Merek. "You can trust me, Merek. I won't let you down. I promise no Saxon will harm you." My voice shook as I spoke, but I lifted my chin, took a long deep breath and stared at the door and waited.

Tristan and Brom were grinning as they ran back to the main group of men. They'd used all of their arrows, and had even managed to get close enough to use those arrows again by pulling them out of the Saxon scum. Brom's sword was bloody from killing six men, as was Tristan's dagger, as he'd cut four men's throats and stabbed one in the eye. His wolf had finished off three, so all in all, it had been worthwhile sneaking to the side of the so called army and causing a little chaos.

Rulf had set up a few traps between them and the enemy, and as they reached the group, they heard the screams of dying men as the traps claimed their legs. Artorius had already used oil to draw a line halfway across the field, so if they should reach that point, someone would light it and hopefully burn half the army.

One of their scouts had finally returned bloodied and shaking as he'd been ambushed on his return. Some of the Saxons had quietly moved to flank them, killing two of the scouts, but Algar had escaped, though a nasty gash down his arm would need stitches. "There are four hundred or so men. Mostly mercenaries, with a small band of Saxon in the centre. Sagarus leads them."

Artorius frowned. "Sagarus? She said she'd killed him?"

Tristan overheard the exchange and shrugged. "My lady was not sure, though she said Sagarus did not move, she was not waiting to see if it were so or not."

"As it should be. No woman should be a victim of this madman. The lady Aemilia is most capable, though killing a man like Sagarus will take more than the gifts the lady possesses, I fear. He is a giant of a man and his evil runs deep. He sacrificed a lot of men to keep us occupied just to snatch the Lady Aemilia away. He failed in his humiliation of her, and has only succeeded in humiliating himself. This battle is to save whatever honour he has left."

Brom shivered. "I have heard tales of him. That his gods bring him back to life, and he sacrifices children to appease them and grant him immortality. Your lady Aemilia was lucky to have escaped."

Artorius gripped his sword. "Immortal or not I shall enjoy cutting his head off and burning his body. The lady may have feared checking, but I do not. It finishes here, we make a stand or this Saxon scum will ruin our women and enslave our children. I for one will not let that happen. Are you with me?"

The roar of his men was like a tidal wave of sound. There may be only two hundred, but it was two hundred of the best fighters and bowmen he had ever known. They knew every trick to whittle down the enemy numbers and, so far between them they had killed over fifty. The enemy were about a quarter of a mile away. He could see them. Most were on foot while perhaps a hundred were on horseback. They would be the main problem but if they charged, the oil would be lit just at the right time and, with God's help, they would be burned alive and a barrier placed between the footmen and his men. They also had the castle to their back giving archers a better reach from the castle walls. They could kill footmen at the back of the ranks and possibly create panic among the Saxons. Never had he thanked the wisdom of Ayleth so much as now. It was she who had urged him to train the women of the village and castle. Now, they had an extra fifty archers to help secure Sagarus' downfall. He had forty men on horses to mow them down if all went to plan. He looked out at the sea of Saxons, raised his arm and let the arrows fly.

CHAPTER 32

John stared hard at his editor. "Are you serious? I have all of this fucking evidence of mistreatment of patients and funding and you want more? What about the tapes? The photographs? What the hell do you want? A video of something taking place perhaps...?"

Michael smiled unfazed by John's outburst. "Actually, that wouldn't be bad. I wouldn't show the patient's face of course, and it would be absolute proof. As it stands, all of this could easily be pushed aside, hidden away. It's not absolute enough for me to go public, John."

John reached over and pushed the two photographs of a patient's bruises taken yesterday. It clearly showed one on her shoulder and another on her upper arm where one of the orderlies had grabbed her hard and pulled her along the corridor to her room. "What about that? I saw it happen and took those pictures myself."

"Yeah, and they'd say she did it to herself, or that you did it to make a point or something."

"What about the conversations I taped of the nurses?"

Michael sighed. "They don't mention anyone in particular, only generally. Okay, it might get a little attention, but nothing major. We need hard evidence of either a video of a patient being abused, or something else that leaves nothing to chance."

John leaned back in his chair and rubbed his hands over his face. He was exhausted and absolutely sick of being at the hospital. He'd thought he'd got enough, but now he had to admit, he hadn't. "Okay, so give me some equipment and I'll bug the doctor's office."

"I can't do that, it's illegal."

"For God's sake! What am I supposed to do then? Turn into a fly perhaps and stick to the fuckin' ceiling?"

Michael thought for a moment. "You said you were in the office when she was having one of her sessions with Miss Emily Rogers, or whatever she was doing. Can you do that again with a video recorder? That way you're hearing it, taping it, and catching it just in case you aren't believed, and if caught, you were only trespassing and you couldn't leave because they came back and you were forced to stay hidden."

John shrugged. "Yeah, I guess I could try, but it'd have to be one of those small ones. I have to say it freaked me out what I was hearing. Emily was so articulate in her descriptions...."

Michael laughed. "Oh, God, don't tell me you believe in all that past-life crap? It's her way of making them believe she's crazy, and this Doctor Griffiths has bought into it. Making her more the fool when we expose them all, patients and medical staff."

"Patients?"

"Yeah, why not? I'll bet Emily Rogers faking a past life is worth something? 'It wasn't me, the bad man from my past made me do it. I was an executioner in another life'. It's all bollocks, John. She killed that man in cold blood and I want the story. Just get the damn thing and let me worry about the rest."

John left the office with a heavy feeling in his stomach. He hadn't started this to get the patients. He'd agreed to it because of the abuse the patients were enduring and nobody believed them. The patients were the victims here, although Emily might be the exception. He still didn't feel comfortable exposing the patients to more aggravation, and besides, he wasn't entirely sure Emily had been faking it. There was something about her voice, and the descriptions that sounded too perfect, and a sadness overlapping everything that freaked him out even more. If she was talking about a past life, that was truly freaky, but not something he was one hundred percent convinced of just yet.

Mary peered into Emily's bedroom and knocked. Getting no response, she knocked again and Emily stirred but didn't wake. Checking Jane was fast asleep she first walked over and checked Jane's pulse, steady and fine as always, as the sleeping tablets kicked in, but on checking Emily's, she found her pulse raced and Emily breathing hard. Touching her forehead, she was surprised to find it sleek with sweat. Pulling back the covers, she found Emily's gown drenched and she immediately pulled the emergency cord.

Within seconds the team was there. Mary explained the situation and the doctor tried to elicit a response from Emily, but nothing worked. She groaned once, but she was either in some deep sleep, or unconscious. Either way, Doctor Hill had her carried out and she was taken to the medical room, where he could examine her better. Her pulse and blood pressure were very high, and her eyes unresponsive and no amount of chest rubbing would get her to respond. As a final resort, he produced smelling salts, but they didn't work either.

"It looks like she's having a serious dream, judging from her behaviour. So we'll keep an eye on her."

"Is she in a dream state?"

"Well, she's responsive in so much as her pupils dilate, and she responds to stimulus and pain, but refuses to wake up. She's either faking or she's so deeply asleep, it's like sleep walking?"

"Faking, surely no one can fake this?" Mary stared down at Emily who continued to sleep. "Has she been given anything?"

The doctor rechecked the charts. "No, nothing. She had a session with Doctor Griffiths but no medication is shown on her chart, so I guess not."

They both looked at each other over the sleeping body of Emily. Mary knew he was thinking the same thing, but refused to voice his concern to a nurse.

"I'll look back in on her in half an hour. Will you stay with her?"

Mary nodded. "Sure, it's my turn for late evening shift, so I'm here till eleven."

Doctor Hill glanced at the clock and smiled. "Okay, see you at half past ten."

Mary watched the door close before moving to sit beside Emily. She picked up her limp wrist and out of habit, took her pulse again and gently replaced it under the cover. It had dropped slightly, but still high.

What was it that had made her look in on Emily? She'd been happily going through her daily routine, checking all of the patients on her floor, but something had drawn her upwards to check the more secure patients. Jennifer, the nurse on duty had been surprised to see her, but said nothing and had gone back to the raunchy pages of her romance book. Mary would never know, but liked to believe Emily's guardian angel had directed her, so for now, she sat back and watched the beep of the monitor that let her know Emily's heart continued to beat.

*   *   *

The shouting was loud even from Merek's room. I could hear what sounded like commands and names being called with varying degrees of urgency. Of course, my Old English was too bad to understand what was being said, though I liked to believe it was along the lines of, 'Pour the oil, light the arrows, and fire on the sons of bitches!' I crept to Merek's door and peeped out, mayhem as people ran here and there. Three women were putting out a small fire near the stable block, and a man stumbled past me with an arrow sticking out of his arm, but he was breathing and moving, so I wasn't too concerned at the moment. I made a mental note to check he was seen by Ayleth in case of infection.

I ducked back inside and slammed the door shut as men rushed past, startling me in their haste. I recognised them from the soldiers who guarded the main gate. They were in charge of protecting the castle, and

I wondered how Tristan and Artorius were getting on in the field. My question was answered as I heard a roar as people cheered from the castle walls and silently thanked whoever was listening.

I also thanked the gods that Artorius had listened to me about the oil in the field. I'd seen it in a film and it'd made a difference in the battle. I wasn't sure if it was historically accurate, but considered that perhaps if it was true then, maybe William Wallace had heard of this battle and got the idea from us. It was a chance I was willing to take to save lives. Artorius hadn't taken my advice regarding making very long spears, but merely smiled politely before leaving to see my oil idea carried out.

I sat beside Merek who hadn't stirred at all and tried to think of anything else I had watched in films that might help our fight. A 'Terminator' would be perfect right now, so long as it was a goodie. Even a gun of any kind would make a difference, but I had no idea when they got invented. Bows, arrows, swords and daggers, axes and spears were all we had at hand for these fighters. Hand to hand combat, face to face with the person you intended to kill. Not like the World Wars where cowards created the war and then sent millions to die by cannons and guns and gas. Not that I'd say no to a cannon right at this moment.

The noises abruptly changed. I could hear distant clacking and clanging, metal on metal. So, the hand to hand battle had begun. I clasped Merek's hand in my own. His felt fairly warm compared to mine, that was freezing and trembling. I bent my head to rest my forehead on our hands and although I didn't believe in God, I prayed to whoever was listening to keep us safe.

CHAPTER 33

Tristan yanked his sword out of the mercenary's stomach and finished him off by cleaving his head in two. He was gasping for breath but he had no time to catch it as another man raced towards him, his arm raised, his sword bloodied and his eyes glaring death. Tristan waited until the final moment before sidestepping and following through with his own sword. It caught the man on his back and he sliced a chunk from his body. The man screamed and fell flat, face down next to his comrade. Tristan barely glanced at them as he moved forward to the next man.

Brom was near to him, fighting two men at once with ease. Tristan ran towards them and sliced the head off one of the opponents who hadn't seen him coming. The other was taken aback long enough for Brom to slice the man's belly and walk away as his guts spilled out, moving onto the next victim. Tristan gave him a nod, and Brom returned it with a grin as he raised his sword in defence. Tristan glanced quickly around and saw his wolf tearing out another mercenary's throat. He gave a high whistle and the wolf released the bloodied corpse and returned to his master's side.

Both men scouted the field and saw Artorius fighting two mercenaries and ran to defend him, slicing men as they ran to his side. The oil had saved many of their men, and the screams of the enemy as they burned alive had died away. Only the grunt of men and the clash of metal were heard among the groans of the dying, and the stench of blood and shit. Of Sagarus they found no sign. The three men fought their way through the enemy along with Dain and Borin, who was using his axe to great effect. Every so often Artorius would raise his arm and any enemy that had got past them were shot down by a hail of arrows. They would win this day, but it troubled all of them that Sagarus was nowhere to be found.

*   *   *

I heard the footsteps and instinctively knew they were coming here. I stood, ready to defend myself and Merek when the door was flung open and a woman stood there, searching the darkened room. Her eyes became accustomed to the dimness, and when her eyes lighted on me, she stepped into the room and began indicating outside, then pointing at me. I guessed what she expected, but I shook my head.

"No, not going. Staying here with Merek...." I pointed to the man lying in the bed, and pointed firmly downwards to the floor. "Staying here."

She obviously understood, but stepped closer and became more urgent in her pointing, so much so, she reached over and grabbed my sleeve and pulled, tearing the seam. I yanked my arm away and stepped back. "No, stay here with Merek." I stared hard at her. "Who are you anyway? Do I know you? You tore my gown, bitch!"

I could see the young woman was becoming very agitated as she nervously glanced between me and the open doorway. Making up her mind, she suddenly pulled a small, long knife from her pocket and thrust it towards me, all the while pointing at the doorway.

Horrified, I stepped back quickly, but the wall was only four feet from my back. I had nowhere to go. "What the fuck are you doing? Who are you?" I shouted over and over, but she didn't understand, but kept waving her knife threateningly, all the while pointing at the open doorway with her other hand.

Abruptly, I realised who she was. A traitor. This woman had given me away to Sagarus' men to save her own skin, and now it seemed she wanted to do it again. Anger flared in me and took over from the fear. I saw my own dagger sitting beside the poison a foot from me. I lunged for it and held it in front of me to ward her off.

I was glad to see her indecision as my dagger was longer than her knife. I hoped she wouldn't guess that I had no idea how to use it. Knife wielding was not something I had ever wanted to learn, but I could remember being given the opportunity. Now I wish I hadn't turned it down. Judging from her meagre attempts at lunging and swishing the air I guessed she wasn't a knife wielding professional either, and so we came to a stalemate. She and her knife were between me and the door. Now I had a dagger, she knew she couldn't force me to go anywhere with her.

"So, bitch, you prefer Sagarus' company to your own people, eh?"

She recognised his name and had the decency to look uncomfortable. I could see the fight leaving her as her constant pointing flagged, her conviction that I should go also waning. Eventually, she stopped and we both stood, knives pointing at each other. "So, what happens now, traitor bitch? Yeah, my dagger's bigger than yours." I knew taunting her was pointless, but I wanted to hurt her. She watched those mercenaries carry me away and calmly closed the door on me knowing what they would do. I despised her for that treacherous act.

She seemed to understand, or at least, she was thinking the same thing, as she slowly backed away, and closed and locked the bedroom door against the growing chaos outside. She slumped against the wooden door, and finally her arm lowered, the knife pointed to the floor instead of me.

"He kill me. First rape, then slow kill...."

"Who are you? I see Ayleth has taught you some of our language. She must have liked you.... Why did you betray me to Sagarus?" My initial shock at hearing broken English, my English, disappeared quickly and I focused on getting information.

She stared at me uncomprehending, so I went over it again with lots of hand gestures, and finally she nodded slowly.

"Sagarus kill family. Me child. He take...." Her face crumpled and I guessed what Sagarus had taken, and my heart abruptly went out to this pathetic woman.

"He keep me to himself. I fail, he give...." She pointed at Merek then outside.

"Sagarus would give you to Artorius?" When she shook her head, I understood and felt sick. "He would give you to all of his men until you die." I tried to breathe deeply to quell the surge of bile that rose in my gut, but I failed and threw up. The terror of the battle and now this gut-wrenching tale was too much to bear.

"I won't let him take you. Artorius will protect you. Besides, Sagarus is dead."

"No. Sagarus have child. Girl. Will kill if no come back...." My statement of Sagarus' death did nothing to quell her terror for her daughter, and I gently repeated it.

"Sagarus alive. Hurt neck, but fight with army." She pointed outside and I suddenly felt sick again. So I had only hurt him. Possibly bruised his windpipe and given him concussion but that wasn't enough. I chastised myself silently for not daring to check his breathing. I took a long shaky breath and returned my attention to this trembling soul in front of me.

"He has your daughter? Is he the father?" I knew the answer even as I asked. "But surely he wouldn't kill his own daughter?"

Her confusion as I spoke was frustrating, so I again repeated everything with hand gestures and she nodded. "Babe. No love for Babe."

I stared at this poor woman who had endured years of abuse only to be impregnated by a monster, who would hold his own child hostage if she didn't deliver me. I think my heart broke at that moment as I contemplated her dilemma—me or a daughter by her rapist? Should I go with her to save an innocent baby? Could I do that? Besides the fact that he would undoubtedly kill the child at some point, if he hadn't already, he would hold the threat over this broken woman for however long he could keep her alive, or how long he wanted her. My sacrifice would make no difference to hers, or her daughter's life, and that was the cruel reality.

I rubbed my eyes with the back of my hand, wiping away the grief of my decision. She watched me, not without some element of pity as she saw me trying to come to a verdict. I finally looked back at her and she knew I'd decided. Tears welled up and fell freely down her cheeks. I saw that she understood, and I think she knew it was a hopeless situation for every female involved. Both she and her daughter would continue to be abused, and killed when it suited Sagarus. There was no hope. Sagarus had given her this meaningless purpose, knowing that it wouldn't work. I would kill her in self-defence, or this woman would kill herself, either way, he was rid of another human being he cared nothing for. I glanced down at the bottle of poison and back at her, and waited.

She took one long deep breath and with a slight nod of her head, she came to a resolution. Afterwards, I thought that she'd already made it long before she entered Merek's room. Pushing herself away from the wall, in three strides, she was within reach of the small table on which stood the small bottle of poison. She grabbed it, pulled out the stopper and with only the briefest of pauses, placed the bottle to her lips and drank. With a yell of disbelief, I reached for her as she fell forward. The bottle clattered from her hand onto the bed and the remnants left a stain on the cloth. It was all I registered as I caught her full weight, and we both crumpled together onto the floor.

*   *   *

"I'm beginning to get quite alarmed at Miss Rogers' continued sleep. She shows no signs of trauma or drug-induced sleep but it is now twelve hours since this was brought to my attention and we cannot wake her."

Doctor Dowling looked over Emily's notes again and shrugged. "Her medication shouldn't be the cause, and I agree with you, Doctor, I cannot find any evidence of foul play to cause this sleeping state. Though I do notice that when shaken slightly, Emily responds as if in a deep sleep, but as yet we have not managed to bring her round fully. Her blood tests should be back shortly, but in the meantime I have contacted Doctor Griffiths as she is the patient's doctor and maybe she can bring some light into this matter."

Doctor Hill raised his eyebrows and offered a non-committal shrug before taking a seat in the lounge. "The nurse, Mary, is very concerned, and has become attached to Emily Rogers. If there should be anything … shall we say, untoward then I doubt we could keep this quiet."

Doctor Dowling slowly leaned back in his chair and gave his friend his full attention. "Untoward behaviour? What are you suggesting?"

Doctor Hill licked his lips nervously. "There has been talk, rumours of late night activity with Miss Rogers. Doctor Griffiths has certainly neglected her other patients these last couple of weeks, stating Emily needed extra sessions to help her come to terms with the murder."

"I see, and just what exactly do you believe has gone on? Off the record of course, for now at least."

"Off the record? I think she's become attached to Miss Rogers and her plight, in what has become a bit of a mess. The CID are not convinced Emily was alone when the security guard was killed, and finding that thumbprint has messed up their investigation. Of course, without Emily's help in telling them what happened that night, we've had no option but to hold her here, for her own good and safety, of course. Jail would be too radical a move, especially if she is innocent.

"Yes, yes I see that, but what of Doctor Griffiths' involvement?"

"Well, she is a lesbian …"

"And?"

"Well, I wonder if she's become attached in another way to Emily Rogers. Not that I'm saying anything sexual has happened … but…."

"God forbid, that's all we'd need is a sexual harassment case on top of this mess, but unless Emily says anything different, we won't go down that particular road. Do you think she's innocent?" Without waiting for a reply he carried on. "It's a hard one to fathom isn't it? If Emily is innocent, then why not say so straight away and walk free? Why stay silent all these months? Shock, do you think, or fear?"

"Perhaps both in the beginning, but I'm not so sure now. I think it's a game. A game she's gone too far with now, and maybe that's why Doctor Griffiths is so taken with her, as she was the first Emily spoke to in all that time."

"Yes, perhaps, but three months is a long time to stay quiet without some reason."

"Not really. I had a patient down in … Oh, Doctor Griffiths, please come in."

Marian stared at both doctors before settling in the chair opposite the desk next to Dr Hill, who watched her carefully. She ignored him and kept her attention on the superior consultant who had asked her to come in.

"So, gentlemen, what's this all about that I'm called in this early …"

*   *   *

Almost an hour later, Marian left the office so angry and humiliated that she could barely breathe. Her hands shook badly and she could feel her cheeks burning, and knew her neck was red. She always got like that when she became angry or anxious, and she was both. How dare they question her personal values, and with Emily of all people. Bloody men!

She walked briskly to her office, unlocked it and went inside, slamming the door loudly behind her. Glancing at the clock, she suddenly felt drained. It was only just gone seven and her day already sucked. They wanted all of her notes from her sessions with Emily and she was to go and view Emily's condition, see if hypnosis was the cause in some way. They all knew it to be a slim chance, but one they had to try so they could hold their heads high and say they had tried everything.

She found her key and pushed it into the locked drawer. For a moment it wouldn't turn, but with some jiggling, it eventually turned and the drawer opened. Emily's notes, both private and professional were in two piles. She took out the professional ones, that had minimal notes on what had occurred in their sessions together. It gave enough information without delving deeply into the fantastic world Emily saw under hypnotic state. She also pulled out the tapes of their sessions, at least, the tapes that showed clearly the 'hour' that she kept, just in case someone else needed to hear the sessions. These showed mumblings and the odd question and answer that concerned the murder, but most was useless.

Her other tape recorder that she kept running constantly held all of the sessions with every tiny detail. Nobody would hear these except herself.

With a quick look around to check everything was in place, she was about to pull out her key when she noticed the small scratch next to the keyhole. Bending down she examined it closer and saw a few tiny grooves embedded in the wood and knew someone had tried to open her locked drawer, and her stomach lurched with fear. Someone was onto her. She quickly collected the papers and tapes together and left her office, locking it behind her, but wondering just how safe that actually was.

CHAPTER 34

Brian walked briskly, ignoring the receptionist, as he headed straight for John, who loitered near the opposite doorway. The receptionist was calling, "Sir, excuse me ... Sir ..." But he didn't look around, his whole focus on getting answers, and hitting someone very hard, and he didn't care which order that came in.

John watched his approach and had the decency to look worried. For a split second his attention moved to the receptionist, who was now calling security. He raised his hand to let her know Brian was with him, turned back to welcome him, but not in time to stop the punch that sent him reeling through the swinging door. The poor receptionist's voice went up a couple of tones in her panic and security came running. Three burly men pulled Brian off him before he could get another punch in.

"What the hell, man ..." John rubbed his jaw and spat out blood onto his other hand. "If I lose a tooth, I'm going to sue your arse ..."

Brian remained motionless, both his arms gripped by security. The third one looked between them both.

"What's going on here? John, you know this man?"

John nodded. "Yeah, he's Emily's brother."

Ed, the head of security, shrugged. "Emily Rogers? Yeah, thought I recognised you, but I don't give a shit who you are. I'm calling the police to sort this out." He turned to his two comrades. "Take him to the office."

At this, Brian struggled. "No way. Take me to see my sister. What have you done? John, is this your fault? What's happened to her? She looks worse, like the walking dead...."

Ed again looked between John and Brian. "What's he talking about? No, doesn't matter, I won't talk about it here, take him to the office."

John watched the three men escort Brian away, who continued to fight them. Halfway across the hall, Ed turned back. "You'd better come too. We'll get a nurse to check your jaw and you can help with sorting this out."

John hesitated a second, but Ed refused to move. It wasn't a question, and he followed the rest of them towards the security office, thinking about what his story should be. The papers he'd photocopied of Emily's sessions were juicy stuff, and he'd only had time to quickly glance through some of them. The poor girl was obviously either a complete loony or Doctor Griffiths was feeding her some bullshit to see if she could make Emily believe she'd had a past life or something, and that was really creepy. He hoped they'd be safely hidden in his locker. He'd only meant to warn Brian about Emily's sessions and then take off to his editor, now he had no idea what Brian would say and considered his options. He didn't blame Brian for the punch. If a hospital was doing mind games on his sister, he'd hit out at anyone he thought responsible. He just hoped Brian wouldn't ruin everything at such a crucial point in the investigation.

*   *   *

Emily stirred in her sleep. Her eyes fluttered open for a few brief moments, but remained unfocused and Mary slowly sat back in her chair and resumed her knitting. Every so often Emily muttered something incoherent and she'd lean forward, her ear to Emily's lips, but nothing she said made sense. Who on earth was Merek? And what did foxglove have to do with anything?

Inspector Richards studied the analysis of the sword and whistled through his teeth. Sergeant Mathews turned at the noise. "What's up, sir?

"This damned sword is apparently one of a kind. The way the blade has been made was unheard of when this one was forged in the fires of Mount Doom." He giggled at his own joke, but abruptly broke off and studied the file eagerly. "Definitely more prints. In fact, it's covered with them, but smudged with blood apparently. DNA was retrieved, but no matches so far."

"Whose blood? The security guard?"

"Yes, but not just his. There were traces of other blood in tiny amounts, as if it's been used to kill before, and then wiped, but not very well. Paul Dawson, the murdered victim, is O positive, this one is B negative. Emily's is O negative so we know it isn't hers either, so ..." He abruptly sat back and slammed the file on the desk.

"So ... we have to let Miss Rogers go?" his sergeant butted in.

Inspector Richards looked annoyed. "Looks that way. We have nothing to hold her, except she was found with the murder weapon in her hand, covered in blood and sitting in her own piss, shaking uncontrollably and sobbing, and screaming so much we had to sedate her. Since that night, she's refused to speak with anyone, until recently with this Doctor Griffiths. In those first few days, Emily was almost catatonic, but the evidence suggested that at the time only she and the security guard had been in the vicinity, because there were no other footprints. No other DNA on the victim, and his skin under two of Emily's fingernails matched scratches on his neck. Emily's hair in his hand suggested there was a struggle, resulting in Emily killing him by chopping his head off."

The Sergeant leaned forward and read the file. "You know, I've never really been convinced of her guilt."

"Yeah, you said at the time, but the evidence argued against your theory. Now, well ..."

"Yes, now, well, I still find it difficult to visualise a small girl like that overpowering a large fifteen stone fella enough to get a good swing with a sword. There's no evidence of any other trauma on his body to suggest he was knocked out or punched."

"True, and the lack of any other footprints suggest they were alone, and yet nothing adds up."

"Yes, that is perplexing. If only Emily Rogers would speak to us, we'd solve a case that's dragged on far too long, and I'm convinced this Doctor Griffiths woman is hiding something."

"Agreed. Get your coat, we'll go over there and see if we can rattle a few cages. Perhaps this new evidence will get her to talk."

His sergeant grabbed his jacket. "Okay, but what about Hitler doc?"

"She can kiss my arse. I spoke with the head consultant again yesterday, and apparently they have concerns about our Doctor Griffiths. He's willing to allow us access to Emily, so long as she doesn't become upset."

"Won't her brother object?"

"No, I doubt it. He wants her out, and will do anything to get that result. At least he's been eliminated from our enquires. I didn't really suspect him. Besides, I got the impression they weren't close. Anyway, the victim's family deserve closure and I intend to help them get it."

*   *   *

It was the stench I feared I might never forget. The wounded kept coming in, like the drip of a tap thankfully and not a gush, but still, it didn't seem to end. Daylight was fading fast and the night chill seeped into my bones. I stood up straight and hugged myself for both warmth and comfort, but saw another man being helped in and my own needs disappeared.

Ayleth was nowhere to be seen, but I had a rough idea where she'd gone. The room had long ago become too full and the courtyard was packed with men, so she had begun moving those who could be moved into the great hall, both for warmth and to be closer to the kitchens for those who could stomach broth.

I thought I might never eat again, as blood and piss, faeces and vomit and dribble emanated from every orifice. The battle had been a success, in that Sagarus and his mercenaries had retreated, but the numbers of our dead were large, and I wondered if this had merely been a strategic fight to whittle our men down. Apparently Artorius had thought the same thing and ordered as many men as possible to keep watch. He expected another, more voracious attack. Sagarus had apparently stayed off the battlefield, which was suspicious, until we learned that he'd been killing our men along the side-lines, knowing the main warriors were in the thick of it. Artorius was on full alert.

Tristan had sought me out, finding me still in Merek's room, sitting on the floor with the body of the young woman. He had pulled me to my feet, looking between me and the corpse, seeing the empty bottle and understanding something of what had occurred. With a quick glance at his friend who lay still in his bed, he pulled me from the room, kissed me briefly, but thoroughly before rushing off again. The woman could wait. His eyes were wild and fierce, his face and body splattered with other men's blood. His wolf's mouth was stained red, but I'd hardly dared to look down at it, as my stomach was in pieces, and I was already close to vomiting.

The air outside was thick with smoke and fear and I searched the courtyard for Ayleth. From my higher position I looked down at the chaos that was happening in the courtyard below me and knew I had to get involved. Closing Merek's door, I headed down the stairs, taking long deep breaths and inwardly telling myself 'I could do this.'

Thankfully, on reaching the last step, Ayleth came into sight, saw me and beckoned me over to help with one of the less injured. He needed a few stitches in his upper arm. Ayleth silently handed me a needle, a length of sheep's gut, and a half-empty wine pitcher. With a nod, she left us. I gawped after her for a moment, my mind not registering what she was asking me to do, until I turned to look at the young man she'd left me with. He was reaching for the pitcher and I handed it to him with a forced smile. Turning my back, I hovered the needle over the nearest candle flame as I'd seen Ayleth do and with shaking hands, I turned back to my first patient and prayed the wine would be enough to help him.

I'd given him five stitches that looked okay and he was still alive, even giving me a broad smile once I'd finished, passing the almost empty pitcher to me with a nod. I'd taken it and finished it in four gulps, before getting up onto unsteady legs to retrieve another full pitcher, pouring a little onto the wound which made him hiss. I quickly apologised, but he abruptly stood, gave me a nod of thanks and disappeared into the main castle. Turning, I found that I had more injured coming in and, with determination, I set to work with my new skill.

I found that I was pretty good at stitching wounds, so something must have sunk in from those long, boring hours doing embroidery in school. It became obvious though that Ayleth only sent the less injured in my direction, the stitching minimal. Pointless in some cases, since once the wound was cleaned I'd found them not to be as deep as expected. Some, if not most, would recover and live, though many would carry the scars of battle. Once my area was sorted, I went to find Ayleth who was in the worst part.

Men here had lost limbs, more with gaping wounds in their stomachs. Ayleth and the women were doing what they could, but really, there wasn't much to do except help the men die painlessly, and as bravely, as possible. A couple near the door were borderline, judging from the lack of blood, and I went to help them any way I could. Judging from their behaviour, I guessed concussion most likely, as they had head wounds and their eyes were weird. I cleaned them up and offered them water but they barely noticed I was there. I wasn't sure what to do, so stayed nearby and watched them whilst helping others get comfortable.

Someone farther down the room began to sing a tune. They sang low at first, as if to themselves, but then it gained momentum and others joined in. It was, for a moment, a pleasant minute, leaning against the stone wall and listening to music. In that moment, I could have forgotten the horror that lay around me, and the terrorising horde that wanted to kill everyone in this castle, and I closed my eyes and just listened.

Images of the woman flooded my head and I remembered where else I had seen her. In Artorius' great hall, serving wine, laughing and flirting with the men. She must have hated that, or had it been a welcome reprieve from the halls of Sagarus, and his vulgar and vile acts? Had every one of her smiles been fake? Inside she must have been terrified, hating every smile, every touch. To pretend so perfectly took skill and years of practice. I couldn't, and didn't want to imagine what life had been like for her as Sagarus' slave girl.

She'd died fairly slowly, and I'd been angry at Ayleth for getting it wrong. This could have been me. I never left her but held her tightly as her heart slowed down and eventually stopped. The battle raged on outside, but I ignored it then. My whole focus became her, and I thanked her for it knowing it was a pathetic thing to do. I wept for her then. I wept for her poor daughter and her fate, and hoped that it would be quick.

Artorius watched his strange guest as she leaned against the wall. Thomas was singing, and it was this sound that had drawn him out to where he now stood at the top of the stairs. Lady Aemilia stood listening, the look on her face told him of her pain and sorrow, as she hugged herself for comfort. She finally opened her eyes and he saw the tears fall and felt an ache in his own heart for this strange woman. He was about to go down to her when her attention was caught by a call nearby from one of the wounded and she turned, wiped her face and smiled down at the soldier.

He moved around the castle, talking to his men, the soldiers, the injured and the grieving, but all the while he found himself watching out for Lady Aemilia. The shadows lengthened and the stars became clearer in the night sky. As scones were lit and the rooms blazed with firelight, he saw her figure move around the rooms filled with the injured. She was beautiful, no denying that, and he felt drawn towards her. She was a mystery, just as Ayleth had been many years before. Both Ayleth and Tristan had spoken of Lady Aemilia's desire to stay under his protection, and that he should trust that she was an innocent.

Yet the more he watched her, the more he was convinced there was something he wasn't being told. The young woman Ava, Sagarus' woman, who'd swallowed the poison, lay with the rest of the dead. There was no denying the wave of sorrow Lady Aemilia had felt for this woman, whom he thought nothing more than a stranger to Lady Aemilia and yet she'd wept bitterly for this woman. The story she'd related to Ayleth had indeed been heart-breaking, but not worthy of a traitorous act in his eyes. She had betrayed him and the inhabitants of his castle, putting their lives at risk for the sake of Sagarus' bastard, and it was this anger that overwhelmed the sadness. Of course he knew of Tristan's love for

Lady Aemilia and they had lain together. He wasn't sure how he felt about that, but he'd had no time to dwell on it as Sagarus had brought his army.

He absentmindedly sucked the back of his hand, where a sharp knife had just cut the skin. A flesh wound, but it bled freely on occasion. He felt bruised and battered, and a dull fatigue pulled at his limbs, but he knew that if he lay down, he'd fall into the deepest of sleeps and he needed to be sharp. Sagarus was not finished. What was it about Lady Aemilia that drew his enemy out into battle? Her beauty couldn't be Sagarus' only reasoning for this slaughter, neither was this lady's killing of his brother. He'd heard of this butcher, knew of his yearning to hold a part of this country and rule it. Was the lady part of that plan? A shame Ava killed herself. He would have enjoyed a conversation with her before death. Of anyone, Ava might have more of an idea of Sagarus' plans and where the lady Aemilia fitted into it.

He walked back into his bedchamber and went over to a large wooden chest. Unlocking it, he stared down at the item he had found at the place they'd encountered the mercenaries whipping the lady. Picking it up he gently touched the odd fabric, sniffed it and stared down at the flowers embroidered into the dark blue material. A strange garment and not one he'd ever seen before, but it belonged to the Lady Aemilia, and it only added to his suspicions that there was more to her story than she was telling.

CHAPTER 35

"Is this all of your notes, Doctor Griffiths?" The consultant, Sidney Brown-West eyed her over the rim of his glasses.

"Of course, it's what you asked for. Emily Rogers' notes and recordings over this last couple of weeks."

Sidney leaned closer and picked up the top file and scanned it. "It doesn't look much for all the hours she's spent in your care ..."

"As you should already be aware, Sidney, I don't keep many notes until I fill out a final file once they've been discharged or moved. As Emily is still with us and still under my care, I saw no reason to broaden my notes. All I need to remember is up here." She quickly tapped the side of her head and stared back defiantly.

"Yes, yes, I've heard of your personal techniques, but I believe they were not regarded as professional enough for this institute, and you were asked to desist from such minimal reports. I see, at least in Emily Rogers' case, you haven't done as was expected of you."

Marian swallowed and felt the heat rising in her throat. She'd forgotten that meeting, but now it all came flooding back. Sidney Brown-

West had been most insistent on full notes being kept on all patients. He believed it aided in any transitions made, which was technically true, but in Emily's case, she had no intention of allowing anyone else near her. "I forgot obviously, being so busy lately, I—"

"And yet, every other doctor in this hospital is able to remember how to do their job correctly."

Marian bit her lip. She hated being interrupted, and considered it downright rude. "That's as may be, but I doubt they've had such a heavy workload as I do. I asked for help over six months ago, but was told that funding was limited, yet I see certain wings have thrived while the secure wing remained untouched." She saw him twitch and knew she'd got him on that. "I would like an assistant, which would free up my time to fill out the files of patients more fully, but as you can see from my record sheets, I've been working quite a few hours of overtime as it is—"

Sidney Brown-West coughed and glanced through the sheets Marian pointed out. His coughing became worse, and she abruptly stood and fetched him a glass of water from the nearby sink. He took it gratefully and with his cough under control, he sat back in his big armchair and regarded her carefully.

"Marian, I believe that you're aware that you've overstepped the professional line with Miss Rogers. I can understand why. She's an exceptional case and one that has interested me since her arrival three months ago, but now that the police are becoming less sure of her guilt, having found more evidence of another person, this needs to be handled delicately. Everything we've done and continue to do with Miss Rogers will be scrutinised by the public along with the board of directors, who met yesterday regarding her continued incarceration. We contacted her brother, who is downstairs with security having punched one of the orderlies."

"Really? I'm surprised he's interested in Emily, considering he's a raging alcoholic and he means nothing to her...." She stopped herself, realising her mistake. Thankfully Sidney overlooked it and carried on.

"Emily spoke to you first, and that must have felt very good for your ego. Ten weeks of silence is hard going and she gave way to you. A special bond was created within that, but I believe you have stepped away from being her therapist to being her friend, which is why strict hours have gone by the by. Is that correct, Marian?"

Her brain was going ten to the dozen as she weighed up her options, but eventually she looked away nervously, and absentmindedly bit her thumb nail. "Yes, I suppose I have, but it wasn't until you said it just now that I can see it. I got too close. I didn't want to believe that I could lose it like that. Even when I spoke with Doctor Hill about it, I didn't want to admit it." Her eyes welled up but she didn't attempt to wipe away the lone tear.

"It happens to all of us at one point or another, Marian. It's nothing to feel ashamed about, truly...." His tone changed on seeing her obvious distress, and her handing him a glass of water had reminded him of how caring she was. "Look, speak with your supervisor. It's been a while according to her, so how about you go and see her now. I made sure Carla was free this morning, in case we could sort this out. You'll need a couple of hours to help catch up your hours lost, but if there is any comeback on the hospital, we can show that we have sorted it out professionally ... yes?"

Marian met his gaze. "Of course. I'll go and see Carla now then. I need a good off-load, I guess. I've felt overwhelmed lately and being so close with Emily...." She stood up to leave. "I assume you've moved my appointments?"

"Of course. You have no appointments today. See Carla and then go home and rest."

"And Miss Rogers? I received a message to check on her, but...." She knew this was shaky ground but she had to know if Emily was lost to her.

"Right now Miss Rogers is asleep in some self-induced state. Someone is watching over her and you'll be kept informed obviously, but in light of recent events, I'm not sure you should continue as her doctor, do you?"

Marian nodded and left the room before she punched the bastard. The crying woman act always got her out of situations with older men, who felt uncomfortable with distressed 'ladies'. Pathetic really, but Sidney was a typical man of the forties. His upper-crust upbringing had got him into all the best schools, mixing with the toffs who knew absolutely nothing of real life, and definitely nothing about women.

She got into the lift for the fourth floor and walked slowly towards Carla's office. She didn't dislike Carla; she just wasn't on her wavelength. Carla was a hippie, a twenty-first century one anyway. Carla's philosophy was live life and be free, and most days could be found doing various therapies outside, barefoot. Of her past, she'd say, "Life threw me quite a lot of shit, but now it's flushed and gone far away, so no reason to keep hold of it otherwise it'll stink!"

Her door was open when Marian arrived and the scent of incense lingered in the hallway. "Darling, Marian, come on in and let's get a cup of herbal tea in you. You look positively knackered, my dear."

Marian grinned sheepishly and allowed herself to be pulled into the warm scented room.

*   *   *

"I want to see my sister."

"I'm sorry, but that's not going to happen while you're in this state, so calm down and we'll see what the doctors say, eh?"

Brian was so on edge he could have hit out at anyone, except he was sitting in a leather chair facing the man's groin. It wasn't done to punch another man in his balls. He glanced across at John, still nursing his jaw. A nurse had already cleaned the wound, a cut inside his cheek, nothing too bad. John caught his eye and raised an eyebrow in a questioning manner. Brian merely glared back.

"Look, the doctors called me this morning. She's unconscious or something. If she dies, then I'll sue all of you for obstruction." He saw his words made the group of guards uncomfortable, but the head of security continued to look indifferent.

"You tell me why you hit him. Do you know each other?"

Brian looked away and shrugged, but John's gaze moved back to him. "So, you do know each other." Eddie frowned and looked between the two. "So, why hit him here, in a secure hospital?"

Brian finally sat back deflated, "He pissed me off. If my sister dies because he couldn't be arsed saving her, then I'll fuckin' kill him!"

John was growing visibly nervous and stood up. "Forget it, mate. I'm not pressing charges, it's just a misunderstanding. I'd better get back to my shift."

Eddie stepped closer and barred his way. "Hang on, what did he mean about saving his sister? You're just an orderly, not a nurse or anything." He stared at John before casually closing the door. "You can stay too. Besides, your shift ended. I know everything that goes on in this hospital, gentlemen, because it is my job to know. So now you're going to fill in the few blanks for me."

*   *   *

One moment I was sitting quietly, holding the hand of a dying man while his daughter slept beside me on a small pallet. She was barely eight years old, but was small and pale from malnutrition, and he was all she had left. Her mother had died last year from a fever.

I felt the stirrings of the air around me and I squeezed his hand tightly, willing him to live, but the hole in his stomach already told me his fate. I was not capable of saving him and neither was Ayleth who'd already been and gone, opening his wound to nature and daring me to argue, but she was right, better a quick death than a lingering agony. I'd opted to stay with him. So far he'd lasted almost an hour, for the most part drowsy from something Ayleth had given him. Occasionally he regained consciousness, calling his wife's name, until my soothing hushes quietened him and he smiled at something beyond me.

I gave up searching for whatever he looked at, obviously not going to see it, but I'd become aware of its presence and I silently thanked whoever it was for coming for him. I worried about the child, but she was fast becoming one of many orphans.

I closed my eyes for the briefest of moments to rest them, as they felt gritty from lack of sleep, and opened them to find Sister Mary bending over me, calling my name with a look of pure joy on her face, and pressing the red button on the wall. Within minutes, doctors surrounded me and I was examined and questioned, but I remained firmly silent.

They told me I'd been asleep for over twenty-one hours. I said nothing, but merely watched them. Eventually they gave up trying to get me to speak and all but Mary left. "You can talk now, they've gone."

I caught her sly smirk and grinned back. "I don't know what they wanted me to say, so...."

"So say nothing, huh? Is that what your mother taught you?" I saw her realisation and reached out and patted her hand before she could apologise.

"No, it's okay, really. My mum did always tell me to say the right thing, and if I couldn't, say nothing. I miss her...." I don't know why I said it. Perhaps because Mary wanted me to. I never spoke of my parents, or their murders, but I'd been aware that people were waiting for me to speak. It wasn't that I couldn't speak, more like I didn't know how to form the words anymore. Their murder had tormented me for years, and no one ever caught. The case remained open, but for me, somewhere around my late teens, I'd had to close it, otherwise I would've gone mad. I thought of them often, but as people I once knew, not as parents, simpler that way.

Mary sat down on the side of the bed. "I'm sure you do, Emily. Do you want to tell me about them?" On seeing me recoil, she gently touched my shoulder. "Okay, no pressure here. Do you want to tell me where you were just now in your dreams?"

"I can't remember. I feel groggy and hungry. Is it time to get up yet?"

Mary saw there was no point in forcing me, so she jumped up and took down my dressing gown from the back of the door. "It's way past breakfast, but for you, I'll find something. Come on."

It took me a while to find my balance. My body felt heavy and as we walked, it felt like I was on a ship, rising up and down, like travel sickness, yet I hadn't travelled anywhere. Had I? My head was here, and my body too, but my thoughts were back with the dying man and his daughter. It appeared that I'd managed to return to that time without Marian's help. It had felt exactly the same, completely real and immersed in his time, with all the sights and sounds and physical feelings. Could I really return on my own or had it been a one off? Twenty-one hours was incredible and I longed to get back, but I did need sustenance. I asked where Doctor Griffiths was, and received a passing comment about workload and gone home.

So, I had gone into a hypnotic state without Marian present. That would annoy her, no doubt. But, oh joy for me if I could do it again. It would mean I could go back and be with him whenever I chose. All those months of willing it to happen had produced nothing but headaches and despair, but now I'd been out of it a day and night.

I wolfed down the tea and crumpets the cook made me, and was enjoying the strawberry yogurt when Brian walked into the canteen escorted on one side by security, and a doctor I didn't recognise on the other, but his white coat and glasses gave him away. Also the way he held himself told me he was someone of importance. Behind them came the two policemen who were in charge of the murder case and they looked grim. I slowly put down my spoon and glanced nervously at Mary, who sat beside me.

"Emily. I'm so glad you're okay." Brian rushed forward, but remembered at the last moment that we were estranged and stopped himself from hugging me, though he looked sad about that.

"Miss Rogers, lovely to see you awake and eating. How are you feeling?"

I stared silently at the doctor and waited for him to continue. "Good, good. Still speaking when it suits you, fair enough. I have two policemen here who would like to talk with you. Do you feel up to that? Nurse Mary can remain if you wish, as can your brother and myself if you prefer...."

"Who are you?"

He looked surprised by my question but smiled warmly. I saw he was a kind man, if a trifle posh with his perfect suit and immaculate hair. "My name is Sidney Brown-West and I am the head consultant here. We met briefly on your arrival, but you were, shall we say, a little distressed, so I wouldn't expect you to remember me. How do you feel today, Miss Rogers?"

I ignored his question and looked up at Brian who watched me with various emotions showing on his face. "Why are you here?"

He slowly knelt down so he was at the same height as me. "I'm here for you, sweetheart. To get you out of here. I'm fighting—"

"I don't think we should jump ahead of ourselves, do you, Mr Rogers?" The Inspector jumped in and stepped forward. "You remember me, Miss Rogers. I'm here for another chat. We can do it with your chaperones, if you like...."

Brian stood up and was about to argue, but Sidney Brown-West whispered something that I didn't catch, and Brian shut up, though he looked far from happy about it.

The inspector waited to see if the doctor or Brian was going to leave, but on seeing that neither was about to budge, he continued, "So Emily, I hear you've been on a sleep fest, feeling better after it?"

Both the inspector and his sergeant sat opposite me on the bench and the inspector took out his notebook. When I didn't answer, he merely looked up and stared hard into my eyes before resuming his reading. "Okay, so I'll presume you're well rested and able to answer questions with, witnesses present. Can you tell me what happened the night Security Officer Paul Dawson was murdered? Who was with you that night? Why were you there?"

"No." After that I refused to answer for the whole hour he questioned me. Brian got angry at both of us. The inspector for pushing, and me for my stubborn refusal to cooperate. Even Mary tried to coax some answer from me, but what could I say? As always, my answer was impossible. I stared down at the table, but didn't see the marks on the wood. I saw the courtyard, the dying. I heard the cries of the wounded and the grieving. I saw him and yearned for him. I didn't want to be here in this lifeless place, not when I could return: and perhaps next time, I would stay.

CHAPTER 36

I sat in the corner of the lounge following the pathetic interview. Aware of eyes upon me, I remained sitting, my knees up to my chest, hugging my legs to my body, trying to go as inward as possible. I'd barely had time to react to my jump from one time back to this, and my insides were doing flip-flops, my mind racing as it fought to catch up.

I wondered about the wounded man and his daughter. I knew how it proceeded, like a film I'd watched before, but there were gaps in my memory and I desperately wanted to return to fill them in. My mind constantly found Tristan's face, and I wanted to weep for being so far from him. I felt frightened for Ayleth and all of the other women within the castle walls. This had happened so long ago, even in my own time frame. I knew how it played out and yet, revisiting it, I experienced the same terror, the same intense sadness and joy at being reunited with these people.

When I returned in that hypnotic state, I was living the moment as if completely new, not returning to a memory. It felt as though my mind had reconnected my body and soul to that instant, so I experienced the emotions raw, wreaking havoc on my head. How long would they be protected before Sagarus invaded again? Could Artorius keep them safe?

Would he? It would probably be fairly easy to check history, though I knew that era was patchy and guesswork at best: there might be something, but would I remember that information when I went back? Under hypnosis, I returned to a point that happened last year. I hadn't been in the hospital then. So, even if I learned something, would it change the course of history for me back then, or would I forget and merely relive what had already occurred?

I remained staring at the wall, though I didn't 'see' it. The wounded man would die, of course he would. Ayleth, Tristan, Artorius were all dead, long gone and rotten by now, yet to me they were as real as Nurse Mary and Brian. I felt the sting of tears and abruptly blinked them away. I knew they were watching me through the cameras. I didn't want to give them anything to use. Yet, all I wanted to do was curl up and sob my heart out for those I might never see again—if what the consultant said was true and Marian's sessions were over. Would my ability to go back also end without her stimuli?

I pushed that aside and considered another problem—Brian. What the hell was he hanging around for now? He looked well, I had to admit that, but years of cleaning up his messes were too difficult to get over just because he wanted to do the right thing. I wondered about that too. Why was he trying to get me out? What was in it for him? I considered the possibility of him getting me out to sell my story. I certainly wouldn't put it past him to do that. He'd looked for an angle about our parents' deaths to get cash when we'd been younger. My reappearance and incarceration would probably get him a fortune.

He'd told me he wasn't going anywhere and that he'd been working on the new building on the other side of the hospital. That was interesting. Brian had always been a good bricklayer, but he'd never been sober enough to keep a job for long. So what had made him take that one? To be near me, he'd said, but I didn't believe that for a second, although it did intrigue me.

And what of Doctor Griffiths? Poor Marian, from what Brian had quickly told me before he'd been escorted out of the canteen, it sounded as though she was in deep trouble. I felt a slight stirring for her, but it didn't last long. Marian, a manipulating bitch, who only ever did anything for her own gain. She only helped others, to feel good about herself. My sessions had given her something new and juicy, and so it had benefited us both. I got to be with Tristan and Ayleth again, and she got an interesting case to help move her up the consultant ladder.

Sidney Brown-West had informed me that Doctor Griffiths was taking a small holiday, which meant they'd suspended her until they decided how best to deal with her. Problem was, I thought I might need her. It was crucial for me to get back and relive my past, but I wasn't convinced that I could do it alone. I'd had a few glimpses and though my latest sleep fest had lasted a long time, I felt completely drained, and I wasn't convinced that I had the energy to return without Marian's aid.

There was so much more to relive, to experience and there was always that possibility that my mind would let me stay. I considered that possibility over and over. My body had been taken back in time, now, through hypnosis, my mind had been given the opportunity to return. What if the two amalgamated and I remained with him. Was that even possible? It felt like it was. Ayleth believed the chances of seeing another time hole had been near on impossible, and yet it had occurred. If I believed enough, surely my mind would begin to believe that I was back with Tristan? If my body couldn't go physically again, then my mind would do just fine.

I sat still, ignoring the tea bell and nurses who ushered the other patients out of the lounge. I focused inward and meditated on a plan, and all the possibilities that might come from that. After losing my parents, I'd gone inward for a few weeks. Shock, they'd said, but I knew it'd frightened Brian. To this day, I have no recollection of what my thoughts were during that time. But I remember a sense of peace in my own bubble, detached from the horror of their deaths.

When the soft touch came, I barely registered it, but the poking became insistent and I finally looked up into the dark brown eyes of the orderly, John, who without any words, pulled me to my feet and escorted me out of the room and my thoughts. He pulled me along the corridors until we reached solitary. I began to pull away, but he held me firmly, leading the way, but instead of a cell, he took me into the small office that held all of the cameras. He sat me down and with a quick glance around, sat opposite me and held out his hand.

"Emily, I'd like to formally introduce myself, I'm John Stoke, a journalist exposing the hospital and their treatment of patients. I've been working with your brother, Brian. I thought it was about time I heard your story. We have about half an hour before another guard will come and check this area, so how about talking to me?"

*   *   *

Brian paced his bedroom. He'd thrown his tie and jacket on the bed, now he undid his shirt, as he could smell his own sweat. He felt fobbed off. That posh consultant, with his two surnames, which he hated, had told him he'd allow him back tomorrow, once Emily was a little calmer. The police upset her. Well, of course they fuckin' had, the bastards! She'd clammed up the moment she'd seen that inspector but he'd had a lot to say to them. So another print meant they were questioning Emily's guilt? Okay, so they had to handle this very carefully, he knew that. Poor Emily had been incarcerated for three months, and it had obviously affected her, but still, she was innocent!

They'd wrecked her brain by doping her up all this time, the compensation would be huge. No, he didn't give a shit about that, Emily was important, and it looked likely that she'd be released into the main hospital for observation before a possible release. He'd found out that she'd been there before. Though fairly secure, the patients had access to outside and it was during one of these outside visits that Emily attempted to abscond, hence the secure wing.

He poured himself a large coke and tried to ignore his craving to add Bacardi to it. Wishing he had some ice, he gulped it down and caught his breath as the fizz tickled his throat. John had quickly disappeared, and despite a brief search for the journalist, Brian had no luck. He'd begun to consider telling on him when he remembered the card John had given him. Scanning his room, he searched pockets until he found the small card with mobile and e-mail on it. Finding his phone, he quickly dialled the number and waited impatiently as it rang out.

*   *   *

Marian drank back her large glass of red wine and poured herself another as she sat riveted to the tapes she'd recorded of Emily. The detail was fantastic, even if they weren't true, her account of life in the sixth century would make a great book. Tristan sounded gorgeous, a man she might consider seducing with his wild manly way. Artorius sounded like the kind, yet strong man who wooed women, slayed the bad men and kept peace in his land. Was there a Guinevere? A threesome with one of these men might prove to be interesting. Though she'd be more interested in the shapely Guinevere, she wasn't one to say no to a man now and then. And where was Lancelot? Characters from medieval stories romanticising a hero of old, and who's to say this Roman Artorius wasn't that man?

Some archaeologists certainly thought so, but it was all conjecture as very little evidence remained of that time, and from her research this Roman commander was in all likelihood fictional. It seemed no scholar could give a clear idea on whom, if anyone, King Arthur was based, but Emily was convincing. This man from the sixth century fought invading Saxons not long after the Romans left Britain to defend itself, and many historians claim that there was someone who may have helped keep the Saxons at bay for a while, until the latter half of the sixth century. Was Emily a reader of history? Having found out as much as possible about her, she expected not, so where had these figures come from?

She picked up an old police file and flicked through the photographs. A friend had managed to get the parents' murder file, which was still open, although the chances of finding the murderer now was minimal. She stopped at a picture taken of Emily from the side. She was young, pale and staring down at the huge mound of flowers well-wishers had left by the hedge. Her brother was standing behind her, but separate, not comforting her. A kind neighbour had her arm around Emily, but she looked as if she barely noticed. Neither of the children showed any remorse to the outside world, no tears had been caught on camera, and it was this that had aroused suspicions in the case, which was pathetic. Neither had a strong alibi, but nothing could be proved.

She stared hard at Emily's face. Was she capable of murder? From the background she'd acquired, Emily had maintained a good relationship with both parents, but Brian had been somewhat volatile until he'd left for college, which his Dad had paid for. Emily looked alone and Marian wondered how long she had felt that way? Long before her parents were murdered, she'd wager.

She had to hear the rest of Emily's story. It niggled at her, like someone only allowed to read half a fabulous book or watch half a film.

Emily may be mad. It might be in her head, but Emily's story was perfect for her studies. Hypnosis was a harmless tool to help people. However, had she tapped into something else with Emily? Had she found a past life, or a safe concept, to help her deal with the murder of the guard? It had become fairly obvious that someone else was involved. This Tristan perhaps? Making him a lover from another century made sense. He would be a killer, a warrior, an acceptable profession to kill someone, also in another century, not touchable to our laws, and safely away while Emily took the rap for his crime. A created warrior who loved her could not be a bad person in Emily's eyes. Perhaps she should go in this direction? On the other hand, it intrigued Marian as to which direction Emily would take her story. She considered writing her theories coming at it from both ends, seeing which one got her further up the chain. First though, she had to find a way to get past Sidney Brown-West and his cronies and that would not be easy.

CHAPTER 37

John finished filling me in on his investigation, but my head was buzzing with so many questions, I couldn't function. I merely stared at him, opening and closing my mouth like a dying fish.

"I know it's a lot to take in, Emily...." John sighed loudly and ran his hands nervously through his hair, whilst double checking the corridor. "But I need you to tell me what's been going on with Doctor Griffiths. I've heard some shit she's been making you sprout, but beyond a few papers I managed to steal and photocopy, I have nothing except you, and you're the best source I have."

"But ... but ... Marian ... she's okay.... She's helping me ..."

John abruptly stood up and paced the small room, his eye forever going to the monitors. "Look, any minute now that fat, useless guard will finally decide to check this area and I'll have to make something up about finding you here. Emily, I really need you to focus, can you do that, or has Marian Griffiths fucked you up too badly?"

I watched him—he was nervous, like a caged tiger glancing in all directions, expectant, waiting for his cue to switch from journalist to his orderly part. I hated him at that moment. He'd watched me. He'd caught me when I'd attempted to escape. He'd been mean and cruel, showing no compassion towards me or any of the other inmates. I recalled his behaviour when Mia died and fought the urge to hit him. Now this whining, jumpy journalist wanted my help for his own career.

I despised journalists. To me they were the dregs of society. They were nothing more than people without a conscience who pushed their way into grieving homes and took photographs at every opportunity, regardless of whether it was in good taste. For months following my parents' deaths, I heard the click of cameras and heard the shout of relentless questions—that were never asked politely, always forceful, implying and rude, hoping to get a reaction. Brian had warned me of showing any reaction in public, and neither of us had given the papers a juicy story, and soon the papers began to turn on us.

Brian. As much as I hated the idea of allowing him back into my life, he and this journalist scum might get me to Marian, my way back to Tristan and the others. I didn't trust my mind on its own without Marian's guidance. I'd managed a few times, but I felt so drained after my twenty-one-hour marathon, I doubted that I could continue alone. I felt so lonely here, life dreary and boring. Okay, since my return, I had been locked up, but I couldn't visualise living outside anymore. Going to work, (if I could find a job) paying my taxes, socialising, finding a boyfriend, getting married, having kids … dull, dull dull! My nerves were on edge all the time, my senses finely-tuned to kill or be killed. I'd learned to live for the moment, as everyone else had done from birth, and now, nothing in this world held any interest.

I felt sure only Marian could take me back to them now, if only to relive the past, which was far more exciting than being in the present. What if I remained in that catatonic state? I'd be happy. My chances of finding another time slip were almost impossible, the one that brought me back to this hell was unbelievable bad luck and I wondered every day how it had affected those I left behind.

"I need Brian. I need you both to get me back to Marian. I mean Doctor Griffiths."

John looked around and licked his lips, unsure. "I don't think I can. She's been suspended while they review your case. The top dogs aren't happy with her behaviour towards you. Was she very unprofessional? No, scratch that, you can tell me in your own words."

His quick change into delving journalist threw me for a moment, but I stopped myself from answering. "I need to get to Doctor Griffiths. Can you help or do I blow the whistle on you?"

John grinned. "I doubt it'll matter. I've got most of what I need, so I was happy to blow my cover."

"You were happy? But not anymore then?" I took a risk and it paid off. I saw him hesitate, and knew someone wanted more. "I'll bet your editor wanted juicier gossip to make the story worthwhile ... right?" I saw I was right and quickly continued, "If you get me to Marian, I might be able to give you what you really need? A chance to see what Doctor Griffiths does in person...."

"Really? You think Marian Griffiths will let me watch one of your sessions and film it? I'm not a fool, Emily, of course she won't. I sneaked in and heard some of the last one and it all sounded a little 'out there'. Were you faking it?"

I ignored his question. "Okay then, don't bother. I'll be let out soon when they realise I'm innocent, and then you'll never know because I'll never tell, and you'll never get what your editor wants."

"Oh yes, and what's that?"

"Proof."

"What's going on in here?"

We both jumped at the booming voice of the security guard on his patrol.

"Nothing, Jerry, just found Emily Rogers who slipped out of the lounge. Wanted some alone time, eh, Emily?"

I merely nodded and let John pull me to my feet, and played docile patient as he pulled me past the guard, who didn't look convinced. As we reached the secure wing, he leaned in casually. "Okay, Emily, I'll get your brother and we'll get you to Marian, but I'm warning you, you'd better not mess with me...."

I smiled politely as he dropped my arm, and I headed for the nearest arm chair, but changed my mind as I saw vomit on the cushion. Instead, I wandered to the large oval window and gazed out, feeling nothing except elation. If Marian was anything to go by, I'd soon be back in the past with my memories and I hoped this time it would be for longer, much, much, longer.

*   *   *

John picked up his messages and found four from Brian. He smiled to himself as he started the car. Brian would be easy to manipulate, desperate to get Emily out of there. But getting to Marian would be another matter. He phoned his editor, who attempted to dissuade him from breaking her out of the hospital, though John could tell he didn't particularly object to the idea.

He drove towards the main high street and pulled into a space on the road. He knew Brian lived in a flat somewhere around here, but couldn't remember which one. He dialled his number and thought about how he would broach the subject of a hospital break. The thought of being arrested made him feel a little anxious, but it would make a great ending to his story of corruption and abuse at the hospital. He could see the headline 'Journalist gets arrested trying to free an innocent woman'. Having spoken to his friends at the police station, he knew some were getting their arses kicked for not pushing for this new evidence sooner. There were questions as to why the thumbprint wasn't found sooner, or if it had been, why it took so long to emerge?

He knew the police on the murder case were at a loss as to any other suspects, as they'd always maintained that Emily was the only suspect— going on the blood spatters on her dress and her fingerprints on the sword. The sword was another puzzle that had archaeologists bouncing off the walls. John had spoken with one of them, a professor Harris who'd tried on numerous occasions to see Emily. He'd wanted to get the sword verified as to where had it come from and how it could possibly be in such perfect order.

He began to form a plan. It would take a lot of luck, but if he could carry it off and film it, then he might just get the answers everyone was desperate to find. "Brian, it's John. Listen, I'm outside on the high street, what number are you?"

"You took your bloody time. What's going on with Emily?" Brian slammed the door after John entered and glared at him.

John merely glanced around the untidy flat, moved an old pizza box from an old armchair, and sat down. "A coffee would be great, and then I want to talk to you about how we can help Emily in a calm manner, okay?"

Brian looked unsure for a second, before going to the narrow kitchen to fill the kettle. "I've got biscuits if you like, with your coffee."

John caught the sarcasm in his voice, but smiled sweetly and played along. "Sure, why not ... chocolate ones?"

He heard a muttered, "Fuck off," and grinned. Brian was an arsehole, but he would be useful, both as muscle and as a scapegoat, if it all went pear-shaped.

Carrying a couple of mugs, Brian placed them on the dirty coffee table and threw half a packet of digestives at John, that he'd carried under his arm. Catching them deftly, John grinned and pulled one out, dipping it into his coffee. He nibbled on it, thinking it was a little stale, but he enjoyed making Brian wait, and wondered how long he could keep it up. Not long, as Brian leaned forward with an impatient sigh. "When you've quite finished...?"

An hour later, John sat back, feeling a little excited, and munched on his third biscuit while Brian sat silent and thoughtful as he stared at the table. John could see his thoughts racing as he contemplated his idea, not seeing the table in front of him.

"It's risky."

John shrugged. "Of course it is, but this way everyone gets their answers and the police have to release Emily."

"Yeah, but what if she slips into one of those comatose things?"

"That's the risk, but even if she did, she comes out of them, eventually. And besides, we'd have Doctor Griffiths there to help bring Emily out. This only happened because they stopped the sessions...." He knew that wasn't technically true, but Brian wouldn't know that.

Brian became quiet again. John got up and made them both another coffee, and made a note on Brian's fridge that he was out of milk. He looked around while he waited for the kettle to boil. The flat was sparse and unkempt, a typical man's pad, but the majority of the furnishings were part of the flat and dated from the seventies, if that. He wondered about Brian's life since his parents' deaths and considered asking about his relationship with Emily, but decided against it, at least for now.

"So, you know this professor? And you can get in touch with this Marian Griffiths?"

John sat down. "Yes, easily."

"All right. Let's do this then ... if you think there isn't another way to prove Emily's innocence?"

"Like I've said, paperwork can take months, as the hospital release her gently into the world. She's been in the secure wing with a bunch of loonies for three months. Regardless of her innocence, it will have affected her."

His words had an effect on Brian, as he saw him open and close a fist. "If I can arrange it, I think the sooner the better, don't you? Then I can expose the lot. The hospital, the doctors, the board, who don't care a jot for the patients, and give Emily's story the voice she deserves."

Brian merely grunted, his attention elsewhere. With one last look around, John rose and let himself out, leaving Brian unmoving in his chair, his thoughts racing on getting his sister back, and the dangers they might have to face.

CHAPTER 38

Marian replaced the receiver and sat down, shocked by the conversation she'd just had with that awful orderly, who'd just confessed he was, in fact, a journalist, though his name was John, John Stokes to be precise. He'd explained quickly about impersonating an orderly to get into the hospital, but he refused to go into too much detail about that. He'd gone on to talk about Emily, and how it would be in everyone's interest to get her back into Marian's care to continue treatment. It crossed her mind that it was a frame of some kind, but right now she couldn't see what angle he might be taking.

"Exactly why is Emily in your interest, Mr Stokes, or whatever you want to call yourself?"

John ignored the obvious bait. "I want to expose the corruption in the hospital. They have kept Emily Rogers locked up in a secure wing with very fragile evidence—"

"Fragile evidence?" Marian interrupted. "She was caught covered in the dead man's blood, the sword in her hand, and in obvious shock, but still...."

"Yes, yes, but they had another thumbprint, and they found that ages ago, so why is she still in the secure wing?"

Marian couldn't answer that. Emily was not a threat to anyone, she was sure of that, as were everyone who cared for her, and yet Sidney Brown-West had repeatedly refused to consider returning her to the main hospital since her attempted escape. Doctor Gilmore, who had his nose constantly up Sidney's arse, agreed with the diagnosis. It was enough to have two doctors' signatures on the forms, to keep her inside.

"I really don't know. Who else is involved? Can we trust this Professor Harris?" She changed the subject, uncomfortable with the realisation that she'd allowed Emily to remain incarcerated (knowing that it was wrong) but purely for her own gain. She briefly wondered what would be in it for Sidney.

John interrupted her thoughts. "Yeah, Professor Harris is pretty enthusiastic about meeting Emily. I didn't go into great detail, only that I could make it possible."

Marian had heard of Professor Harris and his constant attempts to have access to Emily during her incarceration, and she'd backed Sidney in not allowing it. Any line of questioning about that night and everything associated with it could potentially send Emily back into her mute phase and Marian wanted Emily to keep talking.

She had thought a lot over the weeks about the sword and its origins. She liked weaponry, especially if found on old castle walls above ancient fireplaces. They seemed to 'belong' there. Hearing Emily's tale had increased her curiosity. Had she made up this past story to fit the sword's appearance at the crime scene, or could it actually be possible that Emily was telling the truth, that she'd been in the past and brought the sword back with her? Time slips were recorded phenomena. She'd read of people disappearing in front of witnesses, but mostly of people walking into a different time for a few seconds.

Her favourite was about a runner in the middle of a race. He'd been surrounded by witnesses when he seemed to trip and put out his hands to catch himself, but he never touched the ground. He disappeared in mid-fall and was never seen again. Another was of a farmer standing in the middle of his field. A neighbour and his wife were coming up the driveway on their horse and buggy. They could plainly see the farmer standing there, as could his wife and daughter, who were sitting on the farm porch. Suddenly, the farmer cried out and was gone. Everyone ran to the spot, but he'd disappeared, only a dark circle left behind as if the earth had burned. They searched for days, the daughter convinced she could hear her father calling for help. But after a while, his voice faded away and he was never seen or heard from again.

Stories like these intrigued her. She'd read them all her life and even interviewed a lady who'd had an experience in Liverpool. Having got off the train in Lime Street Station, she proceeded to walk her usual route to work which took about ten minutes. After a while, she noticed that she'd been walking for much longer and, on looking around, realised the street looked different, older and dirty, and the people walking past faded and blurred, their dress old fashioned. Looking down, she realised she was walking on a mud path and not the concrete she'd expected to find, but in that same instant, she looked up again and everything was normal.

She'd been convinced she'd had some kind of episode, having mental health issues in the family. She'd been referred to Marian who having spoken to her at length, decided it must have been stress and signed her off for a few days. Now, having spoken with Emily, and heard her fantastic tale, she couldn't help but think back on her old patient.

Unable to remain still, Marian moved around her apartment and found various files of other patients and flicked through them. One or two could be construed as possibilities for time travel. One man was convinced he belonged in the eighteenth century and everything in this world terrified him. Television, radio, vacuums would all send him into a frenzy. Sadly, he'd found a way to cut himself ten months ago and died from his injuries.

The other patient was many years ago, when she'd been newly practising. A teenager had been found wandering a motorway, obviously in some distress and had been brought to the hospital. She spoke a strange language and no interpreter could help. No parents could be found for her and 'Jane Doe' became more and more withdrawn. They believed her to be around seventeen or eighteen years old, but that was really only a guess. Her blood was normal, her brain patterns were normal, but when it became apparent that she was pregnant, she flew into a terrible rage and had to be restrained.

One doctor had voiced the possibility of rape, and that the girl was enraged about this consequence and that she should be treated with compassion. She wasn't, in Marian's opinion, but at that time, she kept quiet, due to her being new. The poor girl had been forced to give birth while in restraints, as every time she was released, she would try to injure herself and abort the child. The child was born too early and died. The girl eventually stopped eating and drinking and was kept alive via machines and force fed. She died eight weeks later and was buried in a small grave, with her child nearby.

She sat back now and considered the two patients and Emily. She hadn't been qualified as a hypnotherapist back then, and it wasn't considered a useful tool by many in the boardroom. The girl had spoken a dialect nobody could understand, so therapy was impossible anyway. Now, Henry had been interesting, but again impossible to treat, as he was so terrified of this world that he spent most of his time sedated while they tried to figure out what to do with him. By that time, it was too late.

Henry had spoken of people and everyday life, claiming he lived in the late seventeen hundreds. A tailor, he had a wife and seven children. During a few brief attempts at getting him to talk, he'd spoken of nothing that couldn't have been researched or found out from television and books, but now Marian found herself reconsidering his ravings.

Emily was more convincing, if she ignored her scientific mind and considered the real possibility of time travel and time holes in space. Emily's stories had real conviction and great detail. Sadly, it was of the dark ages, so not much chance of double checking facts. In fact, if she forgot all logic, Emily's appearance the night she was found could be construed as proof.

The dress she'd been wearing that night was of medieval design. The threads used in the weaving had been very old. Her hair was loose and on her feet she wore leather shoes that had historians arguing over their authenticity. It was decided that Emily's dress was a mixture of what historians considered the most possible way they'd dressed in the sixth century and re-enactment groups' interpretation. The most laughable conjecture had been that Emily was wearing homemade knickers when found and, of course, women didn't wear such things back then, did they? Nobody knew, but who's going to argue with historians?

She'd told John she would telephone back once she'd considered his request. She picked up the phone and dialled the number he'd left. "John, I agree to meet, though I'm not convinced this won't get me into trouble. But you're right, we need to help Emily, and the only way is to find out the truth of that night. My sessions have helped her so far, so it would be a shame to stop them now at such a crucial point in her therapy. So, yes, I'll meet you tomorrow night."

She replaced the telephone before he could say anything, her heart beating fast and hands shaking. This would either make or break her, but Emily's story was just too fascinating to leave alone, and she knew it would haunt her if she didn't try. She shakily poured herself a large measure of Disaronno, found some ice in the freezer and took it all back to her couch.

There was another reason she was considering this action, but wouldn't divulge to anyone just yet. Her friend in the police force made enquiries with regards to an Elizabeth Riley who may have disappeared in nineteen eighty-five. Her case remained a missing person as no foul play had ever been found. She would be in her early sixties if alive. Her partner, Melanie, had never lost hope that she'd be found. Marian put on some music and tried not to think about tomorrow or the possibilities.

*   *   *

I didn't sleep, my head racing with possibilities about my future. I couldn't stay here, I knew that. I had no idea if our old home still belonged to us, but doubted it, unless Brian had continued to rent it out. I could barely remember the three-bedroom home that had been my sanctuary all of my early years. I'd forced myself to forget as soon as I'd left, leaving an alcoholic to manage the place.

I let the tears fall silently as I gazed up at my ceiling, as images of our happy home came flooding back. We had been happy despite two teenagers in the house and Mum and Dad had been so in love. It just wasn't fair. I'd wished over and over that I might get revenge on the bastard that murdered them. But years passed with no leads, no witnesses, no evidence, and my hatred towards the person intensified, knowing whoever it was had got away with it, and justice would never be forthcoming. I would never know who'd taken my parents away, and I'd forced myself to push the intense anger down and hide it, believing that one day whether in life or death, I would have my revenge. What goes around, comes around, I had to believe that.

I quickly wiped my face, and changed my course of thoughts to Tristan and everyone in the past. It didn't make me feel any better. The deep ache in my heart was like the terrible pain I'd felt after losing my parents. What had happened to Tristan in that instant of slipping through time? Had he returned? Had he become lost elsewhere? In that moment, I had thought him here with me, and had turned to look. Confused and disorientated, I'd found myself alone, with only the corpse of Paul Dawson and his blood. I'd fallen to the floor, and remained that way until found by the police. Tristan had gone, lost to me. Inwardly, I screamed and wept for all those whom I had grown to love, and had lost. But mostly, my heart broke for the man who had saved me, and given my life purpose.

I turned towards the wall, my back to the camera in the corner. To anyone watching, I was merely sleeping, but my mind refused to shut down, regardless of the pill they'd given me. I thought of Ayleth and felt such guilt over leaving her behind. Of course, I'd had no choice; still, she had considered the possibility of another time-slip impossible, but it had happened to me within eight months. Fate had given me a new life, filled with love and danger, passion and death, and then ripped me from it.

I'd considered many reasons, and one of them had been finding Ayleth's old girlfriend, if I ever got out of the hospital. I'd explain that Ayleth or 'Betty' had never just left, she'd gone back in time and was still stuck there, though in theory, she should be long dead by now. Yeah, I saw that going down very well. However, I owed it to Ayleth to at least find her and say something. Though in truth, I hated the idea of staying here in this time, and refused to consider the possibility until I had to.

Jane murmured in her sleep and I glanced across at her. I wished I could help her. This was a truly awful place, but I had no idea what Jane saw or felt except the odd insight into her fucked-up mind. Would I end up like her, all messed up and living in my own head? I found the prospect not an unhappy one if it meant I saw and felt Tristan every moment. I closed my eyes and tried to force his image to appear, but it was only fleeting, and I curled into a ball and silently wept for my lost love.

*   *   *

Brian put down his mobile and breathed out deeply. He was shaking at John's words, and what the consequences would be if they got caught. Not knowing what the police were thinking, and what stage they were at, he and John could make things worse if they got caught, or it could all be for nothing and they'd let Emily go anyway. Besides, he also had just a fleeting niggle on his conscience. If, and it was a huge if, Emily had killed this man, he knew what it felt like to crave justice, and hated himself for possibly taking it away from the dead man's family.

Paul Dawson. He'd not really taken that much notice of his name, his only concern had been Emily at the time, but now he tried to visualise him. The photograph in the newspaper had shown a smiling man in his early forties. Slightly chubby, short, military-looking hair and a slight grin on his face, wearing his security guard uniform with pride. He'd barely registered him, not wanting to look at the man if his sister had somehow been a part of his demise. But now, he wondered about the man and his life.

His family, a mother and younger sister, had cried on television and demanded justice for their darling boy, who hurt nobody and preferred his own company and nature walks. He'd had the job as a night security guard for years, and had always been good at it. It'd been hinted at that Paul had a few learning difficulties and worshipped his father, who'd died fairly recently. From what everyone said, he was an innocent man who'd been cold-bloodedly murdered by his sister. Yet, what nobody bothered to question until now was, how could Emily, a five-foot-six, thin young woman, get close enough to decapitate a large man who was apparently good at his job? Yes, she was a black belt, but there was no bruising on him besides around the neck. What the hell was she doing in the old warehouse that night, and where had she been for eight months prior to that? A mystery he hoped would be solved tomorrow night, if all went well.

CHAPTER 39

John left Simon, his editor's, office, with a smirk on his face, and went straight to his own desk to collect his mail, trying to keep himself busy, but it was hard. In only four hours, he'd be breaking the law. Although his editor had agreed to it in principle, he would disown John if it went wrong. Arsehole was always covering his own arse, but John knew he was just as excited about this as himself.

"You know I can't save you if the police catch you?" Simon looked thoughtfully out of the window.

"Yeah I know, but if we get away with this, the story will be worth it." John remained seated, but felt fidgety. He'd barely slept as he went over every detail, and possible outcomes. "But can you get your man to help with the technical stuff or not?"

Simon glanced around and shrugged. "Yes, of course I can get him, but I have to consider his safety as much as yours. So far, the guarantee of this working is fairly minimal."

"No, it's not." John went through everything again and what he needed from the 'tech guy', who did everything from illegal phone tapping, to bugging rooms, to messing with computer screens. John never asked this man's background, and Simon never divulged it.

Eventually Simon nodded. "Okay, stop grovelling, it's embarrassing. I'll make the call, but John, make sure you stick to the schedule. My guy will not wait for you once he's given the times needed, all right?"

"Yeah, that's great. Tell him five on the dot for as long as he can. We should be away before they realise."

Now he had four hours to wait with a stomach performing badly and he ran to the toilets again. The last few months had taken its toll on him emotionally, mentally and in some cases, physically. Afterwards, while popping antacids, he picked up the phone and rang Brian, then Marian, and finally Professor Harris. The scene was set, now it just had to be executed.

*   *   *

Brian paced his flat after talking with John. Four hours would drip by and he doubted he could deal with that. He'd already taken a day off, just in case it went ahead, though the boss wasn't impressed at such short notice and his best bricklayer off. Brian had smiled at his words. He'd never been complimented for his work and had said as much.

"Yeah, well, I mean what I say. You've proven yourself in this job, so don't blow it. One day: and only because you've helped me get ahead of schedule and the bosses are happy. I'll use that time to get the less experienced up to your standard."

"One day. You've got to be fucking kidding me. My skills took years to build, mate! I'll see you on Friday."

"Skills? Bollocks! Bright and early Brian or I'll kick your arse off this project, skills or not."

"Yeah, yeah, okay."

His sister was worth the risk. He owed it to her, but he would feel a small amount of regret if this thing went sour and he lost his job. He'd realised, as his skill had become apparent, that he loved it, and the thought of being good at something and losing it felt harsh. They'd just have to be absolutely sure nothing went wrong.

*　　　*　　　*

I barely ate any breakfast or lunch, aware of eyes watching, and whisperings, as I moved around the canteen, and then the lounge where they had an art therapy class going on. I'd felt obliged to join it and lost myself in an hour of creativity, though my mind was thinking what might have happened if I'd been in my usual session with Marian Griffiths.

When I focused back on the picture, I realised I'd drawn a castle, Artorius' castle, with a figure, his back to the viewer staring up at it from beneath. I knew the figure was meant to be Tristan. Even from the back, his hair colouring, his stance, his sword and clothes told me, and I felt the sting of tears. I yearned for him now more than I had thought possible since Marian's sessions. In some dark place in my heart, I'd grieved for him, for them all, knowing the chances were slim to ever be with them again. I'd remained silent, unable to form words. But since the sessions, I'd found how strong my mind could be, and even reliving my time had brought a joy I had never expected to feel again, as it felt like the first time.

I may never know what happened to them, but I could at least be in their presence again. Even the terrifying parts had made me feel so alive. I just couldn't come back to this monotonous time where people didn't truly 'live' anymore—they merely existed, preferring to give their full attention to computers instead of their own species, and hiding from the actual truth of the world.

I glanced around the room. One patient was attempting to eat some blue oil paint while the tutor and an orderly wrestled him to the ground. Three patients were staring mindlessly at their empty canvas, paint-brush in hand, lost in their own turmoil minds. Four had actually drawn something. In fact, one of them was astoundingly beautiful. A perfect, pink rose in close up with a green leaf and a bumble-bee resting on a petal. A passing nurse admired it, and I admired Jane, the painter of such a beautiful piece. She sat on the floor beneath her artwork whilst rocking herself. She sang something too faint to hear the words.

So Jane had hidden talents? I worried about her remaining here, but there was nothing I could do. At that moment, the tutor saw the picture and came over to admire and praise, while the orderly escorted the paint-eating patient out into the hallway to get cleaned up. I watched as Jane hunched further inward, the tutor speaking softly to her, congratulating her work, and I knew it was the wrong thing to do. Jane wanted invisibility, not admiration, which was her constant war. She obviously had talents and they needed to be expressed, but her mind and body needed to be small and uninvaded. In that moment I could empathise with her.

I felt the hairs on the back of my neck stir, instinct told me I was being watched. I turned towards the source and caught John glaring at me from the doorway. A slight inclination of his head told me to follow him and he disappeared down the corridor. I carefully cleaned my brush and took down my picture, ignoring the 'well done' and 'good job' from the tutor. I caught the eye of one of the nurses, held up my painting and mouthed, 'my room', to which she nodded uninterested, but at least the camera would have caught it so there shouldn't be any questions.

I walked slowly, eyes searching, as John was nowhere in sight. Reaching my room, I opened the door and leaned the canvas against my bed to dry and turned, startled as John appeared in the doorway.

"Be ready to leave by four-thirty today, okay?" He was brisk and turned to go,

"Yeah, okay, but what do I need to know?" I whispered after him.

He quickly scanned the corridor. "You need to know nothing except be ready, dressed and ready to go. Don't do anything stupid and get yourself into solitary. I need you on the hospital floor, so behave."

And he was gone. I sat down heavily on my bed as my legs gave way. Adrenalin rushed through my veins making me shake. Two hours. I didn't know what to do, so I curled up on my bed and waited.

*   *   *

One of the walls had been breached and the Saxons came running into the courtyard. Women and children ran screaming as our men ran to meet them in battle. I stood on the opposite battlement. Artorius was running down with his men, Tristan at his side, roaring their anger at such horror. They sliced the first Saxons they met leaving them to die slowly as they worked their way through the horde. I stood motionless. Shock seeped through every pore at this unexpected turn of events. They'd surrounded the castle, but had kept our gaze fixed elsewhere while they'd breached an outer wall, creeping towards the courtyard like vipers until it was too late.

I finally found my voice and called Ayleth, but she never came, and I searched the throng of fighting men for clues as to what I should do. Run and hide perhaps? Secure myself and others in a room and hope our men won? Merek? His room was close and the fight was nearing his door. I couldn't just stand there and hope for the best. I was a fighter. Maybe not with sword, but I could hold my own and I quickly made my way to his room. I slammed the door shut behind me, dagger in hand, and I backed away, until I felt the hard wood of his bed behind my knees.

I turned to check on him and found Merek as he'd been since his injury, unmoving, but breathing. The wound on his head was closing nicely, with no seeping and no smell. It felt strange being in this room again so soon after the suicide of that woman. I looked down at the floor and saw among the rushes a stain from her body, urine or vomit. I couldn't (and didn't want to) remember. I remained standing with hands shaking and stomach clenched, determined I would protect this man.

The door burst open and I jumped as someone shook me. "Emily?"

I opened my eyes, blinking in confusion as my brain tried to understand the two scenarios in my head. One where I'm fighting for my life in a small room, and here, where a nurse was hovering over me. For a brief moment they seemed to overlap, but I finally focused on the angry nurse. "You're not supposed to linger in your room, Emily, you know that. Come on, get up, night-time is for sleeping."

I slowly sat up and pulled my cardigan closer. The dream, my memory remained with me as I tried to focus and clear my head. Suddenly I remembered and grasped her hand. "What time is it?"

"Nearly four, why? Do you have to be somewhere?"

I blushed and quickly shook my head. "No, of course not, but I do need the bathroom."

She stepped to one side and, like a matron, frogmarched me to the large bathroom. She watched me go in before going about her business, and no doubt to write up her report on me. My being in my room wasn't bad enough for solitary, but I had to be good for just a few more minutes.

I washed my face afterwards and rinsed my mouth out. It felt dry with fear and anxiety, as the memory of that fight refused to retreat. I saw it as clearly as if I were still living it and licked my lips, almost tasting the blood from the split lip I'd received from my attacker. He'd been a small, wiry man, reminded me of a stoat and I said as much, but of course he'd no idea what I was saying. He'd glanced between me and Merek on the bed and had grinned to himself, thinking he had an easy job.

Lunging at me, he'd been surprised by a rip in his shirt as I'd used the dagger. It caught him just on the breastbone so didn't do enough damage, but it did enrage him enough to move faster and slap me hard across the cheek, causing a split lip and a humming in my ears. I'd staggered, but managed to stay upright. I'd kicked out, catching him in his upper thigh, and while he reeled from that, I glanced him a blow to his neck, quickly followed by another kick to his face that sent him flying backwards, his nose broken, gasping for breath.

I couldn't give him a moment to recover and without thinking, I stepped forward and, with one movement slit his throat. Warm blood sprayed on my dress and I stepped back immediately and moved to the top of the bed, fighting back the rising bile. I had to keep my wits about me as more footsteps approached the room. I set my dagger and prepared for battle.

CHAPTER 40

J ohn scoured the recreational rooms searching for Emily. He'd been busy with other patients since seeing her in her room. His disguise as an orderly at least kept his mind occupied while he waited for four o'clock. At five past four Emily was not in her room or any of the lounges. He daren't ask one of the nurses, as they'd be suspicious about an orderly asking for a patient, though he'd already got evidence that that kind of behaviour had taken place last year with Jane and another orderly, who'd been suspended following them being found out. No charges were ever brought against him as Jane hadn't accused him of rape or sexual assault in any of her singing rhymes.

He'd been asked to escort one patient to the men's bathrooms when he saw her loitering outside the ladies. She saw him, but didn't react as he passed her, merely lowered her gaze and slowly walked towards the television lounge. He smiled to himself, checked his watch, and gently pushed the male patient towards the bathroom quicker.

He found Emily easily then and, as four-thirty approached, he put his plan into action. John tried to control the shaking, pounding heart and dry mouth as he walked briskly to the office. With nimble fingers, he switched keys for the outside doors, and slipped a couple of drugs into the coffee he was always asked to make about now.

As if on cue, the nurses and doctors on duty filed into the large office, collecting their coffee mugs with a vague thank-you, and taking a couple of biscuits as a treat before going back to their various posts. John made his way into the television room, gave the nod to Emily and walked towards the back stairs. These weren't guarded as they were electric and had cameras trained on them, as all the exits did, but in a quarter of an hour, the drug would have kicked in, making the staff a little sleepy, and if the 'tech man' was good at his job, all the cameras would be switched to another feed, showing nothing untoward, and this exit would be unlocked.

I caught him up, though kept my distance as he looked up towards the cameras. He pointed towards a bin in the far corner of the corridor, and when I went to see, I found a small plastic bag hidden behind it. Inside were jeans and a jumper, both mine. John turned his back while keeping watch. I changed into normal clothes and stuffed the white pyjamas in the bin.

John looked at his watch, sweat trickled down the side of his face, and he licked his lips nervously. "My watch might be fast, but he'd better be quick. I think the drugs have worked and there'll be chaos any minute."

He was right. I could hear the noise in the nearest recreational room change. The patients seemed more nervous and confused and louder. It would get someone's attention soon. Then I heard a click and John used the keys. The door opened and I rushed through them, with John close behind me. He locked the door and dropped the keys, after wiping them on his uniform.

"Don't we need them?"

He grabbed my hand and pulled. "No, they only work for that door. Besides, if it's all gone to plan, every door should be open in the next five minutes. So let's go."

He was right. We walked quickly down corridors and back stairs. Very few people saw us, and those who did merely glanced our way. I asked about the cameras, but nobody stopped us, and eventually John just said, "They've been dealt with, come on...."

We arrived outside and I stopped for a brief moment. The cold air felt wonderful and I could hear birds starting to wind down for the day. The sun was low, perhaps another hour of daylight left, but I had no time to enjoy the moment as a car pulled up and John pushed me into the back. He kept me lying down with a couple of coats pulled over me.

"Is she okay?" I heard Brian's voice and felt an unexpected rush of gratitude.

"Yeah, she's fine, just drive nice and easy ... that's it, no don't wave to the guard, you idiot. Oh, you know him, do you? Okay, fine, just head out of this road and we'll stop where we planned."

After ten minutes of lying down under stuffy coats, one of which stank of smoke, I was allowed to sit up, and saw that we were heading out into the country. Brian watched me through his rear-view mirror and I managed a small smile.

"It's good to see you, sis." I heard his voice break and he quickly blinked away his tears.

Reaching out, I gently patted his shoulder. "Good to be seen, Brian ... thanks."

I felt that I could be generous towards him now, because if it all went well, I'd be locked in my memories with Tristan, away from all of this, never to return.

We drove for about an hour, mostly in silence, as John directed Brian to turn here and there. We stopped twice to double check we weren't being followed, but finally John was confident enough to direct us to the house Marian had asked him to bring me to.

It was a lovely old house. Stone-built in its own grounds. "Posh! She doesn't live here, does she?" I asked as we pulled up outside a large wooden door.

"No, not on her salary. Apparently, it belongs to an old friend who spends most of his time cruising the sunnier parts of the world, returning here when he has to." John pulled on his coat as he stepped out into the cool spring air.

Brian was handing me a black fleece of his when the door opened, and Marian stood in the doorway. A man I didn't know was hovering nervously behind her. "Welcome, come in, quickly." As I approached, she smiled warmly. "Emily, glad you could make it.... Gentlemen, please close the doors after you and lock them. We don't want to be disturbed now, do we...?" She was watching me carefully all the time she spoke. Now she seemed to remember her other guest. "May I introduce Professor Harris." Looking at me directly, she grinned. "He's dying to meet you."

I let the man shake my hand enthusiastically, and smiled thinly as he went on to talk about his research.

"Now, now, please, Professor, remember what we said. Emily is here to help you, but let's give her some space." Marian's tone had an element of warning, and the professor bowed his head in shame.

"Of course, yes, quite right, poor girl has been through enough. It's just that I'm so excited to finally speak with you."

My head was beginning to spin from all of the excitement and so I was glad when Brian took my arm and gently led me into a large, cosy room filled with all manner of antiques, a roaring fire and a small table of buffet food. Rows of books lined one wall, while the other three were littered with portraits of various people. I gazed around me in awe. The rooms were bare and sparse in the hospital, now being in a full room made me feel a little claustrophobic, and from habit, I moved to have my back to a wall.

"Are you hungry, Emily?" Marian, seeing me move had misinterpreted my movement, but on her words, I did realise I'd not eaten for ages.

With a brief nod, I helped myself to the variety of vegetarian sandwiches, dips and carrot sticks. Marian offered me a cup of tea and sparkling water, while everyone nibbled and drank coffee as they waited for me to feel more settled. I was aware of the tension, the small talk doing little to dispel the pressure.

Eventually, my appetite sated, I turned to the professor, who was nibbling on a cheese roll whilst trying not to outwardly watch me. "So, do you have my sword?"

Without a word, he quickly threw down his meal and lukewarm coffee and almost ran to a box I hadn't noticed. Opening it carefully, he brought out Tristan's sword wrapped in plastic and held it out for me to see.

I wasn't expecting the wave of sorrow that flooded my body, and a noise escaped my lips as I reached out to touch it.

Professor Harris withdrew it. "I'm sorry, but you're not wearing gloves. I know it's in the plastic bag, but it's still evidence of a murder and, well, I'm going to get into so much trouble already...."

I slowly lowered my arm. "That's okay. It's just a shock seeing it after all this time, and it looks in good condition...."

"Yes, about that, you've got every historian and archaeologist in the world flummoxed as to how a sword that dates back to the sixth century could be in such perfect order. It just isn't possible, and yet, here it is...."

I grinned. "Yes, here it is. Is it enough proof perhaps that I have indeed been somewhere?"

"Been somewhere? So you're telling me you got this sword from somewhere? Where did it come from? You see, I have this friend, Lucy, who has a weird gift, and I managed to get this to her before coming here, and she tells me this sword is genuine.... Is it?"

I ignored him, my full attention on the sword. I saw again the perfect carvings, the line of the blade, the handle his hands had held so tightly protecting me. "The sword was made for a man called Tristan by a remarkable blacksmith whose name was Dain. I think a man whose talents were before his time. He could make anything. He's dead now. I've been somewhere and I fell in love with Tristan, and he loved me. I was to be his wife, you see, and he was trying to protect me...." The wave of raw emotion hit me hard and I faltered in my explanations. I needed to go back, retreat inward, but Marian used my silence to interject her own view.

"And we're jumping ahead, aren't we? So, Emily, how do you feel about another session, here, now?" Marian stepped forward and blocked Professor Harris from view, who was looking very perplexed.

I looked around at everyone and took a long, deep breath. "Yes, I'm ready..."

CHAPTER 41

I found it difficult to relax in strange surroundings as people watched me expectantly. Even though they'd been told to remain quiet and unobtrusive, I knew they were there and it unnerved me. The room itself was a comfortable, warm room, and the large settee I lay down on was so soft I could have easily fallen asleep, if I'd been alone. Marian bade me to listen to her voice and breathe deeply, as I always did, and although I felt myself relax, I just couldn't move ahead, and I was becoming flustered. My desperation to return, and remain, with Tristan was hard to control, and Marian saw it immediately.

"Gentlemen, I think it would be better if Emily and I were alone. For both privacy and concentration, don't you think?"

John abruptly stood up. "I want to hear what she has to say, I need to."

"Then leave your own recorder alongside mine."

Brian shrugged. "I'm not sure I want to leave Emily alone with you. I'm still not convinced you haven't messed her head up."

"Oh, Brian, I'm fine, stop fretting, it isn't like you to care so much." I hadn't meant it as an insult, but he heard it and sighed loudly.

"Yeah, okay, maybe you're right. I'll go and make a coffee. You men care to join me?" He was already up and moving through the door. John hesitated, but finally pulled out his own recorder, that was already recording and with a smirk, he followed Brian. Only Professor Harris remained.

"I don't want to leave the sword. It shouldn't be here. I've taken a great risk, so has my friend for helping me get it out of evidence, so I daren't leave it out of my sight, you understand?"

I glanced up at him. He was sweating and looked very uncomfortable. "The sword is important to me, but if you need to take it, then take it with you."

"Are you sure?" He looked relieved. "You don't need it as a prop or something?"

I grinned and shook my head. "No, I don't need it to remember." It did cross my mind that if I somehow managed to get back then what would happen to the sword? It had come from the past, therefore it must still be in the past. If I somehow managed to remain in the dark Ages, would the sword disappear or would it remain in this time? A head wrecker.

Tristan would have found the professor's behaviour quite bizarre and would most likely have clobbered him one. I felt irritated by his possessiveness of my sword; after all, it wasn't his to cherish, it was mine, given to me by Tristan that fateful day. But soon, I hoped it wouldn't matter. Soon I wouldn't care where the sword was so long as I was back with him and I'd forget everything here.

Professor Harris carefully picked up the sword and carried it out of the room. We knew he'd stolen it from the police station, and he was in serious trouble for doing that, but he didn't care. He'd wanted to know about the sword, and part of me wanted to tell him everything, though my need to return was stronger. If I could return tonight, then he could smuggle the sword back into evidence. It seemed their security was pretty light right now due to cuts, but in his own words, 'they'd been bloody lucky, and it was lucky if they could get it back in'.

The men gone, Marian brought her chair closer, blew out a few candles so light was minimal, and I lay back on the comfortable sofa and closed my eyes.

*   *   *

"Are you sure she isn't in her room?" Mary glanced around the recreational lounge again, just in case Emily was hiding, not that she ever had, but still....

"I've looked everywhere. I haven't seen her for hours, no one has." The two orderlies looked worried. They'd fallen asleep on duty, which wouldn't look good to the snobs upstairs, but they'd found out that a couple of other nurses and the doctor on duty had also snoozed so it might be in their favour if they'd been drugged.

"Check the monitors, she couldn't have got out of the doors, they're locked. Besides the cameras would have told us if she'd escaped and Edward already checked them. No one is near them. Damn it! She must be here."

Mary looked down the corridor at the doctor who was shaking his head and rubbing his eyes. It was fairly obvious they'd been drugged. Some of them had fallen asleep, while a few others had merely slumped in chairs, dazed, and lost time. Had to be tranquilisers, but how the hell did Emily get hold of those?

"Doctor? Anything?"

He shook his head. "No, nobody has seen her. I feel so woozy. The room is spinning slightly, as if I'm on an escalator."

"Yeah, well, now you know how it feels for your patients you pump this stuff into." The nurse stormed off to raise the alarm and soon the wards were humming to a loud ringing alarm that brought staff from all directions, the drill if an alarm was pulled.

As they reached Mary and the doctor, it was the nurse who filled them in. "One of our secure patients, Emily Rogers, is missing. We have no idea how, but some of the staff have been drugged, so we've lost about two hours. We've checked the cameras on this level, but she isn't on them using any of the doors or windows."

"Well, that's it then, she must still be here somewhere?" A male nurse called from the next ward.

"We've searched everywhere. I think she had help to get out. Inform security downstairs to check their cameras inside and out please."

"You think someone tampered with the camera? Call the police, now."

"Already done."

At that moment, along with the alarm, they could hear the growing noise of a siren.

*   *   *

Slicing a man's throat was not something I felt particularly comfortable with, but even worse for me, was watching the spread of his blood as it oozed from the wound and covered the rushes, and the smell and feel of its coppery stickiness. "I thought blood stopped pumping out when the heart stopped? You are being awkward...." I chastised him loudly, hoping to make myself feel better as I quickly backed away from the growing pool.

The noises outside continued with thundering feet on boards, men's cries, women's screams, the clash of metal on metal along with the grunts of effort to kill an opponent. Footsteps neared Merek's door and I clenched the dagger. I heard men fighting for breath as they got near, and soon they were just outside the door. I moved closer to the unconscious Merek and waited to fight.

They came as one. Two bodies lunged through the door, still fighting as they struggled to deal the death blow to the other. I recognised Brom and his opponent was just as big, a giant with a nasty-looking scar that ran from his left ear to his nose. His eyes caught sight of me, and that was his mistake. In a fraction of a second, Brom had a small knife embedded under the man's chin, he twisted and the giant choked, gargled his last breath, and went limp, face down in the doorway.

Brom pushed himself up, took a quick look around the room, at the dead man at my feet, my dagger held in front of me, protecting Merek's body. He smiled warmly, wiped blood off his cheek, and left me there. He left the door open, the giant's body acting as a door stopper. I edged forward and looked out. The courtyard was heaving with Saxon and our men, though I thought our men outnumbered theirs, judging from the different leather armour I saw. Of Tristan and Artorius I saw nothing and tried not to worry.

I attempted to push the giant out, but after several minutes it became obvious I couldn't move him. I stepped back into the room just in time, as an arrow pierced the doorframe where my head had been. I flung myself beside the bed, slipping on the blood-soaked floor. Another arrow shot through the doorway, thankfully missing Merek by inches, but hitting the bedpost. I had to move him.

I yanked his arms, but he was a dead weight. Eventually, I pulled out the two pillows beneath his head and piled them on top of his body, along with any covers, and placed his small round shield over his chest. Another arrow hit the wall above his head and I felt justified in what I'd done. I felt utterly exhausted and wanted nothing more than to curl up with Tristan and sleep for days, but a shadow in the doorway made that impossible.

I recognised the man immediately. He had dry humped me when I'd been chained up in Sagarus' castle, much to the amusement of the watching men. He grinned a toothless grin and looked me up and down, and then at the two dead comrades, before returning his attentions to me. I was left in no doubt as to his intentions, held my dagger firmly in front of me and backed away.

"You're gonna' die, you ugly mother-fucking ape!" I spoke as bravely as I could, and hoped he didn't hear the tremor in my voice.

He merely stepped over the giant and raised an eyebrow.

"Yeah, that's right, you're going to end up like these two idiots who dared to mess with me.... Now fuck off and die!"

Again, he merely watched me, frowning as he glanced around the room. He moved his head to see who lay underneath all the blankets and a shield, and grinned maliciously. He slowly drew his sword and stepped forward.

"Merek!" I screamed as he lunged at his body. In one movement I pulled a blanket up and threw it at the man, he caught it just as it reached his face, but it was enough for me to follow through with a lunge myself and I caught him somewhere on his arm. He yelled and jumped back, yanking the blanket away. Blood dripped from a small cut on his forearm, not good enough to stop him.

He came at me then in full force. Striding over the bodies, ignoring the blood, he swung his sword and would have cloven my head off if I hadn't been quick and ducked, making a grab for Merek's shield at the same time, bringing it up in an arch, catching the sword. The jolt of impact made my arm and shoulder go numb. I almost dropped the heavy shield, but managed to hold on and moved away to stand behind him. He swung his sword again and I held up the shield. The blow made me cry out as the pain shot up my arm, making every nerve feel like it was on fire. The shield clattered to the floor and I flung myself backwards as he moved towards me.

His hand clasped around my throat and he spat some words at me that meant nothing, but in my head it was probably something along the lines of, 'I'm going to fuck you hard, bitch, then kill you'. The horror I felt overwhelmed me, but it was quickly followed by my training. I let go of my dagger and used the weapons I was good at, my hands and feet. I clasped his hand, got his finger and pulled back hard, he cried out, but his grip only tightened. My skirt was hindering my legs, but I managed a quick kick to the knee that made him grunt with the impact. In that instant, I punched him in the eye.

It was enough to make him release me and stagger back. I yanked on my skirt to tear it enough to free my legs and I dealt him a vicious kick to the knee again, swiftly followed by a kick to the groin. As he bent over in agony, I kicked his face, sending him flying backwards. He was still conscious, so I went over and dealt him a kick to the neck crushing his windpipe. He died soon after.

Standing over his body, my breathing was coming out in gasps as I fought to control my adrenalin levels. I could smell his piss and stepped away, moving to the back wall, away from the growing number of bodies. I caught movement and turned ready to fight again, I relaxed and looked into the open eyes of Merek, who watched me with interest.

I smiled broadly at him, so glad to see him awake, and I went to him then and took his hand. He squeezed it gently and groaned with pain as his other hand went to his head. "God, yes, stay still. I know you can't understand me, but please lie quietly."

He glanced towards the open doorway and moved as if to get up, but his body fell back onto the narrow bed and a loud groan escaped him. I moved to him immediately and gently eased his body flat. "No, you don't. You can't do anything anyway, Merek, you're not strong enough. I'll protect you."

The sound of fighting seemed less to my ears, and I dared to peek out. The fighting had moved back outside of the castle walls. The courtyard was littered with men in all forms of dying, injured or dead. Most, I was glad to see, were mercenaries.

I ran back into Merek's room to try and tell him. I was in the middle of hand gestures when a shadow fell over the doorway and I immediately turned, ready to fight again, as did Merek, who pulled himself up, dagger in hand, but we both sighed loudly on seeing Tristan, bloodied with a couple of small injuries, but alive and grinning like a cat. He took one look around the room at the corpses and his gaze fell on me. In two strides he had pulled me into his arms and was kissing me passionately. We both heard Merek mumble something, and Tristan broke off our kiss to smile at his friend.

Within half an hour, the bodies had been taken away and thrown with the others of the enemy to be burned. Artorius was striding through the remains of his home with one arm in a sling, Ayleth had insisted he use as he'd dislocated his shoulder along with other minor cuts and bruises. He'd caught sight of me in Tristan's arms and smiled warmly before moving onto a group of men who were having a drink of ale.

By nightfall, I could barely move. Every muscle in my body ached and I yearned for a bath, but I wasn't going to bring up all the water needed and I wasn't going to ask the servants either, who were busy preparing food along with their own injuries. I made do with a bowl of cold water and cleansed myself of blood, sweat and muck as best as I could, using Ayleth's rose soap.

I found another dress as my other was torn, this one navy blue and a bit long. But with a few careful stitches, it was hitched up at the sides and looked quite dashing with my white chemise underneath. Satisfied,

I went in search of Ayleth who I knew I'd find in the makeshift hospital. I was halfway there when I caught her coming towards me. She looked absolutely done in, staggering with fatigue. I stumbled towards her and we clung to each other, sobbing with relief. Finally, we made our way slowly to her small cave, where she too changed from her soiled gown and apron, and washed her hands and face.

"Is it over, Ayleth?" It was a question I'd been desperate to ask, but Tristan had been too busy with bodies and mending walls to ask, and Merek couldn't understand me. I'd remained with him, watching his eye movements and helping him eat some vegetable broth and watered-down ale, which he'd grimaced at, but I'd insisted.

Now Ayleth sat on her bed and shrugged. "It's never over, Emily. Sagarus was not among the dead, though his dead outnumber ours, we still lost a great deal and he knows it. The wall on the east side was breached, which means we are very vulnerable right now. We have been given respite, Emily, nothing more."

My legs felt wobbly and I sat on a stool. "You mean he could come back?"

Ayleth lowered her gaze and put her hands between her knees as if she sought comfort there. "Emily, he will come back, it's just a question of when." She lay back on her bed and sighed. "Now is the time to try and get some sleep. He won't come back tonight. He lost a lot of men and we still have enough to keep watch and fight back." She turned to look at me, "You are safe tonight, Emily, and from what I hear, you killed a couple yourself. You're a wee vixen, eh?"

"Yes, I did, but I don't feel safe. Not while Sagarus is still out there."

"Whether it's Sagarus or another Saxon, Viking, French or English, this country will always be invaded, Emily, we know that from our history. We can't not live waiting for a threat to come."

I was about to argue, but stopped myself and thought about her words. During this century known to us as 'the dark ages' we knew there were many battles and skirmishes between the Angles and Saxons and Vikings. Once the Romans left, Britain became a free-for-all and I was living in the middle of it now.

"How do you do it, Ayleth? How do you live with the fear of attack hovering over you every day?" Emotion stuck in my throat and I swallowed hard. I couldn't crumble now.

Ayleth was watching me with a look of pity. "Emily, you just do, you have no choice. The alternative is to give up and die, and Tristan is a good reason not to give up, I think."

"I hear name...?"

We both jump at the sound of his voice, and I fell into his arms. He held me close and I suddenly felt as if my legs would never hold me again. Tristan must have felt the shift and held me tighter. Ayleth sat up and shook her head. "Dearest Tristan, stealth like a wolf." She said it again in their Old English, and he smiled warmly, pulling me closer, as if he couldn't bear for me to be two inches away, and I was glad. I needed to feel his solid body, to help, as mine felt like liquid.

"Come, eat...."

"I doubt I could eat anything and what about the injured and the walls, don't they need fixing...?"

Tristan looked between me and Ayleth who then translated with a shrug.

Tristan stopped then and held my face between his hands. They smelt of rosemary and I saw then that he'd also washed and was wearing clean clothes. His eyes filled mine and all I saw was his own soft brown eyes. Flecks of gold around the side of his iris gave him a strange wolf-like look.

"You safe, I promise." He smiled then, a soft, loving smile that made my stomach curl with pleasure and my insides flood with warmth, the last thing I expected after such a terrifying day.

"I love you." I hadn't realised it until that moment. I had loved him from the moment he'd saved me, and I had seen it in his own eyes. In that moment I believed I could make a life here with Tristan. He pulled me to him and kissed me thoroughly until Ayleth coughed. "I can't get past while you two are blocking the doorway, and I'm hungry!"

We all laughed and walked back to the great hall together. I was aware of men and women everywhere we walked. All were eating something, or drinking ale, but everyone was armed and watchful, as was

Tristan as he walked across the courtyard. He glanced towards the outer wall, now being guarded by a group of heavily armed men who stood behind a pile of rocks. Two wagons filled the gap made by Sagarus. The hole wasn't as big as I'd thought. Having used some kind of hooks, they'd attached them to a couple of bulls who'd pulled the middle stones away, causing those above to topple, leaving a gap large enough for two men to get through abreast.

That's where most of the men died, as they came through the small gap. They'd been met by a hail of arrows and spears. I heard that Brom had stood beside the wall and decapitated a majority of men as they scrambled through, being pushed and urged on from behind. It was a slaughter and one that Sagarus was willing to accept, but why?

It was a question on everyone's lips as we attempted to eat. Fair play to the servants and cooks, that despite the horror of the day, they'd managed to rustle up chicken and eggs and pork, along with fresh bread and broth for those unable to stomach hard food. I went for the bread and broth and nibbled on some cheese. Artorius offered me a cup of wine, which I accepted gratefully, and we all toasted Merek, who'd insisted on being brought into the hall and now lay on a pallet next to the table.

Talk was loud and excitable as people recounted their own adventures in the battle. I sat quietly and listened, trying to understand a few words here and there, but the language was so quick. Tristan sat beside me, one hand holding mine when he wasn't using it to eat. Artorius, sling still in place, was eating fairly well considering, and caught my eye a couple of times, a slight smile on his lips. I began to sense people in the hall knew something I didn't, and I felt nervous.

Eventually the meal ended and Artorius stood up and spoke for a long time on what I presumed was the battle. He toasted the brave dead and then turned to me. Ayleth interpreted for him.

"Today, I have witnessed a strength I never thought possible. A woman, a stranger, my guest, who is willing to sacrifice herself in order to save one of our own. Lady Aemilia took it upon herself to stand guard over Merek, who was unable to protect himself, and she did indeed protect him. Using her skills as a fighter, trained in this strange fighting method, she fought off attempts on his life, thus Merek is with us today. I give thee Lady Aemilia...."

The hall erupted in uproar and cheers made me blush and took my breath away. Tristan pulled me to my feet and toasts were made to me. Merek, helped by Brom came over and kissed me on both cheeks, handing me a slim dagger I knew meant a lot to him. Ayleth had told me it'd belonged to his sister years ago, and he always kept it on his person. She'd died from a complicated childbirth along with his nephew. I tried to refuse, but he insisted and Ayleth quickly told me it would be an insult not to accept such a gift. I took it with a smile.

I sat down flushed and embarrassed but very pleased. It was a lovely thing to do, yet I couldn't help think that anyone would have done the same as I. I couldn't leave them to murder Merek in his state and I doubted anybody in this room would have allowed it either. I said as much to Ayleth who agreed. "That may be true, Emily, but it wasn't them, it was you. A woman. A stranger. You have no connections here beside me, and it wasn't me you protected, was it? You have proved yourself, Emily. You are well and truly one of the castle now."

A sudden exhaustion took hold of me. The heat and the food and the excitement, on top of a lack of sleep and fighting all day, was taking its toll, and thankfully Tristan noticed. Making our excuses, he escorted me out of the hall. We weren't alone. Most were heading to their beds, or back to sit with their injured. A few looked utterly grief-stricken, and I knew they were going to empty beds and my heart went out to them.

Instead of escorting me up to my bedroom chamber, Tristan moved purposefully towards the little nook where we had first sat alone. It was a chilly night, but I had my cloak, and his body warmth was enough. We huddled together, his arms wrapped tightly around me as we stared up at the stars. The quarter moon was high. I tried talking to him about the North Star, but he didn't understand me very well.

"Well, if I'm staying, I guess I'll have to learn your Old English language...."

He didn't answer but pulled me to him and kissed me. His hands let me know exactly what he wanted, and there in the cold, dark, he entered me quickly and quietly. I gasped as his warm hands touched my naked skin and goosebumps sprang up all over me. "Be my wife."

It wasn't a question, it was a statement, and I held his face in my hands and whispered, "Yes."

CHAPTER 42

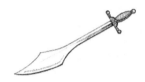

The wall was mended and soldiers walked its length again. Although it had been months since Sagarus had attacked, everyone remained on full alert, sleeping with their weapons, and not straying far from the castle walls. Winter settled on the land, and its cold bite made everything harder to do. Most mornings the water had a thin layer of ice on the buckets, and Ayleth had been forbidden to go to her spring. Either Tristan or Brom would go if they weren't busy, so Ayleth and I spent hours just boiling water again, and again, to get rid of any germs. So far neither of us had become sick, but it felt like a game of chance each time I had a drink of water.

The women thought us very odd at first, but once Ayleth explained about safer water, they began to boil their own, whether it was to humour her or they truly understood we never knew, but didn't care. Nobody could afford to be sick right now, and if it meant boiling water, then so be it. We spent hours knitting and weaving. Merek had fashioned us pairs of knitting needles from bone. Although it repulsed me to touch them, I did enjoy teaching the younger girls how to knit, and so scarves, mittens and socks were made, and even a long woolly jumper was knitted for Artorius by Ayleth to help keep out the chill. Most days my fingers were numb from the cold, but there was always a fire blazing somewhere to defrost my body before moving onto the next task.

I found my place within the castle and had a routine. Most nights Tristan shared my bed, unless I was menstruating, then I insisted he leave me alone. In all my time here, I hadn't missed my monthly period and welcomed it with a sigh of both assurance that I wasn't pregnant, and resignation of the five or six days of feeling dirty and smelly. With no Tampax or panty liners, Ayleth and I fashioned old linen with a type of bog moss inside and tied it to my homemade knickers, of which I now had a full week set. The first few days were horrible with cramps and blood dribbling down my legs on occasion, but I got into a regular habit of a homemade liner, change, wash liner through, leave to dry by fire, wipe with big leaves, start again.

Whilst knitting and weaving garments, we would have long discussions and I was amazed to find that most of the women didn't have regular periods. Ayleth told me it had something to do with their body weight. Most women were thin, unless pregnant. Also, they breastfed their children for a long time, hoping to keep them from starving. None looked ill though, and that was due to Artorius. He looked after his women, and everyone spoke of him with pride that he was their master.

I caught him watching me sometimes and he'd smile, bow and move on. Tristan had asked for his blessing in regards to our marriage and he'd given it gladly, hugging me hard and called me 'sister'. I was accepted by the castle and I felt loved, part of this huge family now, and although I felt fear of what might happen, I could never imagine leaving now.

Winter defrosted into spring, but still it remained quiet. Artorius ventured out to visit other chiefs to talk about peace and living in harmony. Most were happy to support one another. A few felt they deserved more and I'd be on edge whilst the men were gone, expecting Sagarus any moment. He never came and we began to relax a little. Word reached us that the king in the south had allowed more Saxons to settle on his lands. The king, named Cedric, was a Saxon, but he mostly kept himself to himself.

Tristan and I spent as many hours as possible with each other doing a variety of activities. I was attempting to learn their language and was getting fairly good at it. I understood a lot of words now and could have very basic conversations. When not practising or out scouting, Tristan taught me how to shoot, and I had proved myself a worthy archer. My wounds healed well and over the last couple of months, I'd begun showing the men some karate moves and they practised on each other. Most of the time it deteriorated into wrestling matches or playful fights, but it didn't matter.

As we walked past hand in hand on our way to the practice meadow, a couple of men shouted something that Tristan merely grinned at, and I guessed its content and smiled as well. We'd just found out that Sagarus' mercenaries were sick of losing their comrades and many had left his service to find murder elsewhere. Merek, who had made a fairly good recovery, surprised a couple of mercenaries who'd stopped at the nearby village the week before. He'd brought one back alive for questioning, and early that morning he'd given up his secrets before dying a quick death.

I felt elated on hearing the news, but Tristan merely shrugged and acted nonchalant about it. I found out from Ayleth that mercenaries came and went, and I was to remember the Vikings who would come next. I did, and remembered the horrific stories told of plunder and death, and my elation quickly disappeared. I became agitated and nervous, always looking around. Even surrounded by Artorius and his men, I felt vulnerable and jumped at every sound.

Today, Tristan had had enough of my fear and took me out by the river to train. "Best way to fight fear, is to fight better." His wolf trotted beside us, it seemed to have accepted me. Although I distinctly heard a growl every time Tristan bade him stay outside my chamber. He was not welcome inside.

Since that night on the wall, Tristan had made love to me at every given opportunity. Sleep came in fits as I'd wake to find his hands and lips on my body, urging me to wake and open for him. As much as I was weary and ached from the busy day, my body responded to him instantly.

Now we linked arms, and in his other, he held swords made from sticks, his own sword was in its scabbard at his waist, along with an axe and a dagger. He looked a formidable sight wearing only his tunic and trousers, and leather arm shields. I wore my green dress which was slightly cooler than the heavy navy one. Spring was coming quickly, and with it I found myself sweating beneath the layers of clothing. I had put my hair up out of the way. Women around the castle had passed comment on my look, some were curious, others disgusted at my fashion, but none said anything directly to me. I may have been accepted as a fighter in the castle, but some of the younger women were still nervous around me.

I made an effort at every opportunity, but I was never going to undo years of learnt behaviour. Women were encouraged from a young age to look after the husband, the house and the kids. I was not conforming which was suspicious to many women. I smiled and attempted to show interest in sewing and baking and babies, but it just wasn't me. I had come to terms with staying. I think in that instant of wanting to learn the language and make friends, I had subconsciously decided that, but these women would have to meet me half-way.

Ayleth found it all hilarious and said as much. "These women are bred to care, to bake, to cook and to sew. To see a young woman who can't do any of those things is just too weird for these poor girls. I heard talk of you being a witch! Aye, I heard the same thing when I was brought here, but at least I could bloody sew and bake."

I shrugged. "I can't help it, can I? I baked bread, but it came from a packet. I never sewed anything except a button occasionally, and sometimes it stayed on, and as for looking after a man, the lazy sod can do it himself."

Ayleth merely smiled and we continued our lesson, always within hearing of a few girls who were going about their day in the hope that they'd at least know I was learning their language and to watch what they said.

It was a cold crisp day for March and the sunlight glittered off the fast-flowing river nearby. With all the recent rain and sleet the water flowed quicker and louder than normal. I noticed Tristan's behaviour change from carefree to vigilant as we neared the edge. He quickly scoured the area and shook his head. "No here. Further up...."

I saw where he was pointing at, a craggy area across the river was high ground and away from the noise. I understood and followed him willingly. The climb left me slightly breathless and sweating. Once Tristan had done a quick sweep of the area with his wolf, he came back to me and looked me up and down. "Take off dress...."

I smiled. "Really? I thought we were here to fight?"

He reached out and began pulling up my dress slowly. "Hot. More movement...."

I let him pull my dress over my head and he laid it down on a nearby boulder. "I see, so you want me naked so I don't get hot while fighting you? Not the worst reason I've ever heard."

He shook his head as I think he got the gist. "No naked ... no yet...."

I felt my insides warm with his words, and his eyes stared into mine. I could see that he was fighting his urge to ravish me again and my breath quickened. It had only been an hour ago and I still felt his seed between my legs. But, he quickly got himself under control and held out a wooden sword. I took it sulkily and raised an eyebrow questioningly. "And if I'm a good girl, will I get a lollipop?"

For the next hour or so he taught me various moves with the sword and together he moved me through what I could only describe as dance movements, but when fast, became a series of moves that might help me in a fight. When Merek, Brom and Dalibar wandered up later in the morning, I was able to use them as my first guinea pigs, though I was slower with Merek who was still uneasy on his feet if he moved too quickly. Yet, he'd still managed to kill two mercenaries and bring another in for questioning, I reminded myself.

Brom was wonderful and remained patient. Even when I hurt him a couple of times, he'd laugh it off, even feigning chasing me in mock anger. That scared me to death and I wondered how it'd be for any enemy on the wrong side of Brom. By midday my chemise was soaked through with sweat and I saw the reasoning in losing my heavy woollen dress.

After a quick wash in the river to cool down, we all trailed back to the castle and my afternoon was spent helping Ayleth with any injured, which consisted of a burnt finger, a deep cut that needed cleaning and three stitches and a migraine. Along with one young woman who thought she was going into early labour, though thankfully, she didn't. Artorius had sent out word to nearby estates of the Saxon invasions down south and he accumulated a number of allies, who had also been attacked by mercenaries. We had a number of visitors who also took advantage of Ayleth and her knowledge whilst at the castle, so most days were fairly busy.

We settled into a routine such as this for weeks as spring flourished into an early summer and my wedding day fast approached. My periods continued to be fairly regular, something that constantly surprised both Ayleth and myself, with all the sex I was having, but I agreed that it was for the best. I think a tiny part of me hoped that I'd never get pregnant, as the thought of losing a child to a Saxon horde was almost impossible to contemplate, yet women in this time had to endure it.

With the wall rebuilt and the outer moat dug even deeper, alliances made, the men turned their attentions to planting and sowing, along with training more men. I watched them as they turned young boys into fighting men. Some as young as eight were given training in wielding a sword and shield, and shooting arrows. I'd become quite good at archery and was considered good enough to join the men on the wall if danger should arrive. I also argued that more of the women should learn archery, despite there being a small number who were very capable and had helped in the previous battles. Against a number of objections, I took five willing young girls under my wing and began training them. Most days, after their chores, I was allowed an hour with them and, within that short time, all showed promise.

Artorius and I had become firm friends. Through Ayleth he'd informed us of a marriage he was contemplating. An English Baron whose estates ran near Hadrian's Wall was looking for an alliance. Both Ayleth and I were dying to ask if her name was 'Guinevere', but kept our mouths shut in case we changed history. Of course, we didn't really believe in a Guinevere and Lancelot, but better to be safe than change history too much.

Three days before my wedding day, Tristan came for me as usual after he'd scouted the area for any dangers. He'd spent the night, but he was always up and out before I woke. The days were long and busy and most nights I fell into bed exhausted, but content, only to be roused out of slumber by exploring hands and lips. Last night had been no different, and I'd woken to birdsong and an empty bed.

It was to be a morning of sword practice, followed by archery, and then Ayleth and I had scheduled an afternoon of herb lore. We had managed to grow quite a collection for beauty and medicinal purposes. Tristan kissed me fully before escorting me out into the courtyard. We passed pleasantries with the blacksmith, and the baker who gave us pastries to take with us, as I'd missed breakfast. I devoured the vegetable pastry before we'd even reached the pasture and I swigged some cool ale to wash it down.

Tristan laughed and said something about my stomach getting bigger. He wasn't wrong. I'd noticed an increase in my appetite, but I was using more calories with all the manual work I did now, so I'd put it down to needing more fuel. Now I wasn't so sure. My period was due any day. I had hoped to have it finished by my wedding day, but so far it hadn't come. I gently pressed the area above my pelvic bone and thought it felt tighter, rounder, and I knew.

In that instant I felt a maternal bond with my child, and thoughts of my own mother raced into my head. I fought to push them away, but the sudden need for revenge on the monster who'd taken her away from me was overwhelming. I sank down onto my knees and sobbed, wishing the bastard would appear so I could kill him. Silently begging whatever God there was to bring me justice on the murderer of my parents.

Tristan, completely taken aback by this sudden turn of events, had me in his arms within moments, cradling me like a baby, urging me to tell him the reason for my despair. I told him as best as I could about my parents' murder, which I'd already told Artorius anyway to help with my cover story, but now I told him what I had missed out. My grief for them had never diminished, only hidden away, and I'd survived by running from one job to another. He didn't question me about being a slave, as I'd previously said, but held me tightly until my tears dried up and I was able to stand.

"Best way to work off anger and grief...." Tristan held out his sword. "For you."

I stared down at it. His sword was beautifully made. It'd been made for him by a grateful blacksmith years before, whom he'd saved from being taken as a slave. Tristan and Ralf had been too late to save the mother from death, but they'd saved three young girls from being assaulted and enslaved. For that, the blacksmith, a fine sword maker had given him this sword. He now lived within the castle.

"I cannot take it. It's yours. You've earned it, Tristan." I backed away slightly but Tristan reached out and pulled me back to him.

"Yours. You must learn to fight with a real sword now ... I will ask blacksmith to make you your own, but until then, you must strengthen arm."

He was right, of course. I was pretty good with a wooden sword for practice, but real swords were heavier and dangerous. "All right, but only to practise with." I took his sword and held it lengthways to feel its weight. My arm sagged badly after only seconds.

Tristan grinned and produced another sword he often carried in his saddle as a spare. He was directing me where to move so that we could begin practice when they attacked. Three of them, all mercenaries, came at us from behind. Scouts, most likely, who had seen us sitting on the rock, our backs to them. They hadn't seen the sword so it took them by surprise when Tristan pulled his sword free from its scabbard and sliced the first man across his gut. I jumped and pointed Tristan's sword at the man running towards me, but the wolf jumped him from the side and had his throat ripped apart in seconds. Tristan was fighting with the third, but he got the better of him and the mercenary lost half his face with a swipe from Tristan's hidden dagger.

We didn't wait, but turned to run back to the castle. I sensed them before I saw them. A group of six or seven came rushing towards us from the nearby woods. They knew we couldn't let the castle know of them being there. It was kill or be killed. An involuntary scream escaped my lips as I ran full pelt towards the castle walls, but I knew I'd never make it, so did Tristan, who grabbed my arm and pushed me behind him so that he and his wolf stood between me and the group of killers.

They came fast with swords raised and two had axes. My stomach clenched in utter terror, but there was no time to think. I had to save my baby. The wolf leapt at the first man to reach us. His screams penetrated the air, but Tristan was busy fighting three men while two ran past their dying comrade, their eyes fixed on me. They both picked up speed and I waited until the last second then moved to my side, as Tristan had shown me, and their swords met only air, missing me by inches. I felt the rush of their steel and instinctively jumped back and at the same time, I swung Tristan's sword in an arch, cleaving one man's head from his shoulders. The other, partly blinded by the spraying blood, lunged towards me, but the body of his comrade got in the way. It was long enough for the wolf to come to my rescue again. He jumped on the man's back, taking him down. The man shrieked in terror and pain as his hand was ripped off. I turned away but the clash of steel had already finished and Tristan was by my side, pulling my hair away from my face as I vomited the pastry.

314

Tristan was whispering soothing words whilst searching the area for more danger. We heard a shout and Tristan pushed me down behind a huge rock as he acknowledged the whistling sound before I did. Half a dozen arrows littered the ground around us and we both heard a yelp. Tristan turned towards the noise and saw his wolf go down, an arrow sticking out of its back. Without thinking, he ran to his friend and pulled him towards the cover of rocks.

I dared to peep over the rock to watch for any sign of more danger to warn him, but none came and he managed to get the wolf to me without incident. I stared down at the wound, trying to ignore the clenching terror in my stomach, and the nausea that threatened to overtake me again. The wolf was still alive, but the arrow was deeply embedded in his back. I had no vet skills and looked between Tristan and his wolf, unsure what to do.

Suddenly, we were surrounded by men, thankfully ours. The shout we'd heard had been from Rulf who had been on his way to join us when he'd seen the attack and had run to warn the others. Merek was by my side and Tristan was talking to him about me. I could see his attention was on me and Merek nodded. He was still weaker than usual and although his body healed, he had terrible headaches that weakened him for days. On occasion he lost time and I'd tried to explain about epilepsy. He'd started training again with the men, and considering he'd fought three mercenaries, killing two and bringing the third back alive, he was doing pretty good so far. The problem was his patience, and we feared his need to prove himself capable would kill him. I was glad Tristan had done this for his friend. He didn't just trust anyone with his woman and Merek knew that.

Tristan abruptly bent down, kissed me hard and stroked my cheek. Before I could protest, he stood up and was shooting arrows faster than I could count. Brom roared something and, as one, the men ran out to meet the enemy, leaving me and Merek alone again. As the men ran towards danger, Merek pulled me away from the shelter of the rocks and back towards the castle. We could see Artorius leading soldiers on horseback, charging out of the gates. As they passed us, Artorius gave me a quick smile of acknowledgement before roaring his command to his men. I still held Tristan's sword in front of me as we ran. I daren't look back.

There was a flat meadow between us and the castle moat, where I could see men and women scrambling around getting the castle ready to defend itself again. Merek's hand was on my arm, urging me forward. The castle walls were perhaps a quarter of a mile away when I felt it and abruptly stopped. Merek stumbled backwards, but kept his feet and turned to look at me questioningly. For months I had thought about that first day when I'd gone through the time slip, and I had replayed that feeling over and over in my mind, and now, I was standing within reach of another. I couldn't believe it. The chances were unbelievable, Ayleth the perfect example of how rare they might be. And, of course, I had no idea if this would take me back to my time or to another. I had discussed it at length with Ayleth, who liked to believe that time was constant and although we had returned backwards, if we ever got the chance to go through again, she believed time would have moved at the same rate in my own time. So, in theory only seven months had passed since I disappeared in 2015. In theory.

Merek felt it too, and quickly looked around us. His sword drawn, he looked frightened. As did I, because I couldn't see where it was, only feel its tremor and an icy breath of wind that I knew instinctively wasn't from this time. But just in case, I glanced upwards at the blue sky and shielded my eyes from the glare of the hot sun.

We both jumped as Tristan came tearing into us, yanking my hand that Merek had let go to follow him, but I held my ground. Merek said something quickly under his breath, as if saying it out loud would bring it forth, and Tristan stopped pulling me and looked around frowning as he became aware of the change. He could feel it, and he stared hard in every direction, but his attention was caught elsewhere as Brom came running past, the wolf in his arms; they never left anyone behind. For half a second, I didn't comprehend why he'd be running, until I heard, then saw the Saxon army that was emerging from the nearby woodland. I choked on my own breath as hundreds of murderers and rapists thundered towards us, Sagarus leading them on horseback. We turned and ran.

Tristan pulled hard and I had no choice but to follow him. My legs ached from the speed, but I didn't dare stop. We ran until we were in the shade of the walls and there I finally saw it, the shimmering outline of a time slip. It was darker than the shade, almost black, and it felt cold. I could smell the pollution of my time wafting in on the freezing wind. It had built up here, as if a storm raged in another time and a door was open. Tristan came to an abrupt stop and stared at it. I trembled behind him for a brief moment, but then abruptly pulled away from him and quickly scoured the walls for Ayleth, I owed it to her to give her this chance to return—if it did go forward to our time, I had no way of knowing—but I had to offer her that choice, but from my angle I couldn't see anyone. "Ayleth! Ayleth!" I yelled loudly, but Tristan quickly covered my mouth.

"Why? Ayleth?" He pointed at the shimmering dark and began to back away. I pulled my face away from his hand and glanced around quickly, unsure what to do.

"Ayleth! Where are you?" I screamed at the top of my lungs, then looked at Tristan who was reaching out for me. I took a step backwards. Five steps and I'd be inside and away to another time, perhaps my own, perhaps not. Tristan looked between me and the hole and then suddenly, he seemed to understand and he dropped his arm. Ayleth and I came from somewhere else, and this shimmering hole was a way out, a way back.

I saw him swallow hard and glance quickly at the approaching army. They had stopped just past the craggy rocks, and we were still in danger, but I couldn't make that decision to stay or take a chance and go. I was rooted to the spot, with no idea how long the opening would remain. I loved Tristan and if my instincts were right, I was pregnant. I wanted to marry him, but this army was another reminder of why I didn't belong here; and how could I have a child in this chaos? I knew the devastation that was coming with wars upon wars for this land. I doubted I would live long and my child might never survive, but Tristan, how could I leave him....

Tristan suddenly stiffened as a man stepped out of the dark. I turned to look and almost wept when I saw a chubby man wearing a security guard uniform staring around him in terror. Our eyes locked and I started towards him instinctively, to save him, when he raised a gun. The weeks of training took over and with Tristan's sword, I swiped at it, knocking it from his hand and chopping off a couple of fingers in the process. Tristan leapt forward and in one movement had taken his sword from me and in a follow through motion, chopped the man's head off.

His body tumbled backwards into the blackness and I made to grab him. To this day I don't know why. Perhaps to have someone of my time to help me process my decision to stay, because in that instant of seeing the security guard, I had chosen to stay, realising life in any time was dangerous. Or perhaps it was something else, but I had an overwhelming need to have this man and know who he was. I lost my footing and fell forward after the body. I heard a cry and reached out for a hand, as I realised in that second I would lose Tristan forever. I felt the cold steel of Tristan's sword as it glanced off my hand and clattered to the floor beside me and then a hard, concrete floor. "Tristan!"

*   *   *

Marian licked her lips and nibbled her lower lip. Emily was staring into space now, tears streamed down her face as she grieved for her lost love, this Tristan. She turned then at the sound of the door softly opening and Brian looked around. "Is it over? We heard Emily shout, is she okay?"

Marian nodded, unable to speak, as a golf ball of emotion stuck in her throat. The three men tip-toed in and stood by the wall, all staring at Emily.

"Why is she crying? What have you done to upset her? Wake her up...." Brian bent down to look closer.

"She's told me her tale, but it won't help her with the police or I'm afraid, you, Professor. Her story is too impossible to contemplate." Marian cleared her throat and wiped her eyes.

"I want to hear it." John came over and picked up his own recorder.

"It won't help you either, John. The short version is that she believes she has time-travelled and she is crying now, Brian, because she believes that she has lost her true love. A man called Tristan."

"Time-travelling? Jesus! I thought you were helping us solve this murder she is accused of?"

"I had hoped to do that, but it seems she's determined to hide her guilt behind this fantasy that a man called 'Tristan' did it. I'm sorry." Marian went to the telephone and dialled the police. "I'd better let them know where she is. There's nothing else I can do for her, not unless she leaves this fantasy behind."

"What will you say to the police?" John frowned as he waited for his recorder to get back to the beginning.

Marian shrugged. "I'll tell them the truth, of course. Her brother and a journalist broke her out of a secure hospital and brought her to me and forced me to continue her sessions, as you'd become obsessed with finding evidence of her innocence. As for you, Professor Harris, you joined in as you're obsessed with finding out about the sword."

"You bitch! You had no intention of helping Emily, only yourself." Brian moved towards her, but stopped when she began talking to the operator.

Replacing the phone, Marian grinned. "I may be a bitch, but Emily has shown me a great deal, and I can use her as a study. She's a perfect example of how people can lose themselves in fantasy just to retreat from their reality. In Emily's case, she retreated to the sixth century for some reason, before returning to this vegetative state again. I may never have another opportunity to find out why, that will depend on how long this one lasts."

Brian stroked Emily's hair. "The last state lasted weeks ... after our parents were killed." He broke off and cleared his throat. "But she didn't kill that guard...."

Marian watched him closely. "She's done this before, hasn't she?"

Brian ignored the question and went to check outside. "Just tell me she didn't kill the damned guard."

"No, Brian, I don't believe she did. I believe someone else was there. Possibly this Tristan, who she's made into a hero to help her cope with what he did. By making him from the dark ages, where fighting was commonplace, his killing a man who threatened his woman is perfectly acceptable, hence no guilt for the killing, or even witnessing the killing. I will, of course, use this latest information to help the police search for this Tristan character. She gave me a pretty good description." Marian went to the window and stood beside Brian. "I'll need her old files if I'm to help her, Brian. If she has done this before then I have to know."

Brian sighed loudly and wiped a hand over his face. "Yeah, well, she kind of went inward for a while after our parents were murdered, swearing she'd get revenge on the bastard who killed them in cold blood. I'd find her staring at nothing for days, sometimes weeks. I got scared and told our local doctor, who said it was her way of escaping the trauma. Once we started counselling, Emily was fine, at least I thought so anyway. It was like this, but if I clicked my fingers she'd react slightly, but wouldn't come out of it until she was ready."

John sat down heavily on the sofa, quickly followed by Brian and Professor Harris, who still held the sword in its evidence box. "Your sister having episodes as a child doesn't explain the sword or where it came from. Perhaps this Tristan owned it, but how it is in perfect condition is bewildering...."

Brian looked down at the box on the professor's knees. "No, it doesn't, and maybe we'll never know. I wish I could get my hands on this Tristan bastard." He looked at his sister and quickly moved back to her side. He lifted her wrist and then let if fall back onto her lap. Emily never moved. He wiggled his hand in front of her face, but she remained staring ahead as though she wasn't seeing any of them. "And Emily? Where is she now?"

Marian came to stand beside Emily. "I'm not sure. I lost her as she went through the time slip of hers that brought her to the point of the murder in the warehouse, and now, Emily has retreated back into her vegetative phase, which is regrettable." She stepped in front of her patient and clicked her fingers, no pupil movement or jerking. "Emily, I want you to listen to my voice now, it's time to come back to this time, your time, with your brother." No response. Emily was lost to her, for now.

John was listening to Emily's voice on his recorder. He fast forwarded here and there. "Was she pregnant when she was found?"

"Yes, I believe she was, but only two months or so, and she miscarried a week after being in hospital."

"Do you think it was this Tristan's baby?"

Marian watched Emily for a moment before gently wiping away a tear off her cheek. "Yes, I believe it was. Whoever he was, she loved him enough to lie for him, and lose herself in her own fantasy. We may never know why Tristan killed this security guard, or why the horror of seeing it has made Emily retreat into the dark ages, but I believe we know all we can for this case, and now it's time for the police and the hospital to take Emily back into care."

Marian moved towards the door as they heard a car coming into the driveway. "Get your stories straight, gentlemen...."

Brian turned back to Emily and for a moment stared hard at his sister. He quickly glanced behind him at the others, who were getting flustered at the sound of approaching feet, and Marian's voice in the hallway, greeting the police. Now, he gently reached over and wiped the tears from Emily's cheek and, as he watched, he was convinced that she smiled, ever so slightly, but she smiled. "I love you, sister," he whispered, "wherever you are."

EPILOGUE

Paul Dawson rubs his hands together to keep them warm. It's early, the sun barely risen, but sleep has evaded him all night so he got up, got into his car and drove to somewhere random. Now, he realises he's probably made a mistake, nobody will be around here, too quiet.

He pulls out his old gun, and quickly looks around the open field before returning his gaze to the beautiful thing in his hand. It was his father's, something he'd pinched while in the army. He loves holding it. Holding such a formidable tool makes his skin dance and his stomach quiver. His father had shown him just how powerful it could be when he'd pointed it at those whores to make them do whatever he'd wanted, but he'd been weak and then used it on himself before the police could catch him. Now, it was Paul's.

He points it at a nearby tree and pretends to pull the trigger and feels the same exhilaration as when he shot the cat not so long back. Since then he's shot at rabbits, and almost hit a dog, but it'd been too quick. As if on command, he hears a dog bark and looks towards the sound. In the distance, further up the lane, he sees movement, and quickly takes cover in a hedge to wait.

His breathing is quick and his heartbeat races with the possibilities. He's never killed humans before, but it's crossed his mind on any number of occasions, and with another quick glance around, he knows they are alone. He can hear their voices now as they come near him. One of them, a man whistles and calls his dog. "Terry. Come here, boy...."

'Terry? What a stupid name! Reason enough to shoot him,' he thinks and without hesitation steps out of the hedge and begins to shoot.

He doesn't remember aiming, but once the six bullets are fired, he looks down at his handiwork and smiles, pleased with himself. He's got the stupid man twice, once in the head and in the chest. The woman is shot in the neck and is coughing up blood, but doesn't stand a chance of living. He sees there are three dogs, all dead from a single gunshot each.

The walk back to his car takes less than ten minutes and he drives away calmly so as not to draw any suspicions, just as his father has taught him. But he doesn't really need to care, there's no one around, just pure luck he found those two early walkers. He feels so proud of himself. He glances down surprised to see he has an erection. He hasn't had one of those for years and feels even better. Shame he has no whore to use it on.

He drives back into town and after calling into MacDonald's for breakfast, heads home and back to bed, where he falls asleep almost immediately. His nightshift starts again tonight after having a week off for his father's funeral, and his security guard uniform is perfectly pressed and ready for action.

Thank you for taking the time to read this book. If you enjoyed it, please consider telling your friends or posting a short review. Word of mouth is an author's best friend and much appreciated.

ABOUT THE AUTHOR

P J Roscoe is the author of two novels, and several historical articles published in 'Country Quest', a Wales & Border magazine. A Chakradance and drumming facilitator and a qualified counsellor and therapist, she is also a clairvoyant, and it is these experiences that have helped to shape her stories.

http://www.pjroscoe.co.uk/

https://www.facebook.com/pages/PJ-Roscoe/566905963377366

http://bookblogs.ning.com/profile/PJRoscoe

https://twitter.com/derwenna1

Also by P.J. Roscoe:

Freya's Child, available from Crimson Cloak Publishing

Her novel Echoes won the e-book category in the 2013 Paris book festival and Honourable mentions in the New England 2012 and London 2014 book festivals.

Diary of Margery Blake, A novella

Adventures of Faerie-folk - this collection of faerie stories for young children won an Honourable Mention in the Amsterdam book awards in the Children's books section.

Various articles: http://www.thenewsinbooks.com

Love Alters All, short story in anthology of love stories Inevitable Love

Coming soon: Where Rivers Meet.

Time Goes By, short story in the second of the Crimson Cloak Anthologies, Steps In Time http://crimsoncloakpublishing.com/steps-in-time.html

A Mother's Love, short story in paranormal anthology Crimson Timelines, from Crimson Cloak Publishing